"Anyone who ... n of urban fant ... or them as likes ... y good buy."
Thinking About Books

"Waggoner is in possession of a talent that should be taken seriously, and I can't wait for his next book."
The Horror Channel

"Tim Waggoner is well on his way to being proclaimed horror fiction's leading surrealist."
Cemetery Dance Magazine

"Both horror and mystery readers will be delighted by this horror-noir adventure."
Publishers Weekly

"It's hard to say if this singular novel, which boasts a wicked sense of humor to round off the horror, should be eligible for an Edgar Award or a Bram Stoker or both."
Booklist

"Fans of science fiction, fantasy, and horror, fans of noir detective stories and fans of the just plain weird, rejoice! ... *Nekropolis* is something to pick up if you are in the mood for something different and fun."
SF Revu

TIM WAGGONER

Dream Stalkers

A SHADOW WATCH NOVEL

**ANGRY
ROBOT**

ANGRY ROBOT
An imprint of Watkins Media Ltd

Lace Market House,
54-56 High Pavement,
Nottingham
NG1 1HW
UK

angryrobotbooks.com
twitter.com/angryrobotbooks
Perchance to scream

An Angry Robot paperback original 2015

Copyright © 2015 by Tim Waggoner

Cover by Amazing15
Set in Meridien by Argh! Nottingham

Distributed in the United States by Random House, Inc., New York.

ISBN 978 0 85766 372 6
Ebook ISBN 978 0 85766 373 3

Printed in the United States of America

9 8 7 6 5 4 3 2 1

*This one's for my brother, Eric,
my best friend and Jinx's biggest fan*

PROLOGUE

The Maelstrom is all; the Maelstrom is nothing.

The Maelstrom is eternal; the Maelstrom is fleeting.

The Maelstrom is without form or function. Chaos is its natural state, and thus would it ever have remained, but one appeared who could shape the Maelstrom's turbulent energies. The Dreaming began, and with it all of Creation. And the Dreaming continues still, but who can say what might occur if on some far-off day the Dreamer finally awakens?

Pray for sleep everlasting, children.

Pray for dreams without end.

Pray that the Waking never comes to pass.

from *The Primogenium*, book I chapter 1

ONE

I'm not a big beachgoer. I look all right in a bikini, although I'm not going to get on the cover of *Sports Illustrated*'s swimsuit edition anytime soon, and not without some serious help from Photoshop. But in Chicago, "the beach" too often means sweaty tourists, gritty sand, and the nipple-poppingly cold water of Lake Michigan. My idea of a *real* beach is an out-of-the-way island in the Bahamas, but since Shadow Watch agents rarely get vacations, I suppose I'll have to keep dreaming. Get it? *Dreaming?*

Jinx and I sat next to each other, huddled in the large woolen blanket that smelled as if it had been used to wipe King Kong's ass. Our clothes didn't smell much better. Instead of our usual gray suits – standard issue for Shadow Watch officers – we wore thick winter coats, jeans, boots, gloves, and pullover caps. In Jinx's case, the boots were about ten sizes larger than normal to accommodate his gigantic clown feet. It was early December, and the wind coming in off the lake had a nasty bite to it that indicated the city was going to be in for an especially hard winter.

Normally, Jinx's body heat would've kept me warm. Incubi – at least in their Night Aspects – are suffused with Maelstrom energy, and as a result they gave off a significant amount of heat. But tonight, Jinx was wearing a negator collar, which prevented his body from absorbing more than a minimal amount of M-energy. At the moment, he was no stronger or more durable than a human. Unfortunately, he wasn't any saner.

He kept his voice to a whisper as he spoke. "If I cut my wrists right now, do you think I'll bleed to death, or do you think I'll still heal, only more slowly than usual?"

"Don't you dare," I whispered back, knowing full well he might give it a try. "I had a hard enough time cleaning up the mess the last time you slit your wrists. The living room carpet still has stains on it."

"I know. Sometimes they talk to me. They like to tell jokes, but they're not very funny. I laugh anyway, though. I don't want to hurt their feelings."

Jinx might've been joking himself, or he might've been telling the truth. After all, it was *his* blood he was talking about.

The night sky was cloudless and clear, and the stars were so bright, they almost didn't look real. It was sad, but, even though I knew I was looking at the real thing, I couldn't help thinking that the illusory starfield in Nod – called the Canopy – was more beautiful. Sometimes I don't know which world I belong to more, which only makes me feel like I don't really belong to either. I searched for constellations, but it had been a long time since my high school science classes, and I didn't recognize any. At one point, I thought I'd found the

Little Dipper, but there were only six stars instead of seven. No North Star on the end of the handle.

I lowered my gaze and realized Jinx was looking at me. His normal skin tone is clown-white, with bright red lips and blue crescents around his eyes. But his white skin reflects light like nobody's business, and at night he sometimes looks as if he's glowing with a low-level phosphorescence – especially when there's a moon out, as there was tonight. It's a great effect for a lunatic nightmare clown, but not so useful when it comes to going unnoticed during a night-time stakeout. So before heading to Montrose Beach, I slathered flesh-colored makeup all over his face. His disguise wouldn't withstand close scrutiny, especially not in full light, but at least his skin wasn't gleaming blue-white.

"Nervous?" he asked.

He didn't have to ask, though. He was an Incubus, a nightmare given life, and I was his Ideator, the person who'd dreamed him up. We shared a bond that was deeper than that of siblings, or even parent and child. And, even if we hadn't been linked, I'm sure he could read my emotions on my face with ease.

"Yeah," I said. I didn't elaborate. I hoped Jinx would leave it at that, but I knew he wouldn't. If Jinx saw a button labeled DO NOT PUSH, he would immediately push it, keep pushing it until his finger bled, and then destroy the button with a vicious swing of his sledgehammer.

"What's the worst that could happen?" he asked.

"Melody and Trauma Doll will screw up somehow and get killed."

Jinx giggled softly. "I know. I just wanted to hear you say it."

I punched him on the shoulder as hard as I could, and I was gratified to hear him take in a hissing breath through gritted teeth. With the negator collar on, Jinx experienced pain like a human.

I could get used to this, I thought.

The collar was necessary because Incubi can sense each other's presence, especially when in close proximity to one another. Jinx's collar was easily removable – unlike the kind we use on Incubi we take into custody – so it wouldn't prevent him from going into action when the time came. But until then, I intended to enjoy the side benefits.

We had a bottle wrapped in a small brown sack, and we passed it back and forth occasionally, taking turns sipping from it. It was a Jim Beam bottle with water substituted for whisky. Not only were Jinx and I on duty, there was no way in hell I would let him drink alcohol. He was hard enough to control as it was. And the First Dreamer help me if he gets hold of caffeine. When that happens, he's like a combination of Freddy Krueger and the Tasmanian Devil.

Except for the two of us, the beach was deserted – or at least it appeared that way. We'd picked up word on the street that, if you wanted to score some shuteye, Montrose Beach was the place. Jinx and I had been here since ten o'clock, and although I didn't check the time on my wisper – the light from the device would be a dead giveaway that I was a Shadow Watch officer – I estimated it was well past midnight now. A police officer, one of the regular kind, came by to roust us off the beach at one point, but I showed him my ID with its stylized dreamcatcher symbol. He looked at it for a moment without speaking, then told us to have a nice night and left. The Shadow Watch has operatives in every major city on Earth – and some not-so-major – but I knew most of the operatives in Chicago, and that cop wasn't one. Thanks to the Somnocologists who designed it, the dreamcatcher symbol projects an almost hypnotic calming energy that tends to make people more… agreeable. But other than that one encounter, the night had been the very definition of uneventful.

Thanks to the wind, the waves were high tonight, and they broke against the beach with loud, rhythmic *shooshing* sounds. The effect was as hypnotic in its own way as my ID, and if I'd been capable of sleeping, I'm sure I would've dozed off right then. But the sound didn't help me concentrate. It invited me to relax, release my stress, and let my mind wander, none of which I could afford to do. I bit the inside of my cheek hard enough to draw blood, and the pain sharpened my senses once more, but I knew it wouldn't last. I would've killed for a hit of rev, but I was doing my best to stay drug-free these days, and I didn't have any on me.

Where the hell are Melody and Trauma Doll? They should've been here by–

Jinx interrupted my thoughts with a none-too-gentle elbow to my ribs. He nodded to the north, and I turned to see a pair of figures walking along the shore in our direction. Melody was a tall, thin Asian woman with prominent cheekbones, killer eyes, and a smile that could get her gigs modeling for toothpaste ads. Tonight she wore civvies – a black coat and jeans, and her dark hair was tucked under a black-and-white striped beanie cap. Trauma Doll hadn't done anything to disguise herself – which was the point. We wanted any Incubi in the area to recognize her for what she was.

Trauma Doll was Melody's Incubus, and her name suited her perfectly. Her porcelain skin was as white and smooth as polished bone, and, as she moved, small fissures appeared wherever her limbs bent, making soft cracking sounds. The damage healed almost instantly, only to reoccur the next moment she moved. Her only clothing consisted of loops of black barbed wire that encircled her arms, legs, chest, and torso. The wire didn't cover her completely, but, since she possessed no genitals or nipples, the parts that showed weren't especially sexy – unless you had a fetish for life-sized China dolls, that is. She wore her bright orange hair in pigtails tied with blood-stained ribbons. Her sky-blue eyes were anime-large, and they appeared to have been painted on, until she blinked. It was an extremely disconcerting sight, and one I hadn't gotten used to yet. The small nub above her mouth was only a suggestion of a nose, and her too-red lips formed a Betty Boop moue. All in all, Trauma Doll made an imposing, frightening figure, and I wondered what had inspired Melody to ever dream up such a sinister thing.

Then again, I imagine a lot of people wonder the same thing about me and Jinx.

Speaking of Jinx, he sighed as he watched Melody and Trauma Doll approach. "Don't you just love the sound her skin makes as it cracks? It's almost musical."

Of all the problems I've had having a nightmare clown for a partner, I never thought I'd have to deal with Jinx falling for a woman who was made out of porcelain.

"Next thing you'll tell me is how beautiful her skin looks in the moonlight," I said. "All shiny, cold, and hard…"

He scowled at me, but then quickly refocused his gaze on Trauma Doll.

"You know you can't go out with her," I said. "She's a trainee. *Our* trainee."

After the Lords of Misrule had nearly caused the dimensions of Earth and Nod to fuse into a single chaotic mess, the Nightclad Council had decided the Shadow Watch needed more officers – in both dimensions – to make sure something like that could never happen again. Director Sanderson had started a major recruitment drive, and almost all current officers had been assigned a pair of rookies to mentor. Melody Gail and Trauma Doll were ours.

Jinx grinned at me. "You know how I feel about rules."

"The faster they're broken, the better," I said. "But I don't want you doing anything that might interfere with her training."

"Why? Afraid something *bad* will happen?"

"Yes. And you damn well know why."

"Nathaniel," Jinx said, and then surprised me by letting the matter drop. We both fell silent and turned our attention back to Melody and Trauma Doll.

So far, there had been no sign that anyone besides the four of us was on the beach tonight, but when it comes to Incubi, appearances don't mean squat. This fact was driven home to me once again as a patch of sand near our trainees rippled. An instant later a humanoid form rose forth from the sand not more than half a dozen yards from Melody and Trauma Doll. They stopped and turned to face the newcomer. I couldn't make out his features – or if *he* really was a he – so I turned to Jinx.

He reached up and tapped the negator collar around his neck. "Don't look at me. Right now, my eyesight isn't any better than yours."

Shit! I'd forgotten about that damned collar.

The spot where Jinx and I sat was several hundred feet farther back from the water than Melody and Trauma Doll, and even with the half-moon in the sky, I couldn't make out any details about the sand being's form. He/she/it was an Incubus, of course. A human couldn't have risen from the sand like that. But otherwise, I knew nothing. I *hate* not knowing stuff, especially when I'm working and *double* especially when my not knowing something might get someone else killed.

I started to rise to my feet, but Jinx put a hand on my shoulder and gently but firmly forced me to sit back down.

"I thought you'd be all for rushing mindlessly to attack," I said.

"Usually I am, but I'm working on being less predictable."

"But not less annoying."

He grinned at me, but he kept his hand on my shoulder. With the negator collar on, he was no stronger than an average human male, and I thought I could take him. But probably not before he could spring the catch on the collar and remove it. After that, it would be an entirely different story.

I knew Jinx was right to stop me. While I wasn't comfortable letting Melody and Trauma Doll make contact with the shuteye dealer, there was no way Jinx and I could've done it. After our part in stopping the Fata Morgana and the Lords of Misrule, we were too well known throughout the Incubus and Ideator communities in both dimensions. If the two of us had been walking along the beach, the sand-figure would most likely have remained hidden as we passed. We needed to bust the shuteye operation, and, right now, Melody and Trauma Doll – two unknowns – were our best bet.

Relax, I told myself. *Let them do their job. It's what they've been trained for.*

Then again, they weren't fully-fledged officers yet, were they?

Shuteye is one of the most dangerous drugs ever produced in Nod. Once an Ideator brings an Incubus to life, they no longer have any need to sleep. We're linked to our Incubi, and, since they don't sleep, we don't either. We do need to rest several hours each day to continue functioning at peak capacity, however, so we read, watch TV, meditate, whatever, just as long as we're not working. I *hate* resting without sleeping. It's boring as hell, and it's a waste of time. But I'd learned the hard way that if I don't rest, my job performance suffers – which in turn means others suffer, the ones I've sworn to protect. So I do my best to refrain from working three or four hours a day. It's not as much as Somnocologists recommend, but it's about all I can stomach.

I don't miss sleeping all that much. To tell you the truth, I don't even remember what it was like. My life before I became an Ideator and a Shadow Watch officer sometimes seems like little more than – pardon the expression – a dream. But some Ideators would do just about anything to experience sleep again, and some Incubi – who've never slept – are curious about what it's like. Normal sleep drugs, the kind you can get in any pharmacy on Earth, won't work on Ideator or Incubus physiology. And that's why shuteye was created. The drug allows the user to experience a chemical simulation of sleep. Some users begin to exhibit psychotic behavior and become a danger to themselves and others, and some poor bastards go crazy after taking only a single capsule. I know. I've seen it.

Melody and Trauma Doll walked back to the figure who stood motionless as he/she/it awaited them. Melody began talking to the figure, but she kept her volume low. I wished I'd made her wear a wire so I could listen in on her conversation with the dealer, but you can never tell what kind of special senses a particular Incubus might possess. And, if the dealer so much as suspected Melody was an officer, it wouldn't go well for her.

At first, everything seemed to go okay. Melody talked, the sand creature responded. Melody talked some more. The sand creature then reached inside its chest and pulled out a plastic bag containing several small capsules. I couldn't tell how many were in the bag from where I sat, but I guess there were a half dozen, max. The sand creature held the bag out to Melody, while at the same time holding his other hand out palm up, ready to receive payment. And that was the moment Trauma Doll decided to go into action. She shrugged her right shoulder, and the coils of barbed wire wrapped around that arm rippled, loosened, and shot toward the sandy being like a gigantic S&M Slinky, and with a not dissimilar *spronging* sound. The coils lengthened as they encircled the dealer, covering him/her/it from head to toe in an improvised cage.

"That's my girl!" Jinx shouted.

He took his hand from my shoulder, popped the catch on his negator collar, threw it to the side, leaped to his overlarge feet, and began running toward Melody and Trauma Doll, determined not to miss out on whatever action might be left.

As it turned out, Jinx didn't have to worry. Instead of being constrained by Trauma Doll's coils, the sand creature simply stepped out of them, the barbed wire passing through its substance without doing any apparent damage.

"Rookies," I muttered.

I threw the blanket off, got to my feet, and started running after Jinx. I'd kept my trancer tucked against the small of my back, and I drew it as I ran and flicked the activation switch. Melody drew her own trancer the moment the sand creature escaped Trauma Doll's coils, and she fired before the Incubus could attack either of them. A beam of multicolored Maelstrom energy shot from the weapon's muzzle and struck the sand creature in the chest. But either the beam passed through the Incubus' sandy body or else the creature had created a hole in itself for the beam to go through. Either way, the M-energy did the Incubus no damage and continued lancing through the air – straight toward Jinx.

I wanted to shout a warning to him, but there wasn't time. Yet just as Jinx was about to get a face full of M-energy, he veered to the side, and the beam missed him, continuing on for a few dozen more feet, weakening as it went, before finally hitting the beach's upward slope. Sand exploded with a loud chuffing sound. Jinx turned his head to give me a quick grin and a thumbs-up, and then faced forward once more and increased his speed.

I hadn't managed to shout a warning, but Jinx had responded as if I had. I remembered Sanderson telling Jinx and me – during one of our numerous dressing-down sessions in his office – that as Ideator and Incubus, we should have a bond so strong it would be almost telepathic. Since that time, Jinx and I had worked out some, if not all, of our differences, and these days we did function better as a team, better than we ever had before, in fact. So maybe I *had* projected my thoughts to Jinx, at least on some basic level. Or maybe it was nothing more than a coincidence. Right then it didn't matter. I had work to do.

I may be an Ideator, but that doesn't mean I have any special powers beyond having once dreamed an Incubus into existence. Unless you count having life-long insomnia as "special". I ran after Jinx, but I was nowhere near as fast as he was, and I knew he would reach Melody, Trauma Doll, and the sand creature before I would. I briefly considered taking a shot at the shuteye dealer with my trancer. Maybe if Sandy didn't see the energy blast coming, he wouldn't be able to avoid it. But I suck at firing on the move, and I didn't want to hit Melody or Trauma Doll by accident. So I concentrated on running faster and hoped I'd get there in time to do some good.

Our trainees had been startled by the ease with which Sandy had shrugged off Melody's trancer blast, but they recovered quickly. Trauma Doll retracted her coils and they wrapped tightly around her porcelain arm once more. She then thrust her hands toward Sandy, unleashing both her right and left coils. But instead of encircling Sandy, the coils straightened and she scissored her arms back and forth, causing the barbed wire to slash through the creature's substance like a pair of metal whips. At the same time, Melody fired her trancer at Sandy, only this time, she'd flicked the selector switch to wide beam setting, and moved her trancer up and down, spraying Sandy from head to toe with M-energy.

I was impressed. Melody and Trauma Doll were working together in an attempt to disrupt the cohesion of Sandy's substance in order to weaken and perhaps even injure him. It was damned smart. Too bad it didn't work.

Sandy raised his own arms, as if in imitation of Trauma Doll, and he hit the two of them with twin blasts of sand to the face. Melody dropped her trancer, turned her back on Sandy, staggered forward several steps, and fell to her hands and knees. Her trancer's beam winked out as it hit the sand, and it lay there for a split second before it sank into the sand and disappeared. Whatever kind of Incubus Sandy was, he was even more powerful than I'd thought. How much of the beach did the damned thing control? Could the very ground Jinx and I ran on be used against us as a weapon whenever Sandy felt like it? Talk about precarious footing.

The sand-blast had a far more dramatic effect on Trauma Doll. The impact caused the left side of her head to shatter in an explosion of white porcelain shards. She didn't go down, but her arms dropped to her sides and her barbed wire whips fell limp. I'd suspected that Trauma Doll was hollow, but this was the first time I'd had any confirmation. Incubi are tough and they can heal a lot of damage while in their Night

Aspects, but they aren't invulnerable. If their heads are cut off or destroyed, they die. Trauma Doll had only lost half of her head, but I feared she still might be dead – or whatever the equivalent is for a giant animated toy.

I felt like I'd taken a blow to the sternum. My breath caught in my chest, and a cold pit yawned wide where my stomach had been. The thing I had feared the most had happened. Melody and Trauma Doll, rookies under my supervision, had gone down. And neither looked like she'd be getting up anytime soon. Shock gave way to anger – mostly at myself, but it provided the motive force to spur me on to greater speed.

As I continued running toward Melody and Trauma Doll, Jinx let out a bellow of rage, reached inside his jacket, and withdrew a sledgehammer. Part of his clown abilities was being able to store an insane amount of bizarre weaponry on his person, regardless of the size. The sledge – which he called Cuthbert Junior – was his favorite, and without pausing in his run, he lifted the hammer back over his shoulder, then hurled it toward Sandy like it was a steroid-infused tomahawk. Cuthbert Junior was a blur as it spun through the air. As if sensing the sledge's approach, Sandy started to turn to face the oncoming weapon, but, before the creature could do anything, Cuthbert Junior slammed into him with a loud *chuff!* Sand sprayed everywhere, and the sledge continued traveling a dozen more feet before it *thunked* to the ground, only a few inches from the water's edge. Its head sank into the wet sand, its wooden handle pointing skyward. I thought Jinx would go to retrieve Cuthbert Junior, pulling it out of the sand with a moist sucking sound as he shouted something like, *I am rightwise born King of England!*

But instead he ran to the spot where Sandy had been standing, unzipped his pants, pulled out a chalk-white portion of his anatomy I would've preferred not to see – *ever* – and unleashed a stream of urine. The sand sizzled and smoked as Jinx's piss struck it.

As I drew close, I called out, "I think you ought to give some serious thought to seeing a urologist!" Then I ran past him, giving him and his prodigious river of urine a wide berth. I saw the baggie of shuteye capsules lying on the sand. The sand creature must've dropped it when Trauma Doll first attacked. Or maybe it had gotten snagged on her barbed wire as he escaped her trap and was pulled from his hand. Whichever the case, there it was, and, despite my urgent need to check on Melody, I bent down, snatched up the baggie, and stuffed it in my pants pocket. We'd need it for evidence.

I hurried to Melody, who was still on her hands and knees, and crouched next to her.

"Are you all right?" I asked, knowing it was a stupid question but unable to think of anything else to say.

That's when I noticed that the sand directly beneath her face was wet. At first I thought the sand-blast had irritated her eyes and she'd been crying. But then I realized that what I was looking at wasn't the result of shed tears, but rather shed blood.

"I managed to avert my face in time to avoid the full impact." Her voice was strained, and she spoke through pain-gritted teeth. "But a half-blast did enough damage. I can't see out of my left eye." She paused. "I'm not sure I *have* a left eye anymore."

My stomach did a flip at her words. I crouched lower to get a better look at the damage and immediately wished I hadn't. The left side of her face was little more than a mass of blood and ravaged meat. I had no idea if Jinx had destroyed Sandy or if even now the Incubus was working on reconstituting his body, and I didn't care. All that mattered was getting Melody to a hospital.

For an instant, Melody's face seemed to… shimmer is the best way I can describe it. Kind of like the way heat rising off hot asphalt can make the air seem to distort and ripple. It happened so quickly that I wasn't sure if I'd really seen it, and then it was gone, and Melody looked normal again. Well, as normal as anyone *can* look with half of their face reduced to bloody, shredded meat. I told myself that what I'd seen was only a trick of the moonlight, most likely intensified by stress, and I thought no more of it.

Jinx finished his vengeance-piss, shook the dew off the lily, zipped up, and then turned around. At that exact moment a breeze blew in off the lake, and Trauma Doll's half-headless body wobbled, then fell over backwards.

Jinx walked over to Trauma Doll and gazed down at her. Her body remained still, but the scattered shards of what had once been the left side of her head were already beginning to move of their own accord, sliding across the sand to rejoin the rest of her. They traveled slowly, with jerky, erratic motions, as if they were almost too weak to move. Jinx helped them along by moving them closer to Trauma Doll's ragged-edged face and neck with gentle sweeps of his giant feet. The pieces began to adhere to the main body and to one another with soft clinking noises, and I began to hope that Trauma Doll was going to recover. Unfortunately, Ideators don't heal any more swiftly than ordinary humans, and Melody's bleeding wasn't going to stop on its own.

I tucked my trancer into the back of my pants – no way was I going to put it on the sand after what had happened to Melody's weapon. Then I pulled off my jacket, wadded it into a ball, and pressed it to Melody's wound. I helped her shift to a sitting position, and then she took hold of the jacket and held it in place, freeing my hands.

"Thanks," she said, her voice shaky but calm enough, considering the circumstances.

While I'd tended to Melody, Jinx had continued scooping pieces of Trauma Doll's head closer to her body. The porcelain shards were coming together to form larger sections of her face, and a number had rejoined her body to the point where her chin and lower jaw were mostly restored.

As if reading my thoughts, Melody said, "She'll be okay. She may look fragile, but she's one tough bitch." Despite the intense pain she must've been in, Melody's voice held unmistakable pride. I knew how she felt. Kind of.

There was a time when I'd have been holding any number of drugs that I could've given Melody to ease her pain, but all I had was the bag of shuteye capsules.

"How bad does it hurt?" I asked. "Bad enough to risk a shuteye?"

"No!" She almost shouted the word and then, as if embarrassed, she smiled and added, "You don't want me to have to report you for corrupting a rookie, do you?"

I smiled. "Guess not." I glanced over at Jinx. "How's Trauma Doll doing?"

"She'll need another ten minutes or so to finish pulling herself together," he said. Normally, he might've giggled at the bad pun, but he wasn't in a laughing mood just then.

One of Trauma Doll's ears was restored, although none of her facial features had reattached to her body yet. Still, her hand raised and gave me a thumbs-up.

I didn't think it was a good idea for Melody to wait much longer to get medical attention, so I lifted my wisper to my face and spoke into it. The device doesn't look like much, just a simple silver bracelet, but it can do anything a smart phone can, and more.

"Call Connie," I said.

Whenever Jinx and I need a ride, we call Connie Desposito. Her Deathmobile might be one of the most unsafe vehicles I've ever ridden in, but it's faster than ten kinds of lightning, and right now speed was what Melody needed most. But before the wisper could connect with Connie's cell, the sand beneath us began to shudder, and I had a bad feeling that our granular drug dealer wasn't quite finished with us. A large mass exploded out of the sand near Jinx's feet. It slammed into him with a sound like two colliding semis, and the impact sent Jinx soaring into the air. He arced up and out over the lake, then fell toward the water. He landed so far from the beach that I couldn't see where he hit, but I heard the splash. I looked back at the object that had struck him and saw it was a giant fist formed from sand. The fist raised a middle finger toward the lake, and then it shifted, reformed, and became a human figure, only this time it had facial features.

"*Nobody* pisses on me!"

The voice had a whispering quality, like sand sliding over sand, but it was unquestionably male. He turned toward me then, and his expression – already angry –

became downright murderous. I still crouched next to Melody, but, as the sand Incubus started toward me, I stood, drew my trancer, and leveled it at him.

"Do I really need to identify myself as a Shadow Watch officer?"

His sandy mouth twisted into a smirk. "Your clumsy sting operation told me that. Did you seriously think I was going to be fooled by those two?" He nodded to Trauma Doll and Melody. "I could practically smell how green they are."

He stopped when he was within five feet of me. I kept my trancer aimed at him, but he seemed unconcerned. Trancer fire hadn't been any kind of threat to him so far. I glanced at his feet, or rather where his feet should've been. His legs terminated at his ankles, as if his feet were buried in the sand. He was connected to the beach, *was* the beach. And that's when I guessed his name.

"Montrose," I said.

He smiled. "What else?"

"So what's your Day Aspect?" I asked, genuinely curious. "Do you become human or are you *really* the beach?"

All Incubi have Day Aspects, but those aspects aren't always human – or even made of organic material, for that matter.

"Let's just say that in the summertime I get pretty damned tired of people plunking their fat asses down on me."

"So your life sucked so much that you figured becoming a drug dealer would be a step up?"

He shrugged, the motion causing bits of himself to slide off and fall to the ground.

"It's more interesting than lying around and doing nothing all night," he said.

"So why not go live in Nod?"

Since there's no day in Nod, Incubi never assume their Day Aspects. In Nod, Montrose would be free to walk around as a pile of ambulatory sand all he wanted.

"That's boring, too." His voice turned wistful. "Besides, I'd miss the lake."

There wasn't any point in trying to understand Montrose. Incubi don't think like humans do, and we're not always the most rational creatures ourselves. Besides, I didn't have time to keep playing get-to-know-you with him. Melody needed medical attention.

"I shouldn't do this, but you seem like a nice enough guy, and you only tried to sell my colleague a few capsules. How about we go our separate ways and call it a night?"

I kept my tone relaxed, but I didn't lower my weapon.

Montrose didn't take any time to consider his reply.

"Where's the fun in that?"

And that's when I realized how much trouble we were really in. Montrose had swallowed Melody's trancer. He could do the same to us any time he wanted. Hell, he could probably slide his sandy substance into our mouths, down our throats, and into our lungs, asphyxiating Melody and me, and there wouldn't be a damn thing we could do about it. There could be only one reason why Montrose hadn't killed us all by now. The only reason we were still alive was because he wasn't done playing with us yet.

Fabulous.

I wanted to keep his attention off Melody and

Trauma Doll, so I fired a quick blast of M-energy at him, and then I started running north along the beach. I knew my trancer blast wouldn't do much more than slow him down a little, but I'd take however much of a head start I could get. I put all the energy I had into my run, hoping to put as much distance as possible between myself, Melody, and Trauma Doll. I had no idea how big Montrose really was, but Chicago has twenty-eight miles of public beaches, and there was no way he could be *that* big. I hoped.

I have no idea how far I'd gotten before a wall of sand sprang up before me, but I was moving too fast to avoid it. I managed to angle my body so I hit the wall with my right shoulder. I expected the wall to be as solid as rock, but, while it provided some resistance, I plowed through it without much trouble. I was, however, off balance now, and I lost my footing and fell. A pit yawned open beneath me, and, as I tumbled into it, I almost screamed. But before I could do more than fall a few feet, sand rushed up to meet me, and my breath was driven from my lungs as it collided with me. The sand continued moving, taking me with it, and I realized I was being borne skyward by a pillar of sand. Montrose's laughter seemed to come from everywhere and nowhere all at once, and I had the impression that each individual grain of sand was laughing, their tiny voices merging into one eerie, omnipresent sound.

I felt my stomach drop as the pillar – no, the *tower* – rose swiftly into the air. I tried to grab hold of the sand beneath me, to dig my fingers in and steady myself. But the sand that comprised the flat surface of the tower was packed tight, and I couldn't get any purchase on it. I'd lost my trancer somewhere along the line – probably when I'd first fallen into the pit. If I'd had it, I might've been able to blast a handhold with a tight-beam setting. But then again, Montrose would likely just fill the area back in. The tower stopped rising so abruptly that momentum actually carried me several inches higher. Panic gripped me as I felt empty space between me and the top of the tower, and my limbs flailed as my body desperately attempted to find something solid to grab hold of. My momentum gave out, I seemed to hang motionless in the air for an instant, and then I began to fall. I hit the top of the tower belly-first, and I released a most unladylike "Blarg!" It was a good thing I hadn't eaten recently, or more than sound might've come out of me.

I lay there for several seconds, shaking with fear, but I forced myself to calm down. It took every ounce of willpower I had, but I managed to move into a crouching position, and from there I stood. My legs were shaky, but they held me up. From this height, Melody and Trauma Doll looked like actual dolls, and I estimated I was a hundred feet off the ground, maybe more. On my left was the dark expanse of Lake Michigan, and on my right was the city. The buildings were lit up so brightly, they almost seemed to glow, and, even in this moment, when there was no guarantee I'd live through the next few moments, the sight took my breath away. What can I say? I'm a Chi-Town girl born and bred.

Montrose's laughter had faded into the background somewhat, but it hadn't stopped. Now it became louder once more, and I understood why when the tower began to sway. It began gently enough, moving back and forth an inch or two at the most. But with each passing second the tower's range of motion expanded. To make matters worse, instead of following a regular pattern, the tower moved in unpredictable ways: slow circles, fast figure eights… It would jerk to a halt and then start moving again just as abruptly. I spread my feet apart and stretched my arms out, almost as if I were surfing. In a way, I guess I was. Even with the extra attraction afforded by the corrugated soles of my boots, my feet would slide several inches in one direction, and then when the tower changed course, they'd slide in another. The trick was to maintain my balance and not panic. I reminded myself that Montrose wanted to play with me, and that, as long as I amused him, he'd keep me alive. More importantly, the longer I stayed alive, the longer his attention would be off Melody and Trauma Doll.

Since I'd given Melody my coat, all I had to protect my upper body from the cold December air – not to mention the ass-biting wind blowing in off the lake – was a long-sleeved white shirt that was part of my official Shadow Watch uniform. I could feel the cold starting to seep into my bones, slowing me down and making me clumsy.

Evidently I was doing too good a job of not falling, for the sand on top of the tower became softer, looser, and Montrose's laughter rose in volume. I started sliding more then, and even my boots couldn't find me steady footing. Then it happened: my right foot slid out from under me at the same instant the tower jerked in a new direction. My left ankle twisted, and I fell. My left knee hit the tower's surface, followed by my left elbow. The sand had become hard again, and it felt like hitting solid stone. I was too terrified for the pain to register as anything more than a distant annoyance. I flopped onto my back and began sliding headfirst toward the tower's edge. The circular top wasn't especially wide, only ten feet across or so, and I knew I had only a couple seconds to prevent what would most likely be a fatal hundred-foot fall to the beach below.

I curled my fingers into claws and pressed them against the tower's hard surface. My nails tore with piercing pain, but I pressed my fingers down harder. I came to a stop with my head hanging over the tower's edge, and I made the mistake of turning to look down. A wave of vertigo hit me, and I closed my eyes and scooted back to the center of the tower's surface. I got to my feet, fingers throbbing, heart pounding, breath coming in ragged gasps, stomach roiling with industrial-strength nausea. But at least I wasn't dead. Not yet, anyway.

I realized then that the tower had stopped moving, and I could no longer hear Montrose's laughter. A small patch of sand near my feet shifted, bulged upward, and formed into a humanoid face.

"This is the most fun I've had in ages!" Montrose said.

My first impulse was to raise my foot and stomp down as hard as I could on the sonofabitch's face. I almost did it, too, but then I caught movement out of the corner of my eye, and I looked toward the lake. Jinx ran across the water, his already large boots swollen even larger to become miniature pontoons. His boots made loud slapping sounds as he came, and he moved surprisingly fast and gracefully.

So… Jinx can walk on water. I'll never hear the end of that.

Now that Jinx was coming, I knew I only needed to stall Montrose for a few more minutes. I knelt down next to his face, and he frowned in surprise. His face slid back a couple inches, but it didn't disappear into the tower.

"Is that all this is to you?" I asked. "A game?"

As I spoke, I reached toward the front pocket of my jeans, moving slowly and holding Montrose's gaze to keep his attention fixed on my face.

"Of course," he said, his tone indicating that this should be obvious to anyone with even a modicum of intelligence.

I inserted my bleeding fingers into my pocket, fighting to keep the pain I felt from registering on my face.

"It's not a game to me. And it's not to my friends. You hurt them, really badly."

Montrose giggled. "I know."

I slipped the plastic bag containing the shuteye capsules from my pocket. As I palmed the bag, I heard Jinx's splashing footfalls becoming louder. He was getting close to shore.

"So I guess it only matters if something is fun for you, huh?"

I dug my sore, bloody fingertips into the plastic, working to tear a hole in it. My blood made the plastic slippery, complicating the job, but I was determined – not to mention more than a little desperate – and I succeeded. I felt a single capsule fall into my palm. I wasn't sure one would be enough, but I knew I wouldn't be able to get any more before Montrose realized what I was up to.

His expression became puzzled then.

"Well, sure. Isn't that how it is for everyone?"

Shuteye comes in gel-coated liquid doses, and I

pressed what remained of my thumbnail into the semisoft gel coating until I felt it break. I leaned closer to Montrose's face and was relieved when he didn't slide away from me.

"It's not that way for me," I said. "But I have to admit that I'm going to enjoy this."

I lunged forward and jammed my hand into Montrose's mouth.

Despite what I'd said to him, I really didn't want to do this. I'd seen the horrific results of what shuteye could do when someone had a bad reaction to it. But right then shuteye was the only weapon I had at my disposal.

Montrose tried to close his mouth, but I'd caught him off-guard. I shoved my arm down his throat almost all the way up to my shoulder and released the capsule. And then, while he was still too surprised to harden his substance and bite my arm off, I withdrew it and scooted back a couple feet. I had no idea if he had a true digestive system, but I hoped it wouldn't matter.

Montrose's features contorted into a distorted mask of hate. His face rose from the tower's surface, a humanoid body forming beneath it until he stood before me in all his gritty glory. His hands shot toward me, arms lengthening so he didn't have to step so much as an inch forward to reach me. I expected to feel sandpaper-rough fingers wrap around my neck and begin to squeeze. Instead, they fastened over my nose and mouth, and an instant later I felt sand begin to slide up my nasal passages and down my throat. I immediately started gagging – or at least I tried to. The sand was too thick, and there was too much of it. Panic took hold of me, and, if it hadn't been for my training,

I might well have thrown myself off the tower in an attempt to get away from Montrose. Death by, as we call it in the trade, "sudden deceleration trauma" would've been preferable to choking slowly on living sand. But I forced myself to remain standing where I was, and, while there was nothing I could do to fight back the panic, I did my best to endure it.

Just a few more seconds, I told myself. *Just... a... few... more...*

Montrose's face had become a mask of savage glee as he drank in my suffering. But now his features went slack, and, considering what he was made of, I mean *slack*. Lines of sand began running down his face, and his facial features softened as they eroded. The process started slowly, but it picked up speed, and soon his entire body – arms included – collapsed into a lopsided pile on top of the tower. I began hacking and coughing and exhaling air through my nose to clear away the residue that Montrose had left behind. I didn't spend too much time congratulating myself on my brilliant ploy, however. Montrose's body was much larger than the humanoid extrusion that had tried to kill me – and I was standing on it, one hundred feet above the ground. The sand tower remained steady for several seconds after the collapse of Montrose's avatar, but then it began to shake, and I could feel the surface beneath my feet begin to soften. The tower was about to fall apart under me, which meant that I had only one option if I wanted to survive. I ran to the edge and jumped out into space.

As I fell, I relaxed my body and waited. I heard a distant *sproinging* sound, and, an instant later, Jinx – propelled by his powerful shoe springs – came flying toward me. He caught me easily, and, as we plummeted toward the ground, his springs extended once again to soften our landing. We bounced a couple times, and then something strange happened. Stranger than usual, I mean. For an instant – *just* an instant – a wave of dizziness came over me and my vision blurred. When it cleared, I was looking at myself, and I... *she* was staring back at me, wide-eyed with shock. We were descending toward the ground, and I realized that I was holding me. I mean *her*. I glanced at my hands and saw they were chalk-white. I was... Jinx?

The dizziness hit again, accompanied once more by blurry vision. But, just as it passed, I felt a jarring impact. When my vision cleared this time, I found myself looking at Jinx. We were lying side by side on the sand.

"Sorry," he said, his voice devoid of any hint of clownly lunacy. "Guess I didn't stick the landing."

He stood and held out a hand. I took it and he helped me to my feet. I ached all over, but I'd survive. Jinx noticed my wounded hands.

"I thought you didn't go in for manicures," he said, sounding much more like his usual demented self.

I displayed one of my injured fingers to him to show what I thought of his joke. Neither of us said anything about what had happened as we were landing. Maybe we were both hoping it hadn't really happened. Maybe we kept quiet about it because we knew it had.

Jinx and I turned toward the lake and saw a huge mound of sand where Montrose's tower had been.

"I could make an erectile dysfunction joke right now," Jinx said.

"I'd rather you didn't."

Before I could say or do anything else, a loud, low mournful tone came from the direction of the street. Jinx and I turned in its direction to see a midnight-black hearse with eerie green glowing headlights come roaring over the sand toward us. Evidently, my wisper call to Connie's cell had gone through, and she'd heard enough of what was going on to figure out where we were. I couldn't have been more relieved.

I waved to Connie and pointed to Melody and Trauma Doll – the latter of whom had sat up and was putting the remaining shards of her head back into place by hand. Melody, however, was no longer sitting and holding my bunched-up jacket to her face. She lay on her side, very, very still.

I ran toward her and Jinx followed. The Deathmobile came along behind us, and I prayed to the First Dreamer that the fact that a hearse had come to rescue Melody wouldn't turn out to be a bitter irony.

TWO

"How much longer do you think it will be?" Trauma Doll sounded like a lost little girl. She looked to me for reassurance, but I didn't have any to give.

"I don't know."

The three of us – Jinx, Trauma Doll, and me – sat in a crowded waiting room, Jinx next to me, Trauma Doll on the other side of him. The chairs were uncomfortable, the plaster on the walls was cracked, and the floor tiles were yellowed, warped, and covered with unidentifiable stains. The air was cool to the point of being chilly, and it smelled like toxic waste. The lights were overly bright fluorescents, the kind that give you a headache if you sit under them too long and which hum almost below the threshold of human hearing, making you feel increasingly on edge. Most of the others in the waiting room were Incubi of one sort or another, but there were a few humans in the mix. Ideators, probably, but, since some were unaccompanied by Incubi, it was hard to tell for certain.

The staff members were primarily Incubi, and the only way to tell them apart from the other living nightmares in the room was by the white uniforms they wore, although many of those uniforms were so discolored by stains from blood or other less identifiable bodily fluids that there was little visible white remaining. The Sick House is the only official hospital in Nod, but there's no shortage of doctors around. Nightmare physicians and nurses are almost as ubiquitous in Nod as nightmare clowns, and many of the medical-themed Incubi find employment at the Sick House. Their Ideators dreamed them with medical knowledge and skills, and when they assumed full physical existence, they retained those abilities. How in the hell someone *without* medical training can create a being *with* medical training is just one more of the Maelstrom's little mysteries.

Most nightmare docs and nurses look relatively normal, although their features tend to be exaggerated and distorted – pronounced brows, ears that taper to points, bulging eyes, sharp cheekbones, large teeth that are almost, but not quite, fangs. Far worse were the medical devices they carried, most of which looked more like weapons or instruments of torture. Sometimes they carried severed limbs – arms, legs, the occasional head. Once in a while someone would go by dragging a body behind them, leaving a bloody smear in their wake. Needless to say, bedside manner isn't something they worry much about at the Sick House.

Occasionally, something goes wrong with an Incubi's healing ability. Certain drugs can disrupt their ability to absorb Maelstrom energy, and, if they suffer severe brain damage and survive, the same thing can happen, leaving them vulnerable to injury or illness. And there are conditions that can occur to Incubi naturally: fading, of course, being one of the most serious. So it was no surprise to me that there were so many Incubi in the waiting room. Most of the ones present were of the normal type: sharp-toothed, long-clawed, with distorted features. Typical nightmare stuff. But there were a few stand-outs. Something that resembled a skeletal giraffe stood in a corner, the sockets of its skull-head glowing a baleful yellow-green. The giraffe-thing was trembling, its bones making constant clacking sounds. A being made entirely out of various-sized baby heads sat a few chairs away from me, the heads whimpering softly. I studiously avoided looking in its direction. Then there was something that resembled a circulatory system without a body. Veins and arteries formed a criss-crossing cage around a heart that spasmed with loud *squelching* sounds. The heart had a leak in it, and, every time it pumped, crimson fluid jetted through the air and splashed onto the tiles.

Connie had driven us from the beach straight to here. Doors to Nod come into existence each night, but always in different locations. Incubi can sense these Doors – one of the reasons human Shadow Watch officers are paired with them – and the Deathmobile hauled ass to the nearest Door large enough for it to fit through: a garage door of a closed auto body repair shop. We passed from one dimension into another, coming out in the Arcade, the entertainment district in Newtown. The Sick House is located in Oldtown, and the Deathmobile roared through the streets like a mechanical demon to get Melody there as fast as possible. Once we were in Nod, I'd used my wisper to call ahead, and an emergency team was waiting for us outside when we arrived. They whisked Melody away on a gurney, and that was the last we'd seen of her.

Connie had headed back to Earth after dropping us off. She made her living as a freelance cabbie for Incubi and Ideators in Chicago, and she needed to get back to work. Before leaving, she asked me to call and let her know how Melody was doing when I got a chance. I promised her I would.

According to my wisper, we'd been waiting at the Sick House less than an hour, but it felt like much longer. Trauma Doll's face was almost completely healed by now. Faint cracks were still visible here and there though, and I wondered if she was healing more slowly because she was worried about Melody. Jinx's face was expressionless, which, on a clown, is even more frightening than when he smiles. He stared off into the distance and passed the time by eating long roofing nails which he'd found somewhere in his bottomless pockets. He ate them slowly, one at a time, biting off small chunks of metal with soft snapping sounds.

When we'd first sat down, Jinx – who had cleaned the flesh-colored make-up off his face – had tried to console Trauma Doll, but tender emotions aren't exactly his specialty. He tried to distract her by showing her his famous exploding frog trick, but I managed to stop him before he made a mess. He then began reciting limericks, each one filthier than the last. But they only made Trauma Doll cry tiny porcelain tears which fell to the floor with tiny plinking sounds.

"Melody *loves* dirty limericks!" she said, and began sobbing.

Jinx had looked to me for help at that point, but I could only shrug. I'm not exactly the tender type myself. So Jinx gave up and started biting his nails – get it? – again, Trauma Doll eventually stopped crying, and a custodian came by and swept away her tears.

As we waited, I tried not to beat myself up for what had happened to Melody. I told myself that every officer knew the risks of the job, and we were prepared to accept whatever might happen. We lived with the possibility – even the likelihood – of death and injury on a daily basis. We shoved that knowledge to the back of our minds and got on with our work. Melody might've been a trainee, but she was still a member of the Shadow Watch. She'd known what she was getting into. But Melody was my responsibility, and, because I'd made the wrong call, she'd been horribly injured by a living sandblaster. If she died, I knew I'd never forgive myself.

I tried not to think about the last time I'd been sitting here, waiting to find out whether a fellow officer was going to survive a stakeout gone horribly wrong. Only that time, *I'd* been the trainee, and the officer fighting for his life and sanity had been my mentor, Nathaniel Sawyer.

Jinx swallowed the last piece of the nail he'd been working on, and then he turned to look at me.

"You know, this reminds me of the time–"

I hit Jinx as hard as I could on the jaw. Big mistake, since my fingers were still sore as hell. I let out a yelp of pain which was loud enough to cause several of the hospital staff to look my way – a little too eagerly for my comfort. The doctors in the Sick House are known for the *enthusiasm* with which they practice medicine, as well as for their predilection for trying new and often hastily improvised techniques, which are radical at best and psychotically dangerous at worst. I wouldn't want one of the docs to start off treating my hands only to try and transplant a second head onto me for the fun of it.

Jinx and I still wore civvies, so no one in the waiting room gave us a second look. On one level it was nice not to have people giving us nervous glances, but it also felt disquieting. Without my Shadow Watch uniform on, I was just a medium-height human, not particularly intimidating. I like to think that I project a general aura of bad-assness, but the truth is that most Incubi respond not to me but to my uniform, and I didn't like being reminded of that. It's hard enough being a human in a city full of living nightmares without being reminded of how truly vulnerable you are when compared to the average Incubus.

A doctor finally came walking down the hall toward us. He looked like a normal human male, in his late thirties, and handsome enough to be a character in a soap opera. His black hair was thick and mussed just enough to be adorable. Strong chin, full lips, high cheekbones, a brow that could only be called noble. His eyes were forest green and shone with intelligence, compassion, and enough good humor to keep the first two qualities from being boring. As he drew near, he gave us a professional smile that was at once friendly and sympathetic. It didn't offer false hope, but it didn't take away hope, either.

"Hello," he said, in a warm voice. "I'm Dr Arthur Menendez."

His lab coat wasn't stained like the rest of the staff's, and on the left breast was sewn a stylized insignia: a silhouetted profile of a human head enclosed by a multicolored circle. The colors swirled slowly around the head, creating a near-hypnotic effect.

He came straight to me, and briefly acknowledged Jinx and Trauma Doll with smiles and nods before offering his hand for me to shake. I held up one of my wounded hands.

"I'd rather not, if you don't mind," I said. I told him our names, and then said, "You're a Somnacologist. I recognize the insignia on your coat."

Not all humans who are sensitive to Maelstrom energy become Ideators. Some become M-gineers, able to use and shape M-energy, while those more attuned to the mental and emotional aspects of M-sensitivity become Somnacologists.

"Yes," he said. "I've been brought in to consult on Ms Gail's case."

Trauma Doll rose from her seat, her barbed wire outfit shredding the chair's plastic covering as it pulled free.

"Is Melody okay, Doctor? Can I see her?"

Trauma Doll put her hands on Menendez's shoulders, and he nervously eyed the barbed wire coils that wrapped her porcelain body.

"I don't think it's a good idea," he said. "Ms Gail needs her rest."

"But I have to see her!" Trauma Doll said. "I just *have* to!"

She started to cry again, and Menendez relented. I wasn't surprised. He was a Somnacologist. He understood how deep the bond between an Incubus and her Ideator ran.

"All right. You can see her – but only for a few moments."

Trauma Doll smiled for the first time since we'd arrived at the Sick House and nodded.

He gently removed Trauma Doll's hands from his shoulders, then turned and began walking down the hallway. Jinx and I stood, and we followed Menendez down a long corridor, Trauma Doll coming along behind us. The fluorescent lights hummed and flickered overhead, adding nicely to the hospital's sinister atmosphere. Sounds came from the rooms we passed – moans and cries mixed with the electronic tones of medical equipment. The chemical tang in the air was stronger here, and it mingled with a sweet-sour stink that reminded me of rotting meat. I vowed never to get sick or injured in Nod if I could help it.

As we continued walking, I once more experienced a wave of vertigo. As before, my vision blurred, and when it cleared I found myself looking at Menendez's back from a slightly different – and higher – angle. I turned to look at the woman walking beside me at the same moment she turned to look at me. My first thought: *Wow, am I really that short?* My second thought: *I'm in Jinx's body!*

We continued down the corridor, but with each step Jinx's body became more difficult for me to operate. It felt as if his body was somehow trying to reject me, as if I were an invader. I started to lose my balance, and I saw that Jinx – who was in my body – was having similar problems. He weaved as he walked, unable to move in a straight line. He shook his head, as if attempting to clear it, but he started repeating the motion, like my nervous system wasn't cooperating. I reached out, intending to put a hand on his shoulder to help steady him, but, before Jinx's hand was halfway to my body, *his* body did an abrupt spin, and I walked face-first into a wall. The impact didn't hurt much, but the pain was enough to set off a new wave of vertigo. An instant later, Jinx and I were once again back in our own bodies. I didn't bother asking Jinx if he was all right. Smacking into a wall might hurt him for a moment, but it wouldn't do him any damage. And I didn't want to say anything that would alert Menendez to what had happened. But the doctor had stopped walking and faced the two of us. He frowned as he flicked his gaze from me to Jinx and then back again. I thought he might say something, but instead he turned forward once more and started walking again.

Jinx and I looked at each other and mouthed the same word.

Busted.

Before long, Menendez stopped before a room and turned to face us.

He focused his attention on Trauma Doll. "You're Ms Gail's Incubus."

It wasn't a question. Menendez hadn't asked which of the two Incubi with me was bonded to Melody, but he didn't need to. Somnacologists can sense that kind of thing.

He continued, "Because of your deep connection, seeing her in her current state will be difficult for you. Are you certain you want to do this?"

Trauma Doll took no time to consider Menendez's warning.

"I have to see her, no matter what."

Menendez nodded. "Very well. The three of you can see Ms Gail briefly, but, as I said, she needs rest. She's sedated, so she won't know you're here, at least not on a conscious level. Even so, it would be best if you remain as quiet as possible."

He opened the door to Melody's room and gestured for us to enter. Trauma Doll went first, and Jinx and I followed.

One of the worst things about visiting the Sick House is that you never know what you're going to see. If this had been an Earth hospital, we might've found Melody lying in bed, safety rails up, IV in her arm, face wrapped in thick bandages. But the healing techniques used in the Sick House are more unique and specialized – and often quite disturbing.

Melody was wrapped head to toe in white strands of silk-like material. Lines of the silk extended from her body to the walls and ceiling, holding her four feet off the floor. Crouched in one corner of the ceiling was a black spider the size of a large dog, its legs drawn close to its body. The creature remained still as we entered, but I could feel it watching us closely.

Next to Melody, another Incubus sat in a chair. She was an elderly woman in a brown robe, and she was whispering something to herself. I couldn't make it out at first, but as we stepped into the room – careful to avoid the spider's silken strands – I realized what she was saying.

"So good. So *good*…"

She repeated this over and over, without pausing between the words. It was damned eerie, and I couldn't keep from shuddering.

Spider Incubi are probably the most common type of living nightmare. After all, who isn't afraid of spiders? But they come in many different varieties with different capabilities. I wasn't worried that the spider intended to feed on Melody. The Sick House is regulated by the Nightclad Council and monitored by the Shadow Watch. No, she was here for some medical reason, probably because the silken cocoon she'd woven around Melody kept her in some kind of stasis. Since Ideators can't sleep

– not even with the aid of the strongest anesthetics –
other methods had to be employed. As for the old
woman in the robe, I figured her for a Pain Eater, an
Incubus that derives sustenance from others' suffering.
Normally Pain Eaters cause suffering in order to feed,
but this one had found a perfect job that allowed her to
feed without having to harm anyone. Pain Eaters'
victims become increasingly numb the longer they're
fed upon because the Pain Eater takes away their ability
to physically feel anything. As long as the woman
moderated her power, though, she would keep Melody
from experiencing the agony of her injuries. Together
with the spider silk, it was an effective – if creepy –
treatment.

As soon as Trauma Doll saw Melody, she began crying
again. The Pain Eater turned to look at her and gave her
a toothless grin.

"Please, child," she said, in a voice no louder than a
midnight breeze. "I find your pain delicious, but I *am*
working here." Her grin widened. "And a girl has to
watch her figure, you know."

Incubus is a Latin word that means *nightmare*. Over the
centuries, the term came to be applied to an evil male
spirit that visited sleepers in the night and drained life
force from them through sex. Basically, the male version
of a succubus. But Incubi have been around as long as
humanity has, and they adopted the Latin name for
themselves long ago, and they don't give a damn what
modern dictionaries say. But, whenever I encounter
creatures like the Pain Eater, I can see why the whole
notion of draining life force became attached to Incubi
in the first place. It's one of the most terrifying things
that humans can imagine, a being that feeds on their

most primal essence, so it's no wonder they created living nightmares from this dark fantasy.

Menendez gestured that it was time for us to leave. Trauma Doll didn't look happy about it, but she exited the room with the rest of us. Menendez then led us down another corridor until we came to his office. It was a typical doctor's office, which made it atypical for the Sick House. No peeling plastic, no weird stains on the floor... Just a desk with two chairs in front of it. There was a laptop computer on the desk, a stack of manila file folders, and an office telephone. Nothing unearthly or disturbing in any way. On the wall behind the desk was a framed diploma from the Institute of Somnacology, just in case any of Menendez's patients doubted his credentials.

"Please sit," he said, as he closed the door behind us. Since there were only two chairs, Jinx – in a rare display of gentlemanliness – stood leaning against the wall while Trauma Doll and I sat. Menendez sat at his desk and leaned forward, interlacing his fingers on the desktop, his manner professional, but not detached. He cared about Melody. I could see it in his eyes, hear it in his voice when he spoke.

"First the bad news. Ms Gail lost an eye, and she's going to need skin grafts on her face and neck. But let me assure you that her physical injuries – while severe – are not life-threatening.

As you saw, Itsy and Miseria are doing everything they can to keep Ms Gail – if not asleep, precisely – at least unaware of the pain caused by her injuries. The good news: since she was injured by an Incubus, there are traces of M-energy in her wounds. We should be able to manipulate this energy to speed her recovery to some degree, but she'll be out of commission for a couple weeks, at least. From what I understand, the Incubus that hurt her was very powerful. Thank the First Dreamer her injuries weren't even worse than they are."

His words surprised me. In my experience, Somna-cologists tended to be realists. "Are you religious?" I asked.

He smiled. "In my own way. You?"

No one had ever asked me that before. I'd never discussed my feelings on the subject with anyone, not even Jinx. I say – or at least think – *Thank the First Dreamer* all the time. But did I believe?

"I don't know," I said truthfully.

"Fair enough," he said, and let the subject drop.

"So Melody's going to be okay, right?" Trauma Doll asked, sounding equal parts scared and hopeful.

Dr Menendez smiled. "Barring any unforeseen developments, I can almost guarantee it." His smile fell away as he continued. "But she'll recover even faster if you remain near her, Trauma Doll. The bond between Ideator and Incubus is profound and, to be honest, not entirely understood. But we've had significant success in reducing Ideators' treatment time if their Incubi are present during their recovery. And the reverse is also true. Incubi who need help healing recover even more swiftly when their Ideators are close by." He paused and looked at me then. "Although sometimes the bond between the two can become *too* close."

I returned his gaze, keeping my expression neutral. A slight upturn at one corner of his mouth told me he didn't buy my act.

Before he could press the matter further, Trauma Doll said, "Of course I'll stay with Melody. I'll do whatever it takes to help her. I mean, without her, there wouldn't be any *me*."

"Very good," Menendez said. "I'll call a nurse, and she'll tell you what to do to help your friend." He picked up the phone receiver, punched a button on the console, and waited. When someone the other end answered, he said, "Yes, could you come to my office and get Ms Gail's Incubus? She'd like to participate in her treatment. Thank you."

He hung up and a moment later there was a knock at the door. Menendez said, "Come in," and the door opened to reveal a being in a nurse's uniform who looked like she was an ambulatory sea urchin. The nurse let out a series of gurgling noises I didn't understand, but evidently Trauma Doll did, because she nodded and stood up.

"Thank you, Doctor," she said to Menendez. Then she turned to Jinx and me. "I hope you both understand. I have to do this."

"Of course you do," I said. "I'll explain everything to Sanderson."

Trauma Doll didn't have to worry about getting in trouble with our boss. He'd be so pissed at Jinx and me he wouldn't have any anger to spare for her.

She reached out then and briefly touched Jinx's cheek. "I'm going to miss wreaking havoc at your side. Break someone in half for me, will you?"

Jinx smiled. "You got it."

Trauma Doll smiled back, and then she walked out of the office, and the nurse-thing closed the door behind them.

"Thanks for all your help, Doctor," I said, "but Jinx and I have to be going. We need to check in at the

Rookery and make a full report of what happened."

I started to rise from my seat, but, before I could stand, Menendez said, "I'd like to speak with you both a bit longer, if I may. You have a serious problem."

"I've got ninety-nine problems, but a serious ain't one," Jinx said, but he made no move toward the door.

I sighed and sat back down.

"I couldn't help noticing what happened to the two of you as we were walking toward Ms Gail's room," Menendez said. "You both appeared to lose control of your bodies for a moment."

"I've lost control of my bowels before," Jinx said, "but I'm pretty sure that's not what happened this time. Still, I'd better check." He started to undo his belt.

"Please don't," I said. "I've already seen your clown junk once tonight. I really don't need a repeat performance."

Jinx scowled at me, but he refastened his belt. "You're just jealous because you aren't equipped like me." He paused and frowned. "You aren't, are you?"

"Not that I'm aware of," I said.

Menendez didn't remark on our little comedy routine. He did, however, closely observe the interplay between Jinx and me, almost as if he were assessing us. Or diagnosing us.

"Unless I'm mistaken, the two of you experienced what's called Persona Translocation," he said. "A simpler term for it is Blending. In layman's terms, your minds switched bodies. Is this the first time it happened?"

I thought about lying to him, but I figured he wouldn't believe me anyway, so what was the point?

"It happened once before, during the incident when Melody was injured. It lasted only a split second then.

The second time in the hallway was a little longer, but we didn't lose control of our bodies the first time."

"That's because the transference was so brief. The second time your minds attempted to acclimate to their new environments, with awkward and – in the case of Jinx's body – somewhat painful results."

"What caused it to happen?" I asked.

"Blending can occur when the bond between an Ideator and Incubus becomes too strong."

I frowned. "I thought having a close bond was a good thing for Ideators and Incubi. In fact, our boss urged us to strengthen our bond to make us better officers."

"It's true that a strong bond allows for Ideators and Incubi to work in sympatico, creating highly efficient communication and coordinated actions. Definitely an advantage in your line of work. But if the bond becomes *too* intense the boundaries between the separate personalities begin to blur, resulting in Blending. It's a serious enough condition in and of itself, but if a Persona Translocation happened to take place while you were working – say, while dealing with a dangerous suspect – it could prove problematic, to say the least. You said you experienced a translocation before Ms Gail was injured?"

At first I didn't understand what Menendez was hinting at, but then it hit me.

"You think our mind swap had something to do with Melody getting hurt?" I asked.

"Not directly, no. But it's quite possible that neither you nor Jinx was operating at peak efficiency after the translocation. It's difficult to say how that might've affected the outcome of events."

I thought of how Jinx had ended up in Lake

Michigan, and how I'd become trapped atop Montrose's sand tower. Maybe we hadn't been at our best, and Melody had paid the price.

"Please don't blame yourself," Menendez said. "The mind interacts with the Maelstrom in profound and mysterious ways. M-gineers can harness the power to a certain degree, of course, but imagine what we might be able to do if we could *truly* come to understand it. To use it to our – and its – fullest capacity." He broke off with an embarrassed chuckle. "Sorry. Sometimes I get carried away with my work. At any rate, the Shadow Watch has a number of fine Somnacologists on staff, and I'm sure they'll be able to help you deal with your condition. I'm happy to call over to the Rookery and explain the situation to Director Sanderson."

"No! Uh, I mean, thanks, but we'd rather tell him ourselves, wouldn't we, Jinx?"

I turned to my partner, but he'd stopped paying attention somewhere along the way. He'd taken a pair of pliers from one of his pockets and was busy pulling out his fingernails one by one. Considering what had happened to my own fingers during the fight with Montrose, I couldn't help wincing when I saw what Jinx was doing. Menendez noticed, but he didn't comment on it. Why would he? I'm sure he'd seen even crazier behavior from Incubi during his career.

No way was I going to tell Sanderson about our Blending. Not yet, anyway. He'd pull us off duty, and I was determined to find out who Montrose's shuteye supplier was and bring down the whole operation. I wanted to do it for Melody, but also to assuage my guilty conscience. And besides, Jinx and I had only experienced a couple mild, temporary "Persona

Translocations." Nothing too serious so far. If our condition got worse, we would go see the Watch Somnacologists then.

I turned back to Menendez. "Do you have any advice on how to deal with Blending? Just until we get a chance to speak with the doctors at the Rookery, I mean."

"You and Jinx need to get used to being near each other without Blending. Your somnacological systems have to find a balance between disconnection and over-connection while you work. Remaining near each other should help facilitate that process while still allowing you to perform your duties. If you do this, there's a chance that the connection between the two of you will rebalance itself, and you'll have no more problems with Blending."

"And if that doesn't help?" I asked, not sure I wanted to hear his answer.

"If the Blending continues to worsen, you'll both start losing your individual sense of self. You won't know where one of you begins and the other ends. You'll be in danger of losing your minds in an almost literal sense. At that point, the only hope for recovery is permanent separation."

"Permanent?" I echoed.

He nodded.

I turned to Jinx. He was holding up his hand and examining his perfectly healthy nails. He sighed.

"No matter what I do, the damn things keep growing back."

THREE

Menendez gave us his card in case we might need to consult him later. I figured he knew we weren't going to talk to the Watch Somnacologists, and he wanted to make sure we'd at least have some kind of access to help if we needed it. I thanked him and tucked the card into my pocket. He also reached into his lab coat and withdrew a bottle of pills.

"Each of you should take one of these pills two times a day. You can increase the dosage to three or even four pills if your Blending starts to worsen."

"Thanks," I said. I took the pills and put them into my pocket with his card.

"For what?" he asked. "I can't do anything for you both without a full diagnostic workup. Officially." He smiled, shook both our hands, and promised to keep us updated on how Melody was doing.

Jinx and I stopped by Melody's room one more time before we left the Sick House. Everything looked the same as before – Melody still suspended in her silken cocoon, giant spider on the ceiling, creepy robed crone sitting next to her, only now Trauma Doll was present as well. A chair had been brought in for her and she sat next to Melody, on the side opposite from where Miseria sat. One of Trauma Doll's glossy porcelain hands rested on Melody's abdomen, and Trauma Doll's eyes were closed, as if she was in deep concentration. She'd removed her barbed wire, but, while she was technically naked, she looked more like a statue than a living woman, and the effect wasn't particularly erotic.

Jinx started to raise a hand to wave to her, but he stopped. She wouldn't see him, so what was the point? I could feel Jinx's disappointment as if it were my own, and I wondered if that was just a normal function of our link or a sign of Blending. Since neither of us became dizzy and started flailing around, unable to control our bodies, I decided not to worry about it.

I was glad to leave the Sick House and get outside into Nod's perpetually cool air. The star-filled canopy was spread over us, and, even though it was an illusion generated by the Unwakened to protect against the turbulent energies of the Maelstrom surrounding Nod, it was a beautiful illusion. Espial hung in the sky above us as well. It's real – or at least I think it is. No one's ever told me different. Espial functions as Nod's moon, but, since this is a city created by and for living nightmares, an ordinary moon wouldn't do. Espial is a gigantic glowing eye, and it slowly opens and closes its lid over the course of a month, mimicking the moon's cycle in Earth's dimension. Right now it was almost all the way closed, leaving only a mere sliver of light. I liked Espial best when most – or better yet, all – of its mammoth eyeball is concealed. No matter where I am in the city, if Espial's lid is raised far enough, I always have the eerie feeling that it's watching me.

The Sick House, like many structures in Nod, looks like something manifested from a nightmare. Who knows? It might be. There are numerous Incubi who are living buildings. Where do you think stories of haunted houses originally came from? It's a large domed structure formed from a combination of human and animal bones, some bleached white as if they'd been exposed to the sun for months, others gray, cracked, and decaying, while still others have bits of skin, muscle, and tendon attached to them. On Earth, you wouldn't get an ill or injured person within a hundred miles of this place. In Nod, no one so much as blinks an eye at it. There are worse places in town. Much worse.

The Sick House is located on the edge of Newtown, on the Oldtown side. Nightmarish constructions aside, the buildings here tend to look like those from early twentieth century Earth – stately brick buildings, no more than four or five stories. The roads are narrow, traffic minimal, the pedestrians sparse. Most of the Incubi tend to hang out in the Arcade or – if they like their fun sleazy and hazardous – the Cesspit. The vehicles going by in both directions ranged from modern to old-time Earth cars, horse-drawn carriages, and riders on horseback, with the occasional giant anaconda or ball of super-heated gas tossed in for variety. People dream all kinds of bizarre things, so you never know what you'll find confronting you on the streets of Nod.

Once Jinx and I were on the street, I took out the bottle Menendez had given us, popped off the top, and shook out four pills. I gave two to Jinx, and we dry swallowed them. I replaced the cap and tucked the bottle back into my pocket. The pills had a mild medicine aftertaste, but otherwise I felt no effects from them. I know Menendez had said to take one pill twice a day, but I figured it was a good idea to be proactive in treating our condition.

We started walking centerwise, toward the Rookery. We walked in silence for a few moments before I spoke.

"So…" I said, not sure how to approach what I wanted to discuss. "Are you okay?"

"I'm getting a boil on my butt. I'm thinking of naming it Albertus Magnus the Third. Or Steve."

"Thanks for sharing, but I mean how are you handling what happened at the beach?"

Jinx glanced at me sideways. He may act like he's crazy – okay, it isn't an act – but that doesn't mean he's a complete idiot.

"You're really asking me how I feel about Trauma Doll ditching us to stay with Melody."

"Maybe."

He remained silent for a few moments as we continued walking. When he spoke again, there was no hint of lunatic clown in his voice. He sounded like a regular guy. A regular *sad* guy.

"I'm going to miss her, but I understand her decision. I'd do the same thing for you." A hint of dark mischief returned to his gaze. "No way would I want to miss your suffering."

"You're all heart. Wait, I said the wrong body part. You're all asshole."

He let out one of his high-pitched, shudder-inducing hyena giggles.

"So were you two…" I trailed off, hoping Jinx would pick up on the hint.

"Screwing like rabid weasels? In case you didn't notice, she's not exactly anatomically correct. If we tried to do it, she'd end up with a shattered pelvis – literally."

"Stop bragging," I joked. "Besides, she's not an Incubus *all* the time."

Trauma Doll looked much the same in her Day Aspect, even down to a skin complexion so light it resembled porcelain. But during the day she was a flesh-and-blood woman with all the requisite parts in the right places.

Jinx had become a fully Idealized being when I was in my late teens, although he'd manifested a number of times before that, whenever I had a nightmare about him. He'd started life in an adult body, but technically he was only a decade old. In all that time he hadn't shown any romantic interest in anyone, male or female, and I'd come to think of him as asexual. Maybe they hadn't had sex or even held hands, but I knew Jinx had feelings for Trauma Doll. I decided not to press the issue, though.

We were still wearing civvies, but, even if folks didn't recognize me out of uniform, they had no such problem with Jinx. He has, as you might've guessed, quite a reputation in town. Because of this, people tend to make room for us as we walk and avert their gazes as we pass. But Jinx's reputation cuts both ways, so, while it can be a decided advantage when we want people to get out of our way, there are those who consider themselves to be the baddest of badasses, and they are determined to prove it by taking down the toughest clown in town.

So when another clown came walking toward us

from the opposite direction, I instantly went on alert. The fact that she was female didn't make me feel any better. One way or another, regardless of gender or appearance, *all* Incubi are dangerous. She was petite, with candy-red hair, and, while her skin was the traditional clown white, her features were those of someone of African descent. She had dark patches surrounding her eyes and teeth patterns on her lips to make her face resemble a skull. She wore a black-and-white striped sleeveless top, a short frilly black skirt, torn fishnet stockings, and thick-soled leather boots which came up to her knees and were laced in front. She swung her hips from side to side as she walked to keep a hula hoop in motion around her waist. It was made of chrome and razor blades jutted outward from it. Pedestrians gave her an even wider berth than they did Jinx, and, from the look on his face, I knew he didn't like it.

She was chewing pink bubble gum, and she blew and popped a good-sized bubble before reaching us. She stopped in front of us, but continued swinging her hips to keep the hula hoop going. I noticed that the inside of the hoop, which was free of razor blades, didn't actually touch her body.

I glanced at Jinx and raised my eyebrows. He gave a slight headshake to tell me he didn't know the woman. I didn't say anything. This was clown business.

Jinx sighed.

"Normally I'd love to stomp you into paste," he said, "but right now I'm not in the mood. How about a rain check?"

The woman didn't respond right away. Her eyes shone from within their twin black hollows, and she blew another bubble, this one bigger than the last. It kept going until it was almost as big as her head. It popped with a sound like gunfire, and I reached for my trancer out of reflex. I stopped myself before drawing it, though.

When the clown woman spoke, I expected her voice to be high-pitched and squeaky. Instead it was low and husky, as if she was a three-pack-a-day smoker.

"You need to ask yourself one question, Jinx. Are you clown enough?"

She blew another large bubble, popped it, and then, without so much as a glance in my direction, she walked around us, razor-studded hula hoop still spinning.

Jinx and I both turned to watch her depart.

"What the hell was that all about?" I asked.

He shrugged. "Beats me. You know clowns."

He turned and started walking centerwise again. After a moment, I hurried to catch up with him. Yeah, I know clowns. But knowing them and understanding them are two different things.

"So you were unable to take Montrose into custody."

Commander Sanderson stood in front of a framed painting of an hourglass, a new addition to his office wall. Sand flowed downward in a continuous stream, but the top chamber never emptied. I have no idea what his first name is, or if he even has one. For all I know Commander *is* his first name.

"No, sir," I said. "At that point, I was too concerned with getting Melody to the Sick House."

Sanderson turned away from the painting to regard us, his hands clasped behind his back. He looked slightly displeased, but that's his default expression. I can never tell how mad he is until he starts yelling at us. Sanderson – who some people say is *the* Sandman – is a black man in his early sixties, slender, with a neatly trimmed mustache and short hair. He wears the gray suit of the Shadow Watch, but his tie displays the turbulent multicolored energies of the Maelstrom, and, like the hourglass painting, the colors are always in motion.

Jinx and I sat in what I'd come to think of as the "time out" section of the Rookery – the two chairs in front of Sanderson's large wooden desk. I sat with my wounded fingers tucked beneath my legs in the hope he wouldn't notice them. My fingers stung like hell, but I'd treat them later, after Jinx and I got our verbal spanking.

"At least we now know that Montrose exists," Sanderson said. "It's amazing that an Incubus that large and powerful has managed to stay off our radar for so long."

"Maybe he's a relative of yours," Jinx said. "You know, the whole sand thing?" Jinx frowned. "You're not pretending you've never heard of him just because he's family, are you? This cover-up could result in the biggest scandal in Shadow Watch history! It could bring down the entire organization!"

"Or not," I said.

Jinx pursed his red lips. "Good point. I hadn't thought of that."

Sanderson continued as if Jinx hadn't spoken. He has to do that a lot.

"We'll keep an eye on him and see if we can learn who his shuteye supplier is."

"That might not be so easy," I said. "He can disguise himself as part of any beach in the Chicago area, so he can change locations at random. It's possible that he can hide underwater, too, at least close to shore."

Sanderson nodded. "I'll make sure the officers I assign to the surveillance are made aware of those possibilities."

He was taking us off the case? I couldn't believe this was happening again.

"Sir, I know tonight didn't go as planned–"

Jinx gusted out a laugh that sounded like a donkey's bray.

"Understatement, thy name is Audra."

If my fingers hadn't hurt so much, I'd have punched him on the shoulder then. As it was, it still took a supreme effort of will for me to restrain myself.

"In this case, I find myself agreeing with Jinx," Sanderson said.

I was so shocked by Sanderson's words that for an instant a wave of vertigo washed over me, and I found myself looking out through Jinx's eyes. I took the opportunity to slap his face as hard as I could as payback for his snide remark. Sanderson raised an eyebrow, but he was so used to Jinx's odd behavior that he didn't say anything. Another bout of dizziness later, and I was back in my own skull, and Jinx was rubbing his cheek. I smiled. This Blending thing was turning out to have advantages after all.

Sanderson went on. "As I was saying, tonight's operation did not go well, to say the least – and for that, I'd like to apologize."

I blinked several times as I struggled to process what he'd just said. Sanderson turned away, walked behind his desk, and sat down.

"After the two of you stopped the Fata Morgana from merging the dimensions – and saving my life in the process, I might add – I've become somewhat obsessed with strengthening the Shadow Watch so we'd be ready if the Lords of Misrule, or some other power, ever attempted something on that scale again. I decided to step up recruitment of new officers and 'streamlined' their training. I think what happened to Officers Gail and Trauma Doll tonight is proof that I acted rashly in that regard. They simply weren't ready for the level of danger you encountered tonight."

While I'd be lying if I said that I wasn't relieved that Sanderson wasn't blaming Jinx and me for what had happened, I felt a need to defend our trainees.

"To be fair, not many officers could've handled an Incubus as powerful as Montrose," I said.

"You two did. And that brings me to my next point. Since Damien and Eklips died, there's been a void in the Shadow Watch personnel assigned to New York City. I'd like the two of you to fill that void."

If I had been shocked by what Sanderson said earlier, I was absolutely flabbergasted now. Vertigo hit, Jinx and I switched bodies again, and I heard my voice say, "I have to pinch myself to make sure I'm not dreaming!" And then Jinx showed me, as he so often does, why paybacks are hell. He reached up, took a hold of my cheek with thumb and forefinger, and squeezed hard, giving the flesh a sharp twist for good measure. More vertigo, another switch, and suddenly my cheek stung like hell.

Sanderson frowned to the point of scowling, and he looked at me, then at Jinx, then back to me.

Jinx and I needed to cool it. The last thing I wanted was for Sanderson to start suspecting something was wrong with us. More than usual, that is.

"So what do you think of my offer?" Sanderson asked. "We could really use you two in New York."

While Shadow Watch officers move back and forth between Earth's dimension and Nod as necessary, we tend to be assigned a home base on Earth. In cities, for the most part. The larger the concentration of humans, the more combined psychic power there is, and, when they sleep, they subconsciously create pathways to Nod that allow Incubi to cross over and cause trouble. In the hierarchy of Shadow Watch posts, New York was the very top, and to be offered a posting there was a great honor. I should've been jumping up and down with excitement, but I wasn't. I loved Chicago, and I knew it like I knew the sound of my heartbeat. Sure, it's not perfect. There's a significant racial divide and income inequality, but, despite that, it was my town. My home. And you don't leave your home just because it needs fixing. The work Jinx and I did may not have helped directly with Chicago's biggest problems, but we did our best to make sure living nightmares didn't add to the city's woes.

"A bigger city means more stuff to break," Jinx said. "Sounds good."

Sanderson frowned.

"Thank you so much for the offer, sir," I said. "Can we think it over while we keep working on the case?"

"You mean the shuteye situation?" Sanderson asked.

"Yes. It's the least we can do for Melody and Trauma Doll. When Melody gets out of the Sick House, I want to be able to tell her we found the bastards manufacturing shuteye and we burned their fucking operation to the ground." Then, realizing that sounded more than a little crazy – and too much like Jinx – I said, "Sorry. Guess I'm still upset over what happened at the beach."

"Your... enthusiasm is commendable," Sanderson said.

"You mean her stubbornness," Jinx interjected.

I noticed that Sanderson did not disagree with my partner.

"I am not unsympathetic to your feelings in this matter," Sanderson said. "I understand that you have a deeper personal stake in taking down the shuteye dealers due to what happened to Officer Sawyer."

My lips tightened when Sanderson brought up Nathaniel, but I didn't say anything, and he continued.

"But we've had reports that the Lords of Misrule have been active in New York lately. I fear that they may be attempting to recreate the Fata Morgana's technology and finish what she started. I want you and Jinx on *that* case, Audra. Not only because the two of you stopped her before, but because you're more familiar with her than any other officer. That gives you an edge on her."

The Fata Morgana, in the guise of Dr Cecelia Kauffman, had been the psychologist my parents had taken me to see when I'd first started dreaming about Jinx and insisting he was manifesting in reality at night. Kauffman was searching for Ideators that she could use in her plan to merge dimensions, but I'd proven "intractable," so she'd let me go.

Jinx spoke then, and the calm and, above all, rational tone of his voice surprised me.

"Has the Fata Morgana been sighted in New York –

in either of her Aspects?"

Sanderson looked just as surprised as I was. It was a good question. In fact, it was the kind of question I would've asked. Another sign of our Blending?

"No," Sanderson admitted.

Jinx nodded, then glanced at me. I picked up the ball and ran with it.

"So there's no reason for us to go to New York right away, is there? Besides, it took the Fata Morgana years to build her Incursion Engine. You could give us a few days to see what more we can turn up on the shuteye operation, can't you?"

I did everything but add pretty please with sugar on top. I could tell from the sour look on Sanderson's face that he knew I was trying to manipulate him, and he didn't like it one bit.

"You might as well give us permission," Jinx said. "You know she's going to do it, no matter what you say."

Sanderson's sour look got even sourer, but then he sighed.

"Fine. But try to keep the destruction to a minimum, all right?"

Jinx grinned. "No promises."

As Jinx and I left, there was an empty space on the wall where the hourglass painting had been. None of us remembered it ever having been there in the first place.

We went to our lockers and exchanged our undercover civvies for our uniforms. In addition to the gray suit jacket, white shirt, and gray pants, Jinx wore a garish large red tie with white polka dots and huge red-and-white clown shoes. He also sported an outsized daisy on his lapel that was capable of squirting any number of substances, from nausea-inducing to agonizingly fatal. I urge him to always use the former, but hey, accidents happen.

I used the medical kit in my locker to treat my wounded hands, and then I slipped on a pair of dark gray gloves. I winced when the cloth came in contact with my wounds, but the cream I'd put on them was an analgesic as well as an antibiotic, and after several minutes the fiery pain in my fingers had ebbed to a dull throb. Annoying, but I could ignore it. Jinx and I then left the Rookery before Sanderson could change his mind and come looking for us.

Once we were outside on Chimera Street, Jinx said, "So, where do we start?"

I thought for a moment.

"There are only two people we know who were working on bringing down the shuteye operation when the drug first appeared. And, unfortunately, only one is sane enough to talk to us coherently."

"So we need to go back to Chicago," Jinx said. "Unless you feel like visiting Nathaniel. We could take him a new straightjacket. He's probably chewed through his original one by now."

I intended to stomp on one of Jinx's gigantic feet hard enough to break a couple bones, but he anticipated my move and jumped back in time. I ended up stomping only on cobblestone.

I glared at Jinx and in a low, dangerous voice said, "You don't joke about Nathaniel like that. *Ever*. Got it?"

Jinx glared back at me for a moment, but then his expression softened and he averted his gaze.

"Yeah. Sorry."

For Jinx, that was an effusive apology, and, although I was still mad at him, I decided to let it slide.

"Come on. Let's go find a Door."

We started walking again, Jinx moving his head back and forth like a dog searching for a scent. Not only did he have to find a Door, he had to find one that led to Chicago as opposed to anywhere else on Earth. Finding the right Door can take some time, and it doesn't help that the damn things switch location every day.

The neighborhood around the Rookery was one of the oldest in Nod, and the buildings are a mix of architectural styles from Earth's past, from mud and wattle huts to stone walls and thatched roofs, with the occasional Dali-esque nightmare construction tossed in. The Incubi there tend to be old – *really* old – and they dress in the fashion of the country and time period in which they were Idealized. Simple robes and tunics, mostly, but some doublets and leggings as well. Incubi don't age, but Ideators do, and almost all the Incubi who live in Oldtown are on their own and have been for centuries, or, in some cases, millennia. Oldtown has a somber feel to it, and I've always wondered if it's because its denizens no longer have their Ideators with them.

I glanced at Jinx, and not for the first time I wondered what he would do when I died. Some Incubi can't – or won't – go on, and they slowly Fade into nonexistence. Jinx had once told me that was his plan. When I go, he goes. But I didn't want him to become a Fader. I wanted him to live as long and happily as he possibly could. I might not be his mother exactly, and I didn't create him on purpose, but that doesn't mean that I don't care for the big psychotic jerk.

The Rookery isn't the tallest structure in Oldtown, though. That distinction belongs to the building we now approached – the Idyllon. It's a white stone tower surrounded by tall, stately trees whose leaves remain perpetually lush and green. A pathway made of the same white stone as the tower leads to the entrance, which is always left unguarded. People can come and go as they please, and they're free to explore any room or level at any time. The area surrounding the Idyllon is a permanent camp for believers as well as those determined to exploit them. Firstians, as the faithful call themselves, live in tents pitched on the Idyllon's grounds. A mix of human and Incubi, they tend to dress in eclectic, expressive styles, which is a fancy way of saying they're hippies. There are lots of impromptu music sessions, people playing guitar and singing, alone or in groups, and people having serious, thoughtful, and often animated discussions about the finer points of their faith. The more evangelical among them stand on wooden crates or makeshift stages, urging any passing unbelievers to reconsider their faithless ways.

There are always plenty of vendors around, selling wares from stalls or making their way through the crowd, trying to make sales one on one. You could buy just about anything here. Food and drink, clothing and jewelry, cheaply printed copies of the *Primogenium* – usually missing pages – and any number of fake religious relics, the most common of which are bones purported to belong to the First Dreamer. The bones are real enough and had once belonged to someone, but, if they were all put together, they would make a hundred complete skeletons, with parts left over.

A number of the vendors sold more than the wares they had on display. You could find just about any drug for sale, from stimulants like my old favorite rev to jump juice, mem tabs, stunners, tinglies, and more. I should know. I'd bought plenty of rev here over the years. Thinking of rev made me remember what it was like to take a hit from an inhaler of the stuff. The sudden rush of energy that wiped away all traces of weariness. The exhilaration, the feeling that you could do anything, could conquer the whole damned world if you wanted to. I suddenly wanted... no, *needed* a hit. The need was an almost physical ache, and I broke out in a cold sweat and started shuddering.

Jinx looked at me, and I saw sympathy in his gaze that would've been more common to his Day Aspect. It reminded me once again that despite the Jekyll and Hyde nature of Incubi, they were more complex beings than they seemed.

The almost-ache eased, my shaking subsided, and I gave Jinx a nod to let him know I was all right.

Believers and the mercenary-minded weren't the only groups present on the Idyllon grounds. Sometimes non-believers came to taunt believers who – just like many religious folk on Earth – don't react well when confronted with challenges to their faith. Chief among these challengers are the Wakenists, and, as Jinx and I passed through the crowd, we saw one such confrontation taking place quite loudly. Jinx and I stopped walking and watched, in case the verbal argument became a physical one and we needed to intervene.

"Forget for a moment that what you people suggest is madness. You can't wake the First Dreamer because the Dreamer has no physical form. The Dreamer is part of the Great Dream, and may in fact be the Dream itself!"

The Firstian resembled a crow-headed humanoid with bird-claw hands and feet. Despite his beak, he had no trouble forming perfectly understandable words. He wore a tie-dye T-shirt and ragged jeans, and he clutched a worn leather-bound copy of the *Primogenium* close to his chest.

"That's just propaganda that church officials spread so people won't realize that not only is the First Dreamer a physical being, but they keep him hidden inside there!"

The Wakenist, whose body was formed from a tightly packed group of buzzing flies, pointed to the Idyllon. As if mirroring her emotional state – her voice sounded female, at any rate – the flies' buzzing increased in volume. She wore no clothes, but, considering how disturbing her conglomerate insect form was, I wish she had been.

She went on. "They have a secret level, one that they keep hidden not only from the public, but even from their most devoted worshippers. That's where the Dreamer is held prisoner!"

"Absurd!" Crow-Head said. "How could you possibly know this?"

In response, Fly-Girl held up a hand. A single fly detached itself from her hand, buzzed around the crow Incubus' head, then returned to rejoin the rest of her.

"There's nowhere I can't go," she said.

Normally, I wouldn't have thought much of their argument. It was an old debate, probably as old as the Incubi themselves. But this was the first I'd heard anything about a secret level in the Idyllon, let alone from someone who claimed to have been there. Still, I didn't take it too seriously. Conspiracy theories are as prevalent on Nod as on Earth. But what caught my attention was the other people in the vicinity of the arguing pair. One was a tuxedo-clad ventriloquist's dummy, one was a gray-haired woman in a jean jacket and rainbow-patterned skirt, and the third was a large bipedal weasel carrying a wooden rod on which a dozen soft pretzels were threaded. They weren't standing anywhere close to each other, but they were all watching the argument between Crow-Head and Fly-Girl, and, when the latter mentioned having located the supposed secret level of the Idyllon, the three lifted their wrists to their faces and spoke softly into wispers.

I started to feel a little paranoid right then.

I looked to Jinx. "Did you see–"

He nodded.

Fly-Girl continued talking. "The Church keeps the Dreamer locked away so he'll keep dreaming what they want him too. This!" She made a sweeping gesture that caused several of the flies to detach from her arm, and they hurried to catch up with the rest. "This reality, and Earth's, are nothing more than a fantasy conjured by the First Dreamer's mind. The Church wants to keep reality the way it is, and so they force the Dreamer to continue dreaming the same dream. It's slavery! The Dreamer should be free to dream as he wishes. One day the Wakener shall come and rouse the First Dreamer, and then reality will be free to take whatever form it will!"

"Blasphemy!" Crow-Head shouted. He swung his *Primogenium* at Fly-Girl. His clawed hand swept the book through the group of flies that made her head, scaring them. They buzzed furiously as they swarmed around, but her body continued to stand, seemingly unaffected by suddenly finding itself headless. Each of the individual flies had intact heads, I thought. Maybe that's why she didn't appear to be injured.

I decided it was time to step in before the situation could get any worse. I started toward the two Incubi, Jinx at my side. But, just as we reached them, a woman approached from the opposite direction. She was in her sixties, thin-faced, with long white hair that she wore in a thick single braid down her back. She looked like she'd originally come from somewhere in the Pacific Islands on Earth, but I wasn't sure. She wore a white robe which marked her as an official in the Church of the First Dreamer, and the trio of golden stripes around the neck, sleeves, and hem indicated she was a highly placed official.

She smiled kindly as she drew near the two Incubi and placed a hand on each of their shoulders as she reached them.

"Looks like we have a difference of opinion here."

Her voice was kind and soothing. The flies still buzzing in the air grew quieter and began to circle more slowly, but they did not rejoin to form Fly-Girl's head.

Crow-Head bowed before speaking. "Ecclesiastor, this... *woman* was making outrageous claims about the Church. She said–"

The Ecclesiastor tightened her grip on Crow-Head's shoulder and his beak snapped shut.

"It doesn't matter what she said. All are entitled to their views. Diversity in all things is a prime component of the Dream, is it not?"

Crow-Head looked down as if ashamed. "Yes, Ecclesiastor."

She smiled. "Good. Now why don't you go off by yourself to meditate for a while and restore your calm?"

He nodded without lifting his gaze, then turned and shuffled off on his bird feet. The Ecclesiastor remained standing next to Fly-Girl, her hand still gripping the Incubus' shoulder.

"And you, child. I respect your part in the Dream, but now I think it best if you move on."

The flies that had formed the woman's head slowed down even more, and they flew closer together, almost but not quite reassembling into their former shape.

"What if she doesn't want to move on?" I said. Thinking before I speak has never been one of my strengths.

The Ecclesiastor turned to me, smile still fixed firmly on her face, although now it was a bit strained.

"Hello, officer." Her gaze flicked to Jinx. "Officers."

The fact that she didn't acknowledge Jinx right away pissed me off, but it didn't surprise me. Some Firstians view Incubi as lesser creatures, dreams of dreams, as it were. Sure, they were still part of the *Dream*, and that was all well and good – as long as they remembered their place. An Incubus cop? That was getting more than a bit above Jinx's station as far as she was concerned.

The Ecclesiastor returned her gaze to me and continued speaking. "Of course this child is free to do as she pleases. But in the interest of maintaining the peace, she might consider keeping her distance from Heckle until he's had a chance to cool down. That's all I meant to suggest."

Jinx snorted. "Sounded to me like you were telling her to fuck off."

A few cracks developed in the Ecclesiastor's placid expression, but it didn't break, and she didn't rise to Jinx's bait. The flies buzzing around in the space where Fly-Girl's head had been started flying in erratic patterns, but then they quickly settled down and joined together to form the woman's head once more.

"Yes," Fly-Girl said. "I think that would be best. Thank you."

The Ecclesiastor removed her hand from the woman's shoulder, and she turned and walked away.

"I wonder why she bothers walking," Jinx said. "I mean, she *is* made up of flies."

The Ecclesiastor then reached out and clasped my right hand in both of hers. She held my hand tightly and my wounded fingers flared with pain, despite the glove I wore. I couldn't help grimacing. I'm sure she noticed, but she didn't remark on it.

"Thank you for being willing to step in and help, Officer…"

"Hawthorne," I said. "And this is Jinx."

He smiled broadly, displaying a mouthful of jagged yellowed teeth and bleeding gums. A small worm of some kind stuck its head out from between a gap in his front teeth and wiggled, as if it were waving to the Ecclesiastor.

"A pleasure," she said, in a tone which indicated it was anything but. She turned back to me. "I'm Ecclesiastor Withrow, but you, my dear, can call me Constance. Tell me, are you a believer?"

It was the second time that day I'd been asked that question, and I still had no idea how to answer it. While

I pondered my reply, Jinx slurped the worm back into his mouth and began chewing with noisy wet smacking sounds.

"Once you discover the Maelstrom is real and that its energies can be shaped to create... well, *anything*, it's hard not to believe, you know?" I said.

"I do know." Her smile seemed genuine this time. "But that wasn't an answer to my question."

She turned and started walking back to the Idyllon. I looked around for the three people who had presumably alerted her to Heckle's dispute with Fly-Girl, but they were gone. This did not come as a surprise to me. What I *did* find surprising – or at least puzzling – were a half dozen small black objects lying on the ground where Fly-Girl had been standing. I knelt to get a closer look and saw they were flies. Dead ones.

"Check this out," I said to Jinx.

He knelt next to me, and we examined the flies for several moments.

"Maybe she shed them," Jinx said. "Like humans shed skin cells."

"Maybe," I allowed, but somehow I didn't think it was that simple. I straightened. "Come on, let's go."

"Just a sec." Jinx picked up the flies before standing. "Waste not, want not," he said, and popped the entire handful into his mouth, and started chewing.

Then we continued on our way, in search of a Door.

It took Jinx the better part of an hour to find one. By that time, we were in Newtown once more, close to the Maul. Many of the pedestrians wore body armor and carried weapons ranging from claymores to automatic machine guns. The Maul takes combat shopping to the ultimate level, and you can tell those who've just left, because they carry plastic bags filled with purchases and bear numerous bandaged wounds and hobble down the sidewalk at the best pace their broken bodies can manage.

"There," Jinx said, and pointed.

The building was shaped like a giant demon head – pointed ears, curved ram's horns, leering mouth filled with sharp teeth – made entirely of jade. The demon's eyes focused on us, and the leering grin grew wider.

"You've got to be kidding," I said.

Jinx's own grin wasn't much different from the demon head's.

"Nope."

Sometimes Doors manifest as new openings on existing structures. Sometimes they overlap an opening that's already there. This appeared to be one of the latter cases.

"I suppose we have to go through the mouth." I didn't relish the idea of having to pass those teeth, especially if the demon head decided to close its mouth while we did so.

"You should be so lucky," Jinx said.

"Please tell me the Door is in one of the ears."

Jinx kept grinning, and, with a sigh, I started walking toward the demon's huge nose, Jinx chuckling as he followed.

FOUR

I looked around in confusion. One instant I'd been climbing up into a giant demonic nostril, and now I stood in a grassy field, blue sky and fluffy white clouds overhead, tree-covered mountains off in the distance. A dozen kites of various colors and designs filled the air, flown by kids whose parents stood close by.

"It's one of my favorite memories. I have an uncle and aunt who live in Oregon. My parents used to take me to visit them every summer. I loved the windy days the best. As you can see."

He smiled and nodded toward a boy who was running all out, trying to launch his kite skyward. It took a moment before the wind caught it, but after that it rose swiftly into the air. The boy stopped running and turned around to control his kite, a huge grin on his face.

I recognized the boy. He and I had spent hours in therapy – alone and in group – with Dr Kauffman, AKA the Fata Morgana. It was Russell Pelfrey, or, rather, a memory of him. The adult Russell stood next to me, looking exactly like he had the last time I'd seen him. He wore his somewhat cartoonish pirate outfit – purple cape and hood, white shirt with poofy sleeves, tight black pants, brown leather boots, M-energy rapier belted at his waist. He reached up and pulled back the hood, giving me an unobstructed view of his handsome face, puppy-dog eyes, brown hair, and neatly trimmed beard.

I had no idea how to play this. Should I be pissed off that he hadn't so much as tried to contact me since we stopped the Fata Morgana? Should I play it cool and act like it was no big deal to see him? Should I not say anything and kick him in the crotch as hard as I could? Then again, I might have use for that part of his anatomy one day. Best not damage it.

"Where are we?" I asked.

"*Between*," he said. "This" – he gestured to the pleasant scene around us – "is just a backdrop. Decora-tion while we talk."

The wind didn't become any stronger, but it did become louder. And it didn't sound like wind anymore. It sounded like whispering.

"Is that *them*?" I asked.

He nodded. "The Thresholders."

Russell posed as a mercenary called Nocturne, but the mysterious beings called the Thresholders were his real bosses. I had no idea what they were or what their agenda was. Russell might have been an old friend, and he had helped Jinx and me defeat the Fata Morgana, but that didn't mean I could trust him. It was hard to remember that, especially when I looked into his eyes.

Yeah, I know. Sue me.

"So this place – if it *is* a place – is between Earth and Nod. Hey, where's Jinx?" I tried to feel him through our link, but I couldn't sense him at all. I felt a stab of panic, and I had to force myself to remain calm.

"He's here," Russell said. "Kind of. He's not aware of any of this, though. As usual, the trip to Earth will seem instantaneous to him."

"And the Thresholders are doing this because…"

"So we can talk."

"So *now* you want to talk." I'd tried to resist, really I had, but when you're handed that good a straight line, what can you do?

His brow furrowed into an almost-frown.

"My employers are using their powers to hold us in an infinitesimally small fraction of time between dimensions, and you want to start an argument?"

I shrugged. "Seems as good a time as any."

He sighed. "Fine. After we finished foiling the Fata Morgana's plans, word got around Nod that Nocturne was working for the Shadow Watch. I had to restore my cover as a neutral mercenary, and that meant staying away from Shadow Watch officers."

"Including me."

"Yes. I thought about ditching the Nocturne identity completely and establishing another…"

"But Bloodshedder is too distinctive an Incubus," I said. "As long as she was with you, everyone would know who you are. And speaking of your little doggie…"

"She's in Nod. I'll be heading back there when we're done here."

Russell's "employers" were somehow able to transport him between dimensions without the use of Doors, although I had a suspicion they didn't do it often. Maybe it was too difficult and energy expensive.

"You could've sent me a text or a handwritten note. Something."

The whispering grew even louder, and it took on a sharp, angry edge.

I decided to take pity on Russell. "Bosses. What can you do?"

He gave me a relieved smile. But just so he'd know he wasn't off the hook, I said, "But you'll have to make it up to me. Now, since your bosses are working so hard to make this meeting possible, let's get down to business. What do you need to tell me?"

"You've been working on finding out who's manufacturing and distributing shuteye."

"Do you know who it is? Do the Thresholders?" My hopes rose faster than Jinx could crack open a skull with Cuthbert Junior. If Russell could give me that information, I could shut down their entire operation – with the rest of the Shadow Watch's help, of course.

"Sorry. My bosses are very powerful in their own realm, but their influence is limited in other dimensions."

"Of course it is," I said, trying not to sound as disappointed as I felt. "Otherwise, why would they need to employ agents?"

"Right. The Thresholders are also interested in taking down the shuteye ring, and I've been trying to infiltrate the organization for weeks. But I haven't had much luck."

"Because you helped me?"

"Maybe. But I can't even get hold of much information about the operation. I can find street dealers without too much trouble, and I've even located a couple suppliers. But as for manufacturers – nothing."

I asked him for the name of dealers and suppliers he'd identified, but none were new to me.

I quickly filled him in on Jinx's and my encounter with Montrose.

"Sorry about what happened to your trainees," he said. "It wasn't your fault."

"Maybe not, but it sure feels like it was." I hurried on before he could try to make me feel better. I didn't *want* to feel better about what had happened. I didn't think I deserved to. "If you came to me hoping I'd be able to give you information, you're going to be disappointed. I don't know anything more than you do."

"That's what I thought, but it doesn't hurt to check, right? But I also wanted to warn you. Whoever is behind the shuteye ring knows that I've been sniffing around their operation, and they decided to do something about it."

He lifted his shirt to show a large gauze pad taped to his lower right side.

I winced. "I bet that hurt."

"Like a bitch," he said, and then lowered his shirt. I wished he'd kept it up a little longer. I liked the view.

"They – whoever *they* are – sent an assassin after you?"

"They sent two. Real pros, too. If my employers hadn't pulled Bloodshedder and me out of the situation when they did…" He trailed off, but he didn't need to complete the thought.

"So you're warning me to watch my back. Okay. Consider me warned."

If the mysterious *they* could afford to hire assassins good enough to give Russell trouble, that meant they had some serious connections. I automatically suspected the Lords of Misrule, but they were far from the only candidates. The Hand of Erebus, the Red Claw, the

Unbound, the Grim Sleepers… any of them could be mixed up in this.

"Why are the Thresholders interested in shuteye?" I asked.

"Honestly? I don't know." He smiled ruefully. "They aren't big on excess conversation."

"Need to know, huh?"

He nodded. "And, as far as they're concerned, I don't need. But they're deeply concerned, I can tell that much. I get the impression that they fear something big's coming, something that's connected to the shuteye trade. And they're determined to do whatever it takes to stop it."

I sighed. I missed the days when all I had to do was bust petty criminals and try to keep Jinx from killing them.

"So what are you going to do?" I asked.

"I'm going to stay in Nod and make myself a target. If I can keep the bad guys' attention focused on me, they might leave you and Jinx alone."

"What do you think the odds are of that happening?"

"Slim to none," he admitted. "But it's worth a shot. What about you?"

"Jinx and I are going to look up an old friend who dealt with shuteye the last time it hit the streets. We'll see what he can tell us."

Russell nodded as if he knew exactly who I was talking about. Maybe he did.

"I'll keep in touch," Russell said. I must've had a skeptical expression on my face, because he added, "I mean it."

We looked at each other then. There was nothing more to say, and we were hardly going to embrace and kiss. We hadn't even been on an actual date yet. But neither of us wanted to say goodbye.

Feeling confused and uncomfortable, I turned to take in Russell's memory-scape. The sky, the clouds, the mountains in the distance... It was all so beautiful, so peaceful. There were no people now, though. As far as I was concerned, they had never been there in the first place. I had a nagging sensation that something wasn't quite right, but when I turned to mention this to Russell, my vision grayed, went black, and when it cleared I found myself squinting to shut out a sudden explosion of bright sunlight.

I stumbled as I stepped out of the Door, and I felt a hand on my elbow – firm but gentle – steadying me. I opened my eyes slowly to give them a chance to adjust to the light. I glanced over my shoulder and caught a glimpse of a Door set into a wall. It was already fading, and, within seconds, it was gone. Doors usually only exist at night, but they don't always vanish with the first light of day. If they have a particularly strong connection to Earth, they can linger up to a half hour past sunrise, especially if a lot of people in the area are still asleep. It seemed that Jinx had found one such door.

We were standing in an alley, and I could hear the sound of traffic filtering in from the street. I wasn't sure where we were. Hell, we could've been in any city on Earth, but it *felt* like Chicago.

I turned to Jinx. "Thanks."

He smiled and let go of my elbow now that I was no longer in danger of falling over.

"I've been propping you up for years. I'm used to it."

"Ha-ha."

Jinx had assumed his Day Aspect the instant he'd

passed through the Door and into sunlight. I hadn't been looking at him when it happened, but, even if I had been, the change occurs instantaneously, with no apparent transition between the two states. His skin was Caucasian and he was still bald. I've never seen him shave his head – or his face – so, for all I know, he can't grow hair. Maybe if he remained human for more than half a day at a time, he would. He still wore his gray suit, but his tie was now normal size, the colors less vibrant, the polka dots smaller. His giant daisy boutonniere had become a regular-sized flower, and, as it did every time he assumed his Day Aspect, it was quickly drying up. His red-and-white shoes – not to mention the feet within them – had shrunk to a more reasonable size. But more than his appearance had changed. Day Jinx was a very different man than Night Jinx, but, in his own way, he was just as vexing.

"Do you know where we're at?" I asked.

"The Door let us out on North Lake Shore Drive. Not far from the International Museum of Surgical Science." He made a face as he said this. The museum was a favorite of his other self. Night Jinx was always on the lookout for a Door that would allow him to enter the museum after hours. Day Jinx liked museums just fine, but his favorites had a more aesthetic focus.

So we were in the Gold Coast Historic District. A pretty place for tourists to visit and take pictures, but not exactly *my* Chicago. But I couldn't complain. Sometimes you have to take the Door you can get. A week earlier, we'd ended up in Naperville. *That* was exciting, she said sarcastically.

Jinx and I stepped out of the alley, took a left, and continued down the sidewalk. The air was cold, and I

crossed my arms over my chest. I wished I'd thought to
grab a heavier jacket from my locker in the Rookery,
but, since the temperature in Nod never varies, it slipped
my mind. Jinx didn't appear to be bothered by the cold,
but then he usually isn't, regardless of his Aspect.

The Gold Coast is a mix of mansions, row houses, and
high-rise apartments. It's often associated with the
Miracle Mile, although technically it's not part of it. The
vehicles passing by on the street were the best money
could buy, all the brands you'd expect: BMW, Mercedes-
Benz, Bentley, Lexus, Porsche, Jaguar, Ferrari,
Lamborghini… Doctors, lawyers, bankers, and the like,
heading off to work. It's a good life, if you can get it. A
number of the buildings sported holiday decorations –
wreaths on doors, decorated trees in the windows. All
very tasteful. No inflatable Santas, elves, or snowmen.
Far too tacky.

I raised my wisper – so-called because it's powered by
wisps of Maelstrom energy – and called Connie for a ride.
M-tech devices will function during the day, as long as
their charge holds.

"You really think it's a good idea for Connie to come
here?" Jinx sounded uncomfortable, and I knew why.
Day Jinx can be something of a snob at times, and the
Deathmobile's Day Aspect – while much less macabre –
still earned its name, just in a different way.

I ignored his question.

"Russell paid me a visit while we were between
dimensions," I said.

Jinx arched an eyebrow, and I filled him in. As I
spoke, he removed the dead daisy from his lapel and
tucked it in his pocket for later disposal. Day Jinx was
no litterbug.

When I finished, he said, "Assassins. Wonderful. There's nothing I love better than having to keep looking over my shoulder every few seconds."

I smiled. "You should be used to people wanting to kill you by now."

He sighed. "I suppose I am. But it's awfully inconvenient. I was hoping to attend a lecture at the library this afternoon on the history of black performing arts in the city. But I can hardly do so if someone might try to kill me in the middle of the talk. I can't endanger innocent bystanders like that."

Day Jinx was a follow-the-rules and go-by-the-book type. I wondered if he truly cared about the people who might get caught in the crossfire if an assassin tried to take him out during the lecture, or if he was simply following procedure. Probably a bit of both, I decided.

"I think we should avoid going home," I said. "The assassins could be waiting for us there."

Jinx gave me a skeptical look. "You just want to avoid having to go home and rest."

I didn't bother denying it. "I rested yesterday."

"For three hours."

"I did six the day before that."

"Four-and-a-half."

There was no use arguing with him. He's always right when it comes to stuff like that.

"Hey, for me, that's being a good girl, you have to admit."

Jinx wouldn't admit any such thing, but he said, "You probably have a point about staying away from our apartment. And I suppose the sooner we talk with Mordacity, the better."

"You mean the sooner we get it over with, the better.

At least as far as you're concerned."

Jinx didn't comment, but he didn't need to. He and Mordacity didn't get along that well, regardless of which Aspect they were in.

"So did Russell say anything else?" Jinx asked.

I gave him a sideways look. "What do you mean?"

"Did he explain why he hasn't so much as called you since we dealt with the Fata Morgana?"

"You may be my partner, Jinx, but that doesn't mean my love life is any of your business."

"Anything that might have a deleterious effect on your wellbeing is my business. If for no other reason than to make sure you're operating at peak capacity as an officer." He paused, then added, "Besides, Russell's a jerk. You can do a lot better than him."

I couldn't help grinning. "Thanks, Dad."

Jinx made a face at me, but otherwise let the matter drop. I was glad. I'm more comfortable fighting bad guys at his side than talking about personal stuff with him. Facing almost-certain death? No problem. Dealing with my own confused tangle of emotions? *That's* scary.

"How are your hands?"

The sudden change of topic caught me off guard, and for a moment I didn't know what Jinx was talking about. Then I looked at my gloved hands and understood.

"They're sore, but okay."

"You should have a doctor look at them."

"They're fine. And we don't have time to see a doctor."

"If we go to an urgent care facility, it won't take long. It's–" He held up his wisper, moved his wrist in a certain way, and holographic numbers appeared in the air above the device. "–9:46. They shouldn't be busy this early." The holo-display faded and he lowered his arm.

"They wouldn't be able to do anything more for me than I've already done for myself."

I appreciated Jinx's concern, although some of it likely had to do with worries that my wounds might affect my job performance. I decided to tease him a little.

"I *could* try to find someone to sell me some stunners. That would take the edge off."

He scowled and opened his mouth to reply, but then he closed it again and gave me a look that said *Nice try*.

"How about we stop at a pharmacy on the way?" I said, serious this time. "I'll pick up some pain meds, bandages, and some antibiotic cream – the whole works. Sound good?"

"It'll suffice, I suppose."

He smiled slightly when he said this, though, and I knew he was pleased. And to be honest, it's nice having a partner watching out for you, no matter which Aspect he's in.

At that moment a sound like a mountain of scrap metal collapsing filled the air, accompanied by the stench of an oilfield fire. A baby-shit-brown Pinto that looked as if it should've died in the 1970s came rattling down the street toward us, sending property values plummeting by its very presence. Pedestrians, dog-walkers, joggers, and motorists alike gaped in horrified astonishment at the automotive abomination that desecrated their precious Gold Coast. And I grinned from ear to ear, loving every moment of it.

Jinx shook his head.

"You have an odd sense of humor sometimes, Audra."

• • •

On the way to Mordacity's, I asked Connie if she'd heard anything about shuteye being sold on the street.

"Nope. But a drug like that, it's not something people would talk openly about. Especially in front of me. People know I don't discriminate when it comes to picking up fares. Good guys, bad guys... long as they can pay. But it's not exactly a secret that I'm friends with a couple Watch officers. I could ask around if you want. See what I turn up."

"I appreciate the offer, but, if you did that, you might as well be putting a target on your back. Melody and Trauma Doll already got hurt. I don't want to add your name to the casualty list."

I sat in the front passenger seat, while Jinx was crammed into the back. He hugged his knees to his chest in order to keep his feet out of the compost heap of crumpled fast-food bags, empty plastic bottles, and other less-identifiable items. As bad as the Deathmobile smelled on the outside during the day, it was ten times worse inside. A combination of gas fumes, burning oil, sour sweat, greasy salami, and rotting vegetables that seared the inside of your nasal passages and stripped a layer of flesh from your throat. Some Incubi retain a small measure of otherworldly power in their Day Aspects, and I'd always thought the Deathmobile was one of them. I can't believe such a stench could occur naturally.

Connie is heavily pierced and tattooed, and her hair is usually dyed one color or another. Today she sported hot pink, although most of it was hidden beneath a woolen cap. Her elaborate tattoos – she has a race track stretching across her body, filled with images of cars she loves – was hidden by a winter jacket and jeans. She also wore a pair of fingerless gloves. The Deathmobile has no heat in winter and no air-conditioning in summer. I had to grit my teeth to keep them from chattering, and even Jinx looked cold.

We'd already stopped at a pharmacy, and I had a plastic bag of medical supplies on my lap. I had the bag looped around my forearm because I needed my hands to steady myself as Connie drove through the city streets, weaving in and out of traffic as if she were on the Autobahn instead of in downtown Chicago. The Deathmobile doesn't have seatbelts. I'm not sure Connie is even aware of the concept.

The last time I'd spoken with Mordacity, his "office" – for lack of a better word – was located in a rundown building on the Southside. That had been several years ago, but I hoped he was still in the same place. We'd soon find out.

The Southside has a reputation for poverty and crime, but the reality is more complex. Yeah, it has its troubles, but the neighborhoods range from working class to more affluent, and the population is more ethnically varied than in some parts of the city. Mordacity's building was located in one of the rougher neighborhoods, but I wasn't worried about going there. The Southside was nothing compared to the Cesspit in Nod – but that didn't mean I intended to let my guard down.

I asked Connie to drop us off at a corner a couple blocks from Mordacity's building. As loud as the Deathmobile was, I knew Mordacity – along with everyone else in the vicinity – would hear us coming. While Mordacity wasn't an enemy, I didn't know if he still counted as a friend, and I'd rather he didn't receive advance notice of our arrival. Jinx and I climbed out of the Deathmobile, and Connie roared off, the engine making a sound like a pack of pissed-off wolverines caught in an industrial-size woodchipper.

Jinx turned his head, sniffed the shoulder of his jacket, and made a face.

"I'm going to have to burn my clothes. Again."

"Just make sure you're not in them this time."

Jinx gave me a look which said I wasn't nearly as amusing as I thought I was. I get that from him a lot. Hey, can I help it if his Night Jinx sometimes carries out Day Jinx's wishes in unorthodox and potentially fatal ways?

We started walking down the sidewalk toward Mordacity's building. A number of the buildings were abandoned, windows boarded up and graffiti spray-painted on the walls. A liquor store was still open, as was a place called BDBBQ (Best Damn Barbecue). We didn't see many people out. A couple sat on stoops or stood on corners, all of them wearing jackets too light for the weather. They watched Jinx and me with wary eyes. In their part of town, someone wearing a suit usually meant trouble of some kind or another, and two people wearing *matching* suits was even worse. People who drove in cars far less expensive than residents of the Gold Coast also gave us hard, appraising looks. I was glad we'd come here during the day. Jinx and I might be setting off the neighborhood's warning system by our presence, but if I'd come here with Night Jinx… Let's just say a clown in a suit draws quite a lot of attention, almost none of it good.

Mordacity's place was a simple two-story gray stone building, old but in good condition. Jinx and I went inside. There was a small lobby, but no security person on duty. There was a single elevator, and a directory next to it, a black felt board with white plastic letters pushed into it. Madeline's Medical Massage (*medical*, sure) was on the first floor, along with Discount Dental. The second floor had only a single business listed, and it didn't have a full name, just a single letter: M.

I reached out to push the elevator button, but Jinx said, "This old thing will probably make as much noise as the Deathmobile. Besides, it's healthier to take the stairs."

He was right – on both counts. One of the ways for Ideators to help counter the effects of not sleeping was to remain as healthy as possible, which really sucks when your favorite food is carbs with sugar on top. But I chose to be a good girl, and I followed Jinx to the stairs and we started to climb. The stairwell smelled like bleach trying unsuccessfully to mask the smell of urine, but, after being in the Deathmobile, it smelled like spring roses. When we reached the second floor, I opened the door slowly, hoping it wouldn't creak. It made no noise, and I figured the hinges had been oiled recently, probably by Mordacity. He'd want the people who came to see him to feel comfortable, like they could come and go without being noticed if they wished.

We stepped into the hallway, and I eased the door shut behind us. I could hear someone talking softly – a male voice, not Mordacity's – but I couldn't make out what he was saying. There were half a dozen rooms on this floor, but there were no signs or office numbers on any of them, and I assumed they were empty. All but the one at the farthest end of the hall, that is. Jinx and I walked quietly down the hall until we were standing outside the door of Mordacity's... well, *office* wasn't the word he used. He called it his *space*. The door was closed, and there was nothing to indicate what lay behind it, not even an M. But it wasn't necessary. Unless things had changed since we'd last been here – and it looked like they hadn't – Mordacity was the only occupant of the second floor.

Jinx and I listened as the man inside continued to talk.

"...try to understand, but it's not easy to live with day after day. I mean, we were reunited only recently. Yeah, he only leaves for a few days at a time now, and so far he always returns. But what if one day he doesn't come back, and this time he's gone for good? I can't stop worrying about it."

I recognized the voice. It belonged to Abe Chen, and, from his words, I knew the *he* he spoke of was his Incubus, Budgie. I felt suddenly embarrassed for eavesdropping on him. Abe was a good guy, and a friend. He and Budgie had helped us out against the Fata Morgana, and, back in the days when I was using, I could always count on Abe to be carrying a little something extra for me. Like me, he was clean these days, but it sounded as if he were going through a hard time, and I was afraid he might start using again.

I'd just decided that Jinx and I would leave and come back later when Abe stopped talking. The door opened a moment later.

"It's okay. You don't have to wait outside. All are welcome here," he smiled. "You both should know that."

In his Day Aspect, Mordacity was a middle-aged black man with short hair and a goatee that was starting to go gray. He was round-faced, medium height, and stout, and when he smiled – which was often – he resembled an African-American Buddha. He wore an off-white turtleneck, black jeans, and a pair of highly polished black shoes.

It had been several years since we'd spoken, and, although his Day Aspect is a kind, forgiving sort, I hadn't been sure what kind of response Jinx and I would get when we turned up on his doorstep. Now I knew, but, despite his friendly greeting, I still felt uncomfortable. Or maybe it was *because* of his greeting. I think it would've been easier to take if he'd been angry with us.

He stepped aside so Jinx and I could enter. Once we were inside, he gestured toward the circle of metal folding chairs arranged in the center of the room.

"Take a seat, please."

Most of the chairs were occupied, but there were two empty ones. They weren't together, though, so Jinx and I had to sit apart. Dr Menendez had said we should try to keep some physical distance between us, so I figured this was a good first step.

Abe sat opposite me, and he gave me a nod and smiled, then did the same for Jinx. Abe's an Asian man in his early sixties, and he wore a pullover sweater, jeans, and sneakers. He was a little fuller in the face than the last time I'd seen him, and I figured that he'd been eating better – not to mention more regularly – since he'd stopped using. I didn't know any of the other people in the room, not well, anyway. I'd seen a couple of them around, but that was all. There were eight people present, not counting Mordacity, Jinx, and myself, and they varied in age, gender, and race. Ideators and Incubi, but I couldn't tell who was who just by looking at them. Incubi tend to be a bit "off" in their Day Aspects, but not always, and humans can be weird enough even when they aren't Ideators.

Mordacity took the last unoccupied chair and looked at Abe.

"Sorry for the interruption. Go on, please."

Abe glanced at us, clearly uncomfortable, but he started talking again.

"Budgie's a bird, of course, so I understand his need to roam, but I worry about him when he's away. In his Day Aspect, he's so small, and at night... well, he'd certainly give anyone who saw him a fright, and I wouldn't be surprised if people started taking shots at him."

By day, Budgie was a parakeet, but by night he was a huge pterosaur. I could understand Abe's concern.

Abe kept talking, but his words were all variations on the same theme, and I found myself tuning out. I looked around the room, interested to see if anything had changed since my last visit. The same gray carpet covered the floor, but it was a little dingier now. The walls were the same "relocation beige," and the same framed pictures hung there, all paintings or photos of lighthouses. Most of them were night scenes, with the lighthouse's beam cutting through fog. The symbolism was so clumsy it bordered on kitsch. As if the room didn't look enough like the setting of an AA meeting; against one wall was a table with a coffee maker, creamer, and sugar packets, along with an assortment of cookies spread out on a Styrofoam plate. The coffee looked damned tempting. I may not use rev anymore, but I hadn't given up caffeine. That way lies madness.

The others in the group were less comfortable with our

presence than Abe. We were obviously Shadow Watch officers, and a lot of folk with connections to Nod avail themselves of that realm's unique pharmaceuticals, along with other questionable products and shady activities. But Mordacity had vouched for us simply by way of his friendly greeting and invitation to stay, and, if the others never relaxed fully in our presence, no one left and the meeting continued.

When Abe finished speaking, everyone clapped, so Jinx and I did too. Then it was someone else's turn to talk, and after that, someone else's. Jinx and I sat there quietly and listened. Mordacity wouldn't talk to us until the meeting was over. Until then, all we could do was wait. I'd already known the purpose of Mordacity's group session, but, even if I hadn't, it would've become obvious very quickly. Everyone here, whether Ideator or Incubus, had been separated from his or her counterpart. Some were like Abe – Ideators whose Incubi liked to roam. Others were Incubi whose Ideators had died, leaving them to continue living on their own. A few had experienced a falling out with their counterpart for one reason or another, and it was those stories that affected me the most. Roaming Incubi are to be expected since living nightmares are, by their very nature, chaotic. And, while it's sad, Incubi naturally outlive their Ideators since Maelstrom energy is what keeps them alive. But when Incubi and Ideators split up because of some sort of dispute, it strikes me as such a waste. Too much pride, stubbornness, and hurt feelings on either side can lead to years of unhappiness for both parties.

Mordacity was good at his second career, and no wonder. He understood what it was like to be separated from his Ideator.

I did my best to pay attention to the stories people told, but I couldn't keep my mind from wandering. After all, seeing Mordacity for the first time in years reminded me of my own story – one that was in many ways the main reason I'd come here.

"I don't think this is a good idea," I said, in a near-whisper.

Jinx and I stood in the shadow of an alley in the Cesspit. We weren't alone.

"And what in your voluminous and widely varied experience as a Watcher makes you say this?"

Nathaniel smiled and his tone was gently teasing. Still, I knew there was some seriousness to his words. I was, after all, only nineteen and technically still a trainee.

I shook my head. I was unable to put the way I felt into words, but I couldn't escape the feeling that something was wrong.

Mordacity didn't add anything. He tended to defer to Nathaniel, and he rarely spoke in his Night Aspect, preferring to let his actions do the talking for him.

Nathaniel Sawyer was the Shadow Watch's top officer – something of a legend, really – and he had specifically requested to be my mentor after seeing Jinx and me performing "adequately but unevenly" – as our assessment read – during final training exercises at the Watch Academy. When I'd asked him why he made the request, he'd just smiled, and said, "You tell me."

And that, in a nutshell, was what being Nathaniel's trainee was like.

He was a tall, wiry man in his early fifties, with light brown skin and neatly trimmed blond hair. He was always clean-shaven – I'd never seen so much as a hint

of stubble on his face – and his Watch uniform suit was
always freshly pressed and spotless. I tried to play it cool
around him, but the truth was that he intimidated me.
Not because he was mean or anything, but because he
seemed to have his shit together 24/7. He was totally
relaxed and comfortable, even in the most dangerous
situations, and I felt like an awkward child around him.

Mordacity was, in his own way, just as frightening as
Jinx. In his Night Aspect, he resembled a medieval
knight, but, instead of metal, his armor was formed from
ancient, yellowed bone. Thick curving ribs protected his
chest and back, and his arms and legs were encased in
lengths of human bone – ulnae, radii, femora, tibiae…
The bone-like structure was part of his body, more of a
carapace than actual armor, and the effect was eerie as
hell. He had a helmet that grew out of a fleshless
grinning skull, and, for extra-scary effect, crimson
pinpoints of light smoldered within the depths of his
empty eye sockets. He wore a black cape that looked as
if it were made of shadow instead of cloth, and he
carried a long sword – also fashioned from bone – in a
black scabbard belted at his waist. He wore a trancer
holstered at his other hip but, like Jinx, he preferred to
use his personal weapon whenever possible.

I turned to Jinx, hoping he might back me up, but
when I saw him grinning at me, the light from a wide-
open Espial making his white face almost glow, I
shuddered and turned away. I still wasn't used to my
worst nightmare having come to life, let alone being my
partner in my new job.

The four of us were on a stakeout in the Cesspit, and
we'd taken up a position in an alley between a bar called
Blood in Your Eye and a restaurant called Bottom

Feeders. This section of the Cesspit lay on the banks of Lethe, the winding river that flows through Nod. The alley floor was a soupy muck of mud and garbage – the latter of which didn't bear close scrutiny. Sometimes it's better not to know what you're standing in. The air was thick with a stench so eye-burningly acrid it threatened to sear off the outer layers of your skin. Neither Nathaniel nor Mordacity seemed to notice the stink, let alone be bothered by it. Jinx, on the other hand, kept drawing in deep breaths through his nostrils and sighing contentedly, as if he were smelling a bouquet of fresh flowers.

Nathaniel had gotten word from one of his informants that a shuteye dealer named Ocho frequented Blood in Your Eye, and we were here to, as Nathaniel put it, "Have a deep, meaningful discussion" with him. What I couldn't figure out was why we were all standing around in the alley when Ocho was probably inside the bar tossing back cold beer, one after another. I made another attempt to express my reservations.

"What if someone spots us out here and goes inside to warn Ocho? What if he sneaks out the back? What if–"

Unlike Nathaniel, Mordacity wasn't given to enigmatic comments. When he spoke, he told it like he saw it.

"Ocho is a small-time dealer. We're interested in finding out who his supplier is."

Mordacity's voice wasn't what you'd expect to hear coming from a skeletal knight. It wasn't hollow or sepulchral. It didn't sound like a wind blowing through a graveyard at midnight. It was full, deep, and rich. Once, Nathaniel had confided in me that he'd seen the original *Star Wars* as a kid and that "Vader scared the crap out of me." Whenever Mordacity started to creep me out too much, I imagined him saying, "This is CNN." It helped – a little.

"But how is standing in an alley going to help us find the supplier?" I was starting to get frustrated now, and my voice rose to near-normal volume.

Before either Nathaniel or Mordacity could answer, Jinx spoke.

"The supplier won't talk to Ocho inside the bar. They'll meet outside, probably in this alley. If we're patient, they'll come to us."

I was surprised. Jinx wasn't normally one for strategy and tactics, and he *certainly* wasn't one for waiting.

Nathaniel nodded approvingly. "Exactly."

Jinx looked at me then, his grin growing wider and a dangerous gleam coming into his eyes.

"But where's the fun in that?" he said.

He pulled Cuthbert out of his pocket, took a two-handed grip on the handle, and swung the head of the hammer toward Blood in Your Eye's wall before any of us could do anything to stop him.

FIVE

The wall imploded in a shower of shattered brick, creating an opening large enough for Jinx to leap through. I started after him reflexively, but Nathaniel grabbed my shoulder and pulled me back.

"Stay here," he ordered, scowling, and then, without another word, he drew his trancer and climbed through Jinx's makeshift door. Already sounds of fighting came from inside – shouts, cursing, bestial roars, splintering wood, shattering glass, and trancer fire. It didn't take much to set off violence in the Cesspit, and the residents were always ready to give worse than they got.

Mordacity turned to me, and the crimson fires burning within the hollows of his skull blazed brighter.

"Listen to him this time."

And then he drew his bone sword and followed after Nathaniel, leaving me standing in the alley and seething. They'd acted as if I'd done something wrong, but Jinx had been the one who – in typically psychotic fashion – had broken through the wall. Maybe I'd dreamed Jinx into existence, but he was a separate being from me. I had no control over him, so why had

Nathaniel and Mordacity acted like Jinx's latest act of insanity was *my* fault?

I drew my trancer just to feel as if I was doing something, and positioned myself in front of the jagged opening in the wall. Nathaniel might have told me to stay outside, but he hadn't said I couldn't help out from where I stood.

Because of its proximity to Lethe, Blood in Your Eye caters to water-based Incubi, and the bar's clientele that day were no exception. Through the hole in the wall I caught glimpses of creatures covered in fish scales, with webbing between the fingers of their clawed hands, and rows of sharp teeth filling lipless mouths. I saw a man with piranha fish in place of his hands, a reverse mermaid – fish on top, naked woman on the bottom – a man with a ringed lamprey's maw where his face should've been, and a humanoid crocodile with blue-white tendrils of electricity sparking from its teeth.

Jinx stood in the middle of the room, swinging Cuthbert in wide arcs around him and shouting, "Which one of you waterlogged freaks is named Ocho?"

The smart Incubi removed themselves from the path of Jinx's hammer, while the stupid ones ran forward to attack, only to be rewarded with pulped faces and crushed skulls. Nathaniel and Mordacity stood back to back not far from Jinx. Nathaniel fired his trancer in short, precise bursts, each blast striking an Incubus directly between the eyes and causing them to collapse to the floor, stunned. I envied my mentor's aim. Even with all the practicing I'd done, I still mostly just squeezed the trigger and hoped for the best when I fired. Mordacity, as usual, went old school, wielding his long sword with graceful ease, as if it were as light and maneuverable as a fencing foil. For an extra touch of class, he used only the flat of his blade against his opponents to avoid injuring them.

I raised my trancer and took aim at an Incubus who looked like a bloated drowned corpse, covered with tiny crabs nibbling at his discolored flesh. He held a chair above his head and was moving toward Nathaniel, shaking off mini-crabs with each step he took. He obviously intended to brain Nathaniel with the chair, but my mentor was so busy dealing with other opponents that so far he hadn't noticed the Incubus approaching.

"Hey, Crab-Cakes!" I shouted, not knowing whether he'd be able to hear me over the din of the fighting around him. He must have, though, for he turned to face me – I can't say he *looked* at me since the crabs had devoured his eyes – and hesitated.

I fired.

A beam of swirling multicolored power streaked through the air, hit the chair, and reduced it to kindling.

Nathaniel noticed Crab-Cakes then, and dropped him with a quick blast between the man's ravaged eyes sockets. He then spared a second to glance my way.

"Admirable restraint!" he called out, grinning.

I grinned back. No need to tell him that I'd been aiming for Crab-Cakes' chest.

I looked around for another target, but, before I could select one, a slender limb that resembled an octopus tentacle emerged through the gap in the wall and sealed tight to the outer stone. It was quickly followed by several more, and, an instant later, they pulled the rest of the creature's body upward.

"I've seen ugly in this town," I said, "but you're *way* up there on the ick scale."

The Incubus had eight octopus tentacles growing from the neck of a human male's bald head. At least, I *thought* it was supposed to be human. The features were overlarge and distorted: a jutting brow, one big watery eye (the other was concealed by a squint), a bulbous nose, sharp cheek bones, and a bulging chin with a pronounced cleft that made it look like he had a butt on the lower half of his face. The Incubus glared at me with his one good eye, but, instead of responding to my witty observation, he slid down the wall with moist, mucusy sounds, plopped into the alley's foul muck, and then headed toward the street, pulling and pushing with his tentacles, moving with surprising speed. I figured that, while he wasn't much in the looks department, he was no dummy and wanted to get the hell out of there while the getting was good. I forgot about him and turned my attention back to the bar, just in time to hear Nathaniel shout, "That was Ocho! Stop him!"

Nathaniel, Mordacity, and Jinx had done a good job clearing out the bar. Half of the remaining patrons were lying on the floor in various states of semi- or unconsciousness, and in dire need of immediate medical attention. But the tougher half remained on their feet and fighting, keeping my companions busy. There was no one else who could chase after Ocho but me. Thrilled to have a chance to go into action solo and show Nathaniel and Mordacity what I could do, I turned and hauled ass after Ocho.

By the time I reached the mouth of the alley, he was already halfway across the street. His tentacles allowed him to slide through the gray-green street goo as if it were water.

"Stop in the name of the Watch!" I shouted, and then felt like a complete asshole for doing so. Like the less-than-commanding tone of my voice was going to frighten him into giving up.

I ran into the street after Ocho, my shoes splashing in the muck. If anything, it was worse out here than in the alley, and I had to be careful to avoid slipping. If I fell in this shit, who knew how many lethal infections I'd contract?

As I ran, an Incubus came roaring down the street toward me, sending up glop-spray as it came. It was a mechanical creature that resembled a robotic centaur, except, instead of half its body being a horse, it was a motorcycle. The humanoid part rose from where the handle bars would've been on a regular bike. When the Moto-Centaur saw me, he opened his mouth and a shrieking sound like a rotary saw blade scratching across sheet metal emerged. The Incubus kept coming straight toward me, and I knew it wouldn't bother trying to miss me. Incubi aren't much on the whole sanctity of human life thing.

So I aimed my trancer in his general direction and fired. I didn't come close to hitting him, but the energy beam passed near enough to his face to startle him, causing him to swerve. He slid past me – spraying me with muck in the process – then slammed into the front of a business called Savage Salvage. Immediately a pair of Incubi resembling giant Day-Glo lobsters scuttled out of the building and began disassembling the Motor-Centaur, wielding their claws like high-speed precision tools. The

Incubus shrieked once more in his sheet-metal voice, but he didn't shriek for long.

"Sucks to be you," I said, and continued running after Ocho.

He slipped into another alley and shot down it like a tentacled, human-headed rocket. I followed, half-running, half-sliding through the glop. The sheer amount of trash, body parts, and bone fragments in this alley slowed him down a bit, which allowed me to close the distance. As we emerged from the alley, I saw Lethe. Its banks were lined with rusted iron rods atop which were fixed large deep-water fish with mouthfuls of long curving needle teeth, huge blind eyes, and narrow tendrils of flesh protruding from their heads which terminated in bioluminescent nubs. The fish illuminated the rippling surface of the river, and the dark silhouettes of whatever large creatures swam within. Water Incubi use Lethe to travel through Nod – or to lay in wait for prey. Nathaniel's theory was that the shuteye manufacturers, whoever they were, used the river to distribute the drug throughout the city. It was a good theory, but one we might not be able to prove if Ocho escaped.

I knew that, if Ocho managed to reach the water, there was no way I'd be able to catch him. So I stopped running, slid to a halt, raised my trancer in a two-handed grip, took my time to aim, and fired. The beam struck Ocho on the back of his bald head, and his tentacles spasmed as his nervous system struggled to cope with the energy surge. I ran toward him, hoping to get close enough to grab hold of him, but white light exploded behind my eyes and I felt suddenly weightless as the world spun around me. The sensation of motion abruptly ended with a painful jolt, and I thought, *What the hell just hit me?*

I blinked several times, trying to force my blurry vision to clear. When I could more or less see again, I saw Ocho on the bank of the river. His body was no longer twitching, and he was looking at me with a dark smile on his shipwreck of a face. Standing next to him was a massive figure at least eight feet tall. It wore a yellow rain slicker and black knee-high rubber boots. Its head, arms, and legs were thick, bloated lengths of earthworm, and fish hooks the size of small anchors pierced his arms and neck, their metal slick with blood and mucus. Water dripped from his body, and I realized he'd just emerged from Lethe, probably on his way to meet Ocho in Blood in Your Eye.

"Let me… guess." Every time I breathed, it felt like someone jabbed a knife into my lungs, but I kept talking. "You're Ocho's supplier."

"He's called the Angler," Ocho said, in a rough, raspy voice. "And you're going to be his catch of the day!"

The worm-thing had no discernible facial features – no eyes, nose, or mouth – but its head rippled in a way that I took to be assent. The Angler started toward me, walking with an odd, quivering gait on his boneless legs. I wasn't about to let him get hold of me. Being touched by slimy worm-arms would be bad enough, but I didn't relish the thought of those fish-hook barbs penetrating my flesh.

I started to raise my trancer to fire, intending to hold down the trigger and use up the rest of the weapon's charge if I had to, when I realized I was no longer holding the gun. I'd dropped it when the Angler had struck me, and I saw that Ocho now gripped it in one of his tentacles. Fantastic. I'd lost my weapon in the middle of a fight. Nathaniel was *so* going to yell at me. Although, if I didn't do something fast, he'd have to yell at my corpse.

I rose to my feet, my mind racing as I tried to think of some way to fight the Angler. Running away wasn't an option. Not only wasn't it in my nature, I didn't think I'd get very far. I didn't have any weapons beside my trancer, and I certainly didn't have anything specifically designed to deal with worms. No salt to dehydrate him or pesticide to poison him. I made a mental note to encourage Jinx to fill his bottomless pockets with a variety of different and unorthodox weapons. I was beginning to understand that, when fighting Incubi, you never knew what you might need.

I decided that I was going to have to fight barehanded and wondered what it would feel like to punch a guy whose body was made out of giant earthworms. I wondered if I'd get a chance to hit him before he slashed the pointed end of one of those hooks across my throat.

"Stay where you are!"

Nathaniel came charging out of the alley, and, while I wasn't thrilled that my mentor saw me disarmed and barely able to remain standing, I'd be lying if I said I also wasn't relieved as hell to see him.

The Angler turned toward Nathaniel and swung one of his arms like a whip. The hook embedded in that arm tore free and whirled through the air like a shuriken. Nathaniel attempted to dodge it, but it caught him on the right shoulder and sank deep. He cried out in pain, and dropped his trancer. He fell to one knee and gritted his teeth as he fought to shut out the pain.

I looked to the alley, hoping to see Jinx, Mordacity or ,better yet, both appear. But there was no sign of them. I'd later learn that Jinx was so caught up in the frenzy of destruction that he'd had no idea what was happening with Nathaniel and me. As for Mordacity, he did manage to extricate himself from the bar brawl and was on his way. But he wouldn't reach us in time.

The Angler walked past me as if I no longer existed and headed for Nathaniel. I made a grab for him as he went by, but I missed. I'd forgotten that I'd hit my head when I'd fallen, and a wave of dizziness combined with nausea hit me. I fought to retain my balance, and I managed to keep from falling over, if only barely. I did my best to run toward Nathaniel, but all I could manage was a shuffling walk. I wanted to tackle the Angler from behind, but, before I could do more than take a few awkward steps, I felt a warm, tingling sensation wash over me, and my legs suddenly felt as boneless as the Angler's. I fell to the ground again, unable to move, and I knew that Ocho had shot me with my own trancer. On the right setting, trancers can put humans to sleep, but, as an Ideator, a single burst on that setting won't work on me. But the energy could render me immobile, and that's what had happened.

I lay in the muck, unable to do more than watch as the Angler reached Nathaniel. Despite his shoulder wound, Nathaniel rose to his feet and lunged at the Incubus, but the Angler slapped him across the face with one of his boneless arms, and Nathaniel went back down. The Angler wrapped a squirming arm around the hook embedded in Nathaniel's shoulder and tore it free with a single powerful yank. Blood streamed from Nathaniel's wound, and, although I thought he was unconscious, he screamed. I thought the Angler was going to finish off Nathaniel with the hook, but instead he stuck it back into his own arm. Then he reached into one of his slicker's pockets and brought out a plastic container. He pried it open and removed a pill. He closed the container, put it back in his pocket, and then, with the speed of a striking snake, he thrust the tip of his wormy hand into Nathaniel's mouth. Nathaniel gagged as the Angler continued shoving his arm deeper, and I realized that he intended to deposit the pill directly into Nathaniel's stomach.

"Get away from him!"

Mordacity came barreling out of the alley, bone sword held high, the crimson lights in his eye sockets blazing with fury.

Ocho started firing my trancer again, but the beams mostly missed Mordacity, and those that did strike him ricocheted off his bone armor. Ocho dropped my trancer and made for the river, and the Angler withdrew his arm from Nathaniel's throat – minus the pill – and started after his tentacled associate. I wanted to try and grab hold of the Angler as he went past, but I couldn't so much as twitch a finger.

I expected Mordacity to go after the two drug dealers, but Nathaniel's eyes went wide and the cords on his neck strained as he let out a sound like nothing I'd ever heard before. To call it a howl of despair would only be beginning to describe it. It was the cry of a man whose mind and soul had been torn to shreds, and, as I heard it, I felt something break inside me too, and I cried for both of us.

Mordacity forgot about the Angler and Ocho, dropped his sword, knelt in the muck next to his partner, wrapped his bone-encased arms around him and pulled him close. But Nathaniel continued crying out, eyes wild but unseeing, an expression of profound anguish on his face. For an instant, his features seemed to ripple and blur, but I told myself it was due to the tears in my eyes, and nothing more.

I heard a pair of splashes as the Angler and Ocho made good their escape, but I no longer cared about them. All I could do was look at Nathaniel, tears streaming down my face, and think, *My fault. All my fault.*

After the meeting ended, Mordacity took the time to chat with a couple of his… *patients* wasn't the right word. *Clients?* No, he didn't charge for his services. Whatever you want to call the people who came for his help, he spoke with two of them. The rest departed right away, giving Jinx and me uneasy glances as they left. Innocent or not, no one feels comfortable around a law officer in uniform. Jinx moved over to sit with me, and Abe came over to talk with us. He asked us how we were doing, and I answered honestly.

"Up to our necks in shit, as usual."

I asked him how Maggie was. The two of them had started officially dating not long ago.

"She's good. It's, uh, been somewhat challenging seeing her, though. Alone, I mean."

Maggie's Incubus was a powerful – and terrifying – entity known as the Darkness. He was completely devoted to her and never left her side if he could help it. I could see how that could put a cramp in a guy's style.

I'd gotten a Styrofoam cup of coffee when the meeting broke up, and I'd just about finished it. I drained the rest of the coffee, stood, and went over to the snack table to get a refill. Jinx made a face when I came back.

"I can understand drinking that swill when you need a caffeine fix, but choosing to go back for a second cup? That's masochism. And forcing me to smell it? That's sadism."

I asked Abe if he knew anything about who was manufacturing and distributing shuteye, but he said he'd never used the stuff. "It's too damned dangerous," he said. He then left to keep his date with Maggie, and soon after that the two people who'd lingered to speak with Mordacity also departed. It was just the three of us then. Mordacity came over and took the chair where Abe had sat.

"Sorry about that. Not everyone feels comfortable talking about their problems in group." He smiled with genuine warmth. "It's good to see you both. It's been far too long since your last visit."

"It has," I said, unable to remember precisely when that had been. At Christmas, I thought, but I couldn't remember which year.

Day Mordacity was normally a hugger, maybe because at night he was encased in an unfeeling armor of bone. But he made no move to hug either of us. Despite his pleasant demeanor, I wondered if he was angry because we'd stayed away so long. I wondered if I should attempt to break the ice first and go in for a hug, or maybe just reach out and clasp his hands. Then again, my hands were injured. Even covered in gloves, they might hurt if I squeezed his hands and he squeezed back too hard.

But then I looked down at my hands and saw no gloves, no injuries. Just intact fingernails and smooth, unbroken skin. All memory of hurting my hands vanished suddenly, and, although I had a vague feeling that I'd lost something, I couldn't think what it might be, so I decided not to worry about it.

"How have you been?" Jinx asked.

"Okay. The neighborhood's not the greatest, but that makes the building's rent cheaper than it might be otherwise. I usually run several groups a day. No night meetings, though." He smiled ruefully. "I don't have the right temperament for the work then."

"I know what that's like," Jinx said, and both men chuckled.

I was uncomfortable being around Mordacity, especially after thinking back to the night that Ocho and the Angler got away. And, of course, it had been the night that we'd lost Nathaniel. I decided to cover my feelings by getting down to business.

"Shuteye is back on the street," I said.

Mordacity scowled, and suddenly his human face looked as grim as his Incubus one always did.

"Tell me all about it," he said.

I had a third cup of coffee as Jinx and I took turns filling him in. I didn't tell him about my extra-dimensional conversation with Russell, though. I wasn't sure why. Maybe I thought it was too complicated to explain at the time. Or maybe I wanted to keep Russell and the Thresholders – whatever the hell they were – a secret for now. When we finished talking, Mordacity sat for several moments, quiet and contemplative. When he finally said something, it wasn't what I expected.

"You kept finishing each other's sentences."

"We did?" Jinx and I said in unison. We looked at each other, and both said, "Stop that!"

"You're Blending," Mordacity said.

"We saw a Somnacologist, and he gave us some medication." I neglected to point out that Dr Menendez wasn't an official Shadow Watch Somnacologist and that Sanderson hadn't been informed about our condition. Mordacity might be retired, but, once an officer, always an officer. The last thing we needed was for him to rat us out to Sanderson. Then our boss definitely would pull us off the case.

I fought to resist the urge to give Jinx a warning glance. Night Jinx didn't give a damn about rules – unless it was breaking them – but Day Jinx could be a tight ass about "proper procedure." So far he hadn't said anything to me about our not seeing a Watch Somnacologist, but I knew he wasn't happy about it. But Jinx kept quiet, though, and I mentally thanked the First Dreamer.

Mordacity gave me a penetrating look, as if he were trying to zap me with a psychic truth ray. Finally, he said, "Make sure to take your medicine as prescribed. In its own way, Blending is as bad as Separation."

"Forgive me if this is too painful a question," Jinx said, "but did Nathaniel and you ever suffer from Blending?"

"For a brief time when we were trainees. It strikes some Ideators and Incubi earlier than others, if it strikes at all." He grew silent for several moments, and I wondered if he was remembering what it was like to be so closely bonded to a man who had lost his mind on that long ago day on the riverbank. "We got through it, though, and you will too. Before we go any further,

I want to say I know how much you're hurting over what happened to Trauma Doll and Melody. It's never easy when fellow officers are injured in the line of duty, especially when you're close to them." He smiled sadly. "I should know."

"Thanks," I said, not knowing what, if anything else, I should add.

"So… shuteye," Mordacity said. "I'm happy to help you in any way I can, but I'm not sure what I can do. Everything Nathaniel and I learned about the drug and its origin – as little as that ended up being – is contained in records at the Rookery. I don't really have anything to add that's not already in the official record."

Jinx and I had gone over those reports before setting up the stake-out on the beach. I practically had the damn things memorized.

"We're not looking for *official* information," I said.

"I'm sorry, but there isn't anything else I can tell you."

"Thanks anyway," I said, trying not to sound as disappointed as I felt. I turned to Jinx. "So what's our next move?"

He checked the time on his wisper. It was almost three-thirty.

"If I had my way, we'd head downtown and find a cozy little café for a late lunch. But, given the circumstances, I say a stop at Wet Dreams is in order."

"If you'll permit me," Mordacity said, "I'd like to accompany you. I know I've been off the Watch for a long time, but… well, shuteye was the last case Nathaniel and I worked on. I'd like to do whatever I can to help you. And I've known Deacon Booze for many years. He might tell me things that he'd be reluctant to share with you."

Day Mordacity was an intelligent, perceptive man, and Night Mordacity kicked serious ass when he wanted to. Russell had said he'd become the target of assassins after trying to learn the identity of the shuteye suppliers, and that we might end up with the same bull's-eye on our backs if we weren't careful. We could use Mordacity's help.

Jinx, however, was less certain.

"You said it yourself: you *have* been out of the action for some time."

"I have a car. I could drive us."

Jinx grinned with delight.

"Why didn't you say so? It'll be an honor to work alongside you once again."

"Laying it on a little thick, aren't you?" I asked.

"To avoid a return trip downtown in the Deathmobile, I'd lay it on by the ton," he said.

Mordacity frowned in puzzlement. "Deathmobile?"

"Don't ask," Jinx said.

We got up and headed for the door. Mordacity turned off the lights, locked up, and we walked to the stairs. He was just as much into healthy living as Day Jinx was, and I wondered why their Day Aspects, who had so much in common, couldn't get along. And then I remembered. It was because Night Jinx's chaotic rampage in Blood in Your Eye had set off the chain of events that had caused Nathaniel to go completely, irrevocably insane.

I had a feeling there wasn't going to be much conversation during the drive downtown.

Inside, Wet Dreams doesn't look very impressive. Dim lighting, wooden chairs and tables, concrete floor, brick walls with no artwork or even neon beer signs. There's a bar, of course, complete with tarnished brass rail and a large mirror on the wall behind it. The stools there are uncomfortable. I ought to know since my ass has spent a lot of time plopped down on one or another of them. Wet Dreams is open around the clock every day of the year, and there's usually a decent-sized crowd there, no matter what time you show up.

Today was no exception. The bar also tends to be more crowded in bad weather. Some Ideators and Incubi live on the streets, which is a lot easier to manage when you don't require sleep. But rain, cold, and heat drives them inside, and Wet Dreams was one of their favorite destinations. All the tables had people sitting at them, and most of the chairs had been taken, and the barstools were all occupied as well. Wet Dreams' clientele consists mostly of Incubi and Ideators, and normal humans who, for one reason or another, know about us. There's no way to tell who's who, not as long as Incubi are in their Day Aspects, which are almost always human-seeming. At night, however, the place looks like a scene plucked straight from one of Tim Burton's most delirious fever dreams.

I recognized most of the Incubi there. Slynnc, Ms Flat, Luzifer, Groan, Zombeast, Aunt Oon, and more. All looking quite human in their Day Aspects, with no outward hint of the horrors they'd become in a couple hours. A few of their Ideators were present, but not all. Some of the Incubi no longer had Ideators due to a falling out or the Ideator's death. Some of their Ideators were simply at work and would likely stop off at the end of the day.

The air was thick with the sound of animated

conversation, but, as we entered, the room grew quiet and all heads turned to look at us. And then the applause began, punctuated with shouts of "Audra!" and "Jinx!" and various hooting and hollering.

Mordacity smiled. "I hadn't known I was in the presence of celebrities."

"You save a couple worlds from destruction, and everyone makes a big deal out of it." I was extremely uncomfortable with this effusive greeting. I liked it better when people had given Jinx and me the hairy eyeball whenever we walked in.

We threaded our way through the crowded room toward the bar. People I knew – and many I didn't – said hi to me, reached out to shake my hand, stood to give me a pat on the back. Some of them were criminals I'd put away before, and some were criminals that the Shadow Watch had been searching for. They didn't worry about Jinx and me trying to arrest them, though. Wet Dreams is neutral territory. But, even so, their enthusiastic greetings surprised me. Jinx received the same sort of attention, although it was more restrained in his case. His Night Aspect frightened even battle-hardened Incubi, and people tended to be cautious around his Day Aspect because of it. At that moment, I envied him.

Mordacity seemed amused, and a bit wistful.

"This reminds me of the time Nathaniel and I came here after we brought down the Midnight Ravager. So many people wanted to congratulate us personally that it took us close to twenty minutes to cross the room."

We reached the bar a lot sooner than that, and three people graciously vacated their stools so we could sit. One of them – a skinny pale man with red dreadlocks and wearing a Bob Marley shirt – seemed only too happy to give up his seat. He picked up his mug of beer and gave me a smile and a nod as he walked off. There was something familiar and almost mocking about the acknowledgement, but I was certain I had never seen him before. I decided not to worry about it and slid onto the stool he'd occupied. Jinx and Mordacity took the stools on either side of me.

Deacon Booze sauntered up to us, a big grin between his black handlebar mustache and beard. He's a tall man, with broad shoulders, a barrel chest, long black hair which he wears bound in a ponytail, and a booming voice. The phrase "larger than life" was made for him.

"Hail the conquering heroes," he said.

"Fuck off," I muttered.

He laughed and reached below the counter. He brought up three drinks, one at a time, and set them on the bar in front of us. Mine was a steaming mug of black coffee, Mordacity's was some kind of fruity drink complete with a little paper umbrella, and Jinx's was a cappuccino in a fine china cup, served on a silver tray with a small biscuit cookie. He lifted the cup to his face and deeply inhaled the aroma of its contents.

"Bless you," he said to Deacon.

Before I could ask, Deacon turned to me and said, "Don't worry. His is decaf."

If Jinx has any caffeine or alcohol in his system when night falls he becomes even more manic than usual. Kind of like the Tasmanian Devil on crack.

Deacon turned to Mordacity. "Good to see you in here again. It's been a while."

Mordacity smiled, but didn't say anything. I

wondered if the last time he'd visited Wet Dreams was with Nathaniel.

Deacon then turned to Jinx. "Excited about New York?"

Deacon's business – his *real* business – wasn't pouring drinks. It was buying and selling information. And when it came to that product, he was better stocked than anyone in either dimension.

"I'd be lying if I said I wasn't, but right now it's far from certain that we'll accept the promotion."

Jinx carefully avoided looking at me as he said this. The hint of reproach in his voice was so mild, I doubted anyone but me could detect it.

Deacon glanced at me and raised an eyebrow.

Okay, maybe *one* other person besides me.

For a moment, I thought Deacon was going to ask me why we hadn't accepted the transfer yet, but he didn't. Instead, it was Mordacity who wouldn't let the subject lie.

"Nathaniel and I worked in New York for years. It wasn't the easiest post – you can imagine what sort of Incubi *that* city breeds – but we loved it. Is there some reason you're reluctant to go there, Audra?"

"I just need some time to think about it, that's all," I said.

I took a sip of coffee and hoped Mordacity would take the hint. Thankfully, he did.

"So, what brings the three of you into my establishment on this fine day?" Deacon asked. "Might it have something to do with your trip to the beach last night?"

As far as anyone knows, Deacon never leaves the bar. He pours drinks day and night, and no one else works for him. He's a total one-Incubus operation. But he always knows what's going on, in both worlds, so it didn't faze me that he knew about our encounter with Montrose.

"What do you think?" I said.

Deacon's usual veneer of good humor faded and he became deadly serious. "I think it's dangerous to have anything to do with shuteye, whether you're making it, selling it, taking it, or trying to get it off the streets."

Jinx and I shared a look. It wasn't like Deacon to display such emotion. He considered himself a neutral party and he conducted himself as such, which meant he didn't give an indication how he felt about the information he traded in – if he had any feelings about it at all. But it was obvious that this time he did.

"Strong words," Jinx said.

Deacon's smile returned, although it wasn't as broad as before.

"Shuteye is strong stuff," he said.

"I'd say so, considering the number of fatalities it's caused," I said. I glanced sideways at Mordacity. "Not to mention other damage."

Mordacity's lips tightened, but he didn't say anything.

"It was off the streets for years, but it's been making a resurgence lately," Jinx said. "As I'm sure you know. But, despite the Shadow Watch's best efforts, we haven't been able to learn much about who's producing and distributing it."

"That's why we came to you," I said. "If anyone on Earth or Nod knows–"

"No," Deacon interrupted.

I was taken aback by Deacon's response. Normally,

he was unfailingly polite in a cheerful master-of-the-house kind of way. This sort of reaction wasn't his style at all.

A nasty unwanted thought was beginning to burrow its way up from the depths of my mind. Maybe Deacon was so uncomfortable discussing shuteye because he had some kind of connection to it. Could he be dealing out of Wet Dreams? Or at least allowing others to deal? Was it possible that he was in charge of the entire operation? He was rumored to be an ancient, powerful Incubus, and he'd certainly have the connections to run a criminal enterprise and the experience to keep it hidden from the Shadow Watch. I'd never known Deacon to violate his strict policy of neutrality, but that didn't mean he hadn't.

"So you won't help us?" I asked.

He scowled and pursed his lips. He looked like someone who'd just bitten into a pickled lemon.

"It's not that I *won't*," he said. "I *can't*."

"Why not?" Jinx asked.

"Because I don't *know* anything, that's why!"

He shouted this, and his voice cut through the bar's din like a laser beam through soft cheese. Everyone became instantly quiet and turned to look at Deacon. His face had turned a pinkish shade of red from anger, embarrassment, or both. It was amusing in a way, considering that, when the sun sets, Deacon Booze becomes a bipedal pink elephant. But no one in the bar so much as cracked a smile, myself included. Deacon glared at his customers, and one by one they returned to their drinking and conversation, although now their voices were quieter. Most of them were likely discussing Deacon's outburst, maybe wondering if the premier information broker had lost his touch.

I looked at Deacon. "That's impossible. You know something about everything."

Then Deacon did something I'd never seen him do before. He drew a dusty bottle from beneath the counter, along with a pewter mug that looked as if he'd picked it up at a Renn faire. He pulled the cork out of the bottle with his teeth and then poured something that looked like hot tar and smelled like rotting fish into the mug. He started to put the cork back in the bottle, reconsidered, and put the cork on the counter. He then downed the mug's contents in a series of massive gulps that made me think of a predatory animal swallowing large chunks of meat. Watching him made me feel queasy, and, when he finished, he drew the back of his hand across his mouth and almost slammed the mug down on the counter.

"That's what's got my undies in a bunch," he said. "I should've heard *something*. A whispered insinuation. A stray rumor. A half-baked theory."

"So we're talking about an individual – or more likely a group – who is extremely powerful and well-connected," Jinx said.

"If it's a group, it would have to be a small one," I said. "It would be easier to keep the details of the operation secret that way."

"And they would have to be feared," Mordacity added. "Otherwise, their street-level sellers might be tempted to turn on them – for the right price."

"And none have," Deacon said, pouring himself another mugful of the foul tarry substance. "I'd know."

This time he only downed half the muck in one go. Watching him do it still nauseated me, though.

"Who has that kind of power?" I asked.

"Wrong question," Jinx said. "Who has that kind of control?"

"Good point," I admitted.

We all fell silent then and drank our various libations while Deacon moved off to serve other customers. Eventually he returned, finished off his latest mugful of swill, and poured himself another.

After a time, Mordacity said, "The Lords of Misrule? They've recently regained their strength."

"I'm not sure the Lords themselves made a comeback so much as the Fata Morgana did," I said. "The attempt to merge dimensions was primarily a solo project with her in charge."

"She used pharmaceutical research to further her plans," Jinx said. "Perhaps she was behind the initial appearance of shuteye years ago, and now she's returned to the trade after we foiled her last scheme."

"I suppose it's possible." But no one had seen the Fata Morgana since we'd stopped her. She was currently Number One on the Shadow Watch's Most Wanted List, and there was a hefty reward for any information leading to her capture. But so far no one had turned up to collect.

Deacon finished off a third mug of his disgusting drink and belched. Whatever the damn stuff in the bottle was, it smelled even worse on the way back up.

"Why don't you go ask her?" Deacon said. "She's sitting right over there."

SIX

Deacon pointed to a table where a woman sat by herself. She had a martini glass in her hand and half a dozen empties sitting in front of her. I hadn't noticed her among the crowd before this, but, now that Deacon had pointed her out, I took a closer look.

She was the right age – early fifties – and she had the right build: tall and thin. Her long hair was blonde, and she was dressed like Cecelia Kauffman, the Fata Morgana's Day Aspect: blue blazer, slacks, and black heels. But she was significantly thinner than the last time I'd seen her. She no longer wore glasses, her hair was an untended-to rat's nest, and her clothes were wrinkled and in desperate need of a good dry cleaner's attention. No wonder I hadn't recognized her when we'd entered. But now that she'd been pointed out to me, I knew it was her.

Without a word, I rose from my stool, walked over to her, drew my trancer, and placed the barrel against her right temple.

"Hello, Audra." Her voice was rough from too much alcohol, and she seemed completely unconcerned that I was holding a weapon to her head. Her nonchalant attitude pissed me off. I was trying to be intimidating, and the least she could do was look a *little* nervous.

Behind us, Deacon Booze cleared his throat loudly.

"You shouldn't drink that nasty stuff if it's going to gunk up your throat," I said, without taking my eyes off the Fata Morgana.

Deacon wasn't amused. "No weapons, Audra."

I had no idea what Deacon would do if I didn't listen to him. One day I might need to find out, but that day hadn't come yet. I holstered my weapon.

"Sit down," the Fata Morgana said. "Have a drink with me."

Her words were over-enunciated, a sure sign that she was more drunk than she was willing to let on.

"I think you've had enough for you, me, and half the bar." But I slid out a seat across the table from her and sat. No way in hell was I stupid enough to sit next to her.

Her eyes were bloodshot, and her makeup was sloppy. Too heavy in some places, too light in others, and she'd definitely been coloring outside the lines.

"You look like shit," I said, in my usual tactful way.

The Fata Morgana gave me a slightly lopsided smile, raised her martini glass to me in a salute, then gulped the contents down in a single swallow. She put the empty down with the others and signaled for another.

I wasn't sure what to say next. The Fata Morgana is one of the most ancient and powerful Incubi who's ever existed, but I'd first come to know her as the psychologist who'd manipulated and exploited Russell and me, as well as others like us, when we were children. To say I hated her would be a massive understatement. And yet, I couldn't help feeling a small measure of sympathy for the once near-godlike woman sitting before me. She'd been brought low, and she looked it. And, although Jinx and I had been the ones to do it, at that moment I didn't feel especially proud of the result.

"So, what have you and your clown prince been up to lately?" she asked. "Tilting at dragons? Slaying windmills?"

"Something like that," I said. "How about you? Have you been sitting here drinking the entire time since we defeated you?"

I expected some kind of haughty display of bravura, but she simply said, "Yes."

Her reply caught me off-guard. She went on, "I couldn't return to the other Lords, not after being so thoroughly humiliated. And I especially couldn't go looking like *this*."

I frowned. "I don't understand."

Jinx approached the table. He brought with him a fresh martini for the Fata Morgana, placed it before her, and then took a seat.

"During our battle she depleted a great deal of her personal supply of Maelstrom energy," Jinx said. "Until it's restored, she's stuck in one Aspect – this one – no matter what time of day it is or what dimension she's in."

The Fata Morgana nodded. She took hold of her new drink, but didn't raise it to her lips. I had the feeling that she wanted something to do with her hands more than anything else.

"For all intents and purposes, I'm just as human as either of you are right now," she sighed.

Mordacity hadn't followed Jinx over. He remained at the bar, but he'd turned around on his stool and was watching us.

"Did you overhear us talking at the bar?" I asked the Fata Morgana.

"Yes. I wish I *was* the mastermind behind the resurgence of shuteye. It would beat sitting here swilling martinis day after day. You should see the size of the tab I've run up." She shuddered and took a sip of her drink.

Maybe she was telling the truth. Or maybe her story was simply a cover for what she was really up to. Everyone knew her last plan had fallen to ruin, so it was only natural that she be depressed. But what better cover for a new operation? Who would suspect that this beaten woman, scarcely a shell of her former self, remained at full strength and had hopped right back in the saddle after she'd been thrown? One of the Fata Morgana's abilities was the manipulation of perception. Once the sun set, she might still automatically transform into her Night Aspect, but she could make it seem to onlookers as if she hadn't. She was a genius at manipulation, a maestro of deceit. How could anyone believe a creature who had no truth whatsoever in her?

But, strangely enough, I did believe her. And it wasn't because I thought I was seeing a softer side I hadn't known the woman possessed. It was because she had such a monstrously outsized ego that I couldn't see her humbling herself like this, even if it were only part of a ruse.

"So you're investigating shuteye," the Fata Morgana said. "What's wrong, Audra? Your usual drugs not doing it for you anymore?"

"What's it like to have to rely on words as your only weapons?" I countered.

She smiled. "Words can cut deeply enough in their way." She took a small sip of her martini. It seemed she intended to make this one last.

The man with the dreadlocks who'd given up his barstool for me now sat a couple tables over from the Fata Morgana. A lovely black woman with delicate features sat with him. She had a shaved head and multiple ear piercings. She wore a gray T-shirt with the words *This Rent for Space* on it, and jeans tucked into black boots. The ginger noticed me looking his way, and he raised his beer and smiled in acknowledgement. Once again, I wondered if we'd met before, and I raised my coffee cup to return his greeting, just to be on the safe side.

"What can you tell us about shuteye?" Jinx asked.

"What makes you think I'd do anything to help the two of you?" she said.

"Because whatever information you provide will inevitably lead us into trouble," Jinx said, "which means there's a good chance it'll get us killed."

He said this without any outward show of emotion, but there was a gleam in his eyes that told me more accurately than any clock could that sundown was approaching.

The Fata Morgana considered this for a moment, then she smiled in the way a hungry serpent might if it possessed the right facial muscles, and she began talking.

"When shuteye first appeared on the streets several years back, the Lords of Misrule looked into it. A drug that allowed Incubi and Ideators to sleep – or which would at least simulate the experience of sleeping – would be quite a moneymaker. And, of course, if the

Lords controlled the supply and distribution of such a
wonder drug, it would greatly enhance our strength.
A prime consideration given how weakened we had
become by that time. But, despite our best efforts, we
could not discover who created the drug or who was
ultimately responsible for manufacturing and selling
it. We were able to locate a few street sellers, but there
were far fewer of these than we expected. And,
although we questioned them most *vigorously*, they
could tell us little. They knew only the name of their
immediate supplier, an Incubus called the Angler. We
searched for him, but we were unable to find him.
Everyone talked about shuteye, but we couldn't find
anyone who'd actually used it. Anyone who hadn't
died or gone insane, that is. Oh, we found some who
claimed they'd taken it, but when we questioned
them–"

"Which you did *vigorously*, I'm sure," I said.

"Of course, and they all admitted they were lying."

"What about the deaths from shuteye?" Jinx asked.
"And those whose minds were damaged?"

Her lips curled back from her teeth. "Like poor
Nathaniel Sawyer?"

My jaw tightened, but I managed to keep my mouth
shut. I didn't want to give the bitch the satisfaction of
getting a rise out of me.

"We were able to verify those cases," she said. "Just
as the Shadow Watch did. There weren't as many as the
rumors suggested, but there were enough."

"Were you able to get hold of a sample to analyze?"
Jinx asked. The Shadow Watch had done such an
analysis, but I figured Jinx wanted to find out if the
Lords had learned the same about the drug as we had.

The Fata Morgana nodded and took another sip of her martini before answering. "We acquired a number of samples, and I tested them myself. Chemically, there was nothing special about them. They were little more than normal sleep aids, like the kind you can buy over the counter in any pharmacy on Earth. They did possess traces of Maelstrom energy, but the levels weren't very high. Enough, perhaps, to intensify the effect of the drug to a degree, but certainly not enough to cause madness or death. I assume your people discovered the same thing when they analyzed whatever samples they obtained."

"Yes. The assumption was that those pills were fakes that pushers used to scam buyers," I said. "We assumed we never got hold of the real deal."

"A natural conclusion, but an incorrect one," she said. "We were *exceptionally* thorough in our search for shuteye samples, and each pill we obtained and tested gave the same results."

Jinx frowned. "So shuteye is a drug that shouldn't work as advertised, is essentially harmless, and which sometimes drives people crazy and kills them anyway."

"Correct. Which is why the Lords of Misrule decided to forget about shuteye and turn our attention to other interests."

"That's it?" I asked. "You didn't try to figure out why a seemingly harmless pill was having such deadly side-effects?"

"Why would we? The Lords are hardly altruists, my dear. Shuteye had nothing to offer us, and that's all we needed to know."

The Fata Morgana's words frustrated me, but I had to admit that – at least from the Lords' point of view –

the attitude was understandable. All these years the Shadow Watch had believed they'd never obtained a true sample of shuteye to analyze, but, if what the Fata Morgana had told us was true – and I wasn't dumb enough to automatically believe her – the pills they'd tested had been the real thing.

I was about to ask the Fata Morgana another question when I heard a soft skittering on the floor and felt a tug on my pants' leg. I looked down to see a black-and-tan dachshund pulling on the cuff of my slacks. When she saw she had my attention, she let go of my pants leg and looked up at me with what I interpreted as a grim expression. Most importantly, her tail wasn't wagging.

I looked at Jinx. "Trouble's coming."

He frowned, took a quick glance under the table, saw the dog, and then sat up straight once more.

"I see what you mean."

We both drew our trancers and kept them on our laps, where they'd remain hidden by the table.

"Trouble?" The Fata Morgana swallowed the remainder of her martini. "It's just a dog. A Chihuahua or something. I've never really been good at recognizing Earth animals. It's probably someone's pet. People bring all kinds of animals in here. Last week a woman brought in a pelican, of all things. I told her to take her dirty bird out of here, but she thought I meant it as a euphemism for something entirely different. Well, you can imagine her reaction when–"

"Please be quiet now," Jinx said. "Or I'll be forced to bite off one of your lips." He smiled. "You can pick which one. I'm sure they're both equally delicious."

Jinx's sudden nastiness was an indication that sundown was closing in fast. Jinx can be hardest to control when he first shifts into his Night Aspect. He bottles up a lot of insanity while in his Day Aspect and needs to let it out. This is never a pleasant experience for anyone unfortunate enough to be in his vicinity at the time.

Now that Bloodshedder had warned me, she skittered off, presumably in search of her master. I swept my gaze around the bar, but I didn't see Russell at first. Then I noticed a guy sitting at a table close to the entrance. He wore a black suede jacket, a Bears cap, jeans, sneakers, and, to top it all off, a pair of sunglasses.

Smooth disguise, Russell, I thought. Then again, Incubi and Ideators were used to being around people who looked odd, day *or* night, so maybe his disguise wasn't as bad as it seemed. No, scratch that. It was *terrible*.

Jinx saw where I was looking, took a quick glance at Russell, then turned to me.

"If he's here, how much do you want to bet those assassins he warned us about are too?"

"No bet," I said.

I looked to Mordacity. He was still facing us, leaning back on his stool, elbows resting on the bar behind him. At first I thought he had no idea what was going on, but then he tapped his left index finger on the bar three times. His expression never changed and his posture remained relaxed, but I knew that sign well. It was one Nathaniel and he had used to silently communicate to the other that they were alert and ready for whatever came next.

I looked for Deacon Booze, but I didn't see him behind the bar, and he wasn't out among the customers either. I decided he'd probably gone into the back room to get something. That *something* most likely being a weapon. Nothing happened in his bar without him being aware of it.

Jinx and I could play this a couple different ways. We could sit here and wait for the assassins to make the first move, or we could get up and leave the bar and hopefully get out onto the street before they could attack. But the assassins would be expecting us to do one of those two things. Which is of course why we did something entirely different.

Jinx and I stood up.

"Could we have everyone's attention please?" I said.

Everyone kept talking, laughing, and drinking.

Jinx pointed his trancer at the ceiling and fired three blasts. Plaster rained down on our table, and I was grateful he was still mostly Day Jinx. Night Jinx would've set his trancer to high and brought down the entire ceiling.

The customers became quiet after that. I nodded my thanks to Jinx.

"Sorry to interrupt your fun, but there is at least one assassin in here who wants to take out Jinx and me. Now, while I know that some of you wouldn't be all that sorry to see us go–"

"We'd miss *you*, Audra!" someone called out.

Someone else added, "But Jinx can go sit on that hammer of his and take a spin!"

A few people laughed. A few very stupid people, for Jinx noted every one of them, and night was approaching fast.

I went on. "We'd consider it a solid if you'd take a look around and see if you can identify the assassin–"

"Or assassins," Jinx put in.

"–for us. We'll take it from there."

"Why should we?" someone asked. "What's in it for us?"

Before I could answer, Deacon Booze emerged from the back room and came out from behind the bar. He carried a medieval-looking war axe, the metal tempered with multicolored threads of solidified M-energy.

"Ooo, I want one of those," Jinx said. He was practically drooling.

"You are the *last* person in existence who should have one," I said.

"I'll tell you what's in it for you," Deacon called out in a loud voice. "Free drinks for life."

That raised more than a few eyebrows.

"*And*," Deacon added. "I'll answer one question. *Any* question – free of charge. I'll answer it honestly and fully, too. No hints, no half-truths, no omissions."

The room burst into excited conversation, which quickly turned into mass confusion as Deacon's patrons began searching whoever was closest to them for weapons.

Russell took off his sunglasses and grinned at me. Have I mentioned that he has a great smile? Well, he does. Especially when he's using it to show his appreciation for how brilliant I am.

Of course, the frisking swiftly resulted in arguing as friends and acquaintances accused one another of having serious trust issues. This, in turn, led to shouting, which was immediately followed by someone throwing a punch. Things went downhill at warp speed after that.

Deacon walked over to our table, Mordacity following. So far, the fighting hadn't reached us yet.

The Fata Morgana sat and watched the chaos. I expected her to be amused by the violence, but she looked bored.

Deacon sighed. "I just replaced all the tables and chairs last month."

"Rumor is you have a warehouse filled with spare furniture," Mordacity said. "For occasions such as this."

Deacon scowled. "It's the principle of the thing."

The Fata Morgana had been quiet for a while, but now she spoke.

"There are your assassins. Two of them. Well done, Audra."

She inclined her head, and I looked in the direction she'd indicated. Besides Russell – who'd lifted Bloodshedder onto the top of his table so she could bark at anyone who came too close – there were only two other people in the bar who weren't fighting. One was the man with red dreadlocks, and the other was the woman sitting with him. Both were looking at us, expressions neutral, gazes intense. Then, as if by unspoken signal, they stood and drew hand weapons I'd never seen before. They were shaped somewhat like trancers, but they were black – so black that they seemed to draw in the light around them and swallow it.

Jinx and I pointed our trancers at the two of them…

…and, at that precise instant, the sun set.

The change spread rapidly throughout the bar, and beings who'd appeared to be normal men and women became a variety of other things – emphasis on *things*.

Night Jinx grinned, holstered his trancer, pulled Cuthbert Junior from the inside pocket of his jacket, and threw himself into the thick of the melee. I had no

idea if he intended to go after the assassins or seek to
deliver payback to those who'd mocked him earlier.
Either way, he swung his sledgehammer back and forth
in vicious arcs, sending Incubi flying in all directions.

Deacon Booze now had the head of a pink elephant
with long ivory tusks, and he trumpeted his anger, but
no one in the bar took any notice. Mordacity had
transformed into his bone knight Aspect, complete with
sword. I didn't know where the weapon went when he
was in his Day Aspect. I once asked him, but all he'd
done was smile enigmatically. The Fata Morgana
remained in her human guise, proof that she'd told the
truth about her diminished powers. Or proof that she
still had her powers and was projecting a hell of a
convincing illusion of humanity.

Russell was an Ideator like me, so he didn't change,
but his little dachshund suddenly become a huge
demonic hound, furred and scaled, with wicked-
looking spikes jutting upward from her tail. She was
now so heavy that the table collapsed beneath her. She
sprang to her feet instantly, and, like Jinx, launched
herself into the fight. Russell drew his M-energy rapier
from wherever he'd been hiding it, and started to make
his way toward the assassins.

Speaking of the assassins, they had transformed as
well. The male had become a lumpy brown creature
about seven feet tall. He was roughly human-shaped,
although he lacked distinct features. He had no fingers,
only thumbs, and his eyes were hardly more than
holes, his mouth a broad slash. He still had crimson
dreadlocks, only now they looked like they had been
formed out of thick red licorice. He wore no clothing,
but he had three large dark brown buttons on his chest

to suggest a shirt or jacket. I wasn't sure, but I thought the buttons were formed from huge chocolate chips.

Like the male, the female assassin's clothes vanished when she changed. She still retained a basic humanoid form, but she was covered in obsidian scales, and her hands and feet had become curved black talons. Her face had assumed a reptilian aspect – narrowed brow, diminished nose, yellow eyes, and sharp ivory teeth. She looked dangerous as hell.

Both assassins still held their strange dark weapons and now they used them. Beams of shadowy light lanced from the gun muzzles – one headed toward me, the other toward Jinx, who was too busy pounding the snot out of a creature that looked like it was made of hundreds of eyeballs to notice. But there were too many people in the way for them to get a clean shot at either of us.

The dreadlocked assassin's beam struck Lady Grimalkin, a cat-headed woman in a Victorian gown. The energy blast hit her between the shoulder blades, and she yowled in pain. Her body stiffened and she spun around, giving me an excellent view of the fist-sized hole that had been punched all the way through her back and chest. There was no blood, no ragged flesh. The hole's circumference was smooth and dry, almost as if the black beam had cauterized it.

The reptile woman's blast was also intercepted by an unfortunate Incubus. Catermolar looked like a giant green caterpillar with a mouthful of oversized, crooked, yellow human teeth. The beam struck the Incubus in the side of the face, and the front half of its head, gigantic teeth and all, vanished. Incubi can take a lot of damage, but whatever the nature of the strange ebon energy, the injuries it dealt were too much for the Incubi to heal. Both Lady Grimalkin and Catermolar went down and stayed down.

"Jinx!" I shouted. "Get the woman's gun!"

I fired my trancer at the dreadlocked assassin, the beam set on maximum strength. I'm no marksman, but I'm a much better shot than I was when I started out, and I usually hit what I shoot at. But, before the M-energy could strike the assassin, his form blurred and suddenly he was standing next to me. He smashed his dark gun into the side of my head, moving so swiftly that I didn't have time to try to avoid the blow. Fireworks went off behind my eyes, and the next thing I knew I was looking up at the assassin from my vantage point on the floor.

His mouth was stretched into a smile as he spoke in sing-song.

"Run, run, as fast as you can. You can't escape me, I'm the Gingerdread Man!"

He let out a maniacal laugh, or at least that's what I assumed he was attempting to do. It came out sounding more like an asthmatic's wheezing.

I propped myself up on my elbow, my head spinning and throbbing. I'd lost my grip on my trancer when I fell, but I didn't see it close by. It must've slid away when I dropped it, I thought. Or maybe someone accidentally kicked it away. Not that I'd be able to shoot the damn thing straight right now if I still had it.

"Nice try on the laugh, Cookie-Boy, but you've got nothing on my partner. His laugh is so scary that, when you hear it, you'll pee yourself and then the urine will *schlurp* right back into your body because it's too terrified to stay out."

Maybe I was exaggerating, but not by much. I was stalling for time to get my head together enough to do something other than be an excellent target. At that moment, I wondered how Jinx was doing. Had he managed to disarm the reptilian assassin or did she manage to shoot him with her strange weapon and put one or more fist-sized holes in him? And then, as if the thought was a trigger, a wave of dizziness that had nothing to do with the blow I'd taken to the head came over me, and my vision blurred. When it cleared, I found myself looking into a snarling reptilian face, yellow eyes blazing with hate.

"Not *now*," I moaned with Jinx's voice.

The woman snarled and head-butted me. I felt the blow, but it didn't hurt much more than if she'd roughly shoved me. I took a couple steps back, more out of surprise than because of the strength of the blow. Still snarling, the woman lunged forward, claws raised to tear me to shreds. I didn't know what had happened to her weird gun. Presumably Jinx had disarmed her before we'd switched bodies. I didn't have time to worry about details right then. I had to do what I could to save my partner's hide.

I was holding Cuthbert Junior in my right hand, and I brought the hammer up to block the assassin's attack. At least, that's what I intended to do. But, because I wasn't used to Jinx's strength and speed, I ended up hurling Cuthbert Junior toward the ceiling, where the hammer smashed through plaster and became embedded.

The assassin actually paused in her attack to look up at the handle protruding from the ceiling. She then looked at me and sneered.

"Dumbass."

At that moment I couldn't disagree with her.

Jinx has all kinds of nasty toys concealed on his person, any one of which would ruin my opponent's day. But I had no idea where on his body they were stashed, or if they were occupying the same dimensional space that I was at the moment. And, even if I could get my hands on one of his party favors, I'd have no idea how to use it. So I decided to go with what I knew, and I hit the reptile woman in the jaw with a hard right cross, putting every ounce of muscle into the punch that I could. Jinx's body obeyed me, more or less, and although the punch was less than coordinated, it landed where I wanted. The woman's head snapped to the side so hard that, if she hadn't been an Incubus, her neck would've snapped. She staggered to the side but managed to stay on her feet. I suddenly had a new respect for Jinx. I thought of him as a chaotic, uncontrollable, one-man wrecking crew, but if he was *this* strong, the only reason he didn't kill just about anyone he came up against was because, despite all evidence to the contrary, he actually did know the meaning of restraint.

The assassin's lower jaw no longer aligned with her upper, and she worked it back and forth until it popped into place. Then, without missing a beat, she came at me with her claws again. I tried to side-step, intending to grab hold of one of her arms as she went past, spin her around, and then throw her – preferably into something nice and hard, such as the nearest wall. But I still didn't have full control of Jinx's body, and, instead of simply moving a foot or two to the side, I made a fully-fledged leap. I flew sideways through the air for maybe a dozen feet before I collided with an Incubus who resembled a body builder with the head of a naked mole rat, and we both went down. This time the impact hurt a bit more than getting head-butted by the reptile woman, but not by much. No wonder Jinx was always so willing to rush into danger. I could get used to wearing a body this durable.

I jumped to my feet and spared a second to glance in the direction of my real body, which Jinx currently inhabited. The Gingerdread Man was racing back and forth, trying to get to Jinx, but Mordacity, Russell, Bloodshedder, and Deacon had formed a circle around me – around Jinx, I mean – preventing the assassin from getting to him. Jinx was firing my trancer between his protectors, attempting to strike the speedster, but the assassin was too fast, and each shot missed, the energy beams going wild and striking whoever was unlucky enough to be in their path.

As glad as I was to see my friends protecting my body, it also pissed me off big-time. Did they think I was so helpless that I needed *all* of them to come to my rescue? And, with the exception of Bloodshedder, they were all male. Talk about being sexist! When this was over, I was going to have to conduct a few attitude-adjustment sessions.

The Fata Morgana still sat at her table, seemingly relaxed and unconcerned for her own safety, despite her supposed reduction in power. Maybe she was so used to being strong that it never occurred to her that she might be in danger. Or maybe at this point she no longer gave a damn. She noticed me looking at her, smiled, and gave me a wink, as if she recognized who I really was inside.

Before I could pursue that line of thought any
further, Mole-Rat Head rose to his feet, grabbed hold of
my shoulder, and spun me around to face him. His
overdeveloped muscles strained the fabric of his black
turtleneck and black pants. His head was a pink,
wrinkled, ugly thing, and his two protruding front teeth
came to sharp points, as if they'd been filed.

He – or maybe it was really a buff she – made a fist
and drew it back to throw a punch. Before I could make
a conscious move to defend myself, Jinx's overlarge
boutonniere squirted a jet of foul-smelling liquid into
the mole rat's eyes. There was a sizzling sound,
followed instantly by the mole rat's scream. He clapped
his hands to his eyes and, still screaming, began
stumbling around, knocking into people and tables.

I don't know how many times I've told Jinx not to
use acid in his boutonniere, but at that moment I was
grateful that he'd ignored me once again.

Over in one corner stood a group of men and
women, all of whom were doing their best to stay as far
away from the fighting as they could. They were
Ideators like me, but, unlike me, none of them had
been trained to handle themselves in a fight – especially
one involving Incubi. They were smart to stay the hell
back, and I knew that, if they'd been able to reach the
door, they'd have fled the bar as fast as they could.

I was about to turn around and check on the reptile
woman when I felt something sharp rake across my
back. The sensation was followed by a mild stinging,
more like an itch, really. But when I spun around and
saw the reptile woman standing there, blood dripping
from the claws on her right hand, I knew I'd sustained
a serious wound to my back. Jinx healed swiftly in his

Night Aspect, but I realized that I didn't know just *how* swiftly. Would I be in danger of passing out from blood loss if I didn't tend to the wound soon? Or were the furrows the assassin had gouged into Jinx's flesh already in the process of healing? Not that the assassin intended to give me a chance to deal with my injury.

She grinned, giving me an excellent view of her twin rows of sharp teeth. Then she opened her mouth wide and a sulfurous stink filled the air, and I felt heat on my face.

Shit! She's a fire-breather!

I lifted one of Jinx's enormous feet, said a quick prayer to the First Dreamer, and then said, "Go-go Gadget shoe spring!"

A panel on the sole of Jinx's shoe slid open and a coil of metal shot forward and struck the reptile woman in the chest. She flew backwards, her mouth snapping shut as she did, and there was a muffled *whump!* as her fire blast was contained. She soared across the room, miraculously not hitting anyone, until her flight terminated when she smashed into a wall. She bounced off, fell to the floor, and lay there, writhing and howling in pain as smoke poured from her mouth. Even if her mouth and throat could withstand ejecting fire, being forced to swallow it as it ignited was a different matter.

I braced myself with my other leg in anticipation of the spring returning to the shoe, and, when it did, I managed to keep my balance. The longer I remained in Jinx's body, the more I was getting the hang of it. I put my foot back down on the floor and looked up to where Cuthbert Junior was stuck in the ceiling. I was tempted to make a jump for the hammer, but I wasn't sure I had that much control over Jinx's body yet, and I feared there was an excellent chance I'd end up overshooting my mark and getting stuck in the ceiling myself.

I looked back to where the reptile woman had landed, but I didn't see her. I searched for her, but fighting was still going on throughout the bar, and all the combatants obstructed my vision. An instant later I heard an ear-splitting shriek, and a gust of wind blasted past me, knocking me back a few steps. The door then slammed open with such force that it tore halfway off its hinges. I turned to look at "Audra" and the others and saw no sign of the Gingerdread Man. It seemed he, and most likely his dragonish partner, had beat a hasty retreat.

The fighting among the rest of Wet Dreams' patrons continued unabated until Deacon Booze trumpeted an elephant call that shook the entire room. It didn't hurt that he held his war ax over his head at the same time. One by one, the remaining combatants settled down, and, several moments later, the bar was quiet and still. A surprising number of tables and chairs had escaped destruction, and those Incubi who were still conscious – if not altogether unscathed – sat down and looked at Deacon like guilty children who'd just been scolded by an adult. A moment later, the Incubi lying on the floor began to get up, all save Lady Grimalkin and Catermolar. They continued lying where they'd fallen, and I feared they wouldn't be rising again.

Mordacity sheathed his bone sword in its scabbard and went over to check on them. As he did, Jinx came over to me, still wearing my body. He was chewing a mouthful of something.

"That guy really *was* made out of cookie," he said, spraying bits of food as he spoke. "He's a real wimp about getting bit, though. Then again, considering *where*

I bit him, I suppose I can't blame him." He finished chewing and swallowed.

"I can*not* believe what you just did with my mouth."

Now that things had settled down, Russell and Bloodshedder came over to us. Russell's cape was missing a large section on the left side, and I guessed that he'd narrowly avoided getting killed by the Gingerdread Man's strange weapon.

"What's Jinx talking about?" Russell asked me – or at least the person he thought was me.

"Russell!" Jinx shouted, and then grabbed him and planted one right on his kisser.

Concerned – okay, in a mild panic – I pulled Jinx away from Russell. Russell looked confused, but not all that unhappy by what had just happened. Men.

Bloodshedder looked at Jinx and me, her head cocked to the side in confusion. She could sense that something wasn't right, but she couldn't tell what it was.

"Way to go, Audra," Jinx said, giving me a pouty face. "And I was just about to slip him some tongue."

"*My* tongue," I said. "And the only person who gets to make decisions about where and when it gets slipped is me."

"I was just trying to speed things up a little," he said. "I mean, the whole 'will they or won't they' act plays well on TV, but in real life it gets old pretty fast."

I raised a fist, intending to punch him on the arm, but he stepped back and raised both palms in a placating gesture.

"Careful. You hit this body with that fist, and you're liable to break a few bones. And your body doesn't heal as fast as mine."

I lowered my – *Jinx's* – fist, feeling like an idiot.

Jinx smiled. "Maybe now you'll have a greater appreciation for the self-restraint I have to exert day in and day out to keep from murdering you."

I gave him a sour look. "Believe me, I know *exactly* what it's like."

By this time Mordacity and Deacon had joined us. Mordacity confirmed that both Lady Grimalkin and Catermolar were dead, and Deacon said that he'd take care of seeing they received a proper cremation and memorial. The bodies of dead Incubi continue to transform between Day and Night Aspects until they eventually return to the Maelstrom energy from which they were formed. But that process can take days, even weeks, and, in the meantime, it wouldn't do to have Incubi corpses inspected by a medical examiner. On Earth, Incubi make certain that the bodies of their dead brothers and sisters are cremated as soon as possible without being examined, which usually means taking care of it themselves, one way or another.

When Mordacity and Deacon were finished talking, Russell turned to them.

"Do either of you know what the hell's going on with Audra and Jinx?" he asked. "Did the assassins do this to them somehow?"

"It's called Blending," Deacon said. His trunk quivered, and I had the impression he was fighting back laughter. He quickly explained the basics to Russell.

"Oh, my God," Russell said, when Deacon was finished. "Do you mean I really just kissed–"

Jinx grinned and waggled his-my fingers at Russell, who looked like he was going to be sick. Then Russell turned back to Deacon.

"Do you think the same thing could happen to Bloodshedder and me?" He looked at his demonic dog partner, and she let out a yip.

"She said 'You should be so lucky'," Jinx translated.

"We've seen a Somnacologist," I said. "He gave us some medicine to take for Blending."

"Whatever he gave you, it's obviously not doing its job," Deacon said.

Mordacity didn't find anything about our situation amusing.

"I didn't realize your condition was this bad," he said. "If it continues to worsen, you could risk total persona breakdown."

"That doesn't sound good," I said.

"It isn't," Deacon confirmed, all traces of humor gone now. "Your mind and Jinx's will become so intermingled that you won't know where one of you begins and the other ends."

"What's so bad about that?" Jinx said. "Audra and I enjoy being close." He came over and gave me a side hug. "We *lurv* each other!"

I shoved him off me as gently as I could, and I still nearly knocked him on his-my ass.

"The result would be madness for you both," Mordacity said.

Jinx opened his-my mouth, but I said, "No jokes," and, after giving me a dirty look, he stuck my tongue out at me. But he didn't say anything.

"And that's the best-case scenario," Deacon said. "There's a chance you'd both die."

I scowled at Deacon. "Aren't you just a fucking ray of sunshine?"

"So what can we do about it?" Russell said.

"*We* don't have to do anything," I said. "I told you, Jinx and I are under a doctor's care. We'll be fine."

"At the risk of getting called another 'fucking ray of sunshine'," Russell said, "you and Jinx have been inside each other's bodies for at least ten minutes. Have you experienced a switch that's lasted this long before?"

"No," I admitted. "But Doctor Menendez said it might take some time to get our Blending under control."

I didn't want to show it, but Russell's words had scared me. The longer Jinx and I inhabited each other's body, the more I worried that maybe this time we wouldn't switch back. Maybe this time the change would be permanent.

None of the other customers in the bar had said anything since the fighting had died down, and I was uncomfortably aware that everyone in the place was watching us and listening intently to our conversation. Despite the warm welcome Jinx and I had received when we'd entered Wet Dreams, more than a few of the people here tonight had reason to want to get some payback on us. If we remained stuck in each other's body, that meant we weren't up to our full fighting strength, and that made us vulnerable. I wondered how long it would take for word to spread throughout the Incubi community here in Chicago as well as in Nod. Those two assassins might turn out to be the least of our worries. I decided we should change the subject, and fast.

"Does anyone know anything about those strange guns the assassins carried?" I asked.

"I've never seen anything like them," Mordacity said. "But they're deadly as hell, as we saw."

I never would've stirred up shit in the bar if I'd

known the assassins had been packing weapons that destructive. But how could I have known? No one had ever seen anything like them before.

"I tried to knock the lizard lady's gun out of her hand before you and I switched," Jinx said. "But it shattered like glass when Cuthbert Junior hit it. I doubt there's enough left intact to put under a microscope."

I turned to Deacon, but he held up his hands. "Don't ask me. Even if I did know what the damn things are, I'm not going to answer any more of your questions for free – not after the trouble you brought in here tonight!"

I sighed. "How long are we banned this time?"

He thought for a moment, taking a quick glance around the bar as he did. I had the feeling that, if so many people hadn't been watching, he might've let the matter drop. But people *were* watching, and he said, "One month."

"Fair enough," I said.

Deacon nodded, gave Jinx and me a stern look for good measure, and then headed to the bodies of Lady Grimalkin and Catermolar, calling for several Incubi to help him with them. Some of the other patrons took this opportunity to leave. Most were Ideators who'd had enough rough and tumble for one night. The rest were Incubi, who I feared were heading out to spread the word about Jinx's and my Blending problem.

Vertigo took hold of me then, hitting me far worse than it had the last time. When the dizziness faded, I found myself back in my own body looking up at Russell. He'd caught me before I could hit the floor. Jinx, however, hadn't had anyone to catch him, and he lay on his side where his body had fallen. As if she felt sorry for him, Bloodshedder padded over on razor-claw feet and began licking his face with her black forked tongue.

"At least *she* doesn't mind kissing me," Jinx said. He patted Bloodshedder on the head before standing. As he got to his feet, I caught a glimpse of something stuck to the back of his jacket.

I disengaged myself from Russell's arms – a bit reluctantly, I must admit – and walked over to Jinx.

"Turn around," I said.

He frowned, but he did as I asked. His jacket and shirt were shredded and bloody from where the reptilian assassin had raked him with her claws, but the chalk-white flesh beneath looked as if it was well into the healing process. But none of that had drawn my attention. What had was a small piece of memo pad paper that had been taped to his jacket just above where he'd been wounded. There was writing on it.

Are you clown enough?

I removed it and handed it to Jinx. He read, sounding out the words as he went, even though I knew he didn't need to.

"Isn't that what the clown with the hula hoop said to you in Nod?" I asked.

"Yeah. Weird. Did you feel anyone put it on my back when you were inside me?"

"I'm really uncomfortable with you referring to our mind-switch like that, but no, I didn't."

"I didn't feel anyone do it before our switch." He shrugged and tucked the note away in a pocket. Then he scowled. "Hey, where did the Fatty Banana go?"

We all looked to the table where the Fata Morgana had been sitting, but of course she wasn't there.

"Did any of you see her leave?" Russell asked.

We all shook our heads. Then it hit me.

"You remember that she was here. More than that, you remember who she is."

Russell, Mordacity, Jinx, and even Bloodshedder exchanged confused looks.

"Uh, yeah," Jinx said. "Shouldn't we?"

His question caught me by surprise. I was thrilled they remembered the Fata Morgana – and even more thrilled that *I* did. But I couldn't explain why. All I knew is that it came as a great relief to me.

"Of course you should," I said. "Come on, let's get out of here before Deacon gets any more pissed off than he already is."

I started toward the door, and, even though I couldn't see it, I knew the others exchanged one last set of puzzled looks before following.

SEVEN

The assassins weren't waiting for us outside. I didn't think they would be stupid enough to try to kill us again so soon, not when Jinx and I had our guard up and had allies with us. But you never know. As we walked out, Jinx had jumped up and pulled Cuthbert Junior free from the ceiling, and now we were standing in the alley next to the bar. Mordacity's hood had a cape, and he drew it up now to conceal his features, where Russell did the opposite, removing his hood. Bloodshedder stayed behind the rest of us, so that no one could see her from the street.

"Find us a Door, Jinx," I said. I turned to Russell. "That is, unless your masters are willing to save us the trouble and open a portal for us right here."

"Masters?" Mordacity asked. "And by the way, who *is* this young man?"

"Sorry, Mord," Jinx said, twirling his hammer one-handed as if it were a majorette's baton. "Audra's still working on learning her manners."

Mordacity's hand fell to his sword. In his Night Aspect, he was much more of a tight-ass, all knightly code of honor and stuff. He took offense if someone didn't show him the respect he thought a knight of his rank was due, and he *loathed* it when Jinx called him *Mord*. Which was why, during our training period, Jinx had done it every chance he'd gotten.

Russell introduced himself. "I'm Russell Pelfrey, although, on the street, I go by Nocturne. My Incubus is Bloodshedder."

"Nice to meet you. I'm Mordacity."

Russell smiled. "I know who you are. Everyone in Nod does."

"Are you going to ask him for his autograph now?" I asked.

Russell glared at me, but I ignored him.

"He poses as a mercenary," I added. "But he really works for an oh-so-mysterious group that call themselves the Thresholders."

"Oh, *them*," Mordacity said.

I don't know who was more surprised by Mordacity's words – me or Russell.

"How much do you know about them?" Russell asked.

"More than you'd like, I'm sure," Mordacity said. If his bone face had been capable of smirking, I'm sure he would've done so then.

Russell scowled, clearly unhappy with Mordacity's response, but he let it go.

"My *employers* only create portals when necessary," he said. "Otherwise, they prefer we make use of Doors like everyone else."

"Energy conservative, eh?" Mordacity said. "Makes sense. Inconvenient, though."

"All right, Jinx," I said. "You heard the man. No free rides tonight."

Before Jinx could respond, Bloodshedder let out a playful yip, leaped onto the side of the building, and skittered up the wall like a giant insect.

"You're not going to beat me this time!" Jinx stuffed Cuthbert Junior into his pocket, the hammer shrinking and vanishing, or doing whatever the hell it does when he's not using it. Then he started running down the sidewalk, his giant shoes making loud slapping sounds on the concrete as he went. Night had only just fallen, and there were still plenty of pedestrians out walking, and the street was filled with cars. The people on the sidewalk scattered as Jinx barreled toward them, and more than a few motorists honked their horns or rolled down their windows to shout things like, "Run, clown, run!"

Mordacity looked at me.

"He should know better than that," Mordacity said. "Watch officers – especially Incubi – are supposed to keep a low profile when ordinary humans are about. At least the dog was smart enough to take to the rooftops."

"Jinx *is* maintaining a low profile," I said. "He still has his clothes on, doesn't he?"

My stomach gurgled loudly then, and I felt a twist of nausea in my gut.

"I don't think I'll ever forgive Jinx using my mouth to take a bite of the Gingerdread Man. Did he really bite him where I think he did?"

"No comment," Russell said, and my stomach roiled again.

"By the way, thanks for the warning about the assassins," I said to Russell. "If Bloodshedder hadn't alerted me in time, there's a damn good chance Jinx and I would be lying dead on Deacon's floor with a couple bloodless holes in us."

"No problem," he said. "I only wish we'd been able to warn you sooner. But, by the time we learned the assassins' names and found out they'd traveled to Earth, we barely had enough time to get to Wet Dreams before they attacked." Russell added that the female assassin's name was Demonique. It fit her.

"How did you know we'd be at the bar?" Mordacity said, sounding suspicious. He may not have served as an active officer for years, but he still maintained his professional skepticism.

"Bloodshedder tracked you down," Russell said. "She's got quite a nose on her, no matter which Aspect she's in."

"Then she should be able to track the assassins by scent," Mordacity said. "Call her back!"

"I'm not worried about Gingerdread Man and Demonique right now," I said. "I know they were hired by whoever is behind the shuteye operation, but what are the odds they actually know anything about the people who employed them? They were probably hired by a go-between's go-between."

"Of course," Mordacity, said with the affronted tone of someone who's been told by his granddaughter how to suck eggs. "But at least it would be a place to start."

"I've got a better place to start," I said. Although truth was, I wasn't sure I had the guts to follow through on my own idea. "There's one person who's an expert on shuteye that I haven't talked to yet. And it's long past time that I paid him a visit."

Mordacity had no eyes to widen in surprise, but I'd

worked with him enough to read his body language, and I could tell he understood exactly who I was talking about.

Nathaniel Sawyer.

Surprisingly enough, Jinx found a Door first. It was inside a dumpster located behind an Indian restaurant – which happened to be right next to a seafood place – and I figured the warring food smells had confused Bloodshedder's nose, otherwise she would've won.

Jinx held the dumpster lid up for us, beaming proudly at his victory, and one by one we went in. Luckily for us, the lid opened directly onto the black void that marked the boundary between worlds. That meant we didn't have to crawl through garbage to get to Nod. Bloodshedder, who could be as poor a sport as Jinx when she chose, squirted some pee on Jinx's leg before she leaped into the dumpster, instantly spoiling his mood. I went through second to last, unable to keep from grinning at the sight of Jinx's wet pants' leg, and Jinx followed after me.

Sometimes when I pass between worlds, I hear the Thresholders' whispering, but this time I didn't. I was surprised to find that I missed it a little.

The Nodside door opened onto a narrow space that was too small and cramped to be a hallway. There were other doors here, all of them unmarked, all of them ending a foot or so above the floor.

"What is this place?" Mordacity asked.

We were packed shoulder to shoulder, and Mordacity shuffled back and forth, trying to make more room for himself.

I had a bad feeling about this.

I pushed open another of the doors, and inside was a tiny space with a mirror, a small bench protruding from the wall along with several metal pegs. A chill rippled down my spine as I closed the door.

"Please tell me this isn't what I think it is," Russell said.

"It's a dressing room," I told him.

"Fuck!" Russell spat, and Bloodshedder started growling.

Jinx's reaction was somewhat different. He clapped his hands and rubbed them together vigorously, eyes glittering with maniacal glee.

"I don't understand," Mordacity said.

"We're in a department store," I explained. "Which can only mean one thing."

"We're in the Maul." Jinx said *Maul* the way another person might have said *paradise.*

"What so bad about…" Mordacity broke off. "You mean *Maul.* M-A-U-L." He sighed. "All right. Here's how we're going to play this."

I stopped him before he could go any further.

"With all due respect to you as one of our mentors, Jinx and I have developed our own technique for making it out of the Maul alive and more or less intact."

"And what, pray tell, might that technique be?" Mordacity asked.

Jinx's mouth curved into a cruel smile, and his teeth looked sharper than they had a moment ago.

"It's called 'Stay out of Jinx's Way'," he said.

"How much longer is he going to be?" Russell said.

Russell, Mordacity, Bloodshedder, and I sat on the edge of a fountain outside the Maul's main entrance.

Mordacity stood, arms crossed, staring impatiently at the entrance's titanium doors. Bloodshedder lay on the ground, head on her front legs, eyes closed. She looked like she was sleeping, but I knew she'd be awake and rending flesh in an instant if there was trouble.

The fountain outside the Maul has a statue in the middle – a staggered column of large marble skulls perched one on top of the other, with equally large coins clamped in their teeth. Crimson water – at least, I *hoped* it was water – trickled from the skulls' eyes and noses, and ran down the column into a circular basin. A phrase was carved around the base's circumference: *Superesse Emptor*. Let the Buyer Survive.

"He'll be here soon," I said.

Mordacity harrumphed. I'd forgotten how cranky the Maul made him. Unlike most Incubi, he wasn't a fan of mayhem for its own sake. Plus, he hated the fountain. He thought the skulls were an affront to "ossified individuals everywhere," as he'd once told me.

"How long have you and Jinx been…" Russell trailed off, as if searching for the right words.

"Occupying each other's bodily space?" I offered. "Less than a day. I'm hoping we can get the situation resolved soon."

"I hope so, too." He smiled. "The next time we kiss, I want to know for certain that it's really you behind the lips."

I smiled sweetly. "What makes you think there's going to be a next time?"

Before Russell could reply, the doors burst open and an Incubus came flying out. The creature – which looked like an eight foot long trilobite with a scorpion's tail – flew through the air for a dozen yards and landed on the concrete with a loud cracking sound. The Incubus skidded for several feet before it managed to flip over, and then it skittered down the street, moving as if it were jet-propelled. I got a good enough look at it to see that its shell was cracked and its tail was bent at a funny angle.

Jinx came striding forth from the Maul after that, his clothes torn and soaked with blood. In one hand he carried a gore-smeared Cuthbert Junior. In the other he carried a blood-stippled shopping bag. His right cheek was swollen, probably from where the triloscorp had stung him. His gait was a bit wobbly, most likely because his body hadn't neutralized the poison yet.

"Sorry it took me so long," he said. "I forgot where the chocolate shop was."

He came over to the fountain and handed me the bag. I took it gingerly, doing my best to avoid getting any blood on my hands. I peered inside and then looked at Jinx.

"No dark chocolate?"

"They were out."

"Oh, well. Milk chocolate's good, too. Thanks."

I pulled out one of the candies, unwrapped it, and popped it in my mouth. I promptly started making 'mmm' noises that, if Russell's expression was any indication, sounded like I was enjoying myself a little too much. Too bad. Chocolate is an ultimate good and is meant to be enjoyed to the fullest.

After Jinx had cleared a path to the exit for us, I'd sent him back inside to get me a little something from Chocolatears. The Incubus who runs the shop cries her candy, hence the name.

As I chewed, I said, "It's a bit saltier than usual."

"Sucre told me she broke up with her boyfriend last week," Jinx said.

I nodded. "That explains it."

Russell made a face as I tossed a second chocolate into my mouth. "I can't believe you're eating that stuff. It came out of a living being's eyes, you know."

"I needed something to get the taste of gingerbread out of my mouth," I said. "Besides, don't knock it til you've tried it. And it beats Jinx's favorite sweet shop."

Jinx looked at Russell and smiled, revealing chocolate-smeared teeth.

"It's called Eat a Candy Bar Out of My Ass," he said.

As Russell and I stood up to go, I had a sudden feeling that something wasn't right. I turned back to look at the fountain, but it seemed the same as it always had been: basin with the Latin phrase, column of oversized skulls, red liquid running from their eyes, noses, and wide-open – not to mention quite empty – mouths.

I stared at those skulls for a moment, a thought nagging at the back of my consciousness, as if I were trying to grab hold of a memory that remained stubbornly out of reach.

I wasn't the only one staring at the skulls with a puzzled expression. Russell was, too.

"Something wrong?" I asked him.

He hesitated before answering.

"No, I guess not. Let's go."

Even though entering Nod through the Maul isn't the safest way to get there, we'd survived more or less unscathed thanks to Jinx's near-demonic skills at psychotic shopping. You never know where an Earthside Door will lead to in Nod, although Incubi can usually tell where a Nodside Door will let out on Earth. It was a lucky break that we'd arrived in Newtown instead of the Cesspit, or someplace even worse, like the Edgelands.

Ever since his breakdown, Nathaniel had been held in Deadlock, in the wing for the criminally insane, or what Incubi sometimes refer to as "overachievers." After the Angler had forced Nathaniel to swallow the shuteye pill, he'd become a mindless savage, lashing out at anyone who came near him. His condition had improved somewhat over the years, but not enough for him to be released. I hoped he'd be able to talk rationally with us – especially with Mordacity present – but there was no guarantee of that.

Since Deadlock is located in the Murk, there's only one relatively safe way to get there: the Loco-Motive. And we were only a few blocks away from the Arcade station. As we headed for the station, I wished we had time to stop at the Rookery so Jinx could get a new set of clothes. But I didn't want to risk missing the train. And, to be honest, I didn't want to run into Sanderson. Despite the fact that Jinx and I were in his good graces at the moment, I feared he might not approve of our talking with Nathaniel without his authorization. Better to ask forgiveness than permission. For me it's more than a saying – it's a way of life.

One good thing about Jinx's current revolting state was that it caused pedestrians to give us a wider berth than they usually did when they saw him coming. Considering that we didn't know if there were any other assassins gunning for us, the more distance everyone kept from us, the better.

While we were walking, I decided to call Dr

Menendez and check on how Melody was doing. I raised my wisper close to my mouth and said, "Call Menendez."

Russell looked at me, obviously curious as to who I was calling and why, but he didn't ask. It took several moments for the wisper to make the connection, and then I heard his voice.

"This is Dr Menendez."

Russell's eyes narrowed when he heard Menendez speak, but otherwise he kept his expression neutral. Smart boy. Jealousy is *so* unattractive.

"Hi, this is Audra Hawthorne." I gave my full name for Russell's benefit. Menendez and I weren't friends, and there was no reason to make Russell think otherwise. Although I admit it would've been fun to torture him, just a little. "I'm calling to see how Melody's doing."

"Hi, Audra. Good to hear from you. Ms Gail's condition hasn't changed significantly since we last spoke, but that's only to be expected. It's going to take some time for her to recover. I'll be sure to contact you the moment Ms Gail shows any sign of improvement."

"Thank you. I'd appreciate that."

I still felt guilty as hell over what had happened to Melody, but at least she was receiving the best care available in two dimensions. I was about to say goodbye when Menendez said, "How are you and Jinx doing? Have you experienced any more incidents of Blending?"

"A couple," I said. "But they weren't too bad."

Russell gave me a look.

"Okay," I admitted, "they were a *little* bad. Especially the last one." I quickly described to him what had happened to Jinx and me in Wet Dreams.

"I wouldn't worry too much about it," Menendez said when I'd finished. "You're still in the early stages of treatment. You and Jinx should take another dose of the medicine I gave you, and remember to stay near each other."

"Okay, we will," I said

"Good. Keep me posted on your progress, and, as I said, I'll be sure to contact you if there's any change in Ms Gail's condition." He paused, and then in a warmer, more personal tone, said, "Take care, Audra."

"You too," I said, and then ended the call.

We all continued walking in silence for a few minutes afterward. I took out the bottle of medicine Menendez had given me, shook out four pills, gave two to Jinx – who inhaled each through a separate nostril – and dry swallowed mine. After I tucked the bottle back into my jacket pocket, Russell said, "So... about this doctor..."

"Don't start," I said.

Russell scowled, but he didn't say anything more. Bloodshedder, who was padding along at her master's side, let out a snuffle-snort that was the demonic hound equivalent of a laugh.

Before long, we reached the train station and went inside. Outside, the station was a modern-looking glass-and-steel building, although, like so many structures in Newtown, its angles didn't seem quite right, and it hurt your head to look at it for too long. But inside, it resembled something from the late 1800s on Earth. Cracked marble floor, dark brown wooden benches, white brick walls, and a single glass-windowed ticket counter. The benches were filled with Incubi waiting for the Loco-Motive to arrive, and there were more lined up to get tickets.

Mordacity, Russell, and Bloodshedder scanned the crowd, keeping watch for anyone who looked suspicious. More suspicious than normal, that is. Jinx was busy playing with a dead lizard he'd pulled from one of his pockets. He was using it as a ventriloquist's dummy, holding it with one hand while propping it up on the palm of the other and waggling the head back and forth. The lizard introduced itself as Senor Largarto in a high-pitched voice, and it kept up a running commentary on how ugly the Incubi around us were. Mordacity turned his impassive skull face toward Jinx, and I thought he might draw his sword and take off Jinx's head. But he managed to restrain himself and we made it to the ticket window without any of us trying to kill the others.

I didn't feel like waiting in line, so I took out my badge and flashed it at the Incubi ahead of us as I walked directly up to the window. A few people grumbled, but when they saw Jinx – blood still wet on his shredded clothes and making a dead lizard talk – they decided to keep their mouths shut. Jinx, taking the silence as encouragement, began doing Abbott and Costello's famous "Who's on first?" routine with Senor Largarto, causing more than a few people to abandon their travel plans and head quickly for the exit.

The words *Booking and Ticketing Office* were carved into the cement above the window, and the Incubus behind it wore a dark blue uniform jacket with gold trim at the cuffs, light blue shirt, and a dark blue tie. She wore a billed cap, also trimmed in gold, with a badge on the front displaying the letters LM. I assumed the Incubus was female because of the swell of breasts under her uniform. The gender was difficult to determine from her face since she didn't have one. In its place was a gaping hollowed-out wound that stretched from her forehead down to her chin. The edges of the wound were ragged and bloody, and the inside looked like the wet red pulp of a partially emptied watermelon.

I hate watermelon.

I showed the ticket officer my badge, not that I was sure she could see it. "Official Shadow Watch business. We need five tickets for the next departure."

"Six!" Jinx said in his Senor Largarto voice, and gave the dead lizard a shake.

I sighed. "Six tickets. Charge them to the Watch's account."

Since we didn't have Sanderson's permission to speak with Nathaniel, the "official" part was a fib, of course. I hoped Mordacity wouldn't make an issue of it. It was exactly the sort of thing he would've disapproved of in the old days. I sensed he wasn't comfortable with my lying, but he didn't object.

The ticketing officer may have lacked a face, but she still had ears – and hands. She reached out to run her fingers across my badge, and when, in doing so, her skin briefly came in contact with mine, I couldn't stop myself from shuddering. If she noticed, she gave no indication, not that my reaction would've bothered her necessarily. As you might imagine, a lot of Incubi love scaring humans. It is, after all, quite literally what they are born to do.

Satisfied that my credentials were legitimate, the ticketing officer – who wore a nametag on her jacket that said Adorabelle – turned toward a computer keyboard. She rapidly typed a sequence of letters and numbers, and her printer spat out our tickets.

As she handed them to me, I said, "Thanks."

She made a wet gurgling noise that might've meant "You're welcome" or something else altogether.

I stepped away from the window to allow her to serve other customers, and I walked over to the train schedule mounted on the wall. It was an old-fashioned blackboard in a black frame, with information written on it in white chalk. Russell and Mordacity accompanied me, while Jinx continued to regale ticket-buyers with his dead lizard ventriloquist routine, and Bloodshedder sat next to him, watching and occasionally thumping her spiked tail loudly on the floor. There's no accounting for taste, I suppose.

Train Timetable was written at the top of the chalkboard, and below it was a list of stops and times. The Nodian clock begins at thirteen and goes to twenty-five. The Loco-Motive is the only train, and it runs in only one direction: edgewise. The train tracks are a Mobius strip, even though the train travels eternally forward, it makes more or less regular stops at various points in Nod's separate zones throughout the day. According to the timetable, the Loco-Motive was next due to stop at the main station at 22:17. I tapped my whisper and saw that the current Nodian time was 21:19.

I turned to Mordacity and Russell.

"We've got a little less than an hour to kill," I said. "I could use some dinner. Except for coffee and chocolate, I haven't eaten all day."

"I don't eat in my Night Aspect," Mordacity said.

"Right," I said. "The whole animated skeleton thing. I almost forgot. How about you, Russell?"

"I could eat."

From Mordacity's stiff posture – stiffer than usual, that is – I could tell he was irritated.

"I don't understand how you two can be thinking of food right now. You should be staying focused on our mission."

"Easy to say when you don't have blood sugar to get low," I said.

"In our line of work, you've got to eat when you can," Russell said.

Jinx was still putting on his show with Senor Largarto. But, at that precise moment, Bloodshedder sprang forward, snatched the dead lizard out of his hands, and swallowed it down in a single gulp.

"Case in point," Russell said.

"NOOOO!!!!" Jinx wailed

Bloodshedder licked her lips.

Jinx reached into his inner pocket and removed a lily. He knelt down and gently placed it on the floor. He stood and then bowed his head.

"*Domo arigato*, Senor Largarto."

Bloodshedder burped.

Mordacity remained in the station to wait for the Loco-Motive. He promised to call me if it arrived early. I don't think the Loco-Motive has arrived early in the couple centuries it's been in existence, but Mordacity can be kind of OCD in his Night Aspect, so I allowed him his illusion. Besides, there's always a first time, right?

He asked Russell and me to get our food to go and bring it back to the station, not so much because of the train, but because he was uncomfortable having us out of his sight when Gingerdread Man and Demonique might make another attempt to kill us. I told him he had a good point and none of us should be left alone. Russell asked Bloodshedder to stay behind with Mordacity. She pouted because Senor Largarto was little more than a snack for a creature her size, but she brightened when Russell told her he'd bring something back for her. Mordacity didn't seem thrilled at being left with a babysitter, but he didn't protest.

Jinx came with me and Russell. He was unusually subdued, and every now and then he had to choke back a sob. I decided to keep a lookout for any other dead vermin that could replace Jinx's departed ventriloquist's dummy. Not that it would be easy since Jinx is very particular when it comes to dead animals.

There are a lot of restaurants and bars near the Main Station, and we had a fair amount of choice. Most serve food that humans would find hard to digest, if it wasn't outright poisonous to us places such as *Chef Borgia-Dee's*, *Strychnine and Sons*, *Fiberglass Po-Boys*, *Industrial Effluvia and Frozen Yogurt*, and most ominous of all, a place simply called *Buffet*.

I looked at Russell and he shrugged. "Your call," he said.

I sighed. "Buffet it is. May the First Dreamer have mercy on our digestive systems."

Russell and I started heading in the restaurant's direction, but I quickly realized that Jinx wasn't following us. I turned back around and saw him standing there, looking uncomfortable.

"I'm, uh, not really hungry. And I'm still in mourning and everything. Poor Senor Largarto. Taken before he even had a chance to begin properly rotting. I was thinking of stopping in there for a second."

He hooked a thumb toward a place with a glaring neon sign which said *Misery Loves Company*.

"I thought I'd get a cup of coffee." And, before I could protest, he added, "I'll order decaf, I swear!"

"It's been a while since my last dose of caffeine," I said. "Maybe all three of us could go there. They're bound to have something to eat." I looked at Russell. "Sound good?"

"Hey, caffeine is one of the major food groups, as far as I'm concerned."

Jinx looked *really* uncomfortable now. "Look, nothing personal, but it's best if I go in alone." He lowered his voice. "It's not a place for the, er, *un-jesterish*, if you know what I mean."

"It's a clowns-only joint?" I asked.

"Oh no," Jinx said. "Everyone's welcome. But, you know. *Clowns*."

I nodded in sudden understanding. "Anyone *can* go in, but no one but other clowns would *want* to."

Jinx smiled. "Exactly."

I tried to imagine an entire coffee bar packed with nightmare clowns, most of them wired to the ceiling on caffeine. I had absolutely no desire to take a single step toward the place, let alone set foot in it.

I thought for a moment. It wasn't as if Jinx needed my permission. We were equal partners. But Dr Menendez *had* advised us to remain in close physical proximity, and there was the issue of the assassins. I wasn't sure if it was a good idea for us to split up any more than we already had. But it would be for a few minutes, and Jinx was far more damage-resistant than I was, especially in Nod. The sheer amount of Maelstrom energy in the environment would allow him to heal even faster than he could during nighttime on Earth. Besides, no assassin would be dumb enough to enter a place filled with clowns. And no one would hire a clown Incubus as an assassin. They'd be just as likely to kill everyone else in the vicinity – including themselves – as they would their target.

"All right," I said. "But only if you pinky swear you'll restrict yourself to decaf."

For Jinx, a pinky swear is an inviolate vow. I don't know whether it's a psychological thing or part of his intrinsic clown nature, but he literally cannot break a pinky swear.

He nodded, stepped forward, and held out his hand, pinky extended. I stepped forward, did the same, and we locked pinkies and shook our joined hands up and down three times. When we were finished, we broke apart.

"See you back at the station in a few," I said.

Jinx grinned. "Enjoy your rotavirus." Then he turned and headed for *Misery Loves Company*, giant shoes slap-slap-slapping as he walked.

Russell looked at me. "Let's make sure to tell them to hold the rotavirus."

I nodded absently as I watched Jinx head for the coffee bar. There was something about this that was bothering me, but I couldn't put my finger – pinky or otherwise – on what it was.

"There are a lot of humans in here," Russell said. "That's a good sign."

"True. Smells like an orangutan's armpit, though. Kind of spoils a girl's appetite."

"Maybe the salad bar won't be so bad."

"Want to bet on it?"

"Not really."

We started toward the salad bar. The restaurant looked like any generic family buffet place back on Earth – lots of tables and chairs, faded carpet, walls institutional white, and half a dozen serving stations with heat lamps dehydrating already tasteless food.

There were a good number of Incubi present, but Russell was right. At least two thirds of the patrons were human. So, even if the food tasted like overdone ass, it wouldn't poison us. Probably.

We were within a few feet of the salad bar when vertigo hit me again, and the next thing I knew, I was looking at a room filled with chalk-white faces.

"What do you *think* it means?"

The clown who asked this question was short, fat, and heavily tattooed. He wore a black leather vest with no shirt underneath, leather pants, and cowboy boots. Nails had been driven halfway down into the top of his head, and dried blood had crusted around them. And as disturbing as *that* was, the large gauge piercing in the middle of his forehead – a piercing that had removed a section of his forehead – was worse. He'd inserted a clear plastic plug into it so that a portion of his brain was visible.

At first, I had no idea what he meant, but then I realized that Jinx had been holding out a piece of paper for the other clown to inspect. I turned it around to read it, and saw that it was the sign that someone had taped to Jinx's back during the fight in Wet Dreams.

Are you clown enough?

I looked up from the note and fixed Nail-Head with what I hoped was an intimidatingly psychotic glare.

"I think it means that someone's been fucking around with me, and I don't appreciate it."

Nail-Head looked at me for a moment, as if what I'd said surprised him, and then he brayed mad laughter. The other clowns in the bar joined in, filling the place with insane cackles, maniacal giggles, and disquieting chortles. It was a good thing I had Jinx's bladder now, else I might have peed my pants.

I took a quick glance around to get my bearings. *Misery Loves Company* looked like a typically bland corporate coffee shop, a sterile place that tries to be hip but which is completely lacking anything close to personality. I have to admit that the severed clowns' heads hanging from the ceiling by chains was a unique touch, although I could have done without seeing their eyes blink or their tongues licking the tips of the meat hooks protruding from their mouths.

The place was a coulrophobic's personal hell, and, even though I'd more or less adjusted to having a nightmare clown for a partner, that didn't mean I was now in love with clowns. Far from it. The clowns at *Misery Loves Company* were quite diverse in their own way. Both genders and all body types were represented, as were various races – although most had the ubiquitous chalk-white skin of their clan. Some were post-modern, like Nail-Head, while some were old-fashioned, like images brought to life from nineteenth century circus posters or medieval jesters plucked out of time. Their outfits ranged from standard clown looks such as threadbare hobo clothing and candy-colored blouses, to costumes from various Earth cultures – Asian, Hispanic, African… It was like a goddamned Clown History Museum display made flesh and blood.

TIM WAGGONER   177

I recognized several of the clowns present as members of the Bedlam Brothers troupe from the Circus Psychosis, and I also recognized the hula-hooping clown who'd approached us, the first one who'd asked Jinx if he was clown enough.

When the laughter died down, Nail-Head sneered at me.

"We may call ourselves the Unholy Fools, but that doesn't mean we suffer actual ones. You know what your problem is, and you know what'll happen to you if you don't fix it ASA-fucking-P." He jerked a thumb toward the heads dangling from the ceiling.

"You tell him, Lowbrow!" someone yelled, and more laughter followed.

The clowns all held white cardboard cups with plastic lids. Some of them held cups in both hands, and, as they watched me, they sipped their drinks, and I felt my guts turn to iced water. Being surrounded by a room full of caffeinated nightmare clowns was like standing on top of an active nuclear bomb – a situation to be avoided at all costs.

What would Jinx do if he were here? I asked myself.

I leaned close to Lowbrow, bared my teeth, and in my best imitation of Jinx at his most menacing, I said, "I'd like to see you try."

Instantly, every clown in the place pulled a bladed weapon from somewhere on their person: knives, axes, saws, cleavers, and other implements that I couldn't name but which would slice and dice me to bloody pieces just the same.

I held up my hands.

"Empty bravado!" I exclaimed. "That's all it was! I'm well and truly terrified at the moment. If I was wearing underwear, I'd drop several loads in my shorts right now."

Lowbrow held an obscenely large butcher's knife, the blade speckled with rust and old blood. His eyes were wild and his hand trembled, and for a moment I thought he was going to attack. But then his hand steadied and the madness in his gaze diminished. He nodded and tucked his knife away inside his vest. Slowly, and more than a little reluctantly, the rest of the clowns put away their toys as well.

"Consider this your last warning, Jinx," Lowbrow said. "You need to put on your big clown panties and start acting like a true fool. If you don't, we'll be coming for you." He smiled, but there was no mirth in his expression. "Now get your fucking coffee and get the hell out."

I looked at Lowbrow and for a moment I *really* wanted to reach inside Jinx's jacket and see if I could pull out Cuthbert Junior. I had no idea if I could perform that feat of magic while in Jinx's body, but it would feel so sweet to grab hold of Cuthbert's handle and swing the hammer right into the plastic circular window in Lowbrow's head. But I restrained myself, turned, and headed for the counter, where a clown barista held out a cup of coffee for me. Written on the side in black marker were two words: *Decaf* and *Loser*.

This time I did reach for Cuthbert Junior, but just as I felt my fingers close around a wooden handle, vertigo struck, my vision blurred, and, when it cleared, I found myself standing in front of a salad bar, a horrible taste in my mouth. Russell was looking at me oddly.

"I guess you *really* like beets, huh?" he said.

I looked down at my hands and saw they were

covered with purple-red juice. I looked at the bar and saw an empty bowl with a tiny puddle of beet juice in it. My tongue was tingling, and I felt a burning in my chest.

"Jinx, you asshole!" I shouted.

And then before Russell could ask what was happening, I turned and made a dash for the bathroom. I managed to get three-quarters of the way there before the projectile vomiting began.

EIGHT

"I forgot you were allergic to beets. Seriously!" Jinx paused. "Still, I wish I'd been there to see it. When you puke, Audra, you *really* puke. It's truly a thing of beauty." He turned to Russell. "I don't suppose you recorded it with your wisper? I'd love to see the video!"

"Afraid not," Russell said.

Jinx sighed. "Too bad. I could've posted it on SpewTube."

My throat felt as if I'd swallowed ground glass and I had a headache. Worst of all, I couldn't get the damn taste of beets out of my mouth.

The five of us stood on the platform, along with a couple dozen other people, waiting for the Loco-Motive to pull into the station. The train was fifteen minutes late, and Mordacity was beginning to get antsy. Waiting patiently wasn't one of his talents.

Jinx hadn't asked me what had happened in *Misery Loves Company* after we'd switched bodies, and so far he'd shown no sign that he was interested in finding out. I, on the other hand, had a number of questions for him, but now wasn't the best time to ask them. They could wait, but not for too long. I needed to know who or what the Unholy Fools were, and what they meant by the message they'd been sending Jinx. *Are you clown enough?* It had sounded ominous before, and, after my experience at the coffee shop, it had taken on even more sinister overtones.

I would have to find an opportunity to speak to Jinx about it alone. One quality both of his Aspects shared was that they were deeply private people. It would be hard enough getting him to open up to me. No way would he do so if anyone else were around.

A train whistle sounded in the distance, announcing the Loco-Motive's imminent arrival. The sound was more of a shriek than anything else, and it sounded as if it were comprised of a chorus of voices instead of merely one. The night train is a dream archetype that's been around ever since the first locomotives began appearing in England in the early 1800s. It takes an Ideator of uncommon psychic strength – and an equally uncommon level of fear – to bring the larger Incubi into existence, but, even so, a number of nightmare trains have been manifested over the last couple centuries. The Shadow Watch became aware of them, brought them to Nod and – through a process not even the Watch's M-gineers or Somnacologists fully understand – the trains combined into a single nightmarish construction: the Loco-Motive.

The skeleton of some ancient prehistoric beast that never existed outside of dreams forms the train's framework. The bones are lashed together with leathery lengths of tendon with panels of black metal filling in the gaps. An old-fashioned cowcatcher juts from the front of the Loco-Motive, a wicked-looking wedge of highly polished and well-honed steel. The cowcatcher was smeared with streaks of blood and shreds of sinewy meat stuck to the edges, indicating that something had been suicidal enough to get in the train's way. It has a single headlight which blazes a baleful crimson, and smoke the same color billows from its stack. From the way the Loco-Motive looks, you'd expect it to make some sort of ungodly noise as it moves – the rumbling growl of a titanic beast spoiling for a fight, or maybe the labored wheezing of a hodge-podge machine that shouldn't exist, parts grinding and straining, always on the verge of falling apart. But you'd be wrong. The Loco-Motive is almost entirely silent; the only sound it makes is a soft sizzling, punctuated by an occasional loud *pop!* like meat in a frying pan. It's a sound that never fails to unnerve me, and, as the Loco-Motive braked and began to slow, I found myself wishing, as I always did when forced to ride the Loco-Motive, that Nod had a highway system or air travel. But then again, given how chaotic, crippling, and corpse-making traffic can be on the roads in Newtown, maybe it's just as well that Incubi aren't operating vehicles – terrestrial or aerial – through the land.

The stench of burning flesh filled the air as the train stopped, and I swallowed to keep from gagging. After what the beets had done to me, the last thing I wanted to do was start vomiting again.

The door in the first car opened and the Conductor stepped out. He wore the railroad's standard blue uniform and cap, but there was nothing in them. The cap hovered in the air above the collar, giving the impression that it rested on an invisible head. Whatever the hell the Conductor is, he's damn creepy, even for Nod.

Passengers began disembarking and patrons on the platform pushed by them, eager to climb aboard and get settled. Very few of them had luggage of any kind. Incubi tend to travel light.

Mordacity headed for the first passenger car, most likely because it would be easiest to defend if we were attacked. I'd have preferred to take the last passenger car to keep us as far away from the engine's stink as possible, but I couldn't argue with his strategy, and so the rest of us followed.

A lot of the seats were already filled, either by embarking passengers or passengers who had yet to reach their stop. We needed five seats close together, but the most we could find was three. Jinx walked up to a pair of passengers who were sitting by the empty seats, a couple who were conjoined at the face. They only had one nostril between them, but Jinx removed his tattered, gore-stained jacket, draped it over his left arm, and raised his right – making sure to get his armpit as close to the lone nostril as possible. The conjoined couple let out a muffled scream, flung themselves into the corridor, nearly knocking Jinx down in the process, and fled the car as swiftly as their combined bodies permitted. Jinx then donned his jacket once more and with a grin gestured to the now-empty seats.

"*I'm* not sitting there," I said. "Not until the stench dissipates." The Loco-Motive's stink was one thing, but the full unfettered force of Jinx's body odor can strip the paint off a wall at thirty paces.

Mordacity had no sense of smell in his Night Aspect, so he sighed in exasperation and moved past me to take one of the seats the couple had vacated. Bloodshedder surprised me by padding over and squeezing her bulk into the seat next to him.

"I think she likes you," Russell said to Mordacity.

"She likes the bones he's made out of," Jinx said.

As if confirming this, Bloodshedder looked at Mordacity and licked her chops.

Russell, Jinx, and I took the other three seats. Russell and I sat on two seats across the corridor from the others, and Jinx took a seat behind us. An Incubus had the window seat next to Russell, although, since the creature looked like a giant pile of nail clippings without any obvious sensory apparatus, I doubted it had taken the seat for the view.

We sat for several minutes while the rest of the passengers got on and freight was offloaded and new freight was onloaded. Maybe fifteen minutes in all. During that time we kept an eye out for the Gingerdread Man and Demonique – or anyone suspicious – but we didn't see them and no one else set off any alarms.

Nod is a more-or-less flat circle. Oldtown, as you can guess from the name, was the first settlement, and it occupies the center of the circle. The rest of Nod's sections proceed outward in concentric rings, like ripples in a pond. After Oldtown comes Newtown, then the Cesspit, the Murk, and finally the Edgelands. The Loco-Motive's route is an ever-widening spiral that, at least to observers, appears to begin in Oldtown and move out from there. But, since the Loco-Motive's tracks are a Mobius strip, they technically don't have a beginning or an end.

The Conductor stepped onto our car and then the doors closed of their own accord. He didn't shout "All aboard!" or call out our next destination. You need a physical body to produce sound.

The train whistle let out a single, long blast that sounded like the combined wailing of all the doomed souls in Hell. At the signal, everyone took out his or her ticket and held it up. The Conductor walked to the front of the car, and then turned around to face us, if you can use the word *face* to describe the action of a being that has none. He did nothing obvious, didn't raise his arms, didn't so much as twitch his hat, but all of our tickets vanished. I knew from past experience that the same thing had happened in the other passenger cars too.

Normally at that point the Loco-Motive would begin moving. But the train remained still, and the Conductor remained motionless. One by one, we looked around, confused, until we saw one of our fellow passengers sitting in the rear of the car. He was still holding up his hand, and held between his fingers was his still very visible ticket. The Incubus was humanoid, with gray pebbly skin like a rhino and a huge rooster head, which was also covered with gray hide. He was dressed like an extra from *Grease* – black leather jacket, white T-shirt, jeans, and black boots. His eyes were like large black marbles, and they were trained on the Conductor, who appeared to have focused his attention on the Incubus in turn. Rooster-Head began to tremble under the Conductor's scrutiny.

"My ticket's legit, I swear!"

The voice that came out of his beak was an exaggerated stereotype of a Brooklyn accent, the kind you'd hear in a comedy movie from the 1930s or 40s.

The Conductor did nothing. The train didn't move.

Beads of sweat broke out on Rooster-Head's cockscomb.

"I would never try to cheat you with a fake ticket," he said. "Seriously! I mean, who would be stupid enough to do that?" He added a nervous, dry-throated, and thoroughly unconvincing chuckle.

The Conductor began walking now, heading down the corridor toward Rooster-Head, one deliberate footstep at a time.

Rooster-Head began clucking softly as the Conductor approached. When the Conductor was within five feet of him, Rooster-Head stood up abruptly and pulled a gun from where he'd kept it tucked against the small of his back. He trained the weapon – which looked like a standard Earth Glock – on the Conductor and then flicked his ersatz ticket toward him.

"All right, so what if my ticket's phony? What are you going to do about it?"

The Conductor stopped and stood motionless once more. I had the impression he was regarding the freeloading passenger, perhaps trying to come to a decision. He then raised one of his arms – or maybe I should say *sleeves* – and pointed it toward Rooster-Head. There was a sudden *whooshing* sound, and Rooster-Head was yanked off his feet and flew toward the Conductor. His body seemed to lengthen and narrow, almost becoming fluid as it streaked toward the Conductor, entered his empty sleeve, and disappeared. The wind died down, and after a moment the Conductor lowered his arm. He turned and walked slowly back to the front of the car before turning around once more to face us.

The car was dead silent for several seconds after that,

but then Jinx grinned and said, "When I grow up, I want *your* job!"

The Conductor raised his arm again and then, so swiftly did it happen that I might've imagined it, a hand – a gray, pebble-skinned hand – appeared at the end of the sleeve to give Jinx a thumbs-up. And then it was gone.

The Conductor lowered his arm, and then the Loco-Motive finally began to move.

Because of the circuitous route the Loco-Motive takes as it traverses the Rings, the trip to Deadlock would take several hours, so we settled into our seats and did our best to pass the time. None of us could sleep, so napping wasn't an option. We hadn't brought anything to read, except Jinx, who pulled a copy of *Autopsy Monthly* from one of his pockets. I thought Russell was going to lose his buffet dinner when Jinx showed him the centerfold.

Back when I was a trainee, I'd once asked Nathaniel why Deadlock had been built so far from the center of Nod. I thought having the prison closer to the Rookery would've made prisoner transport a lot easier.

"You've seen how chaotic and dangerous Incubi can be as they go about their everyday lives. Imagine what Incubi criminals are like. It's best to keep them as far away from everyone else as possible, and, if that means we officers have to put up with a long train ride now and then, it's a small enough price to pay."

Jinx giggled as he flipped through his magazine, and more than a few passengers got up in search of different seats in other cars. Bloodshedder closed her eyes and allowed her chin to drop to her chest. She might be incapable of sleeping, but she could do a damn good imitation of it. Mordacity had the window seat, and he kept his eyeless sockets pointed at the world outside, no doubt keeping watch for any sign of trouble. He'd have had a fit if either Jinx or I had taken a window seat, given that there were assassins gunning for us, but he had chosen his seat without hesitation. That was Mordacity, always thinking of others before himself. Then again, when you have a body covered with bone armor, you can afford to make yourself a target, I suppose.

"Have you ever seen anything like those weapons the assassins used?" I asked Russell.

"Nope. Whatever they are, they're pretty damned effective, though. Scary, too. It's like that black energy just bores right through flesh and bone, disintegrating it."

"More like unmaking it," I said. "I'll tell Sanderson about the weapons the next time Jinx and I report in."

"And I'll inform my bosses. If someone starts mass producing those things…"

I shuddered. "I don't want to think about it."

"So, you and Jinx have been offered New York," Russell said.

I sighed. "Does *everyone* in Nod know?"

Russell smiled. "You two are famous now, and people gossip about celebrities."

I snorted. "Yeah, well, just wait until the next time we screw up. That'll be the end of our celebrity status."

"Sounds like someone has esteem issues. Is that why you're reluctant to go to New York? Because you shouldn't be. You and Jinx might not be the most orthodox officers that the Shadow Watch has ever seen, but you're both tough as nails and you get the job done. New York would be lucky to have you."

I don't handle praise well, so I just said, "Thanks." After a moment, I added, "I honestly don't know what my problem is about New York. Jinx – Day Jinx, that is – would love living there."

"Me too!" Night Jinx chimed in. "It's bigger than Chicago, which means there's lots more stuff to destroy!" He went back to reading *Autopsy Monthly* after that. He turned the page and began chuckling. I did *not* want to know what he found amusing in that magazine.

"Maybe I just need more time to get used to the idea," I said.

"Maybe," Russell agreed.

I glanced at Jinx, then I turned back to Russell. "I need to talk to him for a few minutes."

Russell nodded. I got up, tapped Jinx on the shoulder, and gestured for him to follow me. He put away his magazine – rather reluctantly, I thought – got up, and followed me toward the rear of the car. There were some empty seats there now, and we took a couple of them.

Only one passenger besides us remained, and he sat all the way in the back of the car. He was a humanoid version of some sleek, black-and-white fur-covered animal. A weasel or ferret, I guessed. He wore a blue one-piece track suit, the kind that zips up in the middle, but his feet were bare. Considering their inhuman shape and size – not to mention the claws jutting from the toes – I could see where he'd have a hard time finding shoes to fit him. His finger-claws were even more impressive. They were each a foot-and-a-half long, and they appeared to be formed from a crystalline substance that gleamed in the train car's fluorescent lights. The claws tapered to wickedly sharp points, and I wondered how he was going to get into Deadlock with them. Visitors aren't permitted to carry weapons, and his were built in. Maybe the prison had an industrial-strength nail clipper.

The creature's face was a twisted distortion of a ferret's, with overlarge eyes that were a deep, disturbing red, wide flaring nostrils, and a mouthful of yellow teeth that were larger, longer, and sharper than a real ferret's. Normally, he would've come across as frightening and intimidating – even to someone as used to Incubi as I was. But he sat hunched in his seat, whiskers quivering, eyes darting back and forth nervously, scraping his finger-claws together with soft *shssk-shssk-shssk* sounds. He glanced at us now and again, but I didn't get the sense he was afraid of us. He didn't appear to be overly fond of sharing a car with Jinx, but then who would? Being enclosed in a tight space with a psychotic clown isn't exactly comfort-making.

I wasn't especially concerned that Ferret-Face might be an assassin sent to attack us. Sure, he had the equipment to do the job. Those claws of his looked deadly as hell. But a professional assassin wouldn't look like he was constantly on the verge of a panic attack. Unless his nervousness was just an act to disguise the fact that in truth he was a stone-cold killer.

I looked at him again and saw he'd started gnawing at the claws on his right hand.

If his nervousness *was* a disguise, it was the best I'd ever seen.

I had a good idea what he was afraid of, and I didn't blame him one bit. I wasn't looking forward to it either.

I ignored Ferret-Face and spoke to Jinx. "You want to tell me what's going on with this 'Are you clown enough?' thing?" I asked. "You know we switched bodies when you were in *Misery Loves Company*."

"Yeah," he smiled. "Mmmm, beets."

My stomach did a flip at the mere mention of the word. "Nice try, but you're not going to distract me like that."

Jinx didn't say anything more for the next several moments, but then he let out a long, defeated sigh.

"Did you know that I'm the first clown to serve in the Shadow Watch?" he said.

"No, I didn't."

"Clowns are one of the most frightening nightmare archetypes. Everybody hates clowns, right? We have a certain image to maintain: scary, psychotic, dangerous…"

"Seems to me you do just fine in all those departments."

"Maybe by human standards. No offense."

"None taken."

"Sure, I'm crazier than a shithouse rat, and I take pride in making some of the biggest and baddest Incubi mess their undies when I laugh. But, ultimately, I'm still a good guy, fighting on the side of the angels and all that. It doesn't sit well with the others."

"The Unholy Fools."

He nodded. "They're the nightmare clown organization. As much creatures of chaos can ever get organized, that is. They'd rather I quit the Watch and rampage through the streets of Nod like the rest of them. Actually, they'd probably like to see my head hanging from the ceiling of *Misery Loves Company* even more. And, if I keep on being a good guy, they'll make it happen."

I wasn't sure what to say. I'd created Jinx, or at least my subconscious had. But once he'd come into existence, he was his own being, able to make his own choices. Still, I couldn't help feeling that I'd steered him toward a career with the Shadow Watch. We were both recruited, but I'd been the one interested in joining. I'd had to convince Jinx by telling him how much havoc he'd be able to wreak as a law officer. At the time, I'd thought I was helping to channel his violent nature toward something positive. Now I wondered if I hadn't done him a disservice, like trying to turn a tiger into a vegetarian.

Before I could say anything more, a loud alarm bell began ringing in the car. I knew the same alarm was sounding in each of the passenger cars. The Conductor hadn't moved since the train began rolling, and, when I say he hadn't moved, I mean he was statue-still, even when the train went through a curve or hit a bumpy spot on the tracks. But now he turned and opened the door between our car and the engine. He closed the door behind him, and, since there was no window in it, I didn't see him enter the engine. No one knows if there's an engineer driving the Loco-Motive or if the machine drives itself. Whichever the case, I knew one thing: the Loco-Motive was preparing to enter the Murk.

It's always night in Nod, even if that night is only a simulation of the real thing back on Earth. But, when you reach the outskirts of the Cesspit, it begins to get even darker. The stars in the Canopy fade until you can't see them any longer, and the darkness becomes more than just the absence of light. It's a thing unto itself, with weight and solidity, a dense black expanse of Something Awful. What little light there was outside the train began to dim, and machinery whirred as metal panels descended to cover the windows. We were unable to see outside anymore, but I knew what happened next. The Loco-Motive's headlight came on, sending a bright yellow beam lancing into the darkness before us. Additional running lights on the sides, tops, and even the bottoms of the cars activated, wreathing the train in a protective nimbus of illumination. The Loco-Motive's engine had been relatively silent during the trip so far, but now it began to thrum as it increased its speed. If you want to survive a journey through the Murk, the best way to do it is to haul some serious ass.

There was another reason the Loco-Motive needed to pick up speed. If it wasn't going fast enough, it wouldn't make it across the Rimline. The borders between Oldtown, Newtown, and the Cesspit are open, and you can pass between them at any point with ease. But the Rimline is more than just a demarcation – it's a barrier created and maintained by the Unwakened to keep the things that dwell in the Murk from invading the rest of Nod. Although the Rimline isn't visible, it's a solid wall of psychic force, and only one object can penetrate it: the Loco-Motive, and then only if it's traveling fast enough. No one knows for certain how the Loco-Motive can cross the Rimline. Some say the Unwakened give it special dispensation. Others say it has something to do with the train's cowcatcher; that it's made of some special substance that allows the Loco-Motive to punch a hole through the barrier and zoom through before the breach can seal itself.

"I *love* this part!" Jinx shouted, his face as eager as that of a roller-coaster enthusiast about to plunge over the top of the highest hill in amusement park history.

I ran back to my original seat, the engine's rumbling increasing in volume and pitch until it was a near-deafening shriek. The alarm continued sounding as we drew near the Rimline, and Russell and I put our feet against the seatbacks in front of us and grabbed hold of them with one hand. Our other hands intertwined without our really thinking about it, but I was glad. If you're about to die a horrible death by slamming full speed into a psychic wall of force, it's nice to have someone to hold hands with as you're smashed to jelly.

Jinx stood sideways in the center aisle, knees bent, arms stretched out, as if he were surfing. Bloodshedder hunkered down in her seat and curled up into a ball, like an armadillo. Mordacity didn't do anything. He just sat stoically and waited.

I knew when the Loco-Motive hit the Rimline, because the train slowed with an abrupt jolt, knocking us forward. It lurched from side to side, as if veering off the tracks. The Loco-Motive began to slow, even though its engine was screaming louder than ever as it strained against the barrier. And then, just as the train came to a full stop, there was a silent popping sensation, a feeling of release as the Rimline gave way, and the train shot forward, slamming us back into our seats. A few moments later the Loco-Motive's speed leveled off, and, while it was still traveling fast, it was no longer going all-out hell for leather. The alarm stopped sounding at that point and the engine shriek died down somewhat, although it didn't return to its more quiet cruising speed.

This passage through the Rimline was no different than the others I'd made – except for holding hands with Russell, of course. We'd managed to remain in our seats, and, while my neck was a little sore, I didn't think I'd sustained whiplash. Mordacity and Bloodshedder made it through fine, but Jinx had lost his footing and had bounced around the car like a giant pinball covered in clown-white makeup. He was now shoved up against the car's rear door, ass over teakettle. He rolled into a standing position, and, while he had some fresh cuts, scrapes, and burgeoning bruises, he looked like he'd survive. He walked back toward his seat, doing his best to straighten the tattered remnants of his jacket.

"That was fun," he said, as he sat behind Russell and me once more. "Now comes my second favorite part of the trip."

The metal panels still covered the windows so we couldn't see outside and, more importantly, so the things out there couldn't see in. Over the sound of the train engine, thumping noises could be heard, as if something heavy struck the car, *many* somethings, coming from all directions.

"What's that?" Russell asked.

He still held onto my hand, but I wasn't about to draw his attention to it. I didn't want to scare him off by making a big deal about holding hands. But then his question sank in, and I frowned.

"Have you ever been in the Murk before?" I asked.

"Nope. Never been to the Edgelands, either. Never had a reason to, until now."

Bloodshedder had uncurled and sat up in her seat once more. Next to her, Mordacity turned to face Russell and answered his question before I could.

"Those noises are caused by the Dark Ones," he said.

"Darkuns," Jinx corrected.

Mordacity sighed. He detested anything approaching slang.

The Dark Ones – or Darkuns, as they've come to be called over the centuries – are primitive, savage Incubi created from the deepest, darkest part of the human subconscious. Amorphous shadow creatures that can alter their shape at will, once they come into existence, the first thing they do is devour their Ideators, merging with them. Because of this, they never Fade. They continue existing decade after decade, century upon century, never aging, never weakening. And they live for one thing only: to feed. When people say they're afraid of the dark, it's these Incubi that they're talking about, even if they don't realize it.

If the Unwakened hadn't created the Rimline to keep the Darkuns separate from the rest of Nod, they'd have slaughtered everyone – Incubus and Ideator alike – long ago. Darkuns are incredibly difficult to kill, so, whenever one is created, the Shadow Watch hunts it down, captures it, brings it to Nod, and takes it to the Murk to release it. Some say the Murk is so thick because it's filled with so many Darkuns. Others say the Darkuns give off darkness, the same way some creatures on Earth give off bioluminescence.

Russell frowned. "I'd heard Darkuns can't stand light, and the train's got lights all over it. How can they get close enough to attack?"

"They don't," I said. "They break off pieces of themselves and hurl them like rocks. They're trying to break the lights so they can get closer."

The thumping noises had increased while we spoke,

and now it sounded as if the train was traveling through a storm of softball-sized hail.

"And if they do break enough lights," Jinx said, grinning, "then they can get in."

"Don't sound so excited by the prospect," Mordacity said. "If the Dark *Ones* gained entrance to this car, we wouldn't last long."

"Sez you, *Mord*," Jinx said.

"So… they throw pieces of themselves, huh?" Russell sounded very much like a nervous man who was trying to sound calm. Bloodshedder felt the same as her master. She hunched down in her seat and whined softly. Russell went on. "Kind of like Quietus, I guess."

Quietus was an assassin who'd served the Fata Morgana. A silent living shadow, he'd killed people with weapons formed from his own substance. As far as I knew, he'd been destroyed when Jinx and I had prevented the dimensions from merging. I hope it was true. He was a cold-hearted and extremely deadly sonofabitch, and both worlds were better off with him gone.

"Quietus might've been related to the Darkuns somehow," I said. "The Darkness too."

"Really?" Russell said. "I mean, he does have *dark* in his name, but besides that…"

"You know how when he opens his robe there's nothing but a black emptiness inside?" I said.

"Yeah, and if someone tries to attack him – or more importantly, Maggie – they might find themselves swallowed up by that void."

I nodded. "Maggie once told me that, when people disappear into that emptiness, they end up here, in the Murk."

"Now *that* would be a nasty surprise," Russell said.

The thumping continued to grow louder and the lights in our car flickered, which was a less than comforting sign. The noise agitated Jinx until he was bouncing in his seat like an over-excited four-year-old. There aren't many things he loves more than fighting Darkuns.

Ferret-Face chose that moment to let out a high-pitched shriek. He yanked his feet off the floor, as if afraid the Darkuns might attempt to enter the car from underneath. He drew his knees to his chest and wrapped his arms around them, as if by doing so he formed a protective barrier for himself. Not that it would help. If a Darkun managed to get inside, nothing short of head-to-toe titanium armor could protect him.

He kept whipping his head around, as if trying to track the movements of the Darkuns outside. His whiskers quivered so fast now that they were blurs, and I thought I could actually hear them making humming sounds. He breathed rapidly, whining with each exhalation, yapping with alarm whenever a Darkun struck a particularly hard blow and outright shrieking if they struck anywhere close to where he sat. He gripped the edge of his seat so tight that his finger claws pierced the metal, and I tried not to imagine what they could do to flesh and bone.

I felt sorry for him, but I was scared myself, and my fear made me snappish as I said, "Calm down, damn it! Everything will be okay!"

His red eyes fixed on me, but I couldn't tell if he'd registered what I'd just said.

Jinx got up from his seat and walked over to sit next to Ferret-Face. The Incubi jumped as Jinx put an arm around his quivering shoulders.

"Don't worry," he said. "If they *do* manage to break in, they'll tear us to pieces so fast, we'll be dead before we know it." He then gave Ferret-Face what I assume he intended to be a reassuring smile, but which instead resembled a lunatic's grimace. I didn't think it was possible to see a being with a fur-covered face go pale, but it happened. The skin beneath his fur turned so white it almost gleamed.

Ferret-Face jumped up from his seat with a strangled cry and ran into the corridor – more to put some distance between himself and Jinx than to escape the Darkuns outside, I think. As for the Darkuns, they redoubled their efforts to break into the car, emboldened perhaps by Ferret-Face's cries of fear. The noise became deafening, and I could feel the engine slow, as if Darkuns weighed it down. I imagined the shadowy creatures clustered along the entire length of the train, so many that they blotted it out entirely, transforming it into another piece of darkness in a realm without light. At that moment, I almost cried out in fear myself.

Up to this point, the Loco-Motive's passage along the tracks had been smooth. But now the car we were in began to sway back and forth, as if the Darkuns outside were attempting to derail it. Ferret-Face's whining became fully-fledged howls at this point, and he clapped his clawed hands over his ears in an attempt to shut out the sounds of the creatures pounding on the car's metal exterior. A useless attempt. I know, because I tried the same thing without success.

Russell looked as worried as I felt, and he'd drawn his M-rapier, more to feel the comfort of it in his hand than because it would do him any good right then. Bloodshedder growled and continuously sniffed the air, as if she could monitor what the Darkuns were doing outside that way. Who knows? Maybe she could. Mordacity didn't appear concerned, but it's hard to appear like anything when your features are made of immobile bone. He sat in his seat next to Bloodshedder, not moving. He'd made the passage through the Murk many more times during his career than I had, and I told myself that I should take a cue from his seeming lack of concern. If Mordacity wasn't worried, then why should I be? The thought helped, a little anyway, until Ferret-Face completely lost his shit.

"We have to get out of here before they kill us!" He screamed these words, pulled his hands from his ears, and ran toward the door.

Panels of reinforced steel had slid down to protect the outside of the door at the same time the smaller panels had locked into place over the windows, but the inside of the door remained unshielded. Ferret-Face began striking the door with those crystalline claws of his, hitting it fast and hard. He quickly sliced through the door and reached the steel panel underneath. I hoped that would stop him, but it didn't. Maybe the protective panels weren't as strong on the inside as they were on the outside. Or maybe his claws were made of stronger stuff than the Darkuns' were. Whichever the case, Ferret-Face cut deep criss-crossing grooves into the steel, filling the air around him with a miniature storm of curved metal shavings.

When Jinx saw what Ferret-Face was doing, he clapped his hands together like an excited little boy.

"This is going to be *fun*!"

Russell and I exchanged glances, and a wordless message passed between us.

Oh, fuck.

I pulled my hands from my ears and started toward Ferret-Face, Russell right behind me. If the terrified Incubus managed to so much as make the tiniest breach in the Loco-Motive's protective barrier, the Darkuns would be able to enter. Their bodies were malleable, like the shadows they resembled, and they would have no trouble squeezing through a crack to get at us. And once they were inside – even if only a handful got through – our survival could be measured in seconds.

Jinx remained in his seat, evidently satisfied to sit back and watch the show. He pulled a fist-sized package out of his pocket. It said Bubba-Wubba on it in colorful letters. He unwrapped a large pink mass, popped it into his mouth, having to dislocate his jaw to get it all in, and began chewing vigorously. I figured he was out of popcorn.

I drew my trancer, flicked the setting selector to sleep mode, and fired a full-power blast at Ferret-Face. The trancer's sleep function works better on humans than it does Incubi, but I hoped the blast would, if nothing else, bring him down from his frenzied panic. At first he seemed unaffected by the trancer's beam – probably due to the massive amount of adrenaline roaring through his system. But soon his exertions began to slow, and I kept firing M-energy at him, hoping he'd lose consciousness soon. His motions slowed even further until he was swaying drunkenly, swinging his claws in awkward, lurching swipes, missing the steel panel as often as he hit it. He staggered backward, swiped the air a couple last times for good measure, and then collapsed. I stopped firing my trancer and holstered it.

"Hopefully, he'll be out for the rest of the–"

A harsh *crack!* sounded, cutting me off. Ferret-Face had sliced dozens of grooves into the protective panel, some of them quite deep. And it was one of those that split open to allow a tendril of darkness to slither through. It moved slowly, waving back and forth, tentatively exploring. It brushed one of Ferret-Face's feet and then froze. But then it moved with lightning speed, wrapping around the Incubus' ankle and pulling him toward the crack in the metal.

This did not look good.

The ebon substance of the tendril began to hiss and bubble, steam rising from it as the light in the car ate away at its darkness. Still, the tendril didn't release its grip on Ferret-Face. I drew my trancer once more and fired a force beam at the tendril. Russell sheathed his rapier and rushed forward to grab hold of Ferret-Face's wrists and tried to pull the Incubus free from the Darkun's tendril. But, no matter what either of us did, the tendril continued withdrawing, pulling Ferret-Face's foot toward the crack in the metal inch by inch. Mordacity ran to help Russell, each of them holding onto one of Ferret-Face's arms. Bloodshedder took hold of Russell's cape and tugged, adding her strength to the struggle. Jinx just chewed his gum and watched. I knew our only hope of saving Ferret-Face was if we could slow down the tendril for the car's light to weaken it or, better yet, destroy it. So I kept firing and Russell, Mordacity, and Bloodshedder kept pulling.

Maybe the Darkun on the other side of the door realized its time was running out, or maybe it was simply eager to feed and couldn't wait any longer.

Either way, other tendrils squeezed through the crack and began to widen it, and then, with a swift yank, the Darkun pulled Ferret-Face toward the expanded opening. Russell, Bloodshedder, and Mordacity were jerked forward; they lost hold of Ferret-Face's wrists, and the Incubus flew toward the opening. The crack was wider now, but not nearly wide enough for Ferret-Face's body to pass through easily. Bone snapped, flesh tore, blood spurted, and then, just like that, Ferret-Face was gone.

As horrible as it was to watch him go, I told myself that at least he'd been unconscious when it had happened. Cold comfort, maybe, but it was something. But my thoughts quickly turned to the problem that Ferret-Face's demise had left us: there was now an opening to the outside – and all the hungry Darkuns who wanted to get inside.

I'd stopped firing when Ferret-Face had been pulled outside, but now Mordacity said, "Use your trancer to block the breach, Audra!"

Trancers aren't lasers and their beams don't produce heat. I couldn't melt the metal and form a patch over the breach, but, if I continuously fired a trancer beam at the breach, I might be able to block the Darkuns from entering. If I could keep doing that until we reached our destination, we'd be safe. Maybe.

But before I could fire again, Jinx stepped past me. He was still chewing his massive amount of gum, cheeks distended like a chipmunk with a mouthful of food, saliva dribbling past his lips. When he reached the door, he leaned his head back and spit out the slimy pink wad. It flew toward the breach, and, when it struck the metal panel, it flattened, plugged the breach,

and stuck fast. It bulged as a Darkun from the other side
– maybe the same one that had taken Ferret-Face –
tried to break through, but the gum-plug held.

Jinx looked at me and grinned, bits and pieces of pink
covering his teeth.

"Bubba Wubba: never leave home without it."

NINE

After a time, the Darkuns' attacks lessened and eventually stopped altogether. The Loco-Motive began to slow, and, although the protective panels over the windows didn't raise and we still couldn't see out, I knew we'd reached our destination. The door that led to the engine opened, and the Conductor stepped back into our car. He pointed his empty sleeve at the side door, and the lock disengaged with a soft click.

We rose from our seats and headed for the exit. Jinx had finished the rest of his spiders, and he crumpled the bag and tossed it over his shoulder. The Conductor raised his sleeve and sucked the bag in as if he had an industrial shop vac hidden inside his clothes.

Jinx giggled. "Man, he is so *cool*!"

The car door opened on its own as I reached it, and bright light flooded in. Knowing what to expect, I squinted and averted my eyes, but the intense light still hurt. We stepped off the car onto a rectangular concrete platform illuminated by tall lamp poles atop which sat what looked like miniature suns. The blazing orbs created an oasis of light in the Murk's darkness, and the illuminated area extended well beyond the platform, revealing the gray, lifeless ground of this region. At the edge of the light, shadowy shapes moved about restlessly. The Darkuns desperately wanted to get at us, but they were held at bay by the orbs' radiance. The orbs' light hadn't failed all the times I'd been to Deadlock, and I had no reason to think it would do so now. But that didn't prevent me from imagining what would happen if the light was suddenly extinguished, and I drew my trancer, just to be on the safe side. Jinx stood next to me and glanced at the Darkuns watching us. I knew he would've loved to whip out Cuthbert Junior and go running off into the darkness to indulge his lust for maximum carnage, but he didn't. Maybe it was because we had a job to do, or maybe it was because there was a chance for even greater mayhem inside the prison. Or maybe it was because he knew I was scared and wanted to comfort me with his presence. Whatever the reason, I was grateful he stayed with me.

I was surprised to see three other passengers disembark from the train. I was instantly on alert. None of them were the two assassins who had attacked us in Wet Dreams, but that didn't mean they weren't different assassins. The others noticed them the same time I did, and Russell and Mordacity drew their swords. Bloodshedder started growling softly, and Jinx pulled out Cuthbert Junior. If the passengers were concerned that we'd armed ourselves, they didn't show it. They seemed far more worried about the Darkuns gathered in the inky blackness beyond the platform's lights. They kept looking around and shuffling back and forth nervously. All three were Incubi. One was a human-sized earwig, another looked like a conglomeration of glistening organs without any skin, muscles, or bones, and the last had a woman's body – trim and well-toned as her tight black shirt and pants revealed – but she had the head of a large, brown-furred, big-eared, and sharp-toothed bat.

The three didn't seem to be together, and, while they checked us out, none of them seemed concerned by us. Given my uniform, maybe they figured we were on official Shadow Watch business, and we only had our weapons out as a precaution. Or maybe they *were* assassins, and they were going to play it cool until they decided to attack.

There were no passengers to get on here, so the Loco-Motive's doors closed, and the engine began to build up steam – or whatever substance provided its power. Crimson smoke curled upward from the train's stack and its high-pitched whistle-shriek sounded. The Loco-Motive slowly edged forward, pulling the cars along behind it. It quickly picked up speed and rolled down its tracks with eerie silence. As the train approached the edge of the protective light nimbus, it seemed to bend at a strange angle, and then it was gone – engine, cars, and all.

"What happened?" Russell asked.

I answered without taking my gaze off the three Incubi standing farther down the platform.

"From our vantage point, the train went back to the beginning of the tracks in Oldtown. To the Loco-Motive, I guess it seemed to just keep going straight."

"Oh," Russell said. "Right. The Mobius-strip thing. So the tracks don't run through the Edgelands?"

Mordacity answered for me. "No one enters the Edgelands by choice."

Jinx gave him a lip-splitting grin. "I do."

"I stand corrected," Mordacity said. "What I should've said is, no one *sane* goes there by choice."

Jinx let out a hyena-giggle, and the three other Incubi on the platform looked suddenly uncomfortable and moved even farther away from us. Maybe they *weren't* assassins, I thought. Then again, Jinx's laughter could scare the hide off a T-rex, so the fact that those Incubi were frightened didn't necessarily mean anything.

"I get why the Loco-Motive doesn't stop directly at Deadlock," Russell said. "Same reason it's located in the Murk in the first place: to discourage prisoners from escaping. How far away is the prison?"

"A couple miles," I said.

"A couple miles in the dark," Jinx added. "With vicious killing machines trying to get at you the entire way." He paused, and then added, "It's glorious."

"Please don't tell me we're supposed to walk there," Russell said.

"The prison sends transportation," Mordacity said. "It's usually here to meet the train, but sometimes it's... delayed."

"By those vicious killing machines Jinx mentioned," Russell said.

Mordacity nodded.

So we stood and waited. Occasionally a Darkun would creep close to the edge of the light and hurl a piece of itself at one of the blazing lamps in an attempt to extinguish it. But the distance was too great, and the chunk of shadowy substance would fall to the ground without doing any harm, and quickly disintegrate in the harsh glare of the lamps.

"Could they try to tunnel to us?" Russell asked. He didn't sound scared, simply curious.

"There's fifty feet of concrete beneath the platform," I said. "And, if one did get through, it would emerge into the light."

Russell nodded. "And light burns them."

"Yes. It doesn't destroy them immediately," Mordacity said, "but it will kill them if it's intense enough."

"Their forms are supposed to be malleable," Russell said. "Is that true?"

"Yes, to a degree," I confirmed.

"Does that mean they can fly?"

I hadn't considered that possibility. "I honestly don't know."

"Because if they *could* fly..." Russell began.

Jinx clapped his hands together in glee. "They could fly *over* the lights and drop something to break them!" He made a whistling sound followed by an uncannily lifelike imitation of an explosion. The sound was so realistic that the trio of other Incubi waiting cried out in alarm and threw themselves to the surface of the platform. After several seconds passed without their horrible deaths by explosive force, they got up and glared at Jinx, who blew them a kiss.

Russell looked skyward, but all that could be seen above us was an unbroken expanse of darkness. I knew he was imagining sleek black shapes soaring through the blackness, chunks of their own bodies clutched in talons, ready to be released when they were over their targets. I knew because I was imagining the same thing.

"I really hope that transport gets here soon," Russell said.

We waited for several more minutes, and luckily no dark bombs fell from the sky. Maybe the Darkuns couldn't fly or maybe they couldn't stand looking downward at the light, and because of this they couldn't aim. Or maybe they simply weren't smart enough to realize they could attempt to destroy the lamps from the air. Whatever the reasons, the lamps continued to blaze with light, undisturbed, much to our relief. Except Jinx's. I'm sure he would've loved to have an excuse to pound Darkuns into paste.

"There!"

Mordacity pointed toward the darkness. At first I didn't see anything, but then I noticed a glimmer of light coming our way. It grew larger as it approached, and soon we could hear an engine's roar, accompanied by the sound of energy weapons discharging.

The transport vehicle surged out of the blackness with a pair of Darkuns clinging to its surface. The creatures' forms were basically humanoid, with large clawed hands and feet, but one had a thrashing tail and the other had an extra arm. As soon as they were in the dome of light, they shrieked in frustration as much as pain, released their hold on the vehicle, and fell to the ground. They rolled several feet, their ebon hides beginning to smoke. When they came to a stop they sprang to their feet and dashed back toward the soothing embrace of darkness.

The prison transport was a sport utility vehicle with a highly reflective metal surface and powerful lights mounted along all sides, the top, and the bottom. The lights were covered by strong metal screens to guard against their being broken. Four metal seats were bolted on top of the transport, each facing a different direction.

Guards were strapped into the seats with criss-crossing thick leather straps. They wore reflective white body armor and white visored helmets with small lamps mounted on top. Each carried a flash rifle, along with several lux grenades on their belts.

As the two Darkuns tried to escape, the guard facing rearward aimed her flash rifle and loosed several bursts of coherent light. The beams missed the three-armed Darkun, but the tailed one was struck directly between the shoulder blades. It screamed, pitched face-first onto the ground, and lay still. Three-Arm didn't look back at its fallen comrade. It kept running like hell until it plunged into the safety of darkness. Smoke rose from the downed Darkun's body as the light continued to eat away at it. It would be completely disintegrated within the space of a few minutes.

The transport slowed as it drew near the platform, and parked a dozen yards away. The rooftop guard facing the front of the vehicle flipped open his visor to reveal a normal-sized head with facial features so small they seemed in danger of being swallowed by the surrounding flesh.

"Let's go," he called out, in a chipmunk squeak of a voice. We filed down the small set of stairs on the side of the platform and walked toward the transport. The other three Incubi preceded us, and another guard exited the vehicle and asked to see their IDs. This guard didn't raise his visor, but I could tell from the inhuman proportions of his body – super-broad shoulders and an almost nonexistent waist – that he was an Incubus. People don't generally carry identification in Nod as Incubi aren't much for rules and regulations. But it can be obtained in the Rookery for those who need it, and no one gets into Deadlock without ID. The Batwoman removed her ID from a pocket and handed it to the guard. He passed the card over his wisper, it beeped, and he handed it back to her, satisfied. He repeated this same procedure for the other two, although, since neither of them wore clothing, the process was more disturbing to watch. The organ mass pulled its ID from between a kidney and liver, and the giant earwig coughed up its card. The guard scanned both IDs without reaction. I guess by this point in his career he'd pretty much seen it all.

When it was our turn, Jinx and I took out our Shadow Watch badges. I intended to vouch for Mordacity, Russell, and Bloodshedder, but, before I could say anything, the guard looked at us – more specifically at Jinx – and took a step back.

"Oh, hell no!" he said.

Jinx flashed the man an unsettling grin. "Have we met?"

The micro-faced guard on the roof said, "The Warden posts pictures in the guard barracks of all the visitors we're supposed to keep a special eye out for."

"Let me guess," I said. "Not only is Jinx on the Warden's list, his name's at the top."

Mordacity turned to Jinx. "What did you do?"

Jinx shrugged. "I have no idea. You know me – I'm a model of decorum and restraint."

The guard on the ground answered Mordacity's question. "The last time he was here, we lost three prisoners."

"They escaped?" Mordacity asked, shocked.

"Not exactly," the guard said, glaring at Jinx.

Jinx continued putting on an innocent act – smiling

politely, face devoid of guile – but he wasn't fooling anyone.

"A few months ago we were transporting a prisoner," I explained. "I guess word had gotten out that Jinx is able to store numerous goodies in his jacket, and some of the inmates thought if they stole it, they'd have access to enough weapons to mount an escape."

Mordacity looked at Jinx. "I imagine that didn't go well for them."

Jinx's innocent expression gave way to arched eyebrows and a cruel smile.

"I think I still have their hands on me somewhere. Would you like to see them?" He reached into his jacket pocket, his arm disappearing up to the elbow as he began to root around.

"No, thanks," Mordacity said. "I've seen more than enough body parts in my career." He turned toward the organ-conglomerate creature and said, "No offense."

The Incubus replied with a moist gurgling sound that might've been *None taken*, but which could've just as easily been *Screw you, Bone-Boy*.

It took some convincing for the guards to allow Jinx to board the transport. In the end, I think they decided it would be less trouble to take him to Deadlock and let the Warden figure out what to do with him. Jinx wanted to ride on top of the transport, but I put my foot down on that. I'd had a hard enough time getting the guards to agree to take him as it was. We all climbed aboard the vehicle. There was a guard behind the wheel and the narrow-waisted Incubus rode shotgun, leaving the rest of us to squeeze in as best we could. It was a tight fit, but we managed. Given that there were six guards in total, not to mention the five of us, I figured that if any or all of our fellow travelers were assassins, they wouldn't try anything right now. I still intended to keep a close watch on them, though.

Once we were all aboard and the doors were locked, the driver put the engine in gear and tromped on the gas. Jinx loves this part of the ride. Me, not so much. The transport left the relative safety of the platform's light and plunged into darkness. The vehicle's headlights cut twin swaths through the black, and the guards on the roof began firing their flash rifles. I had the impression that they did so more as a deterrent than because they actually saw any targets. But before long, pieces detached from the surrounding darkness and flung themselves at the transport. It was difficult to see them as much more than barely glimpsed movement, given that they were black against a black background. But when they passed in front of the headlights or when they were revealed by a burst of illumination from a flash rifle, we caught a glimpse of the Darkuns – clawed, fanged, and lean-limbed. They moved with such speed and ferocity that, as well-armed as the guards were, they had a hard time keeping the creatures at bay. I found myself wishing I had allowed Jinx to ride on top. The guards could've used his help.

I'm not sure how long the ride took. The guards generally try to take the most direct route to and from the station, but the Darkuns don't always make that possible. If enough of them attack at once, the driver is forced to detour around them. The trip could've been as short as fifteen minutes or as long as an hour. But eventually we began to approach a faint glow that grew brighter as we drew nearer. One by one, the Darkuns broke off their attack until the transport was able to move forward unimpeded. Soon Deadlock came into view. When you see the prison for the first time, it's difficult to make out any details because of how bright the light is. Deadlock is a domed structure covered with highly polished reflective steel. High lamp poles ring the dome, with lights mounted to face all directions. As a result, a first-time visitor's impression of Deadlock is a blazing ball of white light, a warm, welcoming beacon of hope shining in a sea of darkness. But a closer look reveals that the prison's light is cold, harsh, and unforgiving, just like the place itself.

The driver pulled the transport up to the main gate and honked the horn three times. The guard in the front passenger seat held his wisper up to his visored face and said, "This is prison transport 306, returning from a pick-up run. Today's password is *okra.*"

I looked at Jinx. "Not the sort of password one's likely to guess."

"It does have that advantage," Jinx said. "But now I'm hungry."

Twin metal doors slid apart, and the transport moved forward.

As terrifying as the Darkuns are, right then I was far more afraid of seeing Nathaniel. What if he was disappointed in the officer I'd become? Worse, what if his condition had deteriorated since I'd last been here? I'd find my answers inside, but, whatever they might be, I didn't think I was going to like them.

Inside the dome, Deadlock looks pretty much like a typical Earth prison – a collection of gray, institutional-type buildings, an exercise yard with a high, sturdy fence, and guard towers erected at regular intervals. As soon as we were inside, the driver turned off the transport's lights. The dome's entire ceiling glows with illumination as bright as day on Earth, so the vehicle's lights were no longer necessary. Battery power was a precious commodity here, one to be preserved at all costs. Incubi don't assume their Day Aspects in this light, though. It's not daylight or nighttime that causes an Incubus to change on Earth. It's the amount of people connecting to the Maelstrom while they dream, bringing Earth's dimension into closer alignment with Nod. Since Deadlock was *in* Nod, surrounded by the ever-turbulent energies of the Maelstrom, Incubi remained in their Night Aspects here, just as they did everywhere else in Nod.

The driver took us around to a building with an unmarked metal door that served as the visitors' entrance and parked.

"Everyone out of the pool," the narrow-waisted guard said.

I was curious what he looked like under his helmet, but he didn't raise his visor, and neither did the driver. Deadlock's guards tend to wear their helmets with the visors down most of the time when they're on duty. I don't know why. Maybe to set them even further apart from the inmates.

We got out of the transport, as did our three fellow visitors. The narrow-waisted guard led us to the door while the guards on the roof began to undo their restraints. I saw that the rear-facing seat was empty, the restraints shredded and dangling. The surviving guards made a point of not looking at the empty seat. It takes a special breed to be a guard in Deadlock. You have to be damn tough – and maybe more than a little crazy.

There was a key-card lock on the wall next to the door, and the guard unzipped his uniform just enough to reach in and pull out a multicolored card from an inner pocket. The card was laminated in a coating of solidified M-energy, and, when he swiped it through the reader, there was a soft crackle of energy discharge followed by a beep. An instant later a series of heavy locks released in sequence, and, when they were finished, the guard opened the door and gestured for us to enter. We walked into an empty room. The walls, floor, and ceiling were all gray stone, and it was lit by humming fluorescent lights.

The room might've been empty of furniture, but not of people. There were eight guards – one for each visitor – all in full white uniforms with visors down. They wore trancers in side holsters and shock batons tucked into their belts. They stood in a row, straight and still, as if at military attention. In front of them stood an Incubus wearing a dark blue suit, white shirt, red tie, and black shoes. The shirt and suit jacket were specially tailored to accommodate his three heads. They were canine – pit bulls, to be exact. The head on the left was white-furred, and it continually sniffed the air, drawing in the scents around it. The right head was tan, and it growled softly, teeth bared ever-so-slightly, its gaze sweeping back and forth as it surveyed its surroundings. The middle head – the one that wore the tie around its neck – was gray and its expression was calm, even contemplative. It's also the only one of the three that, as far as I know, is capable of human speech.

All three pairs of Warden Bruzer's eyes narrowed as they focused on Jinx and me, and the tan head's growling grew even louder.

"Officer Hawthorne, Officer Jinx." The Warden's voice was low and rough, not surprisingly, and had an English accent. Day Jinx once told me the pit bull's ancestors came from England, so maybe that's the reason for the accent. Then again, Incubi are how Ideators dream them, so perhaps the Warden's Ideator had been a Brit. Then again, there might not be any reason for his accent at all. Dreams are funny that way.

Bruzer went on. "I wasn't aware that you two would be paying us a visit today. I received no advance notice from the Rookery."

All three heads scowled at us.

Bruzer wasn't merely a stickler for rules and regulations. He was a merciless, ball-breaking hardass about them. But, before I could think up a suitable lie about why he hadn't been contacted, Mordacity stepped forward.

"It's good to see you again, sir."

He offered a skeletal-armored hand for the Warden to shake. Bruzer's middle face smiled, and, if he'd possessed a tail, I'm sure he would've wagged it.

"Mordacity! This *is* a surprise!" He quickly glanced at Jinx and me. "A *pleasant* one."

His hands were human and unfurred, but they were huge, with long, thick sausage-link fingers. He gripped Mordacity's hand and gave it a couple energetic pumps. It might've been my imagination, but I swear I heard bones crack. Bruzer released Mordacity's hand, and I wouldn't have been surprised to see his fingers crumble to dust. But they remained intact.

"It's been quite some time since we've seen you around here," Bruzer said. He looked at Jinx and me again. "I thought you'd retired from active duty. Did

Sanderson ask you to come back to babysit these two?"

Jinx, smiling sweetly, pulled an object from his pocket and tossed it at the Warden. The guards drew their trancers, but, before they could fire, Bruzer snatched the object out of the air and held it up to his middle face to examine. It was a blue rubber dog bone, and painted on it in white letters were the words *Fuck You*.

"Charming as always, Jinx." Bruzer tossed the toy to the floor, and, while his other two heads paid it no more mind, his tan head looked at it longingly.

Mordacity went on as if nothing had happened.

"We're not here in an official capacity. We've come to see Nathaniel."

"I'm glad to hear that. It's been quite some time since anyone visited Officer Sawyer."

Bruzer's tone remained neutral, but his tan head glared at us and growled, showing how he felt about the situation. Bruzer then turned his attention to the other three Incubi.

"Are they with you?" He addressed this question to Mordacity. In Bruzer's mind, Mordacity would always be a senior officer compared to Jinx and me, even if he was no longer an official member of the Watch.

Mordacity shook his head.

Bruzer motioned and three of the guards moved forward. Each chose an Incubus, gently but firmly took hold of his or her arm – or, in the case of the conglomerate creature, an organ – and led them out of the room. I knew the drill. They would be taken to Visitor Reception where they'd be searched, questioned, and then asked to wait while the prisoners they'd come to see were fetched. Things were going to be a little different for us, though. Nathaniel wasn't allowed out of his cell. We'd have to go see him.

Bruzer used his wisper to call ahead and inform the medical staff that we'd be visiting. When he was finished, he turned to the remaining guards. "You're dismissed," he said, and they turned without a word and left the room.

"Let's go," Bruzer said to us, and he headed for the door.

"That's it?" Russell said, as we followed after the Warden. "I thought Deadlock would have tougher security than this."

I just smiled.

The room opened onto a long corridor, and Bruzer led us to a smaller room next door. There was a single table in it, along with several metal folding chairs. Mordacity, Jinx, and I started removing our weapons. Russell gave me a look, but Bruzer spoke before he could ask any questions.

"No one enters Deadlock armed, not even Shadow Watch officers."

We laid our weapons on the table. Mordacity's sword, my trancer and M-blade, and Jinx's hammer. Jinx didn't stop there. After our last visit, we'd been told that he'd have to divest himself of *all* weapons – literally. He removed his tattered jacket and placed it on the table, then he started undoing his tie. He continued undressing until he was naked except for a pair of pink boxer shorts with My Little Pony characters on them. He'd even taken off his shoes, revealing his enormous chalk-white feet.

Russell surrendered his rapier, as well as a trancer he carried as a back-up weapon. He then removed

Bloodshedder's spiked collar and put it on the table with the rest of our gear.

"One more thing," Bruzer said. He reached into his outer jacket pocket and brought out three silvery lengths of metal that resembled plain necklaces.

Bloodshedder eyed the negator collars and growled.

"Are they really necessary?" Russell asked.

"The fact that I'm in here alone with you testifies to the level of trust I have in you," Bruzer said. "But rules are rules. Only those Incubi on staff are allowed to go about uncollared inside Deadlock."

Jinx walked over to the Warden, took one of the collars, and closed it around his neck. His skin, which had been so white it nearly gleamed under the room's fluorescent lights, became duller, as if an internal energy source had been shut off. Mordacity stepped forward, took a collar, and put it on as well, with a similar effect.

Jinx looked at Bloodshedder, who was still growling.

"It's okay," he said. "These collars are designed so that only humans can remove them. Russell or Audra can take them off us whenever we want."

Bloodshedder didn't look entirely convinced, but she stopped growling.

Bruzer stepped toward her. His white-furred head sniffed the air harder than usual, and his tan head's growling had softened so it was barely audible.

"Allow me," Bruzer said, his voice uncharacteristically gentle. He knelt down and put the negator collar on Bloodshedder as if he were gifting her with a piece of jewelry. Bloodshedder looked confused, but she wagged her spiked tail a couple times. Once the collar was on her, her teeth seemed smaller and less sharp, as did her claws and tail spikes. Bruzer smiled at her before straightening, but, when he turned to the rest of us, his smile was gone and he was all business again.

"Follow me, stay close, and ignore the inmates," he said.

His main head regarded us with a level gaze, but his secondary head was looking at the door and growling again, already on guard.

Two heads, I thought.

I'd seen Warden Bruzer dozens of times over the years, so why should seeing his two heads bother me now? I'd seen plenty of freakier-looking Incubi since I'd first come to Nod. A guy with a pair of dog heads didn't come near to making the list of the weirdest things I'd seen here. But I couldn't keep from staring at the Warden's heads and thinking there was something wrong – *really* wrong – with them.

Bruzer noticed me staring.

"Is something amiss, Officer Hawthorne?" he asked.

You're supposed to have three heads. I wanted to say it, almost did, but I forced myself to stay silent. I had no memory of his ever having a third head, and yet I knew he had. *It was white, and it always smelled the air,* I thought, *like it was trying to sniff out trouble.* I almost remembered this, but not quite. It was like I remembered that I should've remembered, if that makes any sense.

"No, Warden. Everything's fine."

Bruzer eyed me for several more seconds, as if he sensed I wasn't telling the truth. But, in the end, he let the matter go and headed for the door.

Russell looked as if he wanted to say something but wasn't sure if he should. He kept his mouth shut, though, and we all followed Bruzer into the corridor.

Three heads, I told myself. *Three.* It was almost as if I was trying to memorize the fact, as though I was worried I was in danger of forgetting it. Something made me look at my hands, then. Their skin was smooth and unbroken, but, despite their healthy appearance, I couldn't shake the feeling that something was wrong with them too, that they shouldn't be this way. I had no idea what was happening. Maybe after all these years, Jinx's insanity was finally starting to wear off on me. Or maybe it was because of our Blending. Switching bodies back and forth was bound to take a toll on a person's mind. But I didn't think that was it. Whatever was happening was real, and I seemed to be the only one who was aware of it. Except maybe for Russell. The way he'd looked at me after I'd noticed Bruzer was missing a head made me think that he at least suspected something was wrong.

I decided to keep my mouth shut about the situation for the time being. I had no way to prove what I perceived was real, and I feared that if I said anything, Bruzer would slap me in a cell next to Nathaniel's and throw away the key. Maybe if I could get Russell alone, I could ask him if he'd noticed anything peculiar lately and see what he said. Until then, I would keep my eyes and ears open and pay close attention to everything and everyone around me. When the next change… No, that was the wrong word. *Subtraction,* maybe. Or better yet, *excision.* When the next excision occurred, I wanted to make sure I didn't miss it.

I wondered how many *excisions* I couldn't remember and how many more might've occurred and might be occurring at that very moment without my knowledge.

Being unarmed in a prison filled with criminals, quite a few of which I'd helped put away, was nowhere near as frightening as the thought that I could no longer trust reality, even Nod's distorted version of it.

Bringing down the shuteye operation no longer seemed as important as it had a few minutes ago, but I decided I'd keep working the case, at least until I could figure out a way to prove to the others that something far more sinister was happening around us. Until then, I'd fall back on something Nathaniel had taught me long ago. When in doubt, focus on the job at hand.

"Tell me, Warden, do you have any problem with shuteye in Deadlock?" I asked.

Bruzer didn't bother looking over his shoulder as he answered.

"A certain amount of illegal drugs find their way into the hands of our prisoners," he said. "We do the best we can to keep them out and to find and confiscate them when they get in. But we're shorthanded here, and, to be brutally honest, if some jump juice or tinglies slip by us, I'm not going to lose any sleep over it."

"But no shuteye?" I persisted.

Bruzer didn't respond right away. By this point, we'd reached the end of the corridor and come to a metal door with a guard standing next to it. The words *General Population* were painted on the door in white capital letters. Bruzer nodded and the guard pushed a button on a panel next to the door. There was a loud *clank!* as the lock disengaged, and then the guard opened the door for us. We stepped through and into another corridor, where two guards were waiting for us, trancers out and ready for trouble. They wore full body armor and helmets with visors down. They had numbers on their uniforms just below their necks, as all the guards in Deadlock did. 5587 and 6323 were to be our escorts for this visit. The guards took up a position behind us, and we continued forward until we reached a set of stairs that led to yet another corridor.

Deadlock has no outside exercise yard, for obvious reasons. Fully powered Incubi would have a hell of a time trying to survive an attack by an army of Darkuns, but Incubi whose powers were suppressed by negator collars? They'd be slaughtered within seconds. So Deadlock has an inside exercise yard with a basketball half-court, a running track, a weightlifting area, and general space for walking and socializing. The corridor we were in now was a story higher than the yard and had thick bars through which the prisoners below could be observed or, if necessary, shot at. The inmate uniforms are plain long-sleeved shirts, pants, and slip-on-shoes, much like what any prisoners on Earth might wear. The big difference is that Deadlock's inmate uniforms are white, almost blindingly so, and they fluoresce in darkness, making escape attempts even more difficult.

Most of the prisoners were primarily humanoid, but there were quite a few who resembled animals of various types, along with assorted monsters, creatures, and distorted *things* that were absolutely unclassifiable beyond the simple one-word description of *nightmare*. The smell drifting up from the exercise yard made me think of a zoo where the animals had not only never been bathed, but were allowed to roll in their own dung.

A dozen guards ringed the yard, staying close to the walls as they watched the prisoners. They'd move in to take care of any trouble that might arise, but otherwise they kept their distance. They wanted to avoid tempting any of the prisoners to try to steal their weapons. Incubi, collared or not, are chaotic as hell, and they'd snatch a guard's weapons in a heartbeat just to see if they could get away with it.

As we walked down the corridor, we were visible to the prisoners, and it wasn't long before we were recognized.

"Mordacity!" one of the prisoners shouted. "You suck!"

"No, he doesn't!" someone else shouted. "He don't have any lips!"

"I see that prison wit hasn't improved since the last time I was here," Mordacity said.

"Jinx!" someone called out. "When I get out of here, I'm going to hunt you down, rip off your head, and shit down your neck!"

Jinx stopped and walked over to the barred window.

"Who said that?" he demanded.

One of the inmates raised her hand. She had large bulging insect eyes and rigid straw-blonde hair that stuck straight up like the bristles on a broom. Like all the other prisoners, she wore a silver negator collar.

"You and your bitch partner arrested me for indecent exposure!" she shouted.

Russell looked at me.

"She didn't take her clothes off," I explained. "She removed other people's skin. All of it."

"Okay then," Jinx said, "it's a date!" He blew the woman a kiss.

The other Incubi in the yard laughed and Bug-Eyes let out a string of invectives and flipped Jinx a double bird.

Jinx turned away from the window and rejoined us.

"I was joking," he said. "I only have eyes for Trauma Doll."

He reached for his jacket pocket, but, of course, he wasn't wearing his uniform.

"Let me guess," I said. "You were going to show me actual eyes you've been saving for her."

He nodded, and then looked thoughtful. "I wonder if she'd like a pair of giant bug eyes instead."

Bruzer started forward again, and, again, we followed. We walked the length of the exercise yard and then reached another metal door with another armed guard standing in front of it. The guard punched a code on the key panel, the door opened, we stepped through, and then the door shut behind us. The guard on the other side gave the Warden a nod and stepped aside to let us pass. We continued on like this for a while until we reached a corridor with steel doors on both sides. The doors were unmarked, and I knew from previous experience that they weren't cells, but that's all I knew. Bruzer had never told Jinx and me what this area of the prison was for. I'd tried getting some of the guards to tell me on previous visits, but none of them would talk. I'd never seen anyone else in this corridor before, but now a pair of guards big enough to be the Hulk's older brothers were walking toward us from the opposite direction. Between them, locked in a pair of silver manacles, was a creature that looked like a powerfully muscled humanoid wolf, with thick black fur, yellow eyes, sharp fangs, and wicked-looking claws. The wolf was unclothed, and I could see that his legs were bent like a canine's.

Bloodshedder growled upon seeing the wolf-creature, and Jinx wrinkled his nose.

"What's wrong?" I asked him.

"I don't know what that thing is," he said, "but it's not an Incubus."

The wolf-creature fixed its yellow-eyed gaze on Bloodshedder and returned her growl, but then one of the guards cuffed him on the side of the head, and he quieted, although, from the way the prisoner glared at the guard, I knew the wolf would've attempted to tear him limb from limb if he hadn't been manacled.

As we drew closer, I smelled the stink of burning hair, and when I looked at the wolf-creature's wrists, I saw that they had been burned where the silver touched them, as if the prisoner was highly allergic to the metal. I then noticed that the creature wasn't wearing a negator collar.

I looked to Bruzer for an explanation.

"It's a Lyke," he said. "It doesn't belong in Nod. We have an extradition treaty with the dimension where it *does* belong, however."

The guards stopped before one of the doors, and, while one of them keyed in an entry code on the wall panel, the other drew what looked like an ordinary 9mm handgun and pressed the muzzle to the wolf-creature's head.

"The gun is loaded with silver bullets," Bruzer explained.

Russell's eyebrows raised. "Are you saying it's a *werewolf*?"

"Lyke," Bruzer corrected.

The door opened and the guard that had entered the code stepped into the room. He drew his own 9mm and aimed it at the "Lyke" while the second guard shoved the creature inside, keeping his gun pressed to its head the entire time.

"Don't close the door," Bruzer ordered the guards. "We'd like to observe."

The guards did as he ordered, and, when we reached the open doorway, we stopped and peered inside. The room was empty, save for a large oval mirror with a fancy gold frame hanging from the far wall. The mirror's surface was a glossy black, and, although I wasn't sure, I thought I detected shadowy eddies and swirls within the darkness.

The guards marched the Lyke to the mirror, and, without preamble, they grabbed hold of the creature's arms and shoved him toward it. Instead of colliding with the mirror, the Lyke passed through it, entering the blackness and being swallowed by it.

"It's a Door," Russell said.

"Not exactly," Mordacity said. "But similar."

The guards trained their guns on the mirror and backed up slowly, keeping their weapons pointed at the dark glass, as if they feared something might come charging out of it. But nothing did, and, when they returned to the corridor, one of them pulled the door closed, and the locks automatically engaged.

"Good work," Bruzer said.

The guards acknowledged the Warden's praise with nods, and then walked past us, going the way we'd just come from.

I looked to Mordacity.

"You know about that other dimension?" I asked.

"Yes," he said. "But I don't know about all of them."

"All?"

And then it hit me.

There were – I counted quickly – twenty unmarked doors in this corridor.

"You mean all these doors lead to other dimensions?"
I asked.

Bruzer nodded his main head. *He used to have three,* I
reminded myself, although it was getting harder for me
to believe it.

"This *is* the Extradition Department," he said. "The
Shadow Watch keeps the existence of other dimensions
a highly guarded secret. Can you imagine what would
happen if Incubi learned there were others planes of
existence for them to cause havoc in?"

"If that's the case," I said, "then why the *hell* did you
let us look into the room? More specifically, why did
you let *him*?" I hooked a thumb at Jinx.

The Warden turned both of his heads to look at my
partner. Jinx was grinning even wider than he had the
Christmas I'd gotten him the pop-up edition of *History's
Bloodiest Serial Killers*.

Bruzer's second head whined.

"I hadn't considered that," he admitted. He sounded
as if he needed a good stiff drink or ten.

I turned to Russell. "Did you know about these other
dimensions?"

"My employers have hinted at other levels of
existence, but they've never told me anything specific
about them."

I looked at the door again. Twenty different
dimensions… I have a hard enough time keeping two
straight.

TEN

It took another ten minutes to reach Deadlock's medical facility, designated by the oh-so-imaginative name *Medical*. It looks like an Earth hospital for the most part, only with armed guards in full body armor and reinforced steel doors with multiple heavy-duty locks. Healing an injured Incubus should, in theory, be simple. All you have to do is remove the negator collar and let the Maelstrom energies which suffused Nod go to work. Unfortunately, once they were powered up, prisoners invariably attempted escape. So the collars stay on, and Incubi have to heal the torturously slow way that we mere mortals do.

The staff here were medical-themed nightmares, just like at the Sick House. No shortage of that type in Nod. There were few humans on staff, though. Even collared Incubi can be dangerous to humans – especially when those Incubi are convicted criminals – so non-collared Incubi have a definite safety edge when working here.

A doctor was standing outside Nathaniel's door waiting for us. There was nothing to indicate this was Nathaniel's room, though. His name wasn't on the door, and there wasn't even a number. But, although it had been years since I'd last come to visit my former mentor, I had no trouble remembering which room was his. The guilt that I'd been working so hard to keep at bay hit me full force and, without realizing I was doing so, I reached out for Jinx's hand. I thought Jinx might taunt me, maybe ask me if we were going steady now. But he remained silent and gently squeezed my hand in a show of support. Mild dizziness swept over me, and for an instant I was looking through Jinx's eyes, but then the dizziness passed and I was in my own body again. I let go of Jinx's hand. Menendez had told us to remain physically close to one another so we could get used to resisting the Blending effect, but I figured there was no point in tempting fate, especially before we went in to see Nathaniel.

The doctor was a humanoid woman with sickly yellow skin and grossly exaggerated features: huge watery eyes, elephantine ears, a bulbous potato-like nose, and a wide gash of a mouth filled with crooked teeth. She was bald and a pair of bony protuberances shaped like caducei grew from her head. She laughed softly as we approached, a nasally *heh-heh-heh* that was as disturbing as it was annoying. As we drew closer, I was able to make out the letters on her nametag: *Dr Tittering*. The name was appropriate, I thought. I didn't remember seeing her before, though. Maybe she was new, or at least new to me. It *had* been a while since my last visit.

She acknowledged Bruzer with a nod.

"Warden."

I waited to see if she would say anything about his… For an instant, I couldn't remember what the rest of the thought was, but then it came back to me. About his missing head. But she said nothing, and, if her body language was any indication, she saw nothing out of the ordinary with Bruzer.

Doctor Tittering introduced herself and came forward to shake our hands. She continued giggling softly as she took my hand, and I found the touch of her cold, clammy flesh unpleasant. The last time I was so instantly and profoundly disturbed by an Incubus was when I met Penis-Head Harry.

We gave her our names, and, when we were finished, she said, "It's so good to meet you all." Then she let out that disturbing laugh of hers once more, making it sound as if she were looking forward to performing exploratory surgery on us sans anesthesia.

"Especially you," she said to Mordacity. "I think it will do Nathaniel a world of good to see you."

Mordacity's head lowered slightly and his shoulders slumped, and I knew he also felt guilty for having stayed away so long.

"I hope so," he said.

"It looks like you have everything under control here, Doctor," Bruzer said. "If you don't mind, I have other duties to attend to."

"Of course," Dr Tittering said.

Bruzer turned to Mordacity.

"Good to see you again." He glanced at me. "You as well, Officer Hawthorne."

He didn't sound quite as sincere as when he'd addressed Mordacity, but at least he acknowledged me verbally. He merely nodded to Russell and Bloodshedder, and he ignored Jinx completely. He then turned to guards 5587 and 6323.

"Stay with them, please, and render any assistance

they might require." He then frowned at Jinx. "And keep a close eye on him."

The guards nodded and Bruzer turned and walked back the way we'd come.

"We have a love-hate thing going on," Jinx explained to the doctor. "He loves to hate me."

The doctor tittered, whether in appreciation of Jinx's bad joke or because she couldn't *not* titter, I didn't know.

As Bruzer had led us down the corridor, we'd passed a number of staff, as well as a number of prisoner-patients. The former were easily distinguished from the latter by their uniforms. Staff members wore white lab coats, but the patients wore orange shirts and pants, along with white slip-on shoes. No laces, of course. The staff didn't want to encourage suicide, homicide, or any combination thereof. Some of the patients were escorted by staff while others – more than I was comfortable with – were permitted to walk about on their own. I assumed this was because they posed no threat to those around them. At least, that was my hope. There were guards in this wing of Deadlock – there were *always* guards around – but fewer here than anywhere else in the facility.

"Things have changed since the last time I was here," I said to Dr Tittering. "The atmosphere wasn't so... relaxed."

"This is the minimum security section of Deadlock," Dr Tittering said. "The Warden has allowed us to explore less repressive and punitive methods of rehabilitation here. A large part of this exploration is creating a calm, open atmosphere that allows patients to work through their issues without resorting to aggression and violence."

A patient came walking toward us, an Incubus that was at most a foot-and-a-half tall and which resembled a human baby. I couldn't tell its gender, but it had startlingly green eyes, and was kind of cute, but also kind of creepy. Okay – *really* creepy. As the baby walked past us, Jinx said, "You are *so* adorable!"

The baby stopped and turned back to face Jinx. Its tiny hands balled into fists, and its features, once so innocent-seeming, contorted into a mask of absolute rage.

"Adorable?" The baby's voice was rough, raspy, and decidedly female. She sounded like a seventy-year-old who'd been chain-smoking most of her life. "Do you know what I did to the last motherfucker who called me that?" She stomped toward us – actually, toward Jinx – and, as she came, her eyes pulsed with eerie green light and she began to grow. Her physical form remained that of a baby, but she became a *bigger* baby. Her uniform, unfortunately, didn't increase in size with her, and it grew tight and then began to tear at the seams as she continued growing. Two feet tall. Three. Five. Six-and-a-half. She topped out around seven feet by the time she reached Jinx. She was naked now, except for a few tattered scraps of her uniform that clung to her oversized body in several places. Her eyes now blazed bright as twin green fires, and, when she spoke next, she revealed a mouthful of sharp teeth.

"I reached up his ass, pulled out his intestines, and strangled him with them."

Jinx grinned and reached out to pinch her cheek.

"Kids say the darnedest things!"

The giant baby shrieked with fury and threw herself at Jinx. She knocked him to the ground and began kicking, punching, biting, and clawing him. Dr Tittering frantically ordered the guards to intervene.

Jinx giggled while the giant baby assaulted him, as if all she was managing to do was tickle him. This sent her into a wild fury, and she was shrieking and spitting like an animal as the two guards took hold of her by the arms and pulled her off Jinx. She fought to pull free from the guards' grip, and she almost succeeded. But one of the guards pulled a stun gun from his belt holster, jammed it against the baby's neck, and let her have it. The stun gun had been modified to deliver a burst of M-energy instead of electricity, and multicolored power flared bright. The baby stiffened, the green blaze in her eyes extinguished, and she slumped to the floor, unconscious. Once she was down, she quickly reverted to her original size, and one of the guards picked her up and handed her to a passing orderly who held Tantrum as if she was a bomb that might go off at any moment. The orderly hurried off, and the guards stepped back, remaining close but not too close.

Jinx was bruised and battered, but otherwise uninjured. I gave him a hand, he took it, and I helped him to his feet.

"If I ever have children, I want a dozen just like her," he said.

"My apologies," Dr Tittering said. "Tantrum is one of our more… volatile patients."

I looked at Tittering and said, "So, about this calm atmosphere you were talking about…"

She shrugged. "It's a work in progress."

I decided to change the subject. "How's Nathaniel?"

"You've caught him on a good day," she said. "He's lucid. More or less. And it's been almost two weeks since his last violent outburst. I wouldn't advise all of you going in to see him at the same time, though. It's been some time since he's had anyone come to see him who wasn't one of the staff."

I looked at Mordacity. "You should go."

"As should you," he said.

I turned to Jinx, but, since he'd shoved his hand into his shorts and begun playing pocket pool, I quickly turned away. I prayed to the First Dreamer that we wouldn't switch bodies at that moment.

"Bloodshedder and I will look after him," Russell said. "And we have those two for backup." He gestured toward the guards. "We'll be okay."

I didn't like going in without Jinx, but I knew it would be best to heed the doctor's advice. Two visitors would be plenty for Nathaniel, at least to start.

"You've both been to see him before," Dr Tittering said, "so you know what to expect. His condition is essentially the same as it's been all these years. I'll accompany you inside to make certain he's up to seeing you, and then, if all's well, I'll withdraw and leave the three of you alone. If you need anything, I'll be waiting outside. All right?"

Mordacity and I nodded. The doctor tittered, as if delighted by our agreement, and then she turned and keyed in an access code on the panel next to Nathaniel's door. The locks disengaged, and the doctor opened the door and stepped inside ahead of us. Mordacity and I followed.

"Nathaniel? It's Doctor Tittering. You have some visitors."

The basic layout of the room was the same as the last time I'd seen it: bed, night stand with a reading lamp, small bookcase filled with paperbacks. The books were primarily nonfiction and covered a variety of subjects, although the majority of them dealt with Earth history. Another thing that hadn't changed was the smell of oil paint. It was thick in the room, and it stung my nostrils and felt harsh on my throat.

Three-fourths of the walls were covered with intricately detailed paintings that together formed an elaborate hodge-podge mural of mixed-up historical scenes. Napoleon sat astride a World War II-era motorcycle next to the Beatles, who were deep in conversation with a T-Rex wearing bright purple lipstick. The Wright Brothers engaged in a dogfight with Amelia Earhart, while a cosmonaut wing-walked on her plane. Genghis Khan, Cortez, Rosa Parks, Copernicus, Andrew Jackson, William the Conqueror, and dozens more interacted in ways both mundane and fantastical. The depictions were almost photorealistic, and to my untrained eye at least, museum-worthy. There was a table in the center of the room upon which rested neatly organized rows of paint tubes and brushes of varying sizes.

Nathaniel stood before a white section of the wall, brush in one hand, palette in the other, slowly and methodically adding color to the wall one painstaking brushstroke at a time. At first it looked as if he was working on adding to his mural, but a closer look revealed that the only color on his palette – indeed, the only color of paint tubes currently on the table – was white. Nathaniel wasn't working on completing his mural. He'd already done that. Now he was working on covering it over with white. This is what he did, what he had been doing since the day Mordacity, Jinx, and I had brought him here. He painted elaborate scenes that took months, even years, to complete, then he painted over them and, when he was finished, started anew. I wondered how many murals he'd completed during his time in Deadlock and how many layers of paint coated these walls.

Nathaniel wore the standard inmate uniform, but, despite his never-ending painting, there wasn't a single speck of color on his clothes. His hair was a good deal longer than the last time I'd seen him, and he wore it bound in a ponytail that hung to his waist. His beard was fuller too, an unkempt mountain man thatch of hair. Although he was only in his early sixties, his hair and beard were as white as his uniform, but what really made him look so much older than his years was how skinny he was. You've heard the phrase *skin and bones*. Well, he looked like bones and *more* bones.

Nathaniel didn't turn to look at us as he spoke. He continued applying dabs of white paint to the flames of the *Hindenburg*, which also served as an outsize pyre for Joan of Arc.

"Hello, Mordacity. Audra."

I know Nathaniel couldn't sense Mordacity as long as the Incubus wore a negator collar, so I wasn't sure how he knew we were his visitors without seeing us.

As if reading my mind, Mordacity said, "He recognized us by our footsteps."

I couldn't help smiling. Of course he had. Crazy or not, he was still Nathaniel Fucking Sawyer.

"Do you feel up to speaking with them for a bit?" Dr Tittering asked.

Nathaniel didn't answer right away. I couldn't tell if he was considering the matter or if he was so engrossed in his work that her question hadn't registered with him. But finally he said, "Yes," although he sounded distracted, as if he wasn't fully aware of what he was agreeing to.

The doctor looked uneasy, but she turned to us and said, "Call me if you need me."

I expected her to let out another of her creepy titters, but she didn't. She gave Nathaniel a final look before leaving his room and closing the steel door behind her. She did not, however, lock it.

Now that Mordacity and I were alone with Nathaniel, I wasn't sure what to do. I'd come here to learn what, if anything, he might be able to tell me about the shuteye trade in Nod. Information he might've kept to himself and hadn't gotten a chance to share before his chemically-induced breakdown. Or whatever theories or ideas about shuteye he might've developed during his time in Deadlock. Sure, his mental condition was hardly stable, but that didn't mean his mind was inactive. Nathaniel was arguably the best officer the Shadow Watch had ever produced. Surely some part of his mind had continued to work on his last case while he'd been busy painting and unpainting his never-ending mural. But, now that we were here, I couldn't bring myself to ask him any questions about the case. I felt ashamed for having let so much time pass since my last visit, and – as always – I felt guilty for having been the rookie whose inexperience had led to his condition.

If only I'd been able to deal with the Angler on my own, or if he'd managed to force the shuteye capsule on me instead of Nathaniel. Then maybe it would've been me locked up in a room painting whatever fevered visions danced through my drug-addled brain, and Nathaniel and Mordacity would still be out on the street, keeping both Nod and Earth safe. They'd have most likely broken up the shuteye ring years ago, and who knew how much more good they'd have accomplished in that time? More than Jinx and I had, that was for sure.

I didn't feel worthy of being in the same room as this man, and, if Mordacity hadn't been there, I'd probably have done the same thing that I had during my last visit. I'd stand quietly and watch Nathaniel paint for a while, and then I'd leave, without either of us saying a word to the other. But Mordacity spoke now, relieving me of the burden of coming up with a way to get the conversation going.

"Hello, Nathaniel."

Mordacity's voice in his Night Aspect isn't particularly warm, but, if you'd been around him for any length of time, you could've detected the affection in his words. Nathaniel did. Although he didn't turn to look at us, he did pause in his work, paintbrush poised an inch from the wall. He stood motionless for a long moment, before finally resuming.

"It's good to hear your voice, old friend," he said. "How about you, Audra? Do you still talk as much as you did when I trained you? Not that you talked much compared to Jinx. I remember how you used to have to jam a balled-up sock down his throat to shut him up."

I couldn't help laughing.

"He's not quite as bad these days," I said.

"Yes, he is," Mordacity said. "You're just more able to tolerate him. To a fault sometimes, I think."

I didn't feel like getting into a fight with Mordacity, especially because I was afraid he might be right.

"Where are you currently posted, Audra?" Nathaniel still didn't look at us. He just continued adding tiny patches of white to the strut of the Wright Flyer's wing.

"Still Chicago," I said. "But Sanderson's offered Jinx and me the opportunity to transfer to New York." I'm not sure why I told him this, especially when I wasn't all that keen about moving. I guess a part of me wanted my mentor to be proud of me.

"But you haven't leaped at the offer, I take it?"

More brushstrokes.

"I haven't. I'm not sure I want to even take baby steps toward the offer."

A small smile played on Nathaniel's lips for a moment, but then it was gone.

"A sensible reaction. Mordacity and I worked Milwaukee before Sanderson offered us Seattle, then Los Angeles, and eventually New York. Each time we weren't sure moving was the right thing to do. Remember, Mordacity?"

Nathaniel shot his Incubus a quick glance, then returned to his work. It wasn't much eye contact, but it was a start.

"Yes," Mordacity said.

"You get to know a place, it starts to feel like home," Nathaniel said. He paused, then added, "Even a place like this. Makes it hard to want to leave."

Since Nathaniel didn't need to sleep, I wondered if he ever took a break or if he painted around the clock. Presumably he had to at least pause in his work to eat and use the bathroom. But those might've been the only breaks he took. It made me sad to think of him continuously creating, destroying, and then recreating his mural. I felt an impulse to go to him and give him a hug, but I resisted. Although he seemed okay, during one of my earliest visits to see him, I'd tried to hug him and he screamed for ten minutes. At least he hadn't tried to attack me.

"How are you feeling?" Mordacity asked.

"Great," Nathaniel said. "Fit as a fucking fiddle. But, according to the doctors, I'm just as batshit crazy as ever, though."

It wasn't his words that disturbed me so much as the detached, emotionless way he spoke them, as if he were talking about something as routine as the weather.

"I'm sorry it's been so long since my last visit," I said.

"Five years, three months, seventeen days," Nathaniel said. "But who's counting? Don't feel bad, though. I wouldn't visit me either. There's not a lot of space in here. Gets pretty cramped sometimes."

I looked at Mordacity, and, although I couldn't read his immobile features, I could feel the sadness coming off him.

"Audra and Jinx are working a new shuteye case," Mordacity said. "She came to me for whatever insight I could offer, but I didn't have much to tell her. We hope you might be able to help."

Nathaniel continued painting for a while without speaking, and I began to fear that his mind had wandered off and wouldn't be returning any time soon. But he surprised me when he began speaking again.

"It's not shuteye you have to worry about. It's what shuteye is *really* used for."

I frowned. "Incubi and Ideators use it to simulate sleep. Don't they?"

He turned away from the wall for the first time since we'd entered the room and gave me a sly look.

"That's the story." He held up his paintbrush and examined the white-coated bristles. "I'm a bit concerned that this isn't white enough. I mean, sure, it's *white*, anyone can see that, but does this capture the true *essence* of white? People think black represents Nothingness, but black is *something*. Hell, the whole damn Murk is black, and so are all the Darkuns that infest it. But white is blank. It's empty, a canvas waiting to be filled. So I need a really *white* white, and I'm just not sure this is it." He held out the brush for us to inspect. "What do you think?"

I looked at Mordacity, but I couldn't tell what he was thinking or feeling. I turned back to Nathaniel.

"It looks plenty white to me," I said.

Nathaniel broke into a grin, rushed over, and gave me a crushing bear hug. He was still quite strong for someone so thin.

"That's exactly what I'd hoped you'd say! Thank you! Thank you *so* much!"

He held onto me a moment longer before releasing me. When he stepped back, I saw tears in his eyes, and it was all I could do to keep from crying myself.

Nathaniel returned to the wall and resumed painting.

Years ago, before the Angler forced him to swallow the shuteye pill, Nathaniel had gone to art school. He'd tried to live a normal life, even with Mordacity as part of it, but the lure of Nod was too strong, and eventually he and Mordacity were recruited by the Shadow Watch. But in his current mental state, he'd gone back to his art, and, although his endless painting of his old historical scenes was disturbing, I was glad that he had his art to provide whatever comfort for him that it could. At least it was something.

"What did you mean when you said what shuteye is really used for?" I asked.

He didn't turn to look at us, but for an instant – so fast that I wasn't certain I'd really seen it – his features seemed to ripple, as if becoming momentarily fluid. I remembered seeing something similar happening to him right after he'd swallowed the shuteye pill. At the time I'd dismissed it, but now I wondered.

Nathaniel applied several brushstrokes of white before answering my question.

"It's the Discarnate," he said. "They wanted to find a way to return. And they did. They–"

He broke off and doubled over, grimacing in pain. He dropped his brush and palette and clapped his hands to his head.

"Stop it!" he shouted. His voice rose to a shriek as he repeated, "Stop it!"

Mordacity and I both started forward, although what either of us thought we could do for Nathaniel, I don't know. But, before we could reach him, the sound of weapons fire came from the corridor. I recognized the energy discharge of trancers, and I knew the guards were firing at someone. Was there a prison riot in the offing? Or had one or more of the inmates Jinx and I had put in Deadlock come looking for payback? Whatever the case, Mordacity and I had to get out there. But first I reached up and tapped the negator collar around Mordacity's neck. The collar separated, went slack, and fell to the floor.

"Thanks," Mordacity said. As his power returned to him, he seemed to be more *there*. His presence became stronger, the color and angles of his bone armor sharper.

Nathaniel was still holding his head and shouting, "Stop it, stop it!" but there was nothing we could do for him. Mordacity and I hurried for the door, Mordacity in the lead. I knew he intended to shield me from any stray energy blasts since he could withstand a hell of a lot more damage than I could, and, since I didn't have any weapons, I was happy to let him.

He threw open the door and we hurried into the corridor and found ourselves in the middle of a battle. No, *battle* is too dignified a word. This was a slaughter. Dr Tittering lay on the floor, most of her head gone. There was blood everywhere, and her body twitched spasmodically as it attempted to heal itself. As a staff member she hadn't been collared, but, even with access to her full Incubus capabilities, it was doubtful she'd survive an injury that severe. Russell and Jinx hadn't fared much better. Russell lay on the floor, his left shoulder a bloody ruin, the arm hanging by several shreds of meat. He'd lost a ton of blood, and his skin was almost as white as Mordacity's bone armor. Bloodshedder stood next to him and she brushed her neck against the side of his face. At first I thought it was a sign of worry, but, when her negator collar touched his flesh, it sprang open and fell away, restoring her to full strength.

Jinx stood in front of Russell and Bloodshedder, shielding them. Maelstrom energy beams slammed into his nearly naked body, the blasts carving out chunks of chalk-white flesh. His eyes shone with agony, but he laughed maniacally as the energy blasts whittled away at him. He still wore his negator collar, and I knew he couldn't take much more punishment before he went down.

The guards that had accompanied us stood shoulder to shoulder, trancers raised and firing one blast after another. Their helmet visors were up, and I could see the faces of Gingerdread Man and Demonique. Both held expressions of cruel glee and they continued blasting Jinx.

Mordacity and I didn't have time to coordinate our actions, but we were both experienced officers, and we knew what we had to do. Mordacity ran forward to put himself between the assassins and Jinx. I knew Russell could bleed out any moment, but I also knew his best chance of survival was if all our Incubi were up to full power. I rushed up behind Jinx to tap his negator collar, but, before I could reach him, the collar vanished. Literally. One instant it was there, the next it was gone. But I didn't have time for more than a brief *What the hell?* before I was engulfed in fiery agony. While Jinx had been wearing the collar, our link had been shut down. Now it activated again, and I felt Jinx's pain as if it were my own. Maybe it was an aspect of our Blending, or maybe Jinx just hurt so bad that I couldn't help but feel it. Either way, I staggered to a stop and doubled over. My chest and abdomen felt as if they'd been splashed with acid, and the pain was so intense that I had to fight to retain consciousness. My vision grayed out, my head swam, and vertigo washed over me.

When my vision cleared, I found myself in Jinx's body again. I saw that Gingerdread Man had raced forward to intercept Mordacity. The speedster had armed himself with an M-blade, and he flew around Mordacity in a whirlwind blur, striking the multicolored blade against his bone armor with rapid icepick blows. Bits of bone flew off Mordacity as if he were a block of stone that Gingerdread Man was attempting to reduce to rubble with a handheld jackhammer. Mordacity kept trying to grab hold of Gingerdread Man and he raced around, but the Incubus was simply too damn fast.

Demonique now held two trancers. I assumed Gingerdread Man had tossed his to her before rushing forward to confront Mordacity. She stepped to the side to get an unobstructed shot and then continued firing blast after blast of M-energy at me – or, more precisely, at Jinx's body – an expression of frustration on her reptilian face.

"Why won't you just go *down*?" Demonique said.

"Too stubborn, I guess." I still felt the pain of the M-blasts, but it was less intense than before. Without the negator collar blocking access to the Maelstrom energy in the environment, Jinx's body was able to heal super-fast again. Still, there was only so much punishment even he could take.

I heard my voice shout, "Whistle!"

I turned around, giving Demonique and Gingerdread Man a chance to fire at Jinx's back for a change. Jinx, in my body, had straightened and was looking at me with an irritated expression.

"Don't ask!" he said. "Just do it!"

I mentally shrugged, put my fingers between my lips, and let out a loud, shrill whistle. Nothing happened for several seconds, except for Jinx's back taking some significant damage. But then I became aware of a strange sensation, a feeling of excitement and anticipation, as if something was about to happen. I felt more than heard a series of thuds, as if powerful impacts were occurring elsewhere in the prison. Then, over the sound of energy fire, I heard a slap-slap-slap. I turned around and saw Jinx's clothes – clean and restored, looking brand-new – running down the corridor at break-neck speed. They were empty, of course, but they moved as if inhabited by an invisible body. Demonique and Gingerdread Man saw the clothes as they ran past, and they were so surprised by the sight that they stopped firing and gaped. The clothes ran straight toward me, and, when they reached me, they swirled around in a whirlwind of white, gray, and red, and the next thing I knew, I was dressed.

"Right pants pocket!" Jinx shouted.

Without hesitation, I plunged my hand into the pocket and felt a cold emptiness. I had the impression of an impossibly vast space, and then I felt an object in my hand, almost as if someone – or something – had put it there. It felt like the butt of a gun, and when I withdrew the object, I saw I was holding a trancer. Grinning, I tossed it to Jinx, and then I reached into his inner jacket pocket. I experienced the same sensation of cold and emptiness, and then a handle slapped into my palm. I pulled Cuthbert Junior free, turned, and, with a flip of my wrist, I sent the sledgehammer spinning horizontally toward Demonique. The hammer flew too fast for her to avoid, and it slammed into her chest. Despite the body armor that she wore, I heard an extremely satisfying crunch of breaking bones, and I understood why Jinx loves that damn hammer so much.

Demonique went down, and, an instant later, Mordacity finally managed to land a punch on Gingerdread Man, and he joined his partner on the floor. The assassins lay only a few feet apart, and Jinx ran over to them – although, considering how awkward he was in my body, *hobble-lurched* might be a better description – aimed the trancer and fired. A wide angle beam of M-energy sprayed the assassins' heads. They'd been stunned, but were still conscious. Jinx, however, was attempting to remedy this. Trancers can fire energy beams of intense force strong enough to disrupt an Incubus' natural M-energy, but, on lower levels, their energy can put humans to sleep. They can do the same for Incubi and Ideators, if only for a short time. The assassins tried to resist, but, since they were already dazed, they succumbed to the trancer's sleep effect and closed their eyes.

Now that the assassins had been dealt with, I could focus on Russell. I turned toward him only to see that Bloodshedder had grabbed hold of his shirt with her mouth and was dragging him across the floor toward a wavering distortion in the air. I could feel energy emanating from the distortion. It washed over me, making my body tingle, and for an instant I smelled fresh air and green grass, and I heard the sound of children laughing as their kites rose into the air. Before I could say or do anything, Bloodshedder backed into the distortion, yanked Russell in after her, and they were gone. A second later the distortion disappeared, and the only thing remaining was the smeared blood trail on the floor indicating where Russell had been dragged.

The Thresholders – perhaps sensing how badly Russell had been injured – had transported the two of them away, and, although I hated not being able to help Russell myself, I knew his mysterious masters had a better chance of saving his life than I did. I would just have to pray that he'd be all right.

Jinx lowered his trancer, and, satisfied the assassins would remain out of action for the time being, he walked toward me. He looked at me critically, then he straightened "my" tie and adjusted the gigantic lapel flower until it was to his liking.

"I have certain standards to maintain," he said. Then he inhaled noisily and hocked a loogie onto the floor.

"I can see that," I said. I hadn't realized Jinx's clothes could restore themselves, and I was about to ask him if he'd purposely left them tattered and gore-stained before to irritate me, when I realized Mordacity was gone. Jinx and I glanced around quickly, but we didn't see him. I hadn't seen him walk into the spatial distortion, so I knew he hadn't been taken by the Thresholders.

"Check on the doctor," I told Jinx, and then I walked back to Nathaniel's room. The door remained open, and, when I stepped inside, the first thing I noticed was that his walls – both those sections that had his conglomerate historical scenes and those that had been whited over – were splashed with crimson. The sight hit me like a punch to the gut, but it was nothing compared to what I saw standing in the middle of the room. The Incubus was male, thick-bodied and powerfully muscled, with four arms and two legs. He had long shaggy brown hair and a wild tangle of a beard. He had a single large green eye in the middle of his forehead, and he wore the shredded remains of a prison uniform. But it wasn't the sight of a four-armed, muscle-bound Cyclops that disturbed me. What bothered me was seeing Mordacity, or, rather, what had happened to him. Two of the Cyclops' hands held Mordacity's legs and the other two held his arms.

Mordacity's crushed head rested beneath one of his feet, and the rest of his body lay on the floor close by. The Cyclops was drenched in blood, and when he smiled his teeth were a startling slash of white in the crimson mask of his face.

There was no sign of Nathaniel.

"He came back to check on his old friend," the Cyclops said, in a deep voice. "Imagine his surprise when he found me here instead. I've been trying to take over for years, but Nathaniel always managed to resist me. Seeing you and Mordacity at the same time put him off-balance emotionally. It was exactly the opportunity I needed."

He then dropped the pieces of Mordacity as if they were so much trash. He took his foot off the crushed head and with a savage grin kicked the bloody thing into a corner.

"I'll give Mordacity this: he was strong." His four hands curled into fists. "But I'm stronger."

I wanted to demand the sonofabitch tell me who he was. I wanted to force him to tell me what he'd done with Nathaniel. Instead I bellowed in rage and rushed toward him.

And that's when the alarms sounded.

ELEVEN

The Cyclops just grinned as I ran toward him, but vertigo gripped me before I could reach him. The next thing I knew I was back in my own body, kneeling beside Dr Tittering. My fingertips were pressed to her neck, but I couldn't feel a pulse.

A second later, I heard an *oof!* and then Jinx came flying out of Nathaniel's room. He slammed into the corridor's wall, bounced off, and landed face-first on the floor. He moaned something. It sounded like "Give a guy some warning next time," but it was hard to hear with the alarms blaring.

Up to this point, the corridor had been empty besides us and the assassins, but now staff members came running toward us. At first I thought they were coming to help, but they didn't give us a second look, let alone pause in their mad dash. They were all heading in the same direction, and I had the uncomfortable thought that they looked like panicked rats deserting a sinking vessel. I stood and grabbed hold of the first person I could, an Incubus whose bald head was covered with flashing light bulbs. His eyes danced with electric sparks, and the nametag on his white coat gave his name as Jolt.

"What's happening?" I had to shout to be heard over the alarms.

"Riot!" he shouted back, and then he pulled free of my grip and continued running like hell.

Jinx had managed to pull himself to his feet, and the two assassins still lay in the middle of the floor where they'd fallen. I didn't give a damn if they were trampled to death by the panicking staff. As a matter of fact, I kind of hoped they would be.

The blood-soaked Cyclops stepped out of Nathaniel's room, surveyed the chaos around us, and let out a booming laugh.

Jinx stepped over to me.

"Looks like the prisoners found out all their negator collars went poof," I said.

"Negator collars? Do I know what those are?" He frowned. "I seem to have a vague memory. More like an echo of a memory. It's weird." He shook his head back and forth rapidly, as if to dislodge the irritating thought.

Jinx had holstered the trancer when he'd gone to check on Dr Tittering, and I drew it now, aimed at the Cyclops' eye, and fired. I used the weapon's highest setting, and M-energy lanced through the air and popped his giant eye as if it were a lightly poached egg. The Cyclops screamed and clapped two of his hands to his face, as if attempting to hold in as much goo as he could. It didn't help.

I thought seeing a sudden blast of trancer fire would freak out the staff even more than they already were, but none of them seemed to notice. I suppose when you work at a prison full of Incubi whose power-negator collars have ceased to exist, you've got bigger things to worry about than one woman firing a trancer in the middle of a corridor.

The Cyclops continued howling in pain, but I knew his eye would heal soon enough. And, when it did, I intended to shoot it out again. *Then* maybe I'd question him to find out what he'd done with Nathaniel.

Jinx went over to the two unconscious assassins to retrieve Cuthbert Junior. But, as he bent down to pick up his hammer, one of the assassins sat up, aimed a trancer at him, and fired. Jinx managed to dodge in time so that he was only struck a glancing blow on his left shoulder, but the impact was still enough to spin him halfway around. Both assassins got to their feet, but they were no longer Gingerdread Man and Demonique. The Incubi that inhabited their stolen uniforms were the bat-headed woman and the giant earwig, two of the three Incubi who'd gotten off the Loco-Motive with us.

I muttered "What the hell?" or something equally incisive, and raised my trancer to fire at them. But there were too many people in the corridor and I couldn't get a clear shot. The assassins, or whoever they were now, took advantage of the situation and jumped to their feet to join the fleeing staff. I didn't bother trying to go after them. Nathaniel was still missing, and the Incubus that had killed Mordacity might be able to tell me where to find him. Besides, I *really* wanted to shoot out that goddamned eye again.

I headed toward the Cyclops, who was still huddled in Nathaniel's doorway, moaning in pain. Jinx joined me, Cuthbert Junior once more in hand, a black scorch mark on his left shoulder. I nodded at the Cyclops, and Jinx grinned and started forward. Although he wasn't

entirely healed from the assassins' assault – even if I
hadn't been able to sense his condition through our
link, the bloody spots soaking through his once-clean
shirt were a dead giveaway – he was still more than
strong enough to swing his hammer into the Cyclops'
chest and send him flying back into the room. Jinx and
I stepped inside, and I closed the door behind us.
Whatever was happening in the prison, I didn't want
to be interrupted.

I did my best not to look at Mordacity's remains as
we approached the Cyclops. The fucker had risen to his
hands and knees by the time Jinx and I reached him.
His ruin of an eye was no longer bleeding, and, while
he kept the lid down tight so I couldn't see what was
happening, I was certain a new eye was growing in the
socket, slowly but surely.

Just because he couldn't see at the moment didn't
mean the Cyclops was helpless, so Jinx propped
Cuthbert Junior against a wall, reached into a pocket,
and pulled out a small anvil about the size of a softball
with the words *One Metric Fuck-Ton* painted on it in red
letters. He walked over to the Cyclops and dropped the
anvil onto his back. The weight slammed the bastard to
the floor and kept him pinned there. His head was
turned to the side, and I crouched down next to him
and placed the muzzle of my trancer against his closed
eyelid. I pushed and I could feel the liquidy mush
behind the lid give a little. The Cyclops gasped in pain,
but he didn't scream, another sign that he was healing.

"Start talking or I'll start firing," I said.

"Fuck you," he growled.

I jammed the trancer barrel into his eyelid and he
yelped as clear fluid squirted out the sides.

"Where's Nathaniel?" I demanded.

He still didn't answer.

Jinx, meanwhile, had taken in the blood smears on the walls, along with Mordacity's remains. His face was expressionless as he knelt on the other side of the Cyclops and leaned his mouth close to the Incubus' ear. When Jinx spoke, his voice was calm and toneless.

"Mordacity and I didn't get along, but he was my friend. You killed him. If you don't start answering Audra's questions right fucking now, here's what I'm going to do to you."

Jinx leaned even closer, until his red lips were almost touching the Cyclops' ear, and then he began whispering. I couldn't hear what Jinx said, which I consider to be one of the great blessings of my life. The Cyclops didn't react at first, but then he began to tremble all over. Next he whimpered and repeated "No, no, no," over and over. As Jinx wrapped up, the Cyclops released a hot stream of urine that spread out beneath him.

When he was finished, Jinx said, "And just so you know I'm not all talk…"

Moving lightning fast, he opened his mouth, clamped his teeth on the Cyclops' ear, and with a single savage motion tore it off. He turned his head and spat, and the ear flew through the air to hit the wall with a wet smack. It hung there for a second before sliding to the floor.

The Cyclops cried out when Jinx bit off his ear, but then he returned to whimpering. I'd like to tell you that I felt for the one-eyed bastard, but I didn't. Not in the slightest.

"Where's Nathaniel?" I repeated.

"He's right here," the Cyclops said. "He didn't go anywhere."

"Don't screw with us. He's not in the room."

"Yes, he is," the Cyclops insisted. "I'll show you."

Even before his body began to blur and distort, I knew what was going to happen, and I shouted for Jinx to remove the anvil. He didn't question me. Maybe he'd guessed what was going to happen too, or maybe he just felt my urgency through our link. Whatever the case, he pulled a two-foot long hat pin from his pocket and stuck it into the anvil, which then exploded like a balloon, releasing a shower of confetti. The confetti settled not on the Cyclops, but on Nathaniel. Jinx and I helped him sit up. His inmate uniform was still covered with Mordacity's blood and the Cyclops' eye jelly, as was his face and hands, but the fabric had been stretched and torn by the Cyclops' much larger body and now hung even more loosely on him than it had before. He had both his eyes, and they were intact, and the same was true of his ears. I glanced over to where Jinx had spat the Cyclops' ear, half-expecting it to have vanished, but the grisly thing still lay where it had fallen.

"His name is Alkandros." Nathaniel's voice was weak, but there was a focus and certainty to his words that told me that, for the moment at least, his mind was clear. "He is… *was* one of the Lords of Misrule. A very long time ago, back when the Lords first came to power."

Jinx frowned. "That's something like three thousand years ago." He quickly added. "Not that a lunatic clown like me would know something about that. Hyuck!"

"*Hyuck*?" I said. "Really?"

Jinx's white cheeks turned pinkish as he blushed in embarrassment. "I stand by my totally ineffective fake laugh."

Nathaniel smiled briefly. "I'd almost forgotten how much fun it is to watch you two bicker. The bond between Incubus and Ideator is a special one, isn't it?"

He glanced at Mordacity's remains and his expression hardened.

"I don't understand everything that happened to me. But somehow Alkandros' essence entered my body. He was one of the... the..."

"Discarnate," I supplied. "You mentioned the word earlier."

"I did? Yes, I suppose I did. I'm not entirely sure what it means, though. At any rate, when his spirit first entered me, it tried to take over my body, reshape it into his. I fought him, though. And I've continued to fight him all these years." He paused. "It has been years, hasn't it?"

I nodded.

"I thought so. It's so hard to keep track of time in here. I managed to prevent him from taking over... until today." These last two words were filled with sorrow, and he gazed upon Mordacity's remains once more.

I wanted to tell him that it wasn't his fault, that Alkandros had killed Mordacity, not him. But I knew it wouldn't make a difference to how he felt.

"Well, we can't do anything sitting here." Nathaniel struggled to get to his feet, and, when Jinx and I tried to help him, he waved us off. "From the sound of things out there, I'd say all hell's broken loose, and then some."

The alarms had continued to sound all this time, and we could hear people shouting and screaming in the corridor.

"The prisoners' collars vanished," I said. "And, once their powers returned, they started rioting."

Nathaniel looked at me strangely. "What sort of collars?"

I reached into my jacket pocket. I usually keep a couple extra negator collars in there, but the pocket was empty.

I turned to Jinx. "Do *you* remember negator collars?"

He shrugged. "Maybe. Kinda-sorta. I don't know. But if you remember, that's good enough for me."

I smiled at the big psycho. Sometimes he's not so horrible.

Nathaniel held out his hand. "If we're going to go out there, I'm going to need a weapon."

I hesitated.

"If Alkandros takes you over again while you're armed…" I began.

"It's okay," he said. "I don't think he's going to try to come out again anytime soon. And, if he does try, you'll know because I'll start sounding crazy again before it happens."

I thought about it, and, even though my training told me it was a bad idea, I trusted Nathaniel, and so I handed over my trancer. He took it, and then I turned to Jinx to ask him if he had something else in his pockets that I could use to defend myself. But, before I could say anything, Nathaniel took several steps backward – so he'd be out of our reach – and then pressed the trancer's muzzle to his right temple.

At first I feared that Nathaniel hadn't been as

rational as he'd seemed. My fear must've shown on my face, for he said, "I'm perfectly sane at the moment, Audra." He smiled grimly. "In many ways, a truly sane man is the most dangerous of all. It's only a matter of time before Alkandros makes another attempt to manifest. And the longer he has control of my body, the more Maelstrom energy he can draw to himself and the stronger he'll become. It wouldn't take long for him to reach full power, and, once that happened, none of us would be able to stop him. He *is* a Lord of Misrule, after all. There's only one way to stop him. And only one way to make him pay for what he did to Mordacity."

I'd left the trancer's selector switch on high. A full-force M-blast to a human head at point-black range would be instantly fatal.

I felt cold all over and sick to my stomach. "Don't do this, Nathaniel. *Please*. We can find another way."

He smiled. "No, we can't. I'm sorry I'm not going to be around to help you clean up whatever mess you're in. But Mordacity and I trained you two well. You might not be the most orthodox of officers in the Watch's history, but you're two of the best."

As he spoke, his gun hand began to tremble and beads of sweat broke out on his forehead. His face rippled several times, like an interrupted video signal. Alkandros was trying to emerge and stop Nathaniel from killing them both, but Nathaniel was resisting him.

"Remember what I taught *you*."

This last word came out in the deep bass of Alkandros' voice, and for an instant I saw a ghostly image of the Cyclops' face superimposed over Nathaniel's. And then Nathaniel pulled the trigger.

M-energy blasted forth from the trancer, and the body that fell to the floor was Nathaniel's. There wasn't as much as a hint of Alkandros in his face.

I felt numb and hollow. I figured I was in shock, but I didn't care. I wanted to say to hell with whatever shuteye really was, and to hell with whatever was causing bits and pieces of reality to be erased. At that moment, all I wanted to do was kneel at Nathaniel's side and take hold of his hand. But I knew he wouldn't want me to. If I truly wanted to honor him, the best way to do so was to get off my ass and get back to work. I knelt down, touched my fingers to my lips, then pressed them to his cheek. Then I took the trancer from his still-warm hand and stood.

"You ready to go hurt a lot of people?" I said.

Jinx let out a contented sigh.

"Need you ask?"

Jinx and I fought our way through Deadlock one corridor at a time. Jinx used Cuthbert Junior to fracture skulls and pulverize bones, and his lapel flower squirted constant streams of acid at anyone unlucky enough to get in his way. I made do with the trancer Jinx had given me, and, when it ran out of juice, I discarded it, grabbed another from the corpse of a fallen guard, and started firing. Sometimes we fought alongside guards, sometimes we fought with only each other for backup. If the inmates had been organized in even an approximate definition of the word, we would've been overwhelmed in no time. But they fought with each other just as much if not more than with the guards and staff. The Incubi's inherently chaotic nature was as much our ally as it was our enemy.

I don't know how long we fought for, but, after a while, Jinx and I were both covered in gore. We switched bodies often enough that we got used to it and kept fighting with barely a pause in our rhythm. The alarms provided a constant shrill accompaniment to the violence, and after a time we became accustomed to their shrieking. But at one point the lights went out and a few seconds later low-level emergency lighting kicked in. When that happened, the alarms, already loud as hell, doubled in volume.

"Whatever the hell that means," I shouted in Jinx's ear, "it can't be good!"

"Too right!" someone shouted before Jinx could reply.

Bruzer shoved his way through the guards and inmates, none of whom seemed to notice or care about the Warden's presence. He only had one head now, and at first I thought he'd lost the second in battle, but his suit jacket was missing, and his shirt was torn to ribbons, and I could see no sign of a bloody stump where the second head had been attached. Like the first head, it had vanished. Or more precisely, been *excised*, as if it had never existed. The Warden carried a heavy-duty M-rifle, but the shreds of meat stuck in his teeth showed he'd been fighting with every weapon he possessed.

When Bruzer reached Jinx and me, he leaned his remaining head close to ours so he could be heard above the din.

"The second alarm indicates the prison's power supply – *and* its backups – are offline. In short, the lights are out."

Those last few words turned my blood to iced water. If there were no lights inside *or* outside, that meant...

Screams erupted at the far end of the corridor, and people began running toward us, desperate to escape whatever was attacking them.

"Darkuns," I said, so softly that I'm sure neither Jinx nor Bruzer heard me. Not that they hadn't reached the same conclusion on their own. The emergency lighting was enough to see by, but it was nowhere near intense enough to drive back the Darkuns, let alone harm them.

"Follow me!" Bruzer shouted.

He fired several energy blasts from his M-rifle to get people out of our way, then he led Jinx and me to a door. He keyed in a code on the pad, the door unlocked, and he opened it and gestured for us to enter ahead of him. He fired a couple more energy blasts to prevent anyone from joining us, then he entered and yanked the door shut behind him. There was another keypad on this side of the wall, and he destroyed it with a quick burst from his rifle. Metal shattered, sparks flew, and smoke curled forth.

"The doors operate on battery power in case of emergencies," he said.

There were no alarms in this dark, narrow corridor, and it was easier to hear him, although my ears kept ringing from the assault they'd endured since the riot started.

"No batteries for the lights?" Jinx said.

Bruzer cocked his head to the side. "That's a good idea. I wonder why no one ever thought of it."

I sighed. "I'm sure someone did and that those batteries were installed. They just don't exist anymore, that's all."

Bruzer frowned at me, but he decided to let my comment go.

"What about Mordacity and Officer Sawyer? And your two friends?" he asked.

I almost couldn't bring myself to say the words, but somehow I managed. "Russell and Bloodshedder managed to escape, although Russell was seriously wounded. Nathaniel and Mordacity didn't make it."

"I'm genuinely sorry to hear that," he said. "They were both fine officers." He took a deep breath. "Well, let's see if I can at least get the two of you out of here more or less intact."

Without waiting for us to reply, he turned and headed down the narrow corridor at a fast jog. Jinx and I didn't need any further coaxing to follow. The emergency lighting – which I was *very* grateful still existed – provided only dim illumination. Shadows clung to the walls and ceiling, and it didn't take much effort to imagine that they were Darkuns lying in wait to attack. But we made it through the corridor without having our flesh ripped by obsidian claws and teeth, and at the other end was a door. But this one was different than the others we'd seen in Deadlock. It was circular instead of rectangular, and the keypad next to it on the wall had only a single red button.

"This is an emergency exit," Bruzer said. "Outside is a motorcycle with a high-powered headlight and defensive lights mounted on the vehicle's sides and rear. At least, one's *supposed* to be out there. It's possible one of the guards or staff got here before us, in which case..." He trailed off. "No matter. It's still the best chance for survival I can offer you. Remaining in Deadlock at this point would be suicide. I've contacted the Rookery and informed them of the situation, but it will be a while before help can arrive, and by that point there won't be anything left here except Darkuns with full bellies. Good luck to you both."

"Aren't you coming with us?" I asked.

He shook his lone head. "You can ride two on the motorcycle, but not three. And, once the door opens, the Darkuns will swarm it. It'll shut and lock automatically behind you, but it won't keep them out for long. I'll stay here to take out as many as I can."

Nathaniel and Mordacity had already died that day, as had who knew how many others. Maybe Russell too, if the Thresholders hadn't managed to retrieve him in time. I desperately wanted to keep Bruzer from being added to the list of casualties, but I didn't know how to make that happen. And Bruzer was, in a very real sense, the captain of this ship. It was his right to go down with it if he wanted.

On impulse, I gave him a quick hug and a kiss on his fuzzy cheek. He seemed surprised, but pleased. He then pushed me gently but firmly away, and his manner became gruff once more.

"Go."

He made a fist and slammed the red button. The circular door sprang open with a pneumatic hiss, and Jinx and I hurried out before it was all the way open. It was utterly, absolutely dark outside. No emergency lights out here, not anymore anyway. I felt panic rising in me as I realized there could be dozens, hundreds, *thousands* of Darkuns surrounding us, and we would have no way of knowing it. My first impulse was to start firing my trancer randomly in all directions, but its charge was already low, and I couldn't allow my fear to get the better of me. If we hoped to get the hell out of the Murk alive, we'd need every ounce of remaining power the weapon possessed.

The door closed, shutting off the meager light from inside and leaving us in total darkness. I heard the soft rustle of cloth as Jinx rummaged around in his clothes, and a second later I heard the hiss of a match flaring to life. I now saw that, in his other hand, Jinx held a bottle filled with clear liquid. An oily rag was stuffed into the bottle's neck, and Jinx touched the match flame to it. The cloth caught fire and started to burn, and Jinx hurled the bottle toward the ground in front of him. Glass shattered and the Molotov cocktail exploded in a bright burst of flame. Darkuns hissed in anger and drew back from the firelight, and I tried not to think about how many of them there were. The dome's polished metal surface reflected and intensified the light, and we were safe – for the moment.

Unfortunately, there was no sign of a motorcycle.

"Looks like we're walking," Jinx said.

"Are you kidding? Once we step outside the range of the firelight, we're dead."

Before Jinx could respond, we heard the sound of an engine in the distance, and a small pinpoint of light appeared. The sound quickly grew louder and the light brighter as the vehicle approached. It was the emergency motorcycle Bruzer had told us about, and the driver fired bursts from an M-rifle at any Darkun that got too close for comfort. As the driver drew closer, I could see that whoever it was wasn't wearing the reflective white uniform of a prison guard. I knew for certain the driver wasn't a guard when he started firing at us.

The first couple blasts missed. It's a lot harder to shoot accurately from a moving vehicle than people think. I, however, was not moving, and I raised my trancer, aimed, and fired.

The motorcycle's front wheel exploded and the bike flipped forward, launching the driver into the air. The bike tumbled to a stop fifteen feet from where we stood, and the driver hit the ground close by. Most of the bike's running lights had been shattered, but a couple still worked, and they further illuminated the scene, providing additional protection from any Darkuns that might be lurking nearby.

Jinx and I walked over to the downed rider. I expected it to be either Gingerdread Man or Demonique – or the Incubi whose bodies they shared. But it was the organ conglomerate, the third Incubus who'd gotten off the Loco-Motive with us.

"Another assassin?" I said.

"Looks like," Jinx answered. He cocked his head to the side. "I wonder how it managed to drive the motorcycle and fire the rifle without any hands or legs."

"Good question. Let's ask it." I'd kept my trancer trained on the Incubus the entire time, and now I kicked it in the lung. "Sit up. Slowly."

The Conglomerate sat up and looked at us. It had a pair of eyes attached to a brain that rested on top of the pile of organs that formed its body. However it had managed to hold onto the M-rifle, the creature had lost its grip on it when the motorcycle crashed, and it was weaponless.

"Feel like talking?" I didn't see a mouth, but I assumed the creature had some way of communicating.

Jinx smiled at the Incubus. "Please say no."

The Conglomerate glared at us. At least, I think it glared. It was hard to tell since the Incubus didn't have eyelids, or, for that matter, a face.

The words the creature spoke were moist and thick, as if it produced sound by sliding organs against one another.

"I don't have anything to say. But *he* might."

The creature's body rippled and blurred, and it became a humanoid form comprised entirely of sand.

"Montrose?" I said.

His sandy lips stretched into a smile.

"Didn't expect to see me again so soon, did you? You won the last round of our game. Now it's time for Round Two."

But, before Montrose could do anything, Jinx angled the left side of his chest toward him, and a stream of thick liquid shot forth from his lapel flower. The substance struck Montrose in the face, and he staggered back, raising his hands in an attempt to wipe the gunk away. But, as he did so, his hands stuck fast to his face. He managed to tear them free, but huge chunks of his head came away with them, leaving two large depressions in his face. An acrid smell filled the air, and I realized that Jinx's flower was shooting some kind of powerful glue.

Jinx kept up the glue attack, running around Montrose in a circle to cover his entire body and apply layer after layer. Eventually, the stream became intermittent and then with a final gurgling sound, it stopped altogether.

Jinx stopped running around Montrose. He returned to my side and sighed. "I was afraid of that. The works are all gunked up."

He plucked the daisy from his lapel and tossed it over his shoulder. It hit the ground with a gooey plop, and immediately began to wilt. The flower had done its job, though. Montrose looked like he'd been encased in acrylic, and he had been rendered immobile.

We quickly moved to check out the motorcycle. The front wheel had been destroyed by my trancer beam, though, rendering the vehicle useless.

I turned to Jinx. "Why the hell didn't you use that glue on Montrose when we first fought him?"

"I didn't have any then. I picked some up at *Misery Loves Company*, just in case we ever ran into his sandy ass again."

I frowned. "I thought you just made your toys appear. You know, like magic."

He looked at me as if I had just said something incredibly stupid.

"There's no such thing as magic, Audra. You know that. There's only Maelstrom energy. I pick up all my clown supplies at *Misery Loves Company*. They have a supply room in the back. It's the only reason I go in that damn place. Their coffee sucks."

Now that the fighting was over, the Darkuns crept as close as they could to the light without being harmed by it. Jinx drew Cuthbert Junior, but the only weapons I had left were my two fists, and I didn't think they were going to do much against the dark creatures that gathered around us in ever-increasing numbers.

Something came flying toward me out of the darkness. I tried to dodge it, but there wasn't enough light to see clearly, and I didn't get out of the way in time. Something sharp grazed my right shoulder, slicing through my jacket, shirt, and the top layer of skin beneath. The object kept going until it hit the motorcycle seat and stuck fast.

"Fuck!" I clapped my left hand to the wound to slow the bleeding and turned to look at the object that had cut me. It was an obsidian crescent with extremely sharp edges. The light we stood in was strong enough to cause the crescent to emit a sizzling hiss, and then it disappeared in a small puff of smoke. One of the Darkuns had sacrificed a piece of its substance to attack me, probably to probe our defenses. I fired a couple blasts from my trancer into the crowd of Darkuns, but without much effect. The weapon's beam grew weaker with each shot, and I knew it didn't have much power left.

I heard a soft whirling sound, and, before I could react, Jinx swung Cuthbert Junior in front of me. Another black shard, this one shaped roughly like a knife blade, thunked into the hammer's wooden head. Jinx didn't bother trying to dislodge it. He stepped in front of me, Cuthbert Junior gripped tight in his hands, a look of absolute homicidal menace on his face.

"I appreciate the gesture," I said, still pressing my hand tight to my bleeding wound. "But they can attack us from multiple directions, remember? There's no way you can protect me. Not this time."

Another dark shard went flying by me, this one coming way too close to my head for comfort.

Jinx didn't respond to my words. Instead, his brow furrowed in concentration, and I felt an attack of vertigo coming on.

"Are you trying to force us to switch bodies?" I asked.

"Maybe."

I know it sounds weird, but I'd never loved that lunatic more than I did at that moment. He knew I'd have a better chance of survival if I were in his body instead of my own.

"Thanks, but don't."

The sensation of dizziness continued to grow stronger.

"Seriously," I said, in my you-really-don't-want-to-piss-me-off voice.

The vertigo continued for several more seconds before lessening and then going away altogether.

Jinx sighed.

"If you were a *real* friend, you wouldn't stop me from stealing your body."

"Yeah, I can be a real bitch sometimes."

The shards stopped coming, and at first I didn't understand why. But then I realized the fire from Jinx's Molotov cocktail had almost burned itself out, and the remaining motorcycle light was dimming. What little protection we had from the Darkuns would soon be gone, and they'd be free to attack. I could hear the scrape and scuttle of claws as the Darkuns drew closer, along with excited breathing that made me think of hungry, eager wolves. The air around us grew cold, and I could see our breath mist the air. We had only moments left, and I searched for some profound and touching final words to say to Jinx, the nightmare creature I'd inadvertently created and who had become the best friend I'd ever had.

"This blows," I said.

"Hard," Jinx agreed.

The Darkuns edged closer.

"You know, we don't have to stand here and wait for them to come at us," Jinx said.

"That's true."

"We could take the fight to them."

"We could," I said. "It wouldn't last long."

"Maybe not." His red lips stretched into a slow, scary smile. "But at least we'd go out on our terms."

"Something to be said for that," I admitted.

Jinx looked at me. He was grinning, and wild mad light glimmered in his eyes.

"On the count of three?"

I nodded. "One."

"Two…"

I was about to say three, had the tip of my tongue pressed against my two front teeth to make the TH sound, when twin beams of green light cut through the darkness. The Darkuns surrounding us shrieked in terror and agony as their ebon substance began to sizzle and smoke in the beams' unforgiving glare. They fled in all directions as the sound of a powerful but finely tuned engine filled the air, and a moment later a sleek black vehicle pulled up to the wrecked motorcycle and stopped, engine still running. It was a hearse, but not just any hearse. This was the Deathmobile in its Night Aspect, and, while it was an eerie sight with its unearthly green headlights and spectral wraiths that hovered over its roof, I can honestly say that I've never seen anything more beautiful in my life.

The driver's side window rolled down and Connie Desposito grinned at us.

"You two need a ride?" she asked.

"We *were* about to commit a spectacularly futile double suicide," Jinx said, pouting.

"I'll try to find a way to make it up to you," I told him. "When this is over, I'll take you to visit the body farm of your choice."

That perked him right up. "Really? Can we go to the Forensic Anthropology Research Facility at Texas State University? It's supposed to be the largest in the world!"

"Why not?"

Jinx whooped with joy as we walked around to the Deathmobile's passenger side, and I opened the door so we could climb in. I looked into the hearse and saw that the Fata Morgana, in her guise as Dr Cecelia Kauffman, sat next to Connie. She smiled sweetly at us.

Jinx looked at me.

"There's still time to kill ourselves."

I scowled at him.

He shrugged. "Just saying."

TWELVE

The Deathmobile roared over the Murk's rough terrain, but the ride was unearthly smooth. In its Day Aspect, the Deathmobile would've been shaken to bits by driving over the uneven ground, but its Night Aspect had no problems. Its green headlights – which possessed the ability to rapidly age whatever they touched – kept the Darkuns away for the most part, and, if any still tried to attack us, the Deathmobile's wraiths drove them off.

The Fata Morgana and I sat in the front with Connie, while Jinx took the back seat.

Connie kept a first aid kit in the Deathmobile, and she gave it to me so I could bandage my shoulder, which I'd done. I hadn't said anything to Jinx, but I'd been afraid the Darkuns' substance might be poison, but I felt fine, so I figured I was in the clear on that score.

"What happened to you after the fight in Wet Dreams?" I asked the Fata Morgana.

She frowned. "Nothing happened. I merely went to the restroom. When I came out, you and your friends were gone, and without as much as saying goodbye, I might add."

I then asked Connie how she'd known where to find us. "For that matter, how did you know we *needed* finding?"

The Fata Morgana was the one who answered me, though.

"Russell sent me a telepathic message. I imagined he contacted me because he assumed I'd be the only one capable of receiving it. Even with my powers diminished, I still possess my sensory abilities." She pursed her lips in irritation. "More or less."

"She then called me," Connie said. "It was close to dawn by that point, but the Deathmobile and I swung by Wet Dreams to pick her up, and DM was able to locate a Door large enough for us to pass through just as the sun began to rise. We barely made it through in time."

The Fata Morgana continued. "The Thresholders helped him contact me, using whatever arcane powers they possess. Russell said the two of you were in Deadlock and needed help."

Connie picked up the story at that point. "Once we were in Nod, the Deathmobile hauled ass to the Rimline. At first I didn't think she would be able to get through, but the wraiths formed a shell of ghostly energy around her, and that did the trick. Once we were inside the Murk, the Deathmobile caught your scent, and we made straight for Deadlock."

"Sorry," Jinx said. "That's all me. Sometimes it's hard for a clown to maintain his freshness on the run, if you know what I mean."

"You've been spending entirely too much time in my body," I said.

Both Connie and the Fata Morgana gave me a strange look.

"That's *not* what I meant," I said.

"You're still Blending?" the Fata Morgana asked.

"Yeah," I admitted. "It's been getting worse, even with the medicine we got at the Sick House."

The Fata Morgana frowned. "That's odd. If you're undergoing treatment, your condition should be improving. Maybe it'll just take a bit more time." She seemed doubtful, though.

"I understand why Russell might've thought you'd be the only one to pick up his weak signal," I said.."But why did you call Connie, and, for that matter, why did you accompany her? It's not as if Jinx and I are your favorite people."

"Frankly, I did it to amuse myself," the Fata Morgana said. "It's awfully boring being stuck in my Day Aspect all the time. Besides, this way I'll be present when you and Jinx eventually make a mistake. And, with any luck, you'll both die horribly in the process."

"I hate to be the one who brings up the whole logic thing," Jinx said, "especially when I don't use the stuff much myself. But what you said doesn't make any sense. If you wanted us dead, you only had to keep from calling Connie. And, even if you came along with her because you wanted to watch us die, you had an excellent opportunity to do so outside Deadlock, when the Darkuns were about to get us."

Every once in a while, Jinx's brain fires on all cylinders, and it looked like now was one of those times.

"And don't tell us you couldn't stop Connie from saving us from the Darkuns," I added. "I'm sure a wily bitch like you could've found a way to trick her into hesitating before rescuing us, at least long enough for the Darkuns to tear us into bloody bits of confetti."

A haughty – okay, *haughtier* – expression came over the Fata Morgana's face, and for a moment I thought she was going to deny it. But then she lowered her head, as if defeated.

"Fine. Connie, show her your arm. Either one will do."

Puzzled, I looked at Connie. She was wearing a long-sleeved sweater and I couldn't see her arm. She took a hand off the wheel – not that the Deathmobile needed a driver – and pushed up the sleeve on her other arm to reveal clear, unmarked skin. A cold chill ran through me at the sight.

"What happened to your tattoos, Connie?" I asked.

"Not you too!" Connie said. "The Fata Morgana tried to tell me I had tattoos – a lot of them. But I don't have a single tat on my body and no, I'm not going to strip naked just to prove it to you. Sure, I've *thought* about getting tattooed. I had this idea for getting a racetrack inked all over my body, and then having all kinds of cool cars driving around on it." She shrugged. "But I never found the time, you know?"

"Another excision," I said softly.

"Is that what you're calling them?" the Fata Morgana said. She considered a moment. "Not a bad name, actually."

"So you're aware of them, too," I said.

"Of course. As I said before, I may be greatly diminished in power, but I am still a Lord. Before you ask, I have no more idea what's causing them than you do. That's the real reason I accompanied Connie. Whatever's happening, we need to do something about it."

"What do you mean, *we*?" I asked. "With any luck,

Sanderson and the Watch M-gineers –"

"Who are they?" Connie said.

I felt suddenly ill.

"You're kidding." I turned to the Fata Morgana. "Please tell me she's kidding."

"It's true. Sanderson and the Shadow Watch are gone."

My mind reeled. "If the Watch is gone, does the Rookery still exist? If it doesn't…"

The upper level of the Rookery housed the Unwakened, the master dreamers who maintained Nod and protected it from the turbulent energies of the Maelstrom. They also maintained the Canopy, as well as the conditions that permitted life to exist in Nod: gravity, atmosphere, the whole bit, synthesizing them all from the Maelstrom itself. If the Unwakened were gone, if they'd been *excised*, then it was only a matter of time before the Maelstrom rushed in to reclaim Nod, destroying everyone and everything in it.

"Of course the Rookery still exists," Connie said. "That's where the Unwakened are. It's where they've always been."

Relief washed over me. So the Shadow Watch was gone, but the Rookery and the Unwakened had been spared. For the time being, at least.

Jinx frowned at the Fata Morgana. "Wait a minute. Didn't you try to destroy both Earth *and* Nod's dimensions not that long ago? I may be insane, but my memory works just fine."

"The Lords don't want to destroy anything," she said. "We want to provide complete access to the Maelstrom for all beings, so they're free to shape reality as they wish. You can't shape what doesn't exist."

"What about the other Lords?" I asked. "If they're aware of the excisions too, maybe they can stop them."

I was still reeling from knowing that the Shadow Watch no longer existed, and had in a sense never existed. It seemed Jinx and I were the only two Shadow Watch officers left. But, if everyone else in the Watch had been excised, how come we were still here?

"The Lords are a force of chaos," the Fata Morgana said. "We don't exactly work well together. I'm sure the Lords – those who still exist, anyway – are working as individuals to try to determine what's happening and reverse it. I'd be doing the same if I still possessed my full power. Since I don't, I'm forced to rely on you two."

"I'm surprised," I said. "Considering how badly we kicked your sorry ass before, I'd think we'd be the last people you'd want to work with."

"Make no mistake. I hate you two, and nothing would bring me greater joy than to kill both of you as slowly and painfully as I could."

Jinx leaned over the front seat and kissed her on the cheek.

"You say the sweetest things."

She elbowed him in the jaw, but he just laughed as he sat back.

"I decided that if you two could defeat *me*," she said, "then you're my best bet to stop the excisions. I don't have to like you to work with you." She paused. "Come to think of it, I don't like anyone."

I sighed. I really wasn't up for saving the world – worlds – again, but it looked as if I didn't have much choice.

"I suppose we'll have to put the shuteye investigation aside for now," I said.

"Not at all," the Fata Morgana said. "Russell's message said shuteye is related to the excisions, although he didn't say how. I think he tried to tell me, but our connection faded before he could."

"It's those damn mysterious bosses of his," I said, irritated. "If they're so powerful and know so goddamned much, why don't they just show up and fix the problem themselves?"

The Fata Morgana looked at me. "You don't know? Or did the memory vanish?"

"How would I know the difference?" I said.

"Good point," she said.

"I know about the Thresholders," Jinx said.

The Fata Morgana, Connie, and I all looked at him.

"Bloodshedder told me."

I don't speak demon dog, but, since Bloodshedder and Jinx are both Incubi, they don't seem to have any trouble communicating.

Jinx continued. "She said the Thresholders are the spirits of people who died while they were dreaming. They're stuck between Earth and Nod, so they protect access to both dimensions, although they can't enter either. They can only work through agents they recruit, like Russell and Bloodshedder."

"Have either of you spent any time in the Between lately?" the Fata Morgana asked.

"As a matter of fact, I have," I admitted. "And Jinx and I were close to the portal that the Thresholders opened in order to retrieve Russell when he was wounded."

The Fata Morgana nodded, as if I'd just confirmed something she'd expected. "That's why you're able to recognize excisions when they happen and remember what used to exist: your exposure to the energies from Between."

I hadn't been able to remember the excisions at first, although I'd *almost* remembered them. But, when the portal to Between opened in Deadlock, Jinx and I had gotten a good dose of that realm's energy. That must've been what finally did the trick.

"I don't have a clue what any of you are talking about," Connie said. "But I trust you, Audra." She glanced sideways at the Fata Morgana. "And *only* you. If you say these excisions are happening, I believe it."

As we continued driving through the Murk, I told Connie and the Fata Morgana about the riot in Deadlock and what had happened to Nathaniel and Mordacity.

"So Incubi can somehow possess humans?" Connie asked. "That's more than a little kinky, if you ask me."

"More than possess them," I said. "Alkandros was able to transform Nathaniel's body into his own."

"Maybe that's what happened to Gingerdread Man and Demonique," Jinx said. "When they were zonked, they changed into Batwoman and the Human Earwig and got the hell out of there."

It seemed like a crazy idea, but I was used to hearing those from Jinx. But it would explain why the assassins had disappeared and two other Incubi had seemingly taken their place.

"So these possessing Incubi can take over humans *or* other Incubi?" the Fata Morgana asked. "That would make excellent camouflage for assassins. They can literally become someone else."

"And shuteye is connected somehow," I said. "Nathaniel told Mordacity and me that it was used for something other than putting people to sleep. Maybe this is what he meant."

"Perhaps shuteye is how the second personality gets into the body of the first," the Fata Morgana said.

It sounded ridiculous. How could someone's personality – their very essence – be put into something as small and simple as a pill? But Nathaniel's bizarre behavior began immediately after the Angler had forced him to swallow a shuteye pill. And I'd done the same thing to Montrose to stop him, and he'd gained a second personality as well.

"So the people who have a bad reaction to shuteye, like Nathaniel, are those who try to resist the invading personality," I said. "Some die doing so, some go mad, and those who don't or can't resist…"

"They fall asleep and get possessed," the Fata Morgana said. "That explains why there aren't any repeat customers for shuteye. Once you have a second personality in you, the drug's done its work. There's no need for another dose."

"But you said the chemical makeup of shuteye is nothing more than an over-the-counter sleep aid," I pointed out.

"*With* the addition of small amounts of Maelstrom energy," she said. "I dismissed the M-energy at the time, but I shouldn't have. Now I suspect it plays a crucial role in allowing the invading personality to possess its new host. A personality such as Alkandros. My, but I haven't heard his name in ages."

"He told us he was a Lord of Misrule," I said.

"Yes. A bit before my time, though."

"What about the Discarnate?" I asked. "Do you know what they are? Could they be these invading personalities?"

"They're called Faders today. But it's the stage *after* they're completely Faded, when there's nothing left except a disembodied spirit."

"Is that possible?" I asked. "I thought Incubi were just gone after they Faded."

"It's a legend," the Fata Morgana said. "One that was old when I was young. I don't know if it has any basis in fact. I've never met a Discarnate, and I don't know anyone who has. But, if what you say is true, they're real and they've found a way to return to life."

"By time-sharing bodies," Jinx said.

"Life is life," the Fata Morgana said. "People will do anything to extend it, and not just Incubi. Plenty of humans would do the same thing if they had the chance."

I wanted to tell her that it was a damn cynical way to view the world, but I'd be a hypocrite if I said I didn't agree with her.

"So, Russell said the excisions are connected to shuteye?" I said. "I really don't see how that's possible. Possession by Incubus-in-a-pill is one thing, but actually *erasing* parts of reality? That's the big leagues."

I was trying desperately not to think about the fact that Sanderson and the Shadow Watch no longer existed. Their loss was staggering, not only in terms of lives lost, but because, without them, Nod and Earth were defenseless against whatever force was causing the excisions. Jinx and I might prefer working on our own, but we aren't reluctant to call for backup when we really need it, and we sure as shit needed it now. But all we had were a cabbie, her spooky car, and a powered-down super villain who would gleefully watch the rest of us die in agony.

We are so screwed, I thought.

"I'm not saying I believe that pieces of reality are vanishing," Connie said, "but, assuming it's true, if we figure out what's causing it *and* we find a way to stop it, will those missing pieces come back?"

"That," I said, "is a very good question."

We all looked at the Fata Morgana.

"And one that I cannot answer," she said. "Nothing like this has ever happened before. It's almost as if…" She trailed off, a horrified expression coming onto her face. "No. No, it can't be that."

"What?" I said, trying to keep my own fear at bay. If something was bad enough to scare the Fata Morgana, it had to be Bad with a capital B.

"The Wakener."

"It's… not possible," I said. Then in a smaller voice, I added, "Is it?"

"What's a Wakener?" Connie asked.

"Not to mix theologies, but it's like the Devil for Incubi," Jinx said. "Clowns consider him a kind of patron saint of Chaos. Not me, of course. I'm an atheipagagnostic."

"The Wakener is mentioned quite often in the *Primogenium*," I said. "He's the opposite of the First Dreamer, a being who will one day appear and undo the creation that the First Dreamer dreamed into existence."

Connie snorted. "I was raised Catholic, and, if I don't believe any of that stuff, then I'm sure not going to believe there's a First Dreamer and a Wakener."

But, despite her words, there was a note of uncertainty in her voice.

I'd read the *Primogenium* through several times.

When you don't sleep but need to rest and meditate five hours a day, you have a lot of time on your hands. So maybe the excisions were the work of the Wakener, or at least *a* Wakener. And, whether they were religious prophecy come true or just a coincidence, we had to do whatever we could to stop them.

By this point the Deathmobile was drawing near to the Rimline. The border between the Murk and the Cesspit was hard to make out from this side, since you can't see through the darkness. But there's a slight leavening of the blackness. It's not exactly gray, but you can see it if you know what to look for. More importantly, so did the Deathmobile. The sentient hearse didn't slow as it approached the Rimline, and the wraiths wrapped it in a cocoon of spectral energy. Connie had said this was how they'd gotten through before, but I still felt nervous as hell. Without a clear path to follow to the other side, we had no idea what we might hit once we were through. Sure, there might be a road. There might also be pedestrians, other vehicles, buildings... I didn't relish the thought of slamming into them at full speed. But either the Deathmobile could sense what was on the other side of the Rimline or she got lucky because, when we passed out of the Murk, we found ourselves driving down an alley between buildings. The Deathmobile slowed, and, when we reached other end of the alley, she stopped.

The Cesspit is normally a rough, dangerous place, but the scene that greeted us was nothing less than all-out war. Incubi thronged the streets, lashing out at anyone around them with devastating results. Some went old school and fought with teeth, claws, fists, and feet, while others employed knives, guns, broken bottles, or makeshift clubs. Flesh tore, bones broke, and blood gushed, pooling in the streets and running through the gutters like rainwater. A number of buildings in the vicinity had caught fire, and flames rose into the sky, along with billows of black smoke. The streets were so thick with combatants that passage was impossible, and we were stuck in the alley.

This was a Nod in which there was no Shadow Watch to patrol the city. Incubi, because of their dark, chaotic natures and their rapid healing abilities, played very rough at times, and they were less hesitant about breaking the law. Because of this, the Watch could fill Deadlock several times over, so, to reduce prison overcrowding, the less dangerous criminals received a collaring sentence lasting from a few months to several years. But negator collars no longer existed either, and, without the Watch to keep a lid on things, the streets of Nod had become a battleground. Well, more of a battleground than usual. And we were stuck in the middle of it.

"Now this is what I call a party!" Jinx said, excitement and longing in his voice. He watched the violence surging around us like a puppy eager to get out of the car and play with the other dogs.

I felt so overwhelmed and helpless. Jinx and I were the only two Shadow Watch officers left, and, although we'd taken a vow to serve, protect, and bust heads whenever necessary, there was no way we could hope to slow the fighting, let alone stop it.

I was trying to decide what the hell our next move should be when my wisper vibrated. Who the hell could be calling me? All I knew is that it wasn't Sanderson. He no longer existed. I raised the wisper to my face and said, "Answer."

A voice issued from the device.

"Ms Hawthorne? This is Nurse Ooloo. I'm calling on behalf of Dr Menendez. He's currently tied up with a patient, but he wanted me to–"

"Jinx and I are fine," I said. "Thanks for checking on us, but right now we're in the middle of a situation–"

"That's not why I'm calling," she interrupted. "It's Ms Gail. Her condition has worsened. It's quite serious. The doctor thinks you should get here as soon as you can. He's afraid she doesn't have much time left."

I felt cold all over. I tried to speak, but nothing came out.

"Ms Hawthorne? Are you there?'

"I… yes. I am. We'll be there as fast as we can."

"Please hurry."

The nurse disconnected, and I lowered my wisper. I was stunned. When Jinx and I had left the Sick House, Menendez had seemed optimistic about Melody's recovery. Obviously, something had gone wrong, but what? The thought of her dying, after losing Mordacity and Nathaniel, was too much.

"We need to get to the Sick House, Connie. Now."

She shot a dubious glance at the mayhem in the street.

"That's a hell of a lot easier said than done, Audra."

"I understand your concern for the woman," the Fata Morgana said, in a brisk tone that clearly indicated she didn't. "But the life of one officer doesn't matter compared to the potential destruction of Existence itself!"

"The five of us can't stop an entire world of rioting Incubi. But I can go see Melody." I almost added, *One last time*, but I didn't want to say it out loud, as if doing so might make it true.

"And if you don't like it," I added, "we'll be happy to drop you off right here. I'm sure the fact that you don't have your full powers won't be a problem for you."

She looked out the window and saw an Incubus that looked like a featherless ostrich literally kicking the stuffing out of a fanged teddy bear lying in the gutter.

"Thanks," the Fata Morgana said, "but I'm fine where I'm at."

I turned to look at Jinx in the back seat.

"Clear a path," I said.

His eyes glistened, as if he were on the verge of tears. "Really?"

I nodded. "Really. And don't hold back."

He gave me a tentative smile, his eyes shining with a mixture of hope and disbelief.

"Go on," I said. "Do your worst."

His smile became an ear-splitting grin. He opened the Deathmobile's rear passenger door, got out, slammed the door shut, and ran into the street, pulling Cuthbert Junior out of his pocket as he went.

Connie rolled down her window and called out, "Go help him!"

The wraiths that had shepherded us through the Murk and across the Rimline streaked silently through the air after Jinx, and then the fun began in earnest.

Jinx became a blur as he wielded his sledgehammer with devastating force, sending Incubi flying in all directions. The wraiths flanked him, fending off any Incubi which tried to attack from behind, and, when they managed to carve out a small open space, Connie inched the Deathmobile out of the alley. We proceeded this way, moving forward several feet at a time, Jinx and the wraiths making room for us, the Deathmobile blasting its green headlight beams whenever any Incubi came too close, aging them until they were too frail and weak to be a threat.

Jinx's mad laughter filled the air, and more than a few Incubi who heard the blood-curdling sound chose to beat a hasty retreat, clearing even more space for us. Instead of growing tired as he fought, Jinx seemed to draw strength from the havoc he wreaked, and his movements became faster, his blows deadlier, until he was spinning around like a dervish, Cuthbert Junior held out before him like a whirling scythe of destruction. Incubi screamed as they flew through the air, bleeding and broken, and Jinx's laughter increased in volume until it became the only sound we could hear. Never had Jinx seemed more like a monster to me than he did then, but at least he was *my* monster, and in this fashion we made our way through the Cesspit toward Newtown.

As we traveled, we began to see more vacant lots where buildings had once stood, and we even saw several vanish. It happened so quickly. One instant they were there, the next they weren't. Driving became easier as many of the Incubi battling in the street also disappeared, leaving fewer obstacles for Jinx and the wraiths to remove. The Fata Morgana and I witnessed and remembered the people and places that were excised, but Connie didn't. She was completely unaware that anything changed. In a way, her obliviousness was a blessing, as it allowed her to remain calm while she drove.

Newtown doesn't exactly have skyscrapers, but many of the buildings are modern steel and glass and multistoried. It does have a skyline, albeit a modest one, and as we drew nearer I could see that it had changed. Maybe as many as a third of the largest buildings were gone, leaving gaps through which only the Canopy's illusion of stars could be seen.

At least none of the streets were gone – yet – and eventually we reached the Sick House. I feared we'd get there and find an empty space where the hospital had once been, but it was still there, looking as nightmarish as ever. Connie pulled the Deathmobile up to the main entrance, where Jinx waited, sitting on the curb and mopping his brow with a large polka-dotted handkerchief, a gore-smeared Cuthbert Junior lying next to him. The wraiths dove back into the Deathmobile, entering the coffin in the back until such time as they were needed again.

The Fata Morgana and I got out of the Deathmobile, and, immediately, something struck me as wrong. I looked skyward and saw that, while the Canopy's stars were still there, Espial was gone.

I turned back to speak to Connie through the open passenger door.

"Do you mind waiting out here?" I asked. "After this, I want to go to the Rookery and check on the Unwakened."

"Sure," Connie said. Then she added, "It's really real, isn't it? The disappearances, I mean."

"Are you starting to see them?" I asked.

"No. But there's a lot of empty space in Nod. I mean, a *lot*. And while part of me thinks that's perfectly normal, another part is sure it's wrong." She glanced up. "And there's something not right about the sky too, but I don't know what."

"It'll be okay," I told her. "Once Jinx and I see Melody, we'll go to the Rookery. If we have to, we'll rouse one of the Unwakened and see if he or she can tell us what's happening and how to fix it."

I know what you're thinking. If the Unwakened could stop the excisions, why didn't we head straight to the Rookery? Because I was lying to Connie. I had no idea how to wake one of the master dreamers, and, even if I did, I didn't know how dangerous it might be. It was possible the Unwakened were already fighting whatever force was causing the excisions, which would explain why they were happening slowly instead of all at once. If we woke one of them, we might very well weaken the group to the point where they could no longer fight, and that would be the end of everything. But I felt I had to tell Connie something. I couldn't stand the thought of her sitting behind the wheel of the Deathmobile, waiting for us and becoming more frightened with each passing moment.

Connie probably knew I was lying. She's no dummy. But she smiled and nodded, showing me that she appreciated my attempt to reassure her. The Fata Morgana surely knew I was full of shit, but she didn't call me on it, and for that I was grateful.

"What now?" the Fata Morgana asked.

"Now you get back in the car and wait with Connie," I said.

Anger clouded her face, and I thought she might argue, but then the energy drained out of her and she sighed.

"Fine. I'm tired anyway. I'm not the Incubus I once was."

She got back into the Deathmobile, but, before she could close the door, I said, "Do you think you can contact the other Lords?" I almost added, *If any are left*.

"I could try contacting them telepathically, I suppose. But, as I said, I'm rather tired."

"Give it your best shot. At this point, the Lords of Misrule might be Nod's – and Earth's – only hope."

She raised an eyebrow at that, but she nodded, and then, with an effort, she pulled the Deathmobile's door shut.

Jinx tossed his sopping handkerchief aside, and it hit the concrete with a wet *smack*. He picked up a gore-smeared Cuthbert Junior and walked over to join me. He was covered with blood from head to toe, and I wondered if he should start wearing a plastic coverall over his uniform. It would save a ton on dry cleaning.

The two of us started toward the Sick House's entrance.

"Allying with the Lords?" Jinx said. "Sounds like a plan *I* would've come up with."

"Fucked-up times call for fucked-up measures," I said.

"True dat," Jinx said.

The double glass doors opened automatically for us, and we stepped inside. The reception area still had the acrid medicine and bleach odor that hospitals always seem to have, no matter the dimension. But the area was empty, and very, very quiet.

"Maybe everyone's in the rest room," Jinx said.

"Let's go see if Menendez is in his office."

"I'm telling you, we should check the crappers first."

As we made our way through the corridors of the Sick House, we continued to see and hear a whole lot of nothing. We peeked into a few patient rooms, but they were all empty, the beds made as if no one had ever used them.

"I've never slept, so I've never dreamed," Jinx said. "But from what you've told me, and what I've seen in movies and on TV, as well as what I – or at least Sunshine Boy – has read, this is kind of like being in a dream, isn't it?"

Sunshine Boy is how Night Jinx sometimes refers to his Day Aspect.

He went on. "We're walking through a deserted hospital, the only sounds our breathing and our footsteps... I assume this is the sort of experience that humans find disquieting."

"Yeah," I said. "Now that you mention it, this *is* like a scenario out of a nightmare." I wasn't liking where this conversation was going. "Are you suggesting that we're trapped in dream?"

He shrugged. "That's what the Church of the First Dreamer believes, isn't it? That all of us exist inside the First Dreamer's dream? So, what if that dream's gotten messed up somehow?"

Jinx's words shook me to the core. Maybe the Wakening prophesied in the *Primongenium* actually *was* happening. I wanted to tell Jinx that he was full of shit, especially because I was afraid he wasn't. But, before I could say anything, the sound of slow clapping came from behind us.

"I never would've guessed the clown would figure it out." A woman's voice. "You?"

"Never in a million years." Another woman.

I recognized both voices, and when Jinx and I turned around we found ourselves facing Melody and Trauma Doll.

THIRTEEN

Melody aimed one of the strange obsidian hand weapons at us – the kind that bored through flesh and bone as if they were butter – and Trauma Doll was wrapped in her barbed wire coils once again.

"You're looking remarkably well, Melody," I said. Jinx's reaction was less restrained.

"Honey-pie!" He rushed forward, arms spread wide, clearly intending to envelop Trauma Doll in a big bear hug. Trauma Doll's porcelain features twisted into a sneer, and she flicked her right arm. Coils of barbed wire shot forward, she swept her arm sideways, and the wire struck Jinx like a whip. Barbs cut into the right side of his face, shredding his chalk-white skin. Blood gushed from his wounds and splattered onto the tiled floor.

"Aw, sweetie," Jinx said. "I," – he paused to spit out some blood that had gotten in his mouth – "I love you too."

Despite his words, his gaze was ice-cold.

"But before we go any further…" He reached into his pocket and removed a tuning fork. He slapped it against the palm of his hand, and the fork vibrated, emitting a high-pitched tone.

The deadly black weapon began to shake in Melody's hand, and then it exploded in a shower of ebon crystals. She swore and averted her face, but some of the shards still managed to cut into her hand and neck.

"Another toy you picked up at *Misery Loves Company*?" I asked Jinx.

He grinned as he put the tuning fork away. "Yep. Just in case."

Melody turned to face us once more, her neck and cheek stippled with blood. "Null guns are kick-ass weapons, but, unfortunately, they're a bit fragile." She wore a trancer holstered at her side, and she drew it now. "Trancers might not pack the same punch, but they *are* sturdier."

Blood from her wounded hand flowed around the trancer's handle and dripped onto the floor. She glanced down.

"Inconvenient, but easily mended," Melody said. "Especially when you share your body with an Incubus."

Her form blurred and she became the Gingerdread Man. He still held the trancer on us.

"Or two," he said.

His form blurred, and became the bat-headed woman who'd followed us to Deadlock. She grinned. "They call me Badfang," she said, and then another shift occurred and Melody stood before us once more. The wounds on her face, neck, and hand were gone.

"I could've healed the damage Montrose did to me anytime," she said. "All I had to do was let one of the Incubi take over. Their healing powers would've taken care of my injuries within a matter of moments." She smiled. "As you just saw."

"But you didn't, because you didn't want to give yourself – or maybe I should say *selves* – away," I said.

I looked at Trauma Doll. The coils she'd lashed Jinx with had wrapped themselves back around her arm, and Jinx's blood dripped from the barbs.

"I suppose you're Demonique and the giant earwig," I said.

"Sligan is his name," she said, "and yes."

Jinx's facial wound still bled like hell, but was already in the process of healing.

"I'm an open-minded guy," he said, "and ordinarily I'd be willing to explore a polyamorous relationship, but I have a real thing about earwigs. They are, in a word, ass-nasty."

Trauma Doll's body blurred and was replaced by the giant insect. Sligan stood upright, but he fell forward onto his six legs and scuttled toward Jinx, large mandibles click-clacking as he came. Jinx – his wound still looking awful but no longer bleeding – drew Cuthbert Junior and slammed the hammer down on Sligan's head. There was a horrible crunching sound and whitish gunk splattered over the floor. Sligan's mandibles stopped click-clacking, and his segmented legs twitched spasmodically.

"Okay," Jinx said, "*now* we can talk. I think Demonique is kind of hot anyway."

Sligan transformed into Demonique, and she shoved Jinx's hammer aside, moved into a crouching position, opened her mouth wide, and released a gout of flame.

"That hot enough for you?" she said.

The flames engulfed Jinx and he dropped Cuthbert Junior and started jumping around, screaming, "Too hot! Too hot!"

For an instant, I felt Jinx's pain as if it were my own, and I thought we'd switched bodies. But it didn't happen. I still felt our link, but I didn't feel the same irresistible pull to switch that I'd experienced before. Maybe Jinx was purposely keeping me out of his body to spare me pain. Or maybe something else was happening – or, more to the point, *not* happening.

Jinx pulled a giant water balloon the size of a beanbag chair from his jacket and hit himself in the face with it. The balloon exploded, water gushed, and the fire went out, leaving him looking like a scorched and drowned rat.

He looked at Demonique as she rose to her feet.

"Some guys don't like it when a woman comes on too strong, but I consider it a challenge." He grinned, displaying teeth as sharp as a shark's.

Demonique didn't make another move to attack, and Jinx picked up his hammer but kept his distance. He can take a lot of damage, even for an Incubus, but he would use every moment of healing he could get before the fighting began in earnest.

I looked at Melody.

"You both took *two* hits of shuteye?"

She nodded. "Not everyone can host even one Discarnate. Your mentor went crazy with just one in him. But Trauma Doll and I are special."

Demonique blurred into Trauma Doll and grinned at Melody.

"You got that right, sister. Tough as fucking nails, that's us."

"Where's Menendez?" I asked.

"Not here," Melody said. "No one's here, except for us."

"We've got the whole place to ourselves," Trauma Doll said. She smiled. "Lots of room to play."

"I assume you're both Wakenists," I said.

"Yes," Melody said. "Reality is fucked up, especially Earthside. Poverty, war, pollution, climate change, racism, sexism… I could go on, but you get the point. Reality isn't a dream; it's a nightmare."

"Time to hit the reset button," Trauma Doll said. "Start over and get it right this time."

"And how do you plan to do that?" I asked. "Wake up the First Dreamer – assuming he's real and you can actually find him – and force him to dream reality the way you want it to be?"

"He's real, all right," Trauma Doll said. "And finding him is no great trick. He's in the Idyllon, where he's always been."

Her words caught me off guard. "Seriously?"

"Sure," Melody said. "Just like the Unwakened sleep on the highest level of the Rookery, the First Dreamer sleeps at the top of the Idyllon, in the Sacrarium. The Idyllon was the first thing the Dreamer brought into existence. Nod formed around it, and then, once he fell deeper into sleep, he created Earth's universe, and everything in it."

"Only the highest of priests know the truth, though," Trauma Doll said. "The Church doesn't want the truth to get out, or else every Wakenist nutcase would try to break into the Sacrarium and wake the Dreamer."

"So, how did you find out the truth?" I asked.

"Shuteye," Jinx said. "One of the priests took some and became host to a Discarnate."

"Something like that," Melody said. "The Discarnate realized they could control the First Dreamer, they could alter reality and gain new bodies of their own. So shuteye was brought to the Idyllon, and the church's upper echelon was *encouraged* to take it – one way or another. Some died, some went insane, but the majority became hosts for other Discarnate."

"And they began trying to rouse the First Dreamer," I said.

"And they reached out to Wakenists to host other Discarnate to infiltrate various Earth and Nod institutions – such as the Shadow Watch – to make sure no one could interfere with them."

"You were an important assignment for us," Trauma Doll said. "We had to bust our asses to get assigned as your trainees, but, after you stopped the Fata Morgana, everyone thought you two were hot shit, and the Discarnate figured you might be able to stop us if you got wind of what was happening."

"You could've killed us at any time," I said. "Why wait so long?"

"No point in showing our hand before we had to," Melody said. "But, after the incident with Montrose, it was decided you'd become more trouble than you were worth, and we got the word to take you out."

"Who gave the word?" I asked.

"What does it matter?" Trauma Doll said. "You managed to give us a good chase, but it's over now."

"Killing you isn't even going to be much fun," Melody said. "It's not like you're going to give us any challenge."

"Right," Trauma Doll said. "You aren't heroes. Not even close. You're just a couple of screw-ups who get lucky once in a while. But now your luck's run out."

"We may be a couple screw-ups," I said, "but we're

still going to kick your asses. All six of them."

"Five," Jinx reminded me. "I squashed the bug, remember?"

"Right. Forgot about that."

"Besides, since he was a bug, I don't think he technically *had* an ass."

"Point noted."

Melody and Trauma Doll exchanged glances. They no longer looked quite as confident as they had a moment ago.

"You get that we lured you here to kill you, right?" Melody said. "Demonique called you and pretended to be a nurse. You'd heard her voice the least, so we figured you wouldn't recognize it."

"Of course, you won't stay dead," Trauma Doll said. "When the New Dream begins, you'll be brought back into existence. But you'll have had an attitude adjustment."

"You'll like the New Dream," Melody said. "Everyone will. They won't have a choice."

"But that's cool because it will be the ultimate utopia," Trauma Doll said. "Who wouldn't love it?"

"Think of it," Melody said. "No more crime, no more suffering. No more division between humans and Incubi. It's going to be glorious!"

"And how's this New Dream going to come into being?" I asked.

"None of your damn business," Trauma Doll snapped. "You think we're dumb enough to stand here and let you pump us for information?"

Now it was Jinx's and my turn to exchange looks.

"She's kidding, right?" I said.

"If they keep up like they have been, we're going to

know their bank account numbers and their Internet passwords," Jinx said. His face was completely healed by now, and he gripped Cuthbert Junior tight. He was back at full strength and ready for action.

"I think we've gotten all we're going to get out of them," I said.

"I concur." Jinx grinned inhumanly wide. "Time to cause some damage."

He hurled Cuthbert Junior toward Melody. She transformed into Gingerdread Man and, with his speed, easily sidestepped the hammer. The Gingerdread Man's cookie hands were shaped like mittens – one fingerless mass with a thick opposable thumb – and he couldn't fire Melody's trancer, let alone maintain a solid grip on it. The gun fell to the floor as Jinx's hammer flew through the space where Gingerdread Man had been standing and slammed into the wall behind. The sledge bashed a large hole and stuck there, the handle sticking out.

Trauma Doll shot her barbed wire coils at me, and I dove to the side, pain shooting through the shoulder wound I'd sustained when the Darkun's shard had struck me. Without Jinx's healing ability, I couldn't afford to let Trauma Doll's barbs cut into my flesh. The coils lashed through the air over my head as I hit, rolled, and came back up onto my feet. I quickly shrugged off my jacket and wrapped it around my left arm. The cloth wouldn't be much protection against Trauma Doll's coils, but at least it was something.

Gingerdread Man raced toward Jinx, moving inhumanly fast. But Jinx can also move pretty damn fast when he wants to. Before Gingerdread Man could reach him, Jinx raised his right leg and pointed the

bottom of his enormous shoe at the onrushing Incubus.
The shoe bottom flipped open and a coiled spring shot
forward. It struck Gingerdread Man in the stomach and
drilled a large hole through his abdomen. Bits of cookie
sprayed the air, and Gingerdread Man – who'd built up
some serious momentum – continued moving forward.
The result: he broke in two, and both halves fell to the
floor. Jinx's spring retracted, the shoe bottom *snicked*
back into place, and he lowered his foot.

Trauma Doll saw Gingerdread Man go down, and
she forgot about me. She spun toward Jinx, changed
into Demonique, and unleashed a burst of flame at
him. I didn't wait to see what happened. I started
running for the trancer that Gingerdread Man had
dropped. As I ran, I began to feel the familiar dizziness
that told me Jinx and I were on the verge of
exchanging bodies, but I did my best to fight it. Jinx
and I had gotten used to fighting while inhabiting each
other's body, but, if we exchanged now, we'd be dead
within seconds. Not only were Trauma Doll and
Melody dangerous enough on their own, their ability
to allow the Discarnates they hosted to take over their
bodies made them much more deadly. Jinx and I
couldn't afford so much as a moment's hesitation or
confusion if we hoped to survive. So, no Blending. Not
if I could help it.

As I made for the trancer, I caught a glimpse of
Gingerdread Man, or, rather, his two halves. He didn't
appear to be in any pain, but his top half was using its
hands to pull itself toward his bottom. I thought that it
must be inconvenient being a living cookie, and I
wondered what would happen if he were dropped into
a giant glass of milk.

I reached the trancer, snatched it up off the floor, and spun around in time to see Jinx – once again on fire, thanks to Demonique – hurling handfuls of razor-edged confetti at the reptilian Incubus. The confetti swirled around her like a mini tornado, each tiny piece slicing into her scaled flesh again and again, until she was covered with small bleeding wounds. Each wound wasn't much in and of itself, but there were hundreds upon hundreds of pieces of confetti, and they quickly transformed her into a blood-soaked mess. She howled in pain and fury and attempted to burn the confetti with her flame, but there was simply too much of it for her to destroy. Blood pooled on the floor around her feet and began expanding outward.

I would've loved to stand by and watch as Jinx's confetti stripped the flesh from her bones, but I *am* supposed to be one of the good guys. I moved into position so that I was standing behind Demonique and then I raised my trancer. At that exact instant, she transformed into Trauma Doll. Her porcelain skin was unmarked and free of blood, although there was still plenty of it pooled around her feet. The razor confetti continued swirling around her, its edges striking her skin with tiny pinging sounds without doing any harm. From where I stood, I couldn't see her grin, but I could hear it in her voice when she spoke to Jinx.

"What are you going to do now, Lover Boy?"

While the confetti had been slicing into Demonique's skin, Jinx had used another huge water balloon to put out his latest fire. His clothes were scorched and half burned away, and his chalk-white skin was covered with blackened patches, making him look like a human-shaped burned marshmallow. Half of his face was a ruin, and, when he spoke, his words came out slurred.

"I'm going to stand here and watch while Audra drops you like a deadbeat boyfriend."

I fired.

The trancer was set to low, and the M-energy beam that lanced from its muzzle struck Trauma Doll at the base of the skull without damaging her. The impact knocked her out of the confetti tornado and toward Jinx. I thought that he might hit her with his shoe spring, but he stepped aside and watched as she fell face-first to the floor. There was the sound of porcelain cracking, but her body remained intact. Until, that is, Jinx stepped forward, raised his foot, and brought it down hard on Trauma Doll's head. There was a loud *crack-pop!* and shards of porcelain skittered across the floor. Trauma Doll's body spasmed a couple times, and then fell still. When Jinx raised his foot, all that was left of Trauma Doll's head was bits and pieces. One eye had remained mostly intact, though, and Jinx bent down and picked it up.

"I'm sorry, but I have to break up with you. Or maybe that should be break *you* up."

He let out one of his hyena cackles and tucked the eye into his jacket pocket.

In general, I've made my peace with having a psychotic clown for a partner, but sometimes he still makes me want to pee my pants.

While Jinx and I had been dealing with Trauma Doll, Gingerdread Man had managed to pull himself together. His two halves hadn't fused yet, but just their touching each other must've been enough to allow him to switch forms. He blurred and became the bat creature called Badfang.

Badfang jumped to her feet, opened her mouth wide – displaying the sharp incisors that had undoubtedly inspired her name – and released an ear-splitting screech. It felt like someone had rammed white-hot daggers into my ears, and I dropped the trancer and pressed my hands over them in a vain attempt to shut the sound out. Badfang's sonic attack had to be occurring on multiple levels, ultrasonic and subsonic included. I could feel sound vibrations pounding into my body, and I wouldn't have been surprised if I was being shaken apart at the molecular level.

Jinx wasn't faring any better. Incubi tend to have sharper senses than humans, and I know the sound assault was affecting him worse than it was me. He fell to one knee and jammed his fists against his ears, pushing so hard I feared he'd grind the cartilage to a pulp. Agony twisted his features, at least those that hadn't been burned to a crisp.

Badfang's screeching rose in pitch, and the pain – which was already worse than any I'd ever experienced – doubled. But then the air behind Badfang shimmered and Bloodshedder quite literally leaped out of nowhere. Her front paws slammed into Badfang's back and her claws sank deep into flesh. Badfang's sonic attack ceased as Bloodshedder's weight and momentum drove the batwoman to the floor. The impact broke loose a number of her teeth, incisors included, and blood gushed from her mouth. Bloodshedder didn't stop there, though. The demon dog fastened her jaws onto Badfang's neck, bit down, and gave a single, savage shake. There was a sickening crack, and Badfang's body went limp.

Bloodshedder let go of the batwoman, stepped back,

and sat on her haunches, happily wagging her spiked tail. A little thing like a broken neck wouldn't keep an Incubus down for long, but it would take her some time to recover.

I was about to ask Bloodshedder where Russell was – afraid that maybe he *wasn't* anymore – when he stepped out of the shimmering portal. It vanished the instant he set foot on the Sick House's tiled floor. He was dressed in his full Nocturne costume, with a brand-new cape, but with two important differences. One was that he wasn't wearing his M-rapier. It had been left at Deadlock, and evidently the Thresholders hadn't retrieved it for him. The second change was far more striking. His left arm – the one that had been almost torn off at the prison – was bare, and, instead of flesh and bone, it was made of multicolored solidified Maelstrom energy, just as his rapier had been.

"Sorry it took me a minute to come through," he said. "The amount of M-energy my new arm gives off destabilizes the Thresholders' portals a little. Makes going through one kind of like walking through a wall of cold molasses."

My ears rang like hell, and I couldn't quite make out what he was saying. I didn't care, though. I was just glad to see him alive. I wanted to run to him and hug him, but my entire body hurt like a motherfucker, and I feared that, if I tried to take even a single step, I'd scream.

Jinx, of course, was recovering more quickly. He didn't appear to be in pain anymore, and his burns, while still damn nasty, were in the process of healing. Half of his jacket had been burned away, but he still had a couple pockets left. He reached into one, brought out a rev inhaler, and tossed it to me.

I caught it, my body shrieking in protest for making it move.

"I know you don't want to rely on that stuff," Jinx said, "but we've got work to do. Now's not the time to be a martyr."

I caught enough of what Jinx said to get the gist of it. With a trembling hand, I put the inhaler into my mouth and started to activate it. But I didn't. I'd worked too long and too hard to get clean, and I wasn't going to give that up.

"Thanks, but I think I'll play through the pain."

I dropped the inhaler on the ground and stomped on it. The casing cracked, rendering the device useless.

The smile on Jinx's face would've been right at home on his Day Aspect.

I walked – or more accurately hobbled – over to Russell. I started to reach out to touch his new arm, but I hesitated.

He smiled, a little shakily I thought. He was trying to act like what had happened to him was no big deal, but I could tell it bothered him. Who could blame him? It's not every day a guy loses his arm and gets a shiny new one.

"It's okay," he said. "The energy's not volatile in solidified form."

I touched it and found it cold, smooth, and hard as marble. I withdrew my hand, and he flexed his new arm and wiggled the fingers. They moved a little stiffly, but, overall, the arm seemed to work just fine. It was unbelievable. Even the Shadow Watch's most talented M-gineers could only create small objects from solid M-energy. But the Thresholders had been able to craft a working prosthetic arm from the stuff.

"Can you feel anything with it?" I asked. "You know, like a–" I broke off, suddenly embarrassed.

"Real arm?" He smiled to show he wasn't bothered by what I'd almost said. "Not exactly. I can feel pressure, but that's about it. Maybe it'll get more sensitive in time. It's still pretty new."

He flexed his arm again, this time making a fist.

"The Thresholders can do some amazing things, but they're not great with repairing flesh and blood, considering that they don't have any of their own. But they're geniuses when it comes to shaping energy."

There was so much I wanted to say to him. But, before I could speak, I heard the sepulchral sound of the Deathmobile's horn honking, one blast after another, as if she – or Connie – was trying to get our attention. Or worse, sound an alarm.

I picked up the trancer while Jinx ran to the wall and pulled Cuthbert Junior free. Then the four of us started running down the corridor to the hospital's main entrance.

When we stepped out of the Sick House, the scene that awaited us was so disorienting that for a moment I thought Jinx and I were on the verge of switching bodies again.

The rest of the Canopy had disappeared. The black sky was replaced by the turbulent ever-roiling energies of the Maelstrom, swirling colors that combined, broke apart, and recombined in endless combinations, none of which there were names for. The Maelstrom gives off a dim, multicolored light, not very intense, something like dusk on Earth, so we could still see, but not very well.

The Fata Morgana still sat in the front seat of the Deathmobile next to Connie. Connie looked uneasy, but the Fata Morgana looked downright terrified. I knew exactly how she felt.

Jinx, Russell, Bloodshedder and I climbed into the Deathmobile. The others got in the back while I slid onto the seat next to the Fata Morgana.

"It happened when you were inside," she said. "The Canopy just... vanished."

"Can you take us to the Idyllon?" I asked Connie. I didn't know if there was anything we could do to stop what was happening, but we had to try.

She nodded, put the Deathmobile in gear, and pulled away from the Sick House. The streets of Newtown were almost completely deserted now, and I wondered if the situation was as bad on Earth. I decided it probably was even worse. Earth was much bigger than Nod, and, because of this, there was so much more to lose.

"I don't understand what's happening," Russell said. "How is this all possible?"

I gave him the Cliff Notes version of everything that had happened since he'd been wounded in Deadlock.

"So the First Dreamer is real?" he said, when I was finished. "The Thresholders never told me that." He sounded more irritated at his employers than amazed to discover that God was real and slept at the top of Idyllon.

"Or maybe whoever is trying to wake the First Dreamer is able to pick and choose who and what gets excised," Jinx said.

Now *there* was a disturbing thought.

"But if that's true," Russell said, "why are you two still here? Or Bloodshedder and me? As far as we know, we're the only ones who know someone is trying to wake the Dreamer. Wouldn't it make more sense for whoever is pulling the strings to have the Dreamer get rid of us?"

"Maybe whoever it is doesn't have that kind of fine control," I said. "Getting rid of the Canopy, no problem. Focusing on and eliminating individuals might not be so easy."

"And maybe the Dreamer doesn't want us gone," Jinx said.

"So the Dreamer's trying to help us?" I asked.

Jinx shrugged. "How the hell should I know? I'm just a lunatic clown who's evidently not lunatic enough." He crossed his arms and made a pouty face.

Russell gave me a questioning look, and I said, "Long story."

He let it go at that.

Jinx looked through one of the rear passenger windows, casting his gaze upward.

"Huh. There's something you don't see every day," he said.

I hate it when Jinx says things like that.

I *really* didn't want to look out the window, but, of course, I had to. When I did, I didn't understand at first what I was seeing. But after a second, I understood what he was talking about. Tendrils of Maelstrom energy stretched down from the sky – hundreds, thousands of them. They touched the tops of the highest buildings in Newtown, and, wherever they touched, matter dissolved, turning back into the Maelstrom energy it had been created from. Without the Unwakened – who I assumed had been excised now – and without the Canopy, there was nothing to hold the Maelstrom back. It was only a matter of time before Nod, and everyone in it, was destroyed. I'd experienced a lot of emotional blows over the last twenty-four hours or so. The deaths of Nathaniel and Mordacity. The excision of Commander Sanderson and the rest of the Shadow Watch. The discovery of Melody and Trauma Doll's betrayal. The realization that someone was attempting to wake the First Dreamer. And now this: the imminent destruction of the city which, insane as it was at times, had become a second home to me. Not to mention that this destruction would also result in the deaths of Jinx, Russell, Bloodshedder, Connie, the Deathmobile, the Fata Morgana, and myself.

I had been through, as they say, an emotional wringer, and I was wrung the hell out. I had nothing left, so, when I saw the M-energy tendrils reaching downward and beginning to unmake the buildings, I felt no fear, no sorrow, no *This is how the world ends. Not with a bang, but with a whimper*. The only thing I felt was pissed off. Reality had been chugging away for who knew how many billions of years, and now some douche nozzles were going to delete it and overwrite it with their version?

Fuck that.

"We need to get to the Idyllon before the Maelstrom swallows us up," I told Connie. "How fast can the Deathmobile go?"

She looked scared as hell, but she managed a grin. "Pretty goddamned fast."

She tromped down on the gas pedal, and the Deathmobile's engine roared in response. But, just as the hearse leaped forward, an M-energy tendril stretched down in front of us and touched the street. Instantly, asphalt disappeared, along with a huge section of the ground beneath. The tendril slid sideways, continuing to unmake a swath of buildings in its path, but, although it moved out of our way, the damage was done. Connie slammed on the brake, and the Deathmobile skidded sideways as it desperately fought to avoid sliding into the gaping hole that now lay before us. The hearse managed to come to a stop less than a foot from the edge, and Connie let out a shaky breath and patted the dash.

"Good job, girl," she said.

"We're going to have to find another route," Russell said.

"Easier said than done," the Fata Morgana said. She pointed the way we had come, and we all turned to look.

Another tendril – larger and wider than the last – had touched down behind us, unmaking the street as well as the buildings on either side as it came sweeping toward the Deathmobile.

"It was nice knowing you all," Jinx said. He looked at the Fata Morgana. "Except you, of course."

A look of determination came over Connie's face. She leaned toward the Deathmobile's dash, and in a soft voice said, "Get them where they need to go."

The doors to the hearse sprang open. The wraiths exited their coffin, flew around to the sides of the vehicle, and spectral hands reached inside. They grabbed hold of us with their – you guessed it – icy grips, pulled us out of the Deathmobile, and lifted us into the air.

"Wait!" I shouted. "Connie, no!"

But the wraiths carried us away from the Deathmobile with increasing speed. I looked back over my shoulder and saw the other wraiths carrying Jinx, Russell, and Bloodshedder. Not the Fata Morgana, though, and not Connie. I understood what was happening. Connie knew there was an excellent chance the Deathmobile would reach the Idyllon, and she wanted to make sure we did. Several wraiths remained behind, and they wrapped themselves around the Deathmobile, and, just as the M-energy tendril reached the vehicle, there was a green flash of light, and it was gone.

"What happened?" Russell shouted. "Were they destroyed?"

"I don't know." It was clear the wraiths had tried to do something to protect the Deathmobile, Connie, and the Fata Morgana, but I had no idea if they'd succeeded. I hoped they had.

I mentally thanked Connie, and then I faced forward, ready for whatever came next.

FOURTEEN

An increasing number of Maelstrom-energy tendrils reached down from the sky and continued to unmake Nod, and the wraiths had to swerve wildly to avoid them. While the wraiths appeared to be separate ghostly beings with existences of their own, I knew they were in truth only projections of the Deathmobile, but I didn't know how long they could continue to exist apart from her. If they ceased to exist while we were in the air... well, let's just say it wouldn't be happy landings for us.

As we flew, we saw the Loco-Motive sitting immobile on its tracks. Half of its engine was gone, and large sections of the tracks had been unmade. I wasn't sure, but I thought I saw an empty conductor's uniform lying on the ground nearby. We also passed over *Misery Loves Company*. A group of clowns was battling M-energy tendrils in the street outside the coffee shop – Lowbrow and Hula Hoop Girl among them – using every bizarre weapon they could get their chalk-white hands on, but their efforts were futile, and I knew how their fight would end.

Soon the Idyllon's white tower came into view, and

the first thing I noticed was that no Maelstrom tendrils were reaching for it. The sky above the tower was a seething storm of multicolored energy, but it kept its distance.

"Set us down at the edge of the courtyard!" I called out.

I wanted to get our feet back on the ground before the wraiths vanished.

They swooped downward, and for an instant I thought we were going to make it, but then – with less than fifteen feet to go – the wraiths vanished. There was nothing flashy or remarkable about it. No burst of light, no *pop!* as air rushed in to fill the space they'd inhabited. They were here one instant and then they weren't.

And we fell.

Jinx and Bloodshedder landed easily enough, and Russell managed to get his new arm underneath him, land palm-first, spring himself upward, and then come down on his feet like an Olympic gymnast. Show-off. Me? I did my best to tuck and roll, but I hit awkwardly and felt a couple ribs snap. White fire lanced through the left side of my chest, and, when I got to my feet, I couldn't stand straight and I pressed my hand to my side. Bad idea. The pressure only intensified the pain, and I yelped.

"Are you all right?" Russell asked. He started toward me to help, but I waved him off.

"I'll live." I glanced up at the chaotic mass of energy overhead. It was still keeping its distance from the Idyllon, but I didn't know how long that condition would last. We had to hurry.

I knew the disappearance of the wraiths meant the Deathmobile had been destroyed, but I couldn't afford to think about that right then. We had work to do, and not much time to do it in. I had a lot of people to mourn, and I added the Deathmobile to the list. If I survived, I'd honor their memories later. And if I didn't, then it wouldn't matter.

"Jinx, do you–"

I'd been about to ask if he had anything in his pockets that I could use to wrap around my chest for a brace, but, when I saw him, my words died in my throat. Not only were all his wounds healed, his clothing had been restored and cleaned. More than that, he exuded energy, so much that the air seemed to almost crackle around him. His features were sharper, the colors of his skin and clothing more intense. It was as if he'd been turbo-charged and because of it was more *there*. The same thing had happened to Bloodshedder: her body was slightly larger, her scales harder and shinier, her teeth, claws, and tail spikes bigger and sharper. Her eyes blazed with a feral light that I'd never seen in them before. Russell flexed his new arm, and it was glowing now, pulsing with multicolored light as if it had absorbed all the M-energy it could hold and then some.

"Without the Canopy blocking the Maelstrom, M-energy is flooding into Nod," Russell said. "It's obviously having an effect on us."

"I feel *GRRRRRRRREAT!!!*" Jinx said, the last word coming out as a roar that would've done any jungle cat proud.

Bloodshedder let out an excited bark, and her spiked tail thumped the ground, tearing up chunks of the stone courtyard.

I checked my trancer. It was warm to the touch, and

the power readout showed it had a full charge. But I suspected it held even more than that. I decided to keep the trancer until it became too hot to hold. I had the feeling I was going to need it. I realized then that my wisper was warm against my wrist and getting warmer with each second. I slipped it off and dropped it to the ground. I didn't want the damn thing burning its way through my flesh and down to the bone beneath. Russell wore his wisper on his right arm, but he switched it to his left. Jinx didn't remove his. As charged as he was with M-energy, I doubted he felt the device heating up.

"Going into battle with power-ups?" Russell said. "Sounds good to me!"

"Until you three overload and explode," I said. I didn't know if that would happen, but there had to be a limit on how much Maelstrom energy bodies – or prosthetic arms – could hold. I had no idea what would happen once that limit was reached, and I hoped we wouldn't find out.

I made the mistake of trying to stand up straight again, and my ribs screamed at me.

"Uh, Jinx," I said, once I was able to breathe again. "A little help?"

He thought for a moment, grinned, reached into his newly restored jacket pocket, and pulled out a canister of aerosol string. I didn't bat an eye.

"Russell, help me get my jacket off."

I slipped my jacket back on by myself, although it wasn't easy. Jinx's aerosol string was sturdier and more durable than the regular kind, and, while it braced my damaged ribs, it was awkward to move.

My trancer had heated to the point where it was uncomfortable to hold for long, so I'd holstered it. When the time came to use it, I hoped I'd be able to maintain a grip long enough to get off a decent shot.

In the time it had taken Jinx to wrap my ribs, the Maelstrom had enveloped even more of the city, until only the blocks immediately surrounding the Idyllon remained. Sometimes in scary stories there's a part where the protagonist encounters something so big, so awful, so unimaginable that she can feel her sanity slipping away. I'd always thought such scenes were melodramatic exaggerations, but seeing how little of Nod still existed at that moment, I understood that it was possible for one's mind to become so overloaded with horror that it would snap like a toothpick. I understood because I could feel myself losing it. For all we knew, the entire universe was gone, and there was nothing left but the Idyllon and its courtyard. And us. How could the four of us, even with the Incubi super-charged, hope to hold back the Maelstrom from devouring the last crumb of reality left? We couldn't. All we could do was stand there and gape while the multicolored energy rolled in like a measureless wave and engulfed us. We wouldn't die, though. We'd be *unmade*.

It was a near thing, but I managed to hold onto my sanity – but only because I felt Jinx's presence through the link we shared. Our connection was even stronger now, doubtless due to the proximity of so much Maelstrom energy, and I could almost read Jinx's thoughts. He didn't want to be unmade any more than I did, but seeing the Maelstrom up close and personal like this didn't scare him. It thrilled him. He was, at his core, a creature of chaos, and he now gazed upon the full force of ultimate Chaos – the Maelstrom. In a way, it was almost like he was gazing on the face of his god, and it was glorious.

So I used my partner's insanity to bolster my sanity. Maybe it doesn't make sense, but it worked. I felt my panic receding, and, while my fear didn't go away entirely, it became manageable.

Our link went two ways, and Jinx sensed the struggle I'd just gone through. He stepped close to me and put a hand on my shoulder.

"Just another day at the office," he said.

I managed a smile.

"Yeah."

"Look on the bright side," he said. "We haven't switched bodies for a while. I think we've got the Blending thing licked."

Jinx was right. We hadn't switched recently, despite the stress we'd experienced. It looked like Dr Menendez's treatment had worked. But it had been some time since we'd taken a dose of the medicine he'd given us. A thought came to me then, not so much as a rational conclusion but as a gut instinct. Maybe the reason Jinx and I had gotten better was *because* we hadn't taken the medicine lately. I remembered something Menendez had said to us in his office, after we'd paid Melody a visit.

The mind interacts with the Maelstrom in profound and mysterious ways. M-gineers can harness the power to a certain degree, of course, but imagine what we might be able to do if we could truly *come to understand it. To use it to our – and its – fullest capacity.*

"I know who's doing this," I said gently, almost as if speaking to myself. "I know who the Wakener is."

We needed to get inside the Idyllon fast, before it was too late – assuming that time hadn't already come and gone. My mind started swiftly analyzing possible approaches to the tower. The main entrance was out – it was bound to be guarded – and, as far as I knew, there were no other ground-level entrances. There were a number of windows. Jinx and Bloodshedder would be able to jump or climb to them, and, as strong as they now were, they should be able to carry Russell and me with ease. Hell, Russell might be able to climb up by himself with that new arm of his. But the question was, which window should we try?

"Audra?"

Not the highest one. He'd expect that. Probably one in the middle.

"Audra?"

"Not now, Jinx. I'm–"

I broke off when Jinx took hold of my jaw and turned my head toward the Idyllon's entrance. Ecclesiastor Withrow – the priest Jinx and I had encountered the last time we were here – was walking toward us. She appeared unarmed and she was smiling. I was immediately on guard. People are never as dangerous as when they seem harmless.

"Hello, everyone," she said as she reached us. "You've arrived at a most auspicious moment. I dare say the greatest moment of all."

"You mean the moment when a small group of lunatics screw up all Existence?" I said.

Withrow's brow furrowed slightly, and the edges of her mouth turned downward a bit, but she maintained her smile.

"So you're actually a Wakenist?" I said. "Or did you swallow a little pill and end up hosting an unexpected guest?"

"I don't have an Incubus spirit inside me," she said, almost shuddering at the notion. "I don't need one. I *am* a Wakenist, and I joined the Church only so I could get close to the First Dreamer. I once believed that *I* would be the one to wake him." She shook her head. "Foolish pride on my part. I was destined to play a role in the Wakening, yes, but as a servant to the *true* Wakener. He sent me out here to invite you into the Idyllon. He would very much like to speak with you."

"Let me guess," Jinx said. "By *speak with* he really means *kill*."

Withrow looked surprised. "Not at all. True, he hasn't exactly been helping you up to now, but at this point he could kill you all simply by wishing it. He truly does want to talk."

"And *then* he'll kill us," Russell said.

Bloodshedder growled in agreement.

Withrow shrugged. "That's for him to decide. But you might as well accept his invitation. It's not as if you have anywhere else to go."

She gestured toward the sky – or, rather, what had used to be the sky. There was only the Maelstrom now, and, in the time we'd been talking, it had closed in even farther, until now there was nothing left outside the Idyllon's courtyard.

I let out a deep sigh. "Lead the way."

I'd been inside the Idyllon before, as had Jinx. The Church doesn't conduct official worship services, but the bottom floor, called the Gatherum, is open to any and all, as a meeting place as well as a place for meditation. Whenever I'd needed to rest and for whatever reason couldn't get back to the apartment I shared with Jinx in Chicago, I'd come here. The floor is an elaborate tiled mosaic representing the Maelstrom, and the domed ceiling is painted with a starfield on which Earth and Nod sit side by side, the latter rendered significantly larger than it is in actuality. The Gatherum was usually filled with people, both Incubi and humans, all sitting on chairs or at tables, or just standing in small groups, talking. But it was empty now. Normally there was an atmosphere of calm, even tranquility in the Gatherum. But now it was merely silent.

Withrow led us to an elevator and pushed a button on the wall next to it. The door slid open with a soft *ping*, and she gestured for us to enter. As we did, Russell said, "As old as this place is, I figured we'd have to walk up a dozen flights of stone steps."

Withrow stepped onto the elevator last. There were a number of buttons on the inner control panel, but she pressed her thumb to the topmost button, which was unmarked. The button glowed for a moment, and she held her thumb there until it stopped glowing.

"DNA reader," she said. "Only the highest-ranking members of the Church are permitted to enter the Sacrarium." She smiled at Russell. "As you can see, we've made some upgrades over the years."

The door closed and the elevator started to rise. When we reached the top level of the Idyllon, the elevator stopped and the door slid open.

"Welcome to the Sacrarium," she said.

I was expecting… well, I don't know what, exactly. Something enormous, grandiose, awe-inspiring… a place worthy of a being who was, for all intents and purposes, God. But the Sacrarium was nothing more than a simple stone chamber in the middle of which lay a primitive bed made from a heap of palm leaves. Upon the leaves lay a small figure dressed in a plain brown tunic. The figure was barefoot and lay curled up on his side. The chamber possessed no obvious light source, but there was dim illumination nevertheless, enough to see by, but not so strong that it might disturb the sleeper. The figure remained completely motionless, but I could hear soft, regular breathing.

The sleeper wasn't the only person in the Sacrarium at the moment. Sitting cross-legged on the floor next to the bed of palm leaves was Menendez. He smiled as we stepped off the elevator and rose to his feet. He strode briskly over to us, and for a moment I thought he was going to stick out his hand for me to shake. But he stopped in front of me, smile still firmly in place.

"It's good to see you again, Audra. Believe it or not, I'm glad you're here. That all of you are."

Before I could answer, he gave Jinx a nod, and then turned toward Russell. "I'm afraid we haven't met. I'm Arthur Menendez. I am–" He broke off with a chuckle. "I *was* a Somnacologist at the Sick House."

"And now what are you?" Russell asked.

Menendez frowned as he thought. After a moment, he said, "I suppose I'm the Wakener."

Withrow bowed her head. "Yes, my lord. You are."

Jinx took a step toward Menendez, but I took hold of his arm to stop him. We couldn't attack the man, not yet. We didn't know enough about what was going on here. By acting too soon, we could make things even worse than they already were.

Menendez stepped over to the woman, placed an index finger under her chin, and gently raised her head until she looked him in the eye.

"I cannot tell you how grateful I am for everything you've done, Constance. Without your efforts, none of what we've accomplished could ever have come to pass. There might never have been a Wakening if it wasn't for you."

Withrow practically quivered with pleasure at the words of praise from the man she viewed as her messiah. He continued holding her gaze, but he now spoke to us.

"Constance oversaw the distribution of shuteye in the Idyllon. More importantly, she ensured that I was undisturbed during my sessions with the First Dreamer. It took quite a number of them to chip away at his mental defenses. Well, I say *his*, but I'm not certain the Dreamer has a gender. Not as we think of it, anyway."

I looked at the sleeping figure once more. It was small enough to be a child, anywhere between five and ten, I guessed. The Dreamer's physical form leaned toward the younger age, but there was something about the expression on his face that made him seem older. He had short brown hair, but there was a feminine quality to his features, even more than is sometimes normal for young males. His race was impossible to determine from looking at him. While his features never changed, he sometimes looked more European, or Asian, or African, or Hispanic. It was as if he wasn't changing so much as my perception of him did. The child looked so peaceful, so at rest, but most of all, he looked so *ordinary*. There was nothing about him to so much as hint that this was the most powerful being in existence, that the brain inside this small head was somehow connected on a primal level with the Maelstrom and had dreamed all of reality into being.

Menendez continued to look into Withrow's eyes as he spoke once more.

"And when I finally had my breakthrough with the Dreamer, she organized the… dismissal of the Discarnates, as their services were no longer required."

I didn't like the way Menendez hesitated before saying *dismissal*.

"Let me guess," I said. "You were the one who created shuteye in the first place."

Menendez took his hand away from Withrow's face and turned to look at me. He seemed irritated that Russell and I had interrupted his monologue.

"Yes. I first created it as a treatment for patients. It's a mild sleep aid treated with Maelstrom energy to make it effective for both Incubi and Ideators. But eventually I realized I could use it to help the Discarnate. I became aware of them early in my career. They're beings of pure consciousness, and, as a Somnacologist, the interaction of consciousness and M-energy is my specialty, after all. You're familiar with how Faders sometimes attempt to leech life energy from Incubi and even humans to sustain themselves? The Discarnate take it one step further; they attempt to possess the bodies of others. They are, however, rarely successful on their own. Some might view them as monsters, but I took pity on them. All they wished to do was continue to survive, after all, and I wanted to do everything I could to restore them to physical life. To that end, I modified the M-energy in shuteye so that it weakened the user's psychic defenses, allowing a

Discarnated spirit to much more easily enter and share someone's body. It wasn't an optimal solution, I admit, but it worked."

"It's only sharing if someone gives permission," I said.

Menendez went on as if I hadn't spoken. "Eventually, though, I realized that shuteye was only a temporary solution. One day the new hosts would die – sooner rather than later if they were human – and the Discarnate would be without bodies again. There had to be a better way, and then one night I came to the Gatherum to collect my thoughts, and it hit me. If I had the power of the First Dreamer, I could restore the Discarnate to corporeal form. But why should I stop there? I could fix all of Earth's *and* Nod's problems. I would be the first doctor to heal reality itself! But to do so, I needed full access to the Dreamer, which meant full access to the Idyllon. For that, I would need the help of many Discarnate, and that meant I needed more shuteye. The Sick House has – *had* – a pharmaceutical division to develop new medicines. But I could hardly use it to produce the amount of shuteye I needed for my plan."

"So you made a deal with the Angler's supplier," I said. "They'd manufacture shuteye for you, and they'd get to keep some to sell for themselves."

He nodded. "Yes, it was the Hand of Erebus." He made a face. "A criminal organization may not have been the most pleasant of business partners, but beggars can't be choosers. The deal also helped me further my plans, since I inspected every batch they produced and, using my abilities and some devices I designed for the task, I inserted a Discarnated spirit into each pill. As the number of the possessed increased – especially here in the Idyllon – I was able finally to make progress toward my real goal."

"Waking the First Dreamer," I said.

"The Wakening is only the first step," Withrow said. "The true miracle will occur afterward."

"You mean when Doctor Doomsday here hits the reset button on reality," Jinx said. "We already heard this bit from Melody and Trauma Doll."

"Believe it or not," Menendez said, "those two were once my patients. Their problem was the opposite of yours, though. They suffered from Disconnection, a lack of closeness between Incubus and Ideator. I helped them, of course, and, in the process, I discovered how remarkable they were. Their psyches were strong enough to allow them to host a pair of Discarnate each, and the fact they were both Wakenists made them sympathetic to my cause."

"You might understand the basic concept of our plan," Withrow said, giving Jinx a withering look, "but you cannot conceive of the glory that is to come." A look of regret crossed her face, and she sighed. "I only wish I could witness it."

"That sounds rather ominous," I said.

"The presence of other minds only interferes with the Wakener's work," Withrow said. "In the end, there can only be the Wakener and the Dreamer. And so I must depart."

Menendez stepped forward and embraced her. They held each other for a long moment, and, when they broke apart, he said, "You shall be restored in the world to come, I promise you."

She reached up to touch his cheek. Tears glistened in her eyes, but she smiled bravely. "I know."

Menendez then snapped his fingers and Withrow was gone, just like that.

He continued to look at the empty space she'd occupied.

"I'm going to miss her," he said. "At least, this version of her."

"How did you manage that nifty little trick?" I tried to sound nonchalant, but inside I was on the verge of pissing myself with terror. If Menendez had already somehow gained the Dreamer's power, we were well and truly fucked.

"It took quite some doing, but I've implanted a number of hypnotic commands in the Dreamer's subconscious," Menendez said. "Each has a corresponding trigger to activate it."

"I'm bored," Jinx said. "Can I stomp him now?"

"Not yet." We needed to learn as much as we could about Menendez's hold on the Dreamer if we were to have any chance of breaking it. Besides, if we did try to rush him, he might well activate one of his "commands" and cause the Dreamer to excise us from reality, just as he'd done with Withrow. When you're up against someone who's hijacked God's power, the direct approach won't work. You have to get sneaky.

I walked over to the Dreamer and gazed down at him. Menendez joined me, not hurrying, but not taking his time, either.

"Our talking doesn't seem to bother him," I said.

"He's been asleep for billions of years," Menendez said. "If he were that easy to wake, he would've done so long before now."

The others came over and joined us.

"How did you manage to get through to him?" Russell asked.

"I'm a Somnacologist," Menendez said. "Just as you and Audra were born Ideators, I was born with my abilities, which are primarily psychic in nature. When it comes to M-consciousness – the part of all beings that's connected to the Maelstrom – I'm like a master musician playing a relatively simple instrument. But reaching *this* consciousness" – he gestured to the Dreamer – "took all my knowledge and power. Now the Dreamer is on the verge of consciousness, but there's still one problem remaining. Or, I should say, *four* problems."

"Hey, he means us!" Jinx said.

"Indeed," Menendez confirmed. "Melody and Trauma Doll had already managed to infiltrate the Shadow Watch and get themselves assigned as your trainees. But after what happened with Montrose, I decided that I should take a more direct hand in dealing with you. And when I realized the two of you were Blending…"

"You gave us drugs that made the condition worse, not better," I said.

Menendez smiled. "Yes. I'd hoped that your Blending would become such a distraction that Melody and Trauma Doll – and the Discarnate assassins they hosted – would be able to eliminate you without much trouble. But when it became clear that wasn't going to happen, I tried to get the Dreamer to remove the two of you from reality on numerous occasions."

"You did?" I said. "We weren't aware of it."

"That's because none of the attempts were successful. I couldn't figure out why you were immune to the

Dreamer's power. At first I thought that the Dreamer, for whatever subconscious reasons, was protecting you. Now I think it may be because you were exposed to some kind of energy I'm unfamiliar with. I can sense it on you – all four of you, as a matter of fact. I'd love to study it further, but I *am* going to be terribly busy recreating the universe."

I assumed he was referring to the energy from Between. Russell and Bloodshedder had had far more exposure than I, so they were immune to the Dreamer's power. And Russell had kept me in the Between to speak with me in private, and then Jinx and I both got a dose of the Between's energy when the Thresholders opened a portal to rescue Russell. That would explain why Russell and I – and later Jinx – were aware of the excisions when no one else was, and why eventually we could remember them.

"Once you discovered we were immune to the Dreamer's power, you realized we were a much bigger threat than you could ever have imagined," I said. "And, since you couldn't use the Dreamer directly against us, you used him indirectly. You used his powers to excise the negator collars, the lights in Deadlock, and the Shadow Watch, all in attempts to stop us. And of course you had Melody and Trauma Doll – and their other selves – try to kill us along the way. And you armed them with special weapons to give them an edge over us. I assume the null guns were something you had the First Dreamer whip up for you. Too bad the damn things were so fragile."

"Melody and Trauma Doll were stupid enough to lure us to the Sick House and try to kill us there," Jinx said. "If they hadn't done that, we might never have figured

out what was going on." He shook his head.
"Dumbasses."

Menendez scowled. "Yes, well, good help is hard to
find and all that. But enough talk. I've enjoyed our
conversation, but as I said, I have a great deal of work
to do so…"

He clapped twice and the four of us were suddenly
enclosed within a large cage formed of solidified M-
energy. It was virtually indestructible, so of course we
all had to attempt to destroy it. I blasted the bars,
ceiling, and floor with my trancer. Jinx pounded on
them with his hammer. Russell used his arm, and
Bloodshedder employed her teeth, claws, and tail. Our
efforts got us exactly zilch.

Menendez stood by and watched our pathetic
attempts to escape with an expression of mild disdain.
When we finally got it through our heads that we
weren't going to muscle our way out of the cage, we
settled down and Menendez smiled.

"Feel better?"

"Fuck you," I said.

His smile widened. "I'll take that as a yes. Now
perhaps we can get on with things."

"Get on with this, asshole," Jinx said. When his
clothing had been restored by the influx of unshielded
Maelstrom energy, he'd also received a new
boutonniere. He now angled the left side of his chest
toward Menendez, and a stream of liquid shot from the
plastic flower, arced between the bars of the cage, and
struck Menendez in the face. Menendez sputtered and
wiped his eyes, but he remained unharmed. He spat a
couple times and said, "This tastes awful! What is it?
Some kind of acid, I assume."

Jinx frowned, touched his finger to the center of the flower, then quickly drew it away with a hiss of pain.

"I don't get it," he said. "The acid works."

"Not on me, I'm afraid," Menendez said. "When I learned how to influence the First Dreamer, the first thing I had him do was make me impervious to any kind of harm. Just in case someone like you four showed up to try to stop me."

"You know something?" Jinx said. "You're a devious bastard. I respect that."

Menendez bowed his head, as if accepting a compliment.

"So we're at a stalemate," Russell said. "We can't hurt you, but you can't hurt us."

"Not true," Menendez said. "The First Dreamer can't – or won't – do anything to harm you. But *I* still can."

He reached into his jacket pocket and pulled out a 9mm pistol. He didn't aim it at us, but switched the safety off and held the gun at his side.

"A bullet will kill you and Audra as easily as it ever would. And, while I might not have enough ammunition to do any lasting damage to your Incubi, the psychic shock of your deaths would incapacitate them for some time. But I'm hoping it won't come to that."

"Why are you even talking to us?" I said. "You have us trapped. We can't hurt you or interfere with you in any way. Why not just reshape reality and be done with it?" I paused as realization set in. "Wait a minute. It's because you *can't*, isn't it?"

Menendez's face clouded with anger, but he didn't deny it, so I went on.

"Sure, you like to hear yourself talk, but even an egomaniac like you wouldn't be talking this much if you truly had the upper hand. You'd simply make us witness your glorious triumph as you directed the First Dreamer to rewrite Existence to suit yourself. Since you clearly aren't doing that, it can only mean that, for some reason, you can't. And since you *are* talking to us–"

"He thinks there's some way we can help him," Russell said.

"He *did* say he was happy to see us when we got here," Jinx added.

Menendez glared at us for a moment, but then his anger drained away and he looked embarrassed.

"It's true," he said. "I have encountered an… unexpected setback. I've been able to influence the First Dreamer to the point where he is essentially no longer dreaming. But, no matter what I do, I cannot get him to wake all the way and relinquish control of the Maelstrom to me."

"So he won't let you play with his toys," Jinx said. "What a meanie."

"Yes," Menendez said, shooting the Dreamer a dark glance.

"I don't know how in hell we could possibly help you," I said, "but, even if we could, we wouldn't."

Menendez looked at me once more. "Are you certain? Reality as we knew it is gone. Both Earth's dimension and Nod's are no more. All that remains is the Idyllon and the Maelstrom."

"And the Threshold," Russell whispered, but so softly that I don't think Menendez heard him.

"Regardless of whether you approve of what I've done or what I plan to do, right now there is nothing. Nothing! I need access to the First Dreamer's mind in order to take control of the Maelstrom and bring a new reality into existence. I could tell you that it will be a far better reality than the one we had, as much like a paradise as I can possibly make it, but, in the end, isn't any reality better than none at all?"

"If you leave the Dreamer alone, won't he just fall back into a deeper sleep and begin dreaming once more?" I asked. "Reality would begin again on its own."

"As I said earlier, I've brought the Dreamer to a near waking state, but, now that he's there, he seems to be stuck. I can't wake him fully, nor can I return him to deep sleep."

I wondered if Menendez was only telling half the truth. I had no doubt that he was unable to completely rouse the Dreamer on his own. But had he really tried to put him all the way back to sleep? I doubted it. Menendez wanted power, ultimate power, and he wouldn't give up on obtaining it – not when he was so close.

"So where do we come in?" Russell said.

"*We* don't," Menendez said. "*You* do."

Russell frowned, and Bloodshedder growled, low and dangerous.

"It's because of the… strange energy in us." I didn't know if Menendez knew about the Thresholders, but I didn't want to say their name in case he didn't. "It somehow blocks the Dreamer's power. You want to use it against the Dreamer to weaken him so you can break his hold on the Maelstrom and take control of it yourself."

Menendez smiled at me. "You're more intelligent than I thought, Audra. Bravo." He looked at Russell. "I don't know why, but you have more of this energy in your body than the others, even your dog." His eyes narrowed. "At first I thought it had something to do with that arm of yours – fascinating thing, by the way – but I can see it's fashioned entirely from M-energy. This other energy is actually a part of you on the molecular level. It's very strange." He smiled. "But oh so very useful."

"I'm not going to help you," Russell said. "There has to be another way to restart reality other than letting you drive the bus."

"I was afraid you'd feel like that."

Menendez raised his gun, aimed it at me, and fired.

FIFTEEN

The bullet slammed into my right shoulder, and the impact knocked me backward. I fell against the rear bars of the cage, staggered, but I didn't fall. The trancer slipped from my right hand, which no longer seemed to want to grip anything, and I clapped my left hand to the wound to staunch the bleeding as best I could. First my goddamned ribs, and now this! It just wasn't my day. The wound hurt like a bitch, but I was more angry than anything, and that anger helped me deal with the pain.

Bloodshedder lost it. She threw herself against the bars, snarling and snapping. Jinx's reaction was more restrained, but far deadlier. He pulled a pack of cards from his jacket – all jokers, of course – pinched them between his thumb and forefinger, and shot them between the bars. The cards had razor-sharp edges, and they flew toward Menendez like fifty-two flat but still quite deadly shuriken. But the cards lost momentum all at once and fell to the floor.

Menendez grinned and raised the 9mm once more. "I have demonstrated that there is nothing you can do to hurt me. I have also demonstrated that I can hurt you any time I wish. So, Russell, if you do not allow me to

338

use the energy in your body, I'll put a bullet in Audra's head in addition to the one already in her shoulder."

Jinx's face became a mask of hatred that could've inspired a million nightmares. As I looked at him, I thought he started to crouch down, but then I realized what was happening. He was beginning to shrink. Reducing his size was one of his clown abilities. He'd once told me that's how so many clowns were able to fit into those tiny cars they drive. Jinx was planning on shrinking to the point where he could pass between the bars and attack Menendez. In other circumstances, his plan might've worked, but, as Menendez had shown us, nothing we could do would hurt him. Even if Jinx got out of the cage, it wouldn't do us any good.

I stepped toward Jinx. My right arm hurt like hell, so I put my left hand on his shoulder to get his attention. That hand was covered with blood, and it soaked into Jinx's coat, but I didn't care. Jinx looked at me, and I gave my head a slight shake. His shrinking paused, and then he slowly grew, regaining the couple inches he'd lost. He might not have realized why I wanted him to stop shrinking, but he trusted me enough to do as I asked, and that was all that mattered now.

Menendez had been looking at Russell the entire time, and he hadn't noticed my exchange with Jinx. That was good. I had no idea how or if Jinx's shrinking might come in handy, but at least we had one weapon in our reserve.

I looked at Russell then. He'd adopted a cold, almost cruel expression.

"What makes you think I give a shit about *her*?" He said *her* as if it were an especially disgusting and painful venereal disease.

Although I knew he was putting on an act, I still felt a twinge hearing him speak of me like that. After all, he was the closest thing to a boyfriend I had right then. But he'd worked for the Thresholders for years, and during most of that time he'd posed as a cold-blooded mercenary. He was highly skilled at pretending to be something he wasn't, and I thought he had a good shot at fooling Menendez. But the doctor only chuckled.

"Please! I've been observing all of you since you arrived. You and Audra may both repress the hell out of your feelings for one another, but only an idiot couldn't see how much you truly care. So you can drop the act."

I could see the defeat in Russell's eyes then. Menendez could hurt me, Bloodshedder, or Jinx. The 9mm wouldn't do much to the Incubi, but I was certain Menendez had other dirty tricks up his sleeve. And Russell knew it, too. He should've refused to help Menendez, but I knew he would. If I'd been in his position, I'd have done the same.

Russell let out a long sigh, and he almost seemed to wilt. "What do you need me to do?"

A look of satisfaction came over Menendez's face, and I wanted to punch him *so* bad.

"Extend one of your hands through the bars, please."

Russell did so, and Menendez approached the cage. He tucked the 9mm back in his jacket pocket and removed a device that looked something like a tire pressure gauge.

"This is a devitalizer," Menendez said. "Somnacologists use it on patients who've developed an excess of M-energy. It should work for what I have in mind."

He touched one end of the device to the back of Russell's hand and then pressed his thumb to the other end. There was a soft *click*, almost like the sound a ballpoint pen makes. But that was all. While the device's operation wasn't particularly impressive – no flashing lights, no electronic sounds – the effect on Russell was instantaneous and dramatic. He let out a deep moan, his eyes rolled back in his head, and his body fell limp. Bloodshedder yelped in alarm as he collapsed to the floor of the cage, and she rushed over to him and began frantically licking his face. He didn't respond, though. I hurried to him, knelt as best I could, grimacing when both my ribs and shoulder complained. I took hold of his wrist to check for a pulse. He still had one, but it was weak.

I tried to stand, but when I couldn't manage it on my own, Jinx helped me.

"What did you do to him?" I demanded. I didn't bother trying to keep the fear and despair I felt out of my voice.

"I drained that strange energy from his body," Menendez said. "Most of it, anyway. But don't worry. Once I create a new reality, I'll make sure he's whole and healthy once more."

"Sounds like you plan to be a benevolent God," I said, in a bitter voice.

Menendez didn't catch my sarcasm, though. He walked over to the Dreamer, who was still sleeping peacefully on his bed of palm fronds.

"I do. Far more benevolent than this child ever was."

He touched the end of the devitalizer to his wrist as if it were a hypodermic needle and thumbed the switch once more. I half-expected him to throw back his head and draw in a hissing breath as the Threshold energy flowed through him, but his reaction wasn't quite so dramatic. He blinked twice, frowned slightly, and said, "Interesting."

He returned the device to his pocket, then walked over to the Dreamer and sat down on the floor next to him. He crossed his legs and closed his eyes, as if he were preparing to meditate. He then reached out and placed a hand gently on the Dreamer's head. The boy moaned softly, as if he were having a bad dream. He shifted on his bed of palm fronds, momentarily restless, but then he fell still and grew quiet once more. Moments passed, but neither the Dreamer nor Menendez stirred.

"That's it?" Jinx said. "Talk about anticlimactic."

I tried to think, to come up with some plan for stopping Menendez, but I was so weary. I hadn't been able to rest or meditate for well over a day now, and the blood loss from my shoulder wound wasn't helping my condition. I felt lightheaded and my vision swam in and out of focus. I wasn't sure how long I could remain conscious, but probably not more than a few more minutes. We had to do something before I passed out, but I had no idea what. My brain felt clogged with sludge, and my thoughts refused to coalesce.

Luckily, Jinx picked up the slack for me. He tucked Cuthbert Junior away, pulled the can of aerosol string from his pocket, and tossed it to me.

"There's not much left, but there should be enough to make a quick and dirty patch for your shoulder."

He then walked to the edge of the cage and began his shrinking trick again. When he'd reduced himself to twelve inches in height, he slipped through the bars easily. Once on the other side, he quickly returned to his normal size. While he did this, I shrugged off my jacket, unbuttoned my shirt far enough to expose my shoulder wound, shook the can a couple times, and sprayed pink goopy string onto my shoulder wound. It hurt like blazes, but the goop stuck fast and plugged the hole caused by Menendez's bullet. I dropped the can and didn't bother putting my jacket back on or re-buttoning my shirt. I was too damn tired and in too much pain to care.

Menendez sat motionless next to the First Dreamer, his hand on the boy's head. Both of their eyes were closed, and both remained completely still. The atmosphere in the Sacrarium had changed, though. The sourceless light that illuminated the chamber had grown brighter, and the air felt denser and charged with power, like when a violent thunderstorm is imminent.

"What do you think?" Jinx asked. "Should I walk over and bash in Menendez's skull while he's communing with Little Boy God?"

"Menendez's mind is connected to the Dreamer's right now. If he dies while that connection still exists, the Dreamer could experience a severe psychic shock. It could drive him mad or even kill him. If a being like him *can* die, that is."

"So we'd stop Menendez, but reality would be fucked," Jinx said.

"Yep." I thought for a moment. "You're a lot stronger than normal because of all the unshielded M-energy around us. Do you think you're strong enough to bend the bars?"

Jinx shrugged, grabbed hold of two of the bars, and tried to pull them apart. But, although he was stronger than ever before, they refused to yield.

"If you can't break me out of here, can you move the

cage next to the Dreamer's bed?"

Jinx took hold of the bars once more, planted his gigantic shoes firmly on the chamber's floor, and leaned backward. At first nothing happened, but then the cage slid several inches. Jinx put more muscle into it, and the cage slid a few feet this time. He kept at it, and, in fits and starts, he dragged the huge M-energy cage – which had to weigh a literal ton, if not more – to the Dreamer. He slid it to within a few inches of the boy, on the opposite side from where Menendez sat. The noise of the cage being moved hadn't disturbed either the Dreamer or Menendez. Their eyes remained closed, their bodies motionless.

I stepped to the edge of the cage close to the Dreamer and sat down. I turned to look at Bloodshedder.

"I don't know if this is going to work," I said. "But no matter what happens, take care of Russell for the both of us, okay?"

Bloodshedder whined softly, but she thumped her tail once. I got the message.

I turned back to face the Dreamer.

"What are you going to do, Audra?" Jinx asked. "Whatever it is, I don't think I'm going to like it."

"The real fight is taking place inside their minds right now," I said. "I'm going to see if I can get in on the action."

I wasn't a Somnacologist, but I *was* an Ideator. I had a profound connection to the Maelstrom too, just like Menendez, and I also had energy from Between inside me. Nowhere near as much as Russell had, but it might be enough to help me connect with the Dreamer and try to stop Menendez.

"I won't let you do this alone," Jinx said.

"I wasn't planning to," I smiled. "No way I'm going into psychic battle without my favorite crazy clown at my side."

Jinx grinned and sat on the floor next to the cage. I held out my left hand, and he took it. I reached out with my right hand, ignoring the pain in my shoulder as I did so, and took hold of the boy's hand. His skin felt like that of a normal human, warm and smooth. He didn't move or make a sound when I touched him, but his fingers interlocked with mine and squeezed gently. I could feel Jinx through the link we shared, which was stronger than ever. We were ready.

"One for the money," I said.

"Two for the show," Jinx continued.

"Three to get ready…"

"I *like* Times Square," I said.

"It's too Disney for me," Day Jinx said. "It doesn't have any real character."

"You like Broadway," I said.

"Yes, but I *prefer* Off-Broadway."

We stood on the sidewalk in front of the Times Square McDonalds, which was located on Broadway, but not *the* Broadway. The distinction is often hard to explain to tourists. It was half-past noon, and, although it was a clear day and the sun was shining, the December air had a sharp bite to it, and I held a large cup of coffee I'd just bought from Mickey D's, as much for the warmth as the caffeine. I wore a dark gray winter coat over my suit jacket – the Shadow Watch's official winter uniform – but it only did so much to ward off the chill. Jinx also wore a gray coat, but unzipped. He might be (mostly) human during the day, but he rarely gets cold.

"Sometimes I think you buy that swill just to annoy me," he said.

I took a tiny sip of the warm coffee, smacked my lips several times, and said, "Ahhh, that is *good*."

Jinx grimaced and shook his head.

"The next time you're jonesing for caffeine, let me know. There are a dozen places less than ten minutes' walk from here that serve much better coffee."

"Yeah, for ten dollars a cup."

Pedestrians flowed past us in both directions, and there was a steady stream of traffic in the street. Chicago is a busy city, but when Jinx and I first moved to Manhattan, I wasn't prepared for the never-ending tides of people and vehicles. The constant *busyness* of it all still got to me sometimes.

I took a bigger sip of my coffee this time and enjoyed the warmth as it trickled down my throat. Although Christmas was weeks away, a lot of pedestrians were loaded down with shopping bags, and most of the businesses had put up holiday decorations to one degree or another. I've always enjoyed the holiday season, but Day Jinx gets annoyed at the "onslaught of consumerism." But right then, neither of us were in a particularly festive mood. We were working.

"I'm not sure this is the best meeting place," Jinx said. "Approximately three hundred and thirty-three thousand people go through here every day, you know. Probably more right now, since it's the holiday season. We don't even know who we're supposed to meet."

"Nyx said that she'd get in touch with the man and tell him to meet us here during the day around lunchtime. I trust her." I gave him a sideways glance. "And you're hard to miss, even in your Day Aspect."

Nyx – the Greek goddess of the night – was an ancient Incubus who was New York's equivalent of Deacon Booze. She owned and ran Lucidity over on Fifth Street, the premier night club for Incubi in the city. An Apneator – a predatory Incubus that drains sleepers' life force by feeding on their breath as they sleep – had been killing people on Central Park West. Nyx had told us she knew a human who was something of an expert on Apneators, a kind of Van Helsing for sleep-breath vampires, and she'd promised to hook us up with him.

"It's never a good idea to trust Nyx," Jinx said.

"You're still mad at her for cheating on you with Hypnos."

"Maybe I am," he admitted. "But that doesn't make her any more trustworthy."

He had a point. Ancient Incubi always have their own agenda, and rarely does it work to anyone's benefit but theirs. Take the Fata Morgana. She...

I frowned.

"Something's wrong," I said.

"No kidding. I was planning on going to see the new Jasper Johns exhibit at MoMa this afternoon. Instead we're wasting our time trying to catch a fairy tale."

"We don't work in New York," I said. "We still work in Chicago. I mean, sure, Sanderson *offered* us a transfer to New York, but we haven't accepted it yet."

Jinx looked at me as if I'd gone insane. But his incredulous expression only lasted a moment before I saw realization enter his gaze.

"You're right. We're not supposed to be here."

We looked at the people, the traffic, the signs, the buildings, the sky...

"Is any of this real?" Jinx asked.

"Looks real," I said. I inhaled through my nose. "The car exhaust smells real." I reached out and pushed a passerby on the shoulder. The man – a stocky fellow in a thick coat with a scarf wrapped around the lower half of his face – stumbled a bit, shot me a death-ray look, and then kept going.

"Feels real," I said.

"It's *somewhat* real," said a familiar voice.

Jinx and I turned to see Nathaniel and Mordacity – the latter in his Day Aspect – standing behind us, both dressed for the cold weather. They smiled at us, and seeing them like that should've made me happy, but for reasons I didn't fully understand, it made me unbearably sad.

"Just like us," Mordacity said. "We're only somewhat real too."

"You died," Jinx said in a soft voice. "Both of you."

I knew his words were true as soon as he spoke them, although I had no memory of their deaths happening.

"Yes," Nathaniel said. He smiled, but his eyes were serious. "We're… echoes. Memories made flesh."

"You made us that way," Mordacity said. "We're reminders."

I frowned. "Reminders of what?"

"Of what you're doing here," Nathaniel said. "And what this place is."

"This is Times Square," Jinx said. "Such as it is."

"This place is only half-real," Mordacity said. "Maybe not even that much."

He crouched down and touched his hand to the sidewalk. He gripped the concrete, its substance yielding to his hand like putty. He pulled and a portion of the sidewalk peeled away like paper, revealing a roiling strip of Maelstrom energy beneath.

Mordacity stood without replacing the section of sidewalk. The people hurrying past us took no notice of what he'd done.

"Menendez is struggling to wrest control of the Maelstrom from the First Dreamer," Nathaniel said.

"Since they're distracted, you were able to create this place," Mordacity said, then he smiled. "And us."

"Very impressive for your first attempt at being God," Nathaniel said.

As the two of them spoke, my memories came drifting back. I suppose that was the reason that I'd created them in the first place. Like Nathaniel had said, they were reminders.

I turned to Jinx. "You tracking?"

He nodded. "I remember now. I almost wish I didn't, though."

I knew exactly how he felt. The thought that this Half-hattan I'd created was all that remained of Existence was disorienting and terrifying in equal measures.

"This is a wonderful backdrop for the final scene in this little psychodrama," Mordacity said. He turned to Nathaniel. "Isn't it?"

"Oh yes," Nathaniel agreed. "After all, it's drawn from her discomfort about the transfer Sanderson offered. All very symbolic."

Something wasn't right. Their voices had taken on an almost-mocking edge, and slyness had entered their gazes.

"Unfortunately, it won't be long before Menendez realizes you're here," Mordacity said.

"And when that happens, he'll attack, using what you created against you," Nathaniel said.

As if in response to Nathaniel's words, Times Square fell silent. Every pedestrian stopped moving, every engine cut out. The sudden stillness was more than startling. It struck with almost physical force. I'd never experienced a quiet so loud – or so threatening. Then, one by one, pedestrians began to turn toward us, faces expressionless, eyes cold and dead.

Nathaniel and Mordacity smiled. Their teeth were black, and very, very sharp.

"Oops," Nathaniel said. "Too late."

Dark clouds rolled in from all directions and blotted out the sun. Shadows descended on Times Square, and, as they did, the men, women, and children around us took on the mantle of darkness, becoming featureless shadowy creatures with lean bodies, curving talons, and wicked teeth.

Darkuns.

Nathaniel and Mordacity became Darkuns too, and they flexed their claws, as if eager to begin rending our flesh.

Jinx and I drew our trancers, wordlessly moving back to back. We didn't wait for the Dreamers to attack. We started firing. Great swaths of M-energy erupted from our weapons, obliterating any Darkuns unfortunate enough to be in the way. The energy outburst was a hundred times greater than normal trancers were capable of producing. Maybe that was due to our being in an oasis of semi-reality in the middle of the Maelstrom, or maybe it was because I had created these trancers to be super weapons. Whatever the reason, I was grateful we had something to give us a fighting chance.

I knew the Darkuns Nathaniel and Mordacity had

become were in the first wave that attacked us. They
were dead, but, since they hadn't been fully alive, I told
myself that I shouldn't feel bad about their deaths. But
I did.

How many people had Jinx said passed through
Times Square in a day? Over three hundred thousand?
It seemed like at least that many Darkuns swarmed
toward us from all directions. Jinx and I kept firing,
turning in slow circles as we did to make sure we didn't
miss any of the shadowy monstrosities coming at us.
We kept at it for what seemed like hours, but the
onrushing tide of Darkuns never let up. Thankfully,
our trancers showed no sign of losing power, and I
wondered if they were able to draw directly on the
Maelstrom's energy instead of on rechargeable power
packs. I was grateful my mind had designed them this
way, and also grateful that my body no longer suffered
from the injuries I'd sustained to my ribs and shoulder.
Evidently my new status as a demigod came with some
nice perks.

After what seemed like more hours mowing down
Darkuns, Jinx said, "This isn't going to work."

"Seems to be working so far," I said.

"It's a stalemate. We keep destroying Darkuns and
Menendez keeps making more."

He was right. And, while I wasn't sure if Jinx and I
were here in a physical sense or if we were just psychic
projections of our personalities, and our real bodies
remained in the Sacrarium, I could still feel myself
growing weary. But the hordes of Darkuns that
continued rushing toward us remained as fresh as ever.
If this kept up much longer, Jinx and I would make a
mistake – stumble, maybe lose our grip on our weapons

– and the Darkuns would be on us. I didn't know if we'd die for real if we died in this half-place my mind had created, but I didn't want to find out.

"You're fighting like we would in a normal battle," Jinx said. "You need to start fighting like a Dreamer."

He was right. My original intent in linking with the First Dreamer's mind was to be able to fight Menendez on his own terms. I'd forgotten that, but luckily I had my partner to remind me.

As Jinx and I continued firing at Darkuns, I thought a single word: *sunshine.*

The clouds parted and light poured down into the Square. The Darkuns' ebon flesh sizzled and smoked in the harsh, unforgiving rays of the sun, and they screamed in agony. They attempted to flee, but the streets were so thick with the creatures that they couldn't move fast enough. A handful made it to alleys or doorways, but the sunlight was under my control, and it found them wherever they were. In a short time, the Darkuns – all of them – were gone, without leaving behind so much as a scorch mark on the pavement to show they'd ever existed.

Jinx and I stopped firing and lowered our trancers. He grinned at me.

"That's my girl!"

I smiled back weakly, suddenly overcome by tiredness beyond anything I'd ever experienced before. You've heard the old expression *bone-tired*. Well, I was weary down to the cellular level. Being a god takes a lot out of a girl.

The city had fallen silent once more. The streets were filled with overturned and damaged vehicles, the result of the constant waves of attacking Darkuns, but there were no people. Despite the fact that the electronic billboards on One Times Square continued displaying ads, Manhattan felt dead. The quiet was soon broken by the sound of a single pair of hands clapping. Jinx and I turned toward the sound and saw Menendez winding his way through the maze of abandoned vehicles as he crossed the street toward us.

"I knew you were resourceful, Audra," he said, "but I had no idea that you'd be able to follow me into the Dreamer's mind. I'm very impressed."

I considered raising my trancer and blasting him, but I didn't bother. He wouldn't have revealed himself if he could be killed that easily.

Menendez stopped when he reached the edge of the curb. Less than five feet separated us.

"But this is as far as it goes," he said. "The Dreamer is on the verge of waking, and, once that happens, his control over the Maelstrom will end, allowing me to assume control."

"And then you'll create Paradise." I couldn't help sneering as I said this.

"Or the next best thing to it," he said. "And, if I don't get it right the first time, I'll just start over and try again. And again and again until I'm satisfied. After all, it's not so much the destination as it is the journey, right?"

The thought of Menendez creating, destroying, and re-creating reality after reality filled with living, breathing beings that he would destroy on a whim when it suited him sickened me.

"What about taking responsibility for that which you create?" I asked. "Once something becomes real–"

"Something is real only when *I* say it is," he interrupted. "That's what it means to be God."

"Sounds more like what it means to be an asshole," I said.

"We don't have to be enemies, Audra. We could work together to create a new reality. Perhaps you're right about caring for that which we create. You could be my conscience. You could provide the empathy that I lack."

I turned to Jinx. "Is he hitting on me?"

"Maybe, but, if I had to guess, I'd say he's still having trouble waking the Dreamer on his own, and he's trying to manipulate you into helping him."

"Pretty sleazy," I said.

"Extremely."

Menendez's façade of reasonable calm gave way and his face became a mask of fury.

"I *don't* need your help," he said. "And as for your obnoxious sidekick…"

Menendez pointed a finger and Jinx was engulfed in a bright flash of white light, which was immediately followed by a deafening crack of thunder. I was knocked on my ass, and for several seconds I couldn't see or hear anything. I thought I was dead, but, since I could think anything at all, I realized I probably wasn't.

When my vision cleared, I saw Jinx lying on the sidewalk, the pavement around him scorched black. Steam rose from his body, and he was shaking all over, as if in the throes of an epileptic fit.

Menendez gazed upon Jinx with a smug smile.

"Smiting one's enemies with a bolt of lightning might be cliché, but I had no idea it would be so satisfying."

Jinx wasn't dead, not yet, but I didn't think he was going to last much longer. I had to do something, so I did the first thing that popped into my head.

Night, I thought, and I thought hard.

Darkness descended on Manhattan and stars – bright, crisp, and glittering – appeared in the sky above us. The city's streetlights came on, and the electronic billboards added to the glow with their blazing sales messages.

Night Jinx sat up, steam still rising from his body. He let out a loud whoop.

"*Day*-um, son! That was a real kick in the pants! Do it again!"

I reached out and helped Jinx to his feet. His flesh was almost burning hot.

"Maybe later," I said.

"Spoilsport."

Menendez looked even angrier than he had before. He raised a hand, but, before he could deliver another smiting, I flicked a finger toward him, and he flew into the street and slammed into an abandoned taxi. He bounced off and fell onto the street, and the asphalt flowed over his hands and feet and solidified, trapping him. Whatever protection Menendez had gotten from the First Dreamer in Nod didn't work here, not when I had access to the same power he did.

"Nice," Jinx said.

"Thanks."

"Can you make him explode just by thinking it? That would be so cool!"

"We'll see."

We walked over to where Menendez lay, and he raised his head to look at us.

"A little telekinetic force, some minor matter manipulation… Child's tricks," he said.

"Hey, give me some credit," I said. "I did turn day into night."

Jinx pulled Cuthbert Junior out of his jacket pocket,

and a slow devastating grin spread across his face.

"You know something, Menendez? Lying there with your head raised like that, you remind me of a golf ball sitting on a tee."

Before I could stop him, Jinx switched his grip on Cuthbert Junior and held the sledge like a golf club. He then took a step toward Menendez, pulled the hammer back, yelled "Fore!" and swung. I had to admit, his form was perfect.

Menendez's head tore free from his body in a spray of blood and went flying through the air. It arced toward One Times Square and smashed into one of the electronic billboards. The screen exploded in a shower of sparks, and Jinx yelled, "Home run!"

"That's baseball," I said.

Jinx shrugged. "Whatever."

I looked down at Menendez's headless body, blood pooling outward from the ragged stump of his neck.

I holstered my trancer. "You know that empathy of mine he talked about?"

"Yeah."

"I'm not really feeling it so much right now."

Jinx grinned and rested Cuthbert Junior on his shoulder.

"So, what do we do now?" he asked.

"I'm not sure. Maybe if we leave here, the Dreamer will fall back into a deep sleep, and his dream will start up where it left off. And with any luck, everything that was excised from reality will be restored."

"What if he starts a new dream?"

"I guess we'll be gone," I said. "Unless we're part of the new dream somehow."

"I wouldn't worry about that. You have a much more immediate problem. Namely, me."

Menendez's voice echoed all around us. It came from the air, vibrated forth from the buildings, and from the asphalt beneath our feet.

"I'm a Somnacologist, most likely the strongest that's ever lived. There's no way you can defeat me by manipulating the Maelstrom. I was born to understand it, interact with it, control it. You're an Ideator, Audra. All you've done is bring one nightmare to life. You're a one-trick pony, and it's a pretty pathetic trick at that."

"Hey," Jinx said. "I resemble that remark!"

Menendez, head restored, broke free from his asphalt shackles and stood.

"The Maelstrom is Chaos," he said, his voice normal once more. "It's wild, raw potential. Anything can be done with it. Anything at all. It's madness on a cosmic scale. How could someone like you ever hope to wield it, let alone control it?"

Menendez's hand shot out and fastened around my throat. Jinx swung Cuthbert Junior off his shoulder and into striking position, but, before he could attack, Menendez gestured with his other hand. Cuthbert Junior transformed into a huge serpent that swiftly encircled Jinx in its coils. The snake was white, its only markings – blue half-moons over the eyes, red lining its mouth – mirroring Jinx's coloring. Jinx struggled to break free, but his movements only allowed the snake to constrict tighter and soon Jinx couldn't move at all.

"Do you like the way the snake looks?" Menendez said. "I thought it was a nice touch."

I struggled to speak, but I couldn't get anything out. I drew my trancer, jammed it into Menendez's stomach, and pulled the trigger. Nothing happened.

"I'm blocking your access to the Maelstrom," he said. "Your weapon won't work on me now, not unless I wish it."

I dropped the trancer and pounded on Menendez with my fists, kicked him as hard as I could, but his body was like a rock, and my exertions didn't do anything except use up what little air remained in my lungs.

"I get stronger with each passing moment, Audra," he said. "Right now I exist on multiple levels. While I've been tussling with you here, I've also been continuing to work on rousing the First Dreamer. The closer to full consciousness he comes, the less of the Maelstrom he commands and the more I do. Soon, I'll control it all, and *I'll* be God. Then nothing can stop me." He smiled. "Ever."

I opened and closed my mouth, desperately trying to speak.

"I suppose you have some last defiant words to spit in my face. Well, why not? Perhaps I'll find them amusing."

He loosened his grip on my throat, just enough for me to be able to draw in some air, but not enough for me to break free.

"No… defiance," I rasped. "Just a… question."

"Get on with it."

I couldn't turn my head to look at Jinx, so I shifted my eyes toward him.

"Are you… clown enough?"

Jinx frowned.

"Are you clown enough?" I repeated.

Understanding dawned in his eyes, and a huge grin split his face.

"Yes," he said, in a soft voice. Then stronger, "Yes, I *am*."

He closed his eyes and the clown serpent transformed back into Cuthbert Junior. He snatched the hammer out of the air before it struck the ground, and then he tucked it away in his jacket pocket.

Menendez stared at him in confusion. The man's grasp slackened enough that I was able to pull free, but he barely noticed.

"How did you do that?" he demanded.

"It's simple," Jinx said. "You said it yourself. The Maelstrom *is* Chaos. And who understands chaos better than a clown?"

"Not just any clown," I said. "*The* clown."

Jinx smiled and bowed to acknowledge my words.

"I've had quite enough of you two," Menendez said. "Time to finish this."

"I agree wholeheartedly," Jinx said.

He started walking toward Menendez. As he did, the night sky gave way to the swirling multicolored vortex of the Maelstrom. The ground trembled beneath our feet, and the buildings of the not-quite-real Manhattan collapsed into gray and black dust. Clouds of it rose into the air, piles of it slid into the street. The abandoned and wrecked vehicles became dust as well, and the streets broke apart in fragments and fell away, tumbling downward into the turbulent energies of the Maelstrom below. Everything – the vast mounds of disintegrated buildings and thousands of vehicles – all fell into the Maelstrom where they were re-absorbed. The only thing that remained was a small section of asphalt, barely large enough for the three of us to stand on.

"Don't feel too bad," Jinx said. "There's no way you could compete with me in the crazy department. I my thing, after all." Jinx's eyes widened as if a tho occurred to him. "But I might be able to help you with that!"

He reached up and touched his index finger to his forehead. He pushed and his finger passed through flesh and bone as if they were no more substantial than pudding. Once his finger was all the way inside, he wiggled it around a couple times, and then withdrew it. The finger was covered with bloody gobbets of brain.

As the crimson-rimmed hole in his head began to close, Jinx grinned at Menendez.

"Let me give you a piece of my mind."

He jammed his finger into Menendez's head, and the man's eyes went wide with shock. When Jinx withdrew his finger, it was clean. He then licked the tip of his finger and rubbed Menendez's forehead wound, as if he were a mother giving her child a quick spit-clean. When he was finished, the skin on Menendez's forehead was smooth and unmarked.

Menendez didn't do anything for several seconds. Then he chuckled. His chuckle turned into a laugh. His laugh became a loud donkey's bray. And then he was roaring with deep, loud belly laughs. But there was no merriment in his eyes. There was only terror and desperation. The belly laughs gave way to high-pitched shrieks that sounded as much like screams as they did laughter. Tears streamed from his eyes, and his laughter dribbled away into deep, body-wracking sobs.

I'd like to tell you that I felt sorry for him, but I'd be

he might fall to his knees, but instead he

off the edge of our tiny asphalt island.

sobbing as he plummeted toward the

Maelstrom, and then the energies swallowed him and he was gone.

Jinx stepped to the edge of the asphalt and looked down.

"Some people just can't take a joke."

I walked over to him and put a hand on his shoulder.

"Good work," I said. "Disturbing as all hell, but good."

Jinx grinned at me. "All part of the service."

We stood in silence for several moments, looking at the Maelstrom roiling all around us.

"So what now?" Jinx asked. "Do we join hands and say 'Let there be light'?"

"I don't know. I guess we–"

We were back in the Sacrarium. The cage was gone. I sat cross-legged on the floor next to Jinx. Russell lay unconscious close by, and Bloodshedder lay with her head on his chest, looking at us. Menendez lay in a fetal position on the other side of the First Dreamer, shivering and drooling.

The Dreamer was sitting up and looking at me sleepily.

"Would you mind keeping it down, please? I'm trying to sleep."

He yawned, closed his eyes, and settled back onto his palm-frond bed.

SIXTEEN

Several days later, Jinx and I were walking along the shore on Montrose Beach. It was early morning, the sky overcast, the waters of Lake Michigan gun-metal gray. Snow flurries drifted down, only to be tossed and scattered by the wind coming off the lake. The wind was cold, and I wished I had some lip balm. I could feel my lips chapping with each passing second.

I was bundled up in a warm jacket, ski cap, scarf, and gloves. Jinx, in his Day Aspect, walked alongside me. He wore a winter coat, although his wasn't as heavy as mine, and he wore a stylish flat cap to cover his bald head.

"How are you feeling?" he asked.

My right arm was in a sling, and I wore a compression wrap around my chest. Thank the First Dreamer for heavy-duty pain meds.

"My ribs still hurt, and the cold is making my shoulder ache, but I'll survive."

"That's not what I meant."

"I know."

I would love to tell you that, when the Dreamer went back to sleep, reality was restored. And it was – mostly.

Earth's dimension had returned to its previous state, as
had Nod. And every person or object that had ceased
to exist while Menendez had tried to wake the Dreamer
had come back. But those things that had happened as
a *result* of the excisions hadn't been undone. Nathaniel
and Mordacity were still dead, and Connie, the
Deathmobile, and the Fata Morgana were missing. I
assumed that meant something had happened to the
Deathmobile before the M-energy tendril could
unmake her. But what that was exactly, I had no idea.
All I knew was that, so far, there had been no sign of
the hearse, Connie, or the Fata Morgana. I tried not to
assume the worst, but, truthfully, I didn't hold out
much hope for their return.

The Shadow Watch had started investigating the
Discarnate, searching for anyone who'd been possessed
by the spirits against their will. The Watch M-gineers
had rigged a device to detect the Discarnate, but finding
them would be far from simple. They knew how to hide
too well.

Menendez was still alive, but his mind had been
completely shattered by Jinx's contribution to his brain.
He'd been taken to Deadlock, and Warden Bruzer –
who had survived the riot and Darkun attack on his
prison and once more had three heads – had locked
him away in a maximum security cell, where he would
remain for the rest of his life. It didn't seem like a severe
enough punishment for a man who'd almost destroyed
reality itself, but I supposed it would have to do.

Jinx didn't ask me again how I was feeling, but I
could feel him waiting for me to address the question.
Since the moment the Dreamer returned to sleep, we'd
had no more trouble Blending, but I'd been able to read

his moods even better than before, and the reverse was true. He knew I would talk when I was ready. I wasn't quite ready, though. Not to talk about what was really bothering me, so I decided to stall.

"Are you disappointed we're not going to New York?" I asked.

I'd decided to turn down Sanderson's offer, and Jinx had gone along with my decision without saying a word.

He considered a moment before answering.

"Yes and no. On the one hand, it *is* New York. On the other, I'm not sure it would feel like home. Not the way Chicago does."

I smiled. "You keep talking like that, and, next thing you know, you'll end up a Bears fan."

Jinx sniffed. "I highly doubt that."

We continued walking in silence for several moments. And then I was ready.

"Don't you find it hard to believe in anything anymore?" I asked. "I mean everything – the sky, the lake, this sand" – I kicked up a bit to underscore my point – "is all part of some kid's dream. It's not *real*."

"It's as real as it ever was," Jinx said.

"Somehow, I don't find that comforting."

"Incubi have to deal with some of the same feelings," he said. "After all, we're created when an Ideator unconsciously shapes the raw material of the Maelstrom and brings it to life. I am, in a very real sense, your dream come true."

"Don't flatter yourself," I muttered.

He smiled. "A poor choice of words, perhaps, but you know what I mean. You created me, the Dreamer created you… Who knows where the Dreamer came from? Life is filled with questions, Audra. If we're lucky, we might discover some of the answers before it's over for us."

"And if we're unlucky, we might discover answers we'd rather not know."

"True."

Ecclesiastor Withrow reappeared soon after the Dreamer went back to sleep. Jinx and I took her into custody, and I called Sanderson – who had also popped back into existence – and gave him a quick rundown of the situation. Withrow was now safely ensconced in a cell in Deadlock, as were her Wakenist and Discarnate accomplices. For the time being, the Idyllon was under the protection of the Shadow Watch, and it would remain that way until such time as the Nightclad Council could determine what should be done.

"But that's not what's really bothering you, is it?" Jinx asked.

"It's childish, but I'd hoped that when the Dreamer went back to sleep, *everything* would be fixed."

"By everything, you mean Nathaniel, Mordacity, Connie, and the Deathmobile. Maybe even the Fata Morgana."

I nodded. I felt tears threatening, and told myself it was just the wind in my eyes.

"Yeah."

"Me too," he said.

There really wasn't anything more to be said. The Dreamer moves in mysterious ways, I suppose.

I heard a yapping and I turned to see Bloodshedder, in her dachshund Day Aspect, running down the beach toward us, tail wagging. Russell followed behind her. He was dressed in jeans and sneakers, and wore a thick brown jacket. His left arm – which during the day became an ordinary prosthetic one – rested motionless against his side, the hand tucked into his jacket pocket.

I bent down to pet Bloodshedder, grimacing as my ribs protested, and she immediately rolled over so I could give her a belly rub. At moments like these, it's hard to remember that at night she's a vicious killing machine.

I stood when Russell drew near. Bloodshedder still lay on her back, and she wiggled her front paws to indicate she wanted more belly rubs. Jinx crouched down to comply.

I smiled at Russell. "I was wondering when you were going to show up."

I leaned toward him and gave him a kiss. Nothing too passionate, but definitely more than a friendly peck.

"Sorry I've been gone. The Thresholders had work for Bloodshedder and me. Their dimension wasn't harmed when the Dreamer woke, but its boundaries became... I guess *fuzzy* is the best word for it. They needed us to help repair them."

"So now you're a dimensional engineer," I teased. "Is there no end to your talents?"

"I refuse to answer that question on the grounds that it might get me slapped." He turned to Jinx and said hello. Jinx acknowledged him with a nod. He tried to stand, but Bloodshedder wiggled her paws again, and Jinx sighed and resumed rubbing her belly. Her body relaxed and her eyes closed in satisfaction.

"How's the arm?" I asked.

"Still working fine – at night. As for days.... I'm still getting used to it."

His M-energy arm functioned somewhat like an

Incubus. During the day, it changed into an ordinary analogue of itself – in other words, a mundane prosthesis.

I walked around to his right side, and I took his right hand with my left one.

"Walk with me," I said.

He smiled. "My pleasure."

As soon as we started down the beach, Bloodshedder rolled onto her legs and trotted after us. Relieved of his belly-rubbing duties, Jinx stood and followed.

I know that one of the worst ways to end a story is to write, *And it was all a dream*, but in this case, it's true, on multiple levels. And the hard thing about dreams is they all end sometime. But for now, *this* dream continues. And that's enough for me.

ACKNOWLEDGMENTS

Thanks to my agent Cherry Weiner, my publisher Marc Gascoigne, and to my editor Phil Jourdan. All of them have helped make this a better book.